Copyright © 2020 by Douglas Edwardson

All rights reserved.

Cover design and illustration by Janette Ramos

Library of Congress Control Number: 2020922448

ISBN 978-0-9885082-5-5

Printed in the United States of America

Published by Giraffix Media

This is a work of fiction. Names, character, places, and incidents either are the product of the author's imagination or are used fictitiously. Any resemblance to actual persons, living or dead, events, or locales is entirely coincidental.

~ THE SWORDSPEAKER SAGA ~

TRUESILVER

DJ EDWARDSON

GIRRAFIX

KNOXVILLE

For my son Hezekiah

S.D.G

Contents

THE LANDS OF
WARDING

TINESPLITTER
ISLE

BRITTLE
BAY

BRITTLE

REGNIR

WHITEWIND

NOATH

DUNACH

SICKLEWOOD

LOST
HYLLS

GRENDOCK

KEVEL

GRETTLING

WINDLE

CASTING
LIMMRING

JABBLE

HAMLICK

TILLER

RIPPLING

SHEENWATER
SEA

Prologue

SPARKFALL

Like all good stories, this one begins in a library. Now, this library was at the top of a tower. The tower was only three stories tall, so it was hardly the most impressive in the land, but it did sit atop Wardhill, the highest hill in the city of Charring, so the view was rather nice. Though the tower was only about ten years old, it was already starting to lean. The person who built it, the daysman (something like a mayor) of Charring, built it in a hurry, and in a bad location where the ground was weak. And the city of Charring, struggling under the high taxes of the fane, had not been able to afford good stone like the kind used in the buildings of Madrigal or Gilding, or even in past times when Charring knew better days. No, all they could afford was shiftrock, which is brittle, frail, and unreliable—just about the worst kind of rock there is for building.

The tower had to be built because the old residence of the daysmen was struck by lightning and burned to the ground. This made all the people who knew the old building sad because it was very charming and beautiful and didn't lean. Charring seemed to have a lot of fires for some reason. Perhaps they ought to have named it something else.

When the mansion burned down, the current Daysman wasn't there. He was off negotiating with merchants and officials in Madrigal. He spent as much time as possible outside Charring, because he did not like it there. Not one bit.

"He thinks he's too good for us," was what most people in Charring said about him. And they were right.

You see, Tadgart Ilk (for that was the Daysman's name, though everyone just called him Ilk) thought his arrival in Charring was the greatest injustice he had suffered in a long line of injustices.

"Sending me off to this backwoods sinkhole at my age, and after all my years of faithful service," he said to himself. He often muttered like that, since he was the only person with whom he never disagreed.

He was muttering all sorts of things to himself one night in mid-spring, on the sixteenth of Faring, when he stood in his library, leaning over his podium-like desk on the top floor of his leaning tower. He often worked at this desk like that, because when he sat down he tended to fall asleep (he was getting on in years).

So, standing there, half-grumbling and half-dreaming how he could convince Fane Sathe to recall him back to the sunny, southern climes of Verisward, he almost jumped out of his fancy, yet uncomfortable, clothes when the tea kettle let out a *sssssswwweeeeeEEEEE*, whistling through the floorboards from below. At that point, he was about three-quarters asleep, for even standing did not always suffice in keeping him awake. He had already started to drool on his copy of *Convincing Codicils* when the kettle wrenched him back into the waking world.

And it was a good thing that he jerked awake at that moment. After cleaning off his drool from the page, he tightened his robes against the chill and noticed the open window. It had come unlatched again, pesky little thing. Sighing a pitiful sigh and grumbling a familiar grumble, he shuffled over to close it before lumbering downstairs to silence that infernal kettle. But when he got to the window, he forgot all about the kettle. Off in the distance, at the edge of the foothills to the north, toward the pathetic little village of Furrow, an incandescent mote, bright as noon but small as a candle flame, fell upon the world of Kiln.

Sparkfall.

Every night, great sparks streaked across the sky, leaving tiny glittering trails to mark their path. They were always moving, never fixed, and at times their paths brought them down into the lands of Warding, never to return to the skies again. Such was the case tonight. Sparkfall happened often enough, but within traveling distance? Where you could see it for yourself? Some people went their whole lives without seeing where a spark fell. In fact, this was the first one Ilk had seen this close in all his sixty-eight miserable, ill-humored, woebegone years. Even better, no one else from Charring could have seen where it landed, for most of the buildings were nestled farther below, at the base of the Hemming Hylls, packed safely behind the shadow of the city walls.

"This is a sign, a portent," he said to himself. "If I can find where that spark fell, perhaps there will be a nugget of gold, or a ball of Spark itself." Ilk believed in the Spark, you see. Not just in the sparks that traversed the evening skies, but in the Spark itself, which moved all creation and sustained it and gave it form and being. This was one of the few things to his credit. Though he thought of the Spark as a sort of energy or source of power, what is commonly referred to as magic, and of course the Spark isn't that at all.

Whether it was true sparkfall or not, he had to investigate. If it was anything valuable, he should be the one to discover it. It might catch the notice of the fane, perhaps even earn him a post as the daysman of a more important city (or at least a warmer one).

"Perhaps this is the break in fortune I have been looking for!"

Even better, this little investigation would take him away from Charring. That fool of a fielder, Hyndric, would be more than happy to take over for him in his absence (in truth, he mostly ran the city anyway).

The only question was whether or not to lug along that thick-headed oaf, Yasec, the daysman's official protector. There had been raids by the dreaded haukmar harriers along several of the major byways since the spring thaw.

"It will be safe in the hills, most likely," he reasoned. "There haven't been any reports of haukmar sightings this far south."

Besides, Yasec and Hyndric talked about everything, especially when it came to Ilk's affairs, and, more importantly, Yasec only took a bath once a year. No, far better to save the discovery for himself. If it was a chunk of gold, Yasec might run off with it. Those fool commoners were always looking for a way to take advantage of their betters.

Ilk dumped his copy of *Mostly Important Portents* into his satchel, along with some spare quills, sheets of vellum, and ink bottles. Adjusting his nynnian spectacles (which, for all their ingenuity and craftsmanship, always slipped down his nose), he opened the library door and descended the stairs.

It was indeed a most important sign Ilk had witnessed, but he never found the sparkfall. It was not meant for him. But he did find something that changed his fortunes, as well as the fortunes of a great many others.

Chapter 1

DEATH ON THE WETHERBONE TORS

Roony was dead. His body lay in the matted turf beside Old Slick Rock. Kion stared at the sight in quivering disbelief.

What was he going to tell his mother? This was all his fault.

"You thick-headed, ornery old cur." Kion stamped the ground.

Ornery. That was the word to describe Roony. He head-butted Kion every chance he got, always looking for moments when Kion was preoccupied to charge in and knock him flat. Though Kion, at seventeen, towered over the pudgy creature, Roony still managed to get the best of him. The only time the ram was happy was when Kion was flat on his back. He'd been a thorn in Kion's side ever since the day he first picked up a cudgel. He was the most belligerent, obnoxious, cantankerous old sheep in the Wetherbone Tors.

And today, Kion had decided to pay him back. Roony had it coming, of course, but not like this. This was not at all what Kion had in mind when he spied the ill-tempered ram heading for the small copse of hawthorn trees at the edge of the pasture. Roony had somehow managed to escape the pen—again—and Kion had decided to teach him a lesson *and* pay him back for all the head-buttings in one ultimate reckoning. He just hadn't counted on it being so ultimate.

It being dusk, and knowing Roony's senses were not what they once were, Kion sped off at an angle to reach Old Slick Rock before the ram. Old Slick Rock was a massive stone, halfway between the sheep pen and the trees. It was almost as tall as Kion and three times as long. He easily reached the stone before the doddering old ram.

Kion crouched, waiting for just the right moment to scare the wool off the old head-butter. He stayed there for the longest time, trembling in anticipation. The ram's hooves clunked to the rhythm of impending doom. He ambled closer...closer. Kion roared out from behind the rock. Roony's eyes rolled up in his head, and he went stiffer than Old Slick Rock itself. The ram tipped over, stone dead before it hit the ground. It was the last thing Kion expected. And now Roony lay on the hard-packed ground, no longer the orneriest, but certainly the stiffest sheep in the Wetherbone Tors.

"Scared to death," Kion muttered. "Mother's never going to believe this."

Despite his tussles with Roony, Kion loved his sheep, he really did. He could tell what they were thinking most of the time by the look in their eyes or the way they moved. Sometimes he liked to imagine what they would say if they could talk. If Roony could have talked, his last words would have been, "Joke's on you!"

But there was nothing funny about this joke.

"Kion!" his mother called from the cottage. "Kion Bray, it's time for supper!"

How was he going to tell her? He could leave the body there and hope a fox or a mountain lion came for it during the night. But he'd have to answer for the missing sheep either way. His mother would want to know how a predator had gotten into the pen again.

"Kion! Can you hear me?" she called.

He would just have to tell her. Knowing her, she'd forbid him from going into Furrow to see Strom Glyre. The Bladewarden was the greatest warrior in the Four Wards. The thought of not meeting his hero made Kion's neck flash with heat. He would probably never get a chance like this again. When did anything important ever happen in Furrow? But he still had the tournament. Roony's death wasn't a big enough mistake to cost him that. Or was it?

"Coming, Mother," he called back.

Roony may have been dead, but he might still get the best of Kion one last time.

Mother froze halfway between the oven and the table, like an elegant statue glowing in the light of the tallow candle on the windowsill. The only thing still moving was the soup sloshing around inside the three bowls cradled in her arms. They teemed with enticing scents, which wafted through the single room of their tiny wattle and daub cottage. At least she didn't drop the bowls.

"He what?" she said, blinking profusely as though she had just turned from stone to flesh. "You expect me to believe that Roony died from fright? Kion, that's the silliest excuse I've ever heard. He's old, but honestly. Wait, you're serious, aren't you?"

Tiryn sat tucked away in her usual corner. Her mouth inched open wider and wider. If she kept going, she would swallow the moon.

"Poor Roony," she said in that tender way she always used when she talked about the sheep. Tiryn was too soft-hearted for her own good. She cried every time they lost one of the flock, especially when it was a lamb. At fifteen, she should have grown out of it, but she was still as flighty as a songbird. If only she could be more like Mother—kind when she needed to be, but strong when hard times came. Then again, Kion wasn't quite sure he wanted his mother to be all that strong just now.

"I didn't mean to kill him," Kion said.

Mother set the bowls on the table. "Of course you didn't. But we're down to thirty-three sheep. We can't afford to lose any more."

"I know, Mother. Believe me, I wish I'd never jumped out from behind that rock."

His mother motioned him over, and he slid into her arms. The strong scent of wood smoke, ginger root, and lilacs wrapped itself around him like a soothing balm.

"I love you, Kion. But you still have to face the consequences of your actions," she said.

He pulled away.

"What? No! Please, Mother—"

Tiryn snickered in the corner. Kion had a theory that she lived for moments like this, seeing him get his comeuppance. "You stay out of this," he said.

"I wasn't laughing at you, Kion, I was just—the thought of poor Roony toppling over like a dried-out shirt on a clothesline —it's actually sort of funny. If it wasn't so sad, I mean." Her eyes sparkled with a sheen of moisture, somewhere between laughter and tears. Flighty. You never knew what you would get with Tiryn.

"Mother, please don't keep me from fighting in the tournament," Kion said.

His mother gazed into his eyes. "You don't think I'd be that harsh, do you? No, it was an honest mistake. Honest, but unwise. And so it needs consequences."

Kion cringed. Here it came. "So, what's my punishment?"

Mother paused, gathering her resolve. She disliked punishing him almost as much as he disliked receiving it. "You're going to have to stay home tonight and chop up the carcass."

He knew it was coming. That didn't make it any easier.

"But I'll miss seeing Strom!"

"I'm sorry, but you killed Roony. It falls on you to butcher him. And you know we can't let the meat go overnight. It'll barely fetch two nicks as it is, but if we leave it sitting, we'll be lucky to get half a nick and some flour."

"But—but I have to pick up my sword from Zinder. If I don't get it back tonight, I won't be able to practice tomorrow, and who knows when I'll have time to go into town to pick it up again."

"Nevertheless, that is what you must do."

Kion opened his mouth, then snapped it shut again. Anything he said at this point was only going to get him into more trouble. He hated to admit it, but the punishment was fair. Why couldn't she show him mercy, just this once?

"Yes, Mother," he said.

He had his back to Tiryn, but he was certain her smile was as big as the moon.

That night it took Kion a long time to fall asleep. By the time he'd butchered Roony and cleaned up, his mother and sister were already in bed. Mother lay buried in a lump of wool blanket to the left of the door. Tiryn's hammock wrapped around her like a cocoon near the table. The wash basin, stove, and cabinets—all dark, featureless shapes—rested along the far wall, opposite where Tiryn slept.

Kion crawled into his own hammock to the right of the door. It sagged so low it brushed against the two pinewood chests underneath. These held all their worldly possessions, apart from what they used for shepherding or gardening. Those were stored outside in the shed. Kion's hammock had been sagging for the better part of a year, ever since he hit his growth spurt. He'd been meaning to raise it, but he never seemed to remember until he was too exhausted to care.

Tonight was no different. If anything, he was more exhausted than usual. And yet sleep would not come. All he could think about was Strom Glyre the bladewarden, the most celebrated warrior of the age and hero of the Battle of Fane's Falling, camped out in the village of Furrow, just a short trek to the south. If only Kion could see greatness, just once in his life, something he could hold onto during the cold, rainy days, the hard, bony walks over rubbled country, and the lonely, quiet nights of sorrow.

Strom was said to be tall, no doubt even taller than Kion, though Kion was taller than most boys his age. But it was the face, the eyes—that was what Kion wanted to see most. That was what truly told you the measure of a man—his character, the tenor of his heart, whether he was someone men would fight and die for. Kion could picture Strom's gaze, gallant and peerless, yet kind. He was decked out in full armor, glistening and gleaming, his ancient sword hanging at his side. According to Zinder, that blade had been passed down from bladewarden to bladewarden, ever since the fanedom began a thousand years ago. Zinder knew a thing or two about blades. He was the village blacksmith, and the finest one in all of Casting Selvedge, which comprised the three villages of Furrow, Windstern, and Roving. And he was a nyn to top all comers. Nothing rivaled nynnian craftsmanship. How a nyn of his abilities wound up in a little village like Furrow was a mystery to Kion. He doubted if even his mother knew the whole story.

But what mattered most at that moment was not Zinder's past, but that the lucky little nyn was getting to see Strom Glyre, and Kion was not.

"Roony…" Kion muttered through clenched teeth. "You cost me my one chance to see a true hero."

Kion turned on his side and let his arm fall over the edge of his hammock. He brushed his fingers against the chest below. The battered wooden box held his father's helmet, along with Kion's ribbons from past tournaments, some shiny pebbles, a few arrowheads he'd found in the Tors, and other knickknacks. Kion had planned on bringing the helmet to Strom to have him blademark it. Famous captains sometimes blademarked the helmets of their best men, or as a way to honor the fallen. If Strom blademarked that helm, it would have restored some measure of honor to his father's name, at least in Kion's thinking. The villagers said his father hadn't been a real soldier, just his company's musician. Worse, some said he had played the song for retreat against orders after Fane Galbraith was killed, and that he'd nearly cost the Warding army the Battle of Fane's Falling.

"I know what they say isn't true. I know you stayed brave to the end..." Kion whispered in the dark.

But being a musician and a coward were only two of his father's faults in the eyes of the villagers. His father was also a shepherd, as, of course, was Kion. And that was almost as bad as being a coward. Shepherds were the most despised people on the Tors. If the sheep didn't give enough wool, people went without a new coat or blanket. If the crops failed, people went without food and died. Good farmland was rare, not just in the Tors, but in most of the North, so rare that some referred to these lands as the Pebbled Steps. The soil was rocky and so were the people—well, the ones in Furrow, anyway.

Too poor to own their own land, the shepherds lived up in the rugged, windswept hills surrounding the village. They struggled to find good pasture and keep their sheep safe from predators and disease. No one except the other shepherds understood how they suffered. They earned barely enough money to pay the wealthy families who owned their houses, and most of what was left went to the fane's taxes, which only grew year after year.

But the tournament was Kion's chance to change all this. If he won, the villagers would know that the Brays were fighters and that shepherds had just as much honor as anyone else. Maybe Strom would even hear about it up in the fortress of the Clefts at Roving, where he was headed after he left Furrow. Maybe if Kion won, Strom would recruit him to join one of the fane's marches. They could always use another blade to help them push back the haukmarn. With Strom up at the Clefts, the fane surely meant to deal with them once and for all. And soldiers made good pay, from what Kion had heard, far more than shepherds, at least. He would miss his mother, but it would be worth the sacrifice. If his father could give everything for people who treated him like a traitor, Kion could sacrifice for his family.

He rolled onto his back. The soft, familiar rhythm of his mother and sister's breathing filled the dark. In vain he listened for the deep, full breathing of his father. The absence of the sound pressed in on his ears like being underwater. It had been ten years since he died, but the older Kion got, the more the ache grew. Maybe winning the tournament would make it go away. Maybe it would make everything better.

Amidst all his exhausted wrestlings, he drifted off to sleep at last.

But somewhere, close to midnight, a voice spoke into his dreams. It filled him with warmth, but a restless warmth, the kind you get on the cusp of a fever.

"I awake, but only just...My vision is yet dim, so very dim...Come to me and I shall be whole again...Listen to my voice...The call is sent...Awake, glaivebond, awake and take me up once more..."

But Kion did not remember these words, not until it was too late.

Chapter 2

DAY OF INNOCENTS

K ion pulled the sheep pen door shut, bedraggled and weary from a long day of rain and wind upon the Tors. The weather had forced him to shelter the sheep in the crags for several hours to keep them from slipping into a ravine or getting caught in a mudslide. It had been two days since Roony's death, but the absence of the ram's pestering brought little relief. It was the same as always: work, work, work, and more work after that.

He went to the cottage and stood with the door halfway open but didn't go in.

"Mother, I'm going to skip dinner tonight," he said.

She looked up from stirring a pot on the stove. Something savory bubbled inside, but he resisted its pull.

"Are you sure?"

"Yes."

Tiryn sat snug in her corner, reading her diary and humming softly. Off in her dream world, like usual. The diary was one of the few luxuries they had, a gift from their well-off relation in Charring, Aunt Lizet. The crotchety old crone had a soft spot for Tiryn and nothing but spite for Kion. Mother said it was because Kion looked so much like his father. Aunt Lizet had never approved of his mother's marriage, but Kion didn't care what some rich old maid thought about his family. She never even bothered to visit, though Furrow was only a three-day journey from Charring. Which was perfectly fine with Kion.

"I'm too tired to be hungry," he added. In truth, he was starving, but he had to practice. His sword was still at the smithy, so his wooden one would have to do.

"All right," Mother said, far too easily. She never let him skip meals. Something must be wrong. He was tempted to ask but thought better of it. Best to get going before she changed her mind.

"I'll be in at dark." He started to close the door.

"Oh, by the way, Zinder sent your sword back," she said. "I had to run into market today, so I picked it up for you. He said he might even stop by to spar with you."

Kion let out a shout loud enough to blow off the thatched roof. "Fire and ice! Good old Zinder!" He could always count on his friend to light a spark on his darkest days.

Tiryn's eyes peeped mischievously from behind her book, but she looked away as soon as Kion caught her. But he was in too good a mood to be bothered by her antics.

He rushed inside and gave his mother a hug so tight she let out a squeak. "Thank you, Mother. You put it in the shed?"

"Yes, son." Her eyes shone brightly. She lived for the joy of her children.

He fairly flew to the shed. Zinder was just about the best friend a boy could have. Sure, he was older, but he acted Kion's age most of the time.

Kion found the sword bundled neatly in a burlap cloth on one of the crates in the shed.

He unwrapped it eagerly, noting that Zinder had oiled the leather scabbard as well.

Not far off, Zinder's familiar whistling and the jostling of his wagon and harness drifted up the path.

"Just in time for me to thank him," Kion thought.

He stepped outside, drawing the sword with relish so he could admire the freshly sharpened blade. It was as good as the day his father had first received it. Better, even.

As the blade caught the fading rays of the sun in a cold shine, Zinder's white-bearded smile came bouncing up the hill. He was seated in his cart, drawn by his faithful mule, Crusty. Belonging to the rare race of nyn, Zinder was little more than half Kion's height, though he was twice Kion's age. While not as strong as full-grown men, nyn could nevertheless outwork most folk due to their boundless energy. Sometimes Kion wondered if Zinder ever slept. That nynnian energy was on full display as Zinder's arm waved like a ribbon in the breeze. His face beamed, a giddy look on his pointy-nosed face. He had on a sky-blue shirt with a black scarf bunched around his neck and a matching set of black leather gloves. His white leggings had ruffles along the sides, and his polished black boots came up to just below the knee. He caromed around in the cart, as bright and lively as a firefly in a bottle. Enthusiasm and glee bubbled inside his mischievous eyes.

Kion was about to wave back when an odd, oozing sensation seeped onto his hand. The longer he noticed it, the stickier it got, until he sheathed the sword and had a look. His hand was covered in some sort of translucent ointment. So was the sword grip. What had happened? Had the bindings on the grip over-heated in the smithy?

Zinder's popping, roaring, cackling bursts of laughter answered his questions. "Happy Innocent's Day," he shouted.

Innocent's Day. How could he have forgotten? It was the first day of the month of Avring. Zinder terrorized him like this every year!

"Zinder, you vile rogue!"

Kion tossed the sword on the turf and tore off for the cart.

Zinder reined in Crusty and leapt to his feet, then doubled over, laughing.

Kion quickly closed the distance, but Zinder recovered and ran to the back of the cart, his face turning pinker by the moment.

Kion growled as he lunged at his traitorous friend. "You laugh like a newborn piglet!"

"At least my hands are clean!" Zinder jumped back,

squealing in a rather swine-like manner. Whether intentional or not, it made Kion's insult all the more appropriate.

Kion had had enough. He vaulted into the cart. He almost caught Zinder, but the little fellow was too quick. He tumbled over the edge of the wagon and took off sprinting around the cart. Kion hopped down and thundered after him. By now, the shock and sting of Zinder's prank had worn off, and he was laughing too. Zinder's ridiculous cackling was too contagious.

They darted and danced around each other, until Zinder started to lose a step on his younger, long-legged pursuer. In a last, desperate effort, he made a dash for the shed. Kion overtook him in a heartbeat, tackling him from behind.

Once he had Zinder on the ground, he tried shoving his sticky hand into his friend's perfectly groomed beard.

"No! No! No! Please! I claim the right of Innocents!" Zinder cried.

Kion had to let up. Those were the Day of Innocents rules, going back as far as the holiday had been in existence. You couldn't retaliate if you were genuinely fooled. At least not until next year. Kion would have to think of something exceptionally devious for his little friend. And next year he would not forget!

"All right, you rascal," Kion said. "You bested me in trickery. But you'll not fare so well when it comes to swords. I challenge you to a match."

He rose and offered to help Zinder up with his sticky hand.

"Ah, lad, you never give up, do you?" Zinder said.

Kion laughed and helped him up with his other hand.

"You're a great boaster, I see, when it comes to battle skills." Zinder dusted himself off and arranged his hair back into a careful side part. "But we shall see if I can't pull off a trick or two!"

"Indeed, we shall," Kion said, eager for the challenge. "But first, let me clean off my hand and the hilt. You wouldn't want to fight me with an unfair advantage."

Zinder gave him a half-cocked smile. "Says who? I'll take all the help I can get!"

And off they went to the well.

Dusk settled across the Tors. The scraggly hawthorns scattered amongst the rocks and turf sighed wearily in the wind.

Kion and Zinder sat on Old Slick Rock, their vambraces cast aside. A cool breeze ran through their damp hair and feathered against their necks. Kion had gotten the better of Zinder in their sparring, but that was nothing new. He'd been besting his friend regularly since he was fifteen. Now, at seventeen, he never lost.

"It's too bad we can't practice in real armor," Kion said.

"True. But you smell ripe enough as it is!"

"Zinder!" Kion was sensitive about this topic. He never washed unless his mother made him. If he smelled good enough for her, that was all that mattered.

"Sorry, sorry, that was poor taste." Zinder blushed in honest regret. "Sometimes my wheels get ahead of my wagon. But you know, if you'd clean up a bit more often, those farmers would have less to heckle you about." In saying this, he moved slyly upwind of Kion.

"I don't have time for things like that. The tournament's almost here. I need every spare moment I can get to practice."

"I know, I know. But you're right about the armor. It would do you good to train in it. If I had the coin, I'd forge you a nice breastplate," Zinder said, scrutinizing his short blade for nicks. "It's such a shame I missed the bladewarden's visit. I hear that if a smith gets in good with one of the companies, he can practically forge his own gold."

"Oh, no, you missed him too?" Kion said. And here he had been so jealous.

"It was a bitter stroke, but it couldn't be helped. I had some last-minute business that took me over to Windstern. When coin comes calling, the door is always open." Zinder took out his sharpening stone and slid it along his blade. The blade was shorter than Kion's by more than a foot, but of much finer make, for Zinder had forged it himself. Its thick steel glittered cold but bright. It had a clever guard about the hilt that covered the wielder's hand. Kion's sword had been freshly sharpened, but it was still the same modest blade his father had used in the war.

Kion frowned at the mention of Windstern. "You can't keep making these trips, Zinder. You're going to run afoul of the haukmarn sooner or later. There have been three raids already this spring." The haukmarn. The very thought of them raised the hair on the back of Kion's neck. These were the monsters who had killed his father. Kion had never seen one himself, but everyone in Casting Selvedge had heard of their savage deeds. Gray-skinned and dim-witted, they were eight feet of muscle and wrath. One of their harriers was said to equal two men in battle.

"A nyn's got to do his business, haukmarn or no. Until it's full-out war, I'll keep plying my wares," Zinder said.

"Do you think it will come to that—actual war?"

Zinder paused in his sharpening, pondering. "It's hard to say. The haukmarn have conquered these lands before. And who knows but that their allies, those disgraceful noathryn to the west, won't join in with them again, and then we'd really be in a press. One thing's for sure: the haukmarn won't rest until they conquer the Four Wards once and for all. They may come out in open war fifty years from now, or they may come tomorrow, but come they will."

"What's keeping them from coming now? Why are they content to only raid farms and harass travelers?"

"Ah, that's where their weakness lies, you see. Their leader died in the War of the Claws, same as ours. But where we just appointed the next fane, they dissolved into petty bickering and infighting amongst the various tribal claws. Without a strong leader, all they can manage is the occasional raid from a single claw or two. They're no longer united. And those raids you mentioned were in early spring. They've quieted down in the last month."

"Maybe they got wind that Strom was headed to Roving and went into hiding."

Kion imagined what it would be like, marching with Strom and his men into the Fortress of the Clefts, which protected Roving and the Tors to the south. He pictured the crenellations lined with archers and spearmen, their gaze fixed and grave, scanning the hills for any sign of their ancient enemy.

"As likely as not, you've hit it there," Zinder said. "He'd rout 'em just like he did those raiding parties at Fennigar and Seabrim!"

"Or when he rode through the night to catch those noathryn marauders camped out in the Hemming Hylls." Kion stared off. Another picture flashed before him. It was of Strom atop a majestic black steed, his sword lifted high as he burst through the fog and into the flank of the shocked and hapless ranks of the noathryn warriors.

"Rich is the man who lived to see one of those glorious victories." Zinder sharpened his blade with extra vigor, as if he were preparing to fight alongside the bladewarden himself.

"You at least talked to some of the folk who saw him, didn't you?" Kion said.

"Shar's Dome! Of course I did!" Zinder puffed out his chest. "A smith's shop is second only to the market for gossip."

"What did they say?" News at last! For a wide-eyed shepherd boy who'd never left the Tors, this was the next best thing to seeing the bladewarden himself.

"Well, he didn't blademark anyone's helmet, if it makes you feel any better. He spent most of his time with his men out on the commons, chattering away with Fielder Lorris. You can imagine what that was like. Lorris acted like he'd been promoted to Highgild! After the feast—if you can call it that, for it was nothing more than honey bread and stock stew—Lorris took him over to that new stronghold he's been building, 'in case of inva-sion,' as he says. Ho! As if Furrow would last one minute if the haukmarn came howling down from the hills. But he had his day in the sun. Enough to last him 'til the Seven Fires Festival and then some, no doubt. Speaking of the festival, do you think you'll be ready come time for the tournament?"

"I try not to think about it," Kion said. "Every time I do my insides start shaking."

Zinder poked him in the chest. "If you weren't nervous, then I'd worry. A little fear keeps the blade sharp and the wits sharper. Fear can stall the hasty strike, make you wait for just the right moment, and then"—Zinder made a slashing motion with his hand—"you dart in with the blade and teach *them* a little fear, see?"

For someone as pedestrian with a blade as Zinder was, he certainly gave wonderful advice.

Far-off tinkling sounds turned their heads to the north. In the fading light a stocky figure limped along, guiding his sheep out of the woods to the west. The tinkling was from the sheep bells. Zinder stopped his sharpening to stand and get a better look.

"Is that Rike?" Zinder asked. Kion couldn't tell for sure. It was too far away, but it couldn't be anyone else. He was headed towards Rike's farm.

"Must be," Kion said.

Zinder gave the figure an energetic wave, but Rike didn't return it. Bit by bit, he disappeared with his sheep over the far hill.

"Dreary fellow," Zinder said. "But you shepherds do like to keep to yourselves, I suppose."

"Rike's even more guarded than the rest of us, but he's not a bad sort," Kion said. "Mother's been making an extra effort to be kind to him since his wife passed away last winter. He's been coming over for dinner once an eight-mark. In fact, he's coming over tomorrow night if you'd care to join us."

"Oh, now, don't tempt me. You know I never like to miss out

on a chance at your mother's cooking. But it's the first four-mark of the month and there's new orders coming in. I'll be working until the lanterns go out. Besides, I don't think Rike much cares for me. I always try to be friendly when I see him, but he passes by like I wasn't there." He crept back down and put away his sharpening stone.

"A shameful way to treat Furrow's favorite son," Kion said grandly.

"It's hard to imagine how he could fail to acknowledge someone of my obvious magnificence." Zinder thrust his hands behind his back and pointed his chin so high he could have passed for a weather vane.

Kion hopped off the rock. "Careful, if you grow any more magnificent, they might elect you fielder of the village and make you fend off the haukmar harriers all by yourself!"

Zinder flourished his sword in the air. "Bring on the howling hordes! One nyn is worth a hundred men!"

Laughing and joking, they headed back to Zinder's cart, and Kion saw him off.

Chapter 3

MUSIC AND MEMORIES

The potato soup was especially good on the evening of Rike's visit. Mother put in extra cream. And Tiryn's bread was better than usual. Not that Kion let her know.

A sweet, snug aroma hummed through the cottage. The heat of the oven joined with that of the four souls packed together around the little whitewood table. Rike was nothing like Kion's father, but it felt good having a man in the home.

Rike spoke sparingly, but the glimmerings of a smile crossed his face on a few occasions, and his dark gaze softened somewhat as the evening drew on. He was most approachable when talking about shepherding and sheep.

"I haven't seen you in the southern woods for a few days now; have you found some good pasture up north?" Kion asked.

"I have. A new valley I hadn't seen until this spring." As Rike spoke, Mother refilled his cup from the water pitcher. "Thank you, m'lady," he said.

"I thought it was mostly just rock up that way," Mother said.

Rike took a few sips as he gathered his thoughts. They bunched together on his brow, as if he had to compose the words, letter by letter, in his mind before he answered. "Rain changes things. We had those downpours during the month of Kalbrin. I thought I'd have a look."

"That makes sense," Kion said. "A mudslide made it, then?"

"Looks like."

Tiryn stared at their guest in open fascination. When it came to conversation, unless she knew someone fairly well, she took it all in with her eyes and ears and hardly said a word. Rike had been coming over for several months now, ever since his wife died, but Tiryn still acted as shy as a field mouse. Kion tried to catch her eye on several occasions and signal her to stop staring so much, but she was too enrapt to notice.

"I never thought a little rain could change things so quickly. Just shows how much I have to learn, I suppose," Kion said.

"Rike is one of the most experienced shepherds on the Tors. There are a few who are older, but none more skilled," Mother said.

Rike shifted in his seat and gave the door a meaningful glance. He had as hard a time taking compliments as Mother did in refraining from giving them.

"Mother said you helped my father get started here after they got married," Kion said to keep the conversation from stalling.

Rike gave a reserved nod. The look in his eyes grew vague and distant.

"What was my father like? Do you have any memories of him?" Kion said, hoping to draw Rike out.

Rike stared into his soup bowl. For long moments he said nothing, spellbound by his unspoken thoughts. "Dorn was...a good man," he said at length. Sadness mixed with terror upon his face. His head snapped, and his eyes locked on the door. "I'm sorry, but I...I must be going."

Kion nodded understandingly, though he didn't understand at all.

"Would you like some more bread?" Mother hurried to break the awkward tension.

"No, thank you, m'lady. It was delicious, but no...I'm fine."

Rike leaned forward to get up, but Mother placed a hand on his arm.

"Tiryn was going to play some music after dinner. We were hoping you'd stay and listen."

Tiryn nodded expectantly. She was shy about most things, but not about her music.

Rike's face flashed in embarrassment, as if he had just spilled his soup or broken the crockery. "That is very kind, but I must be going. I have things to do back at the farm." He rose and gave quick nods to each of them. "Thank you for the meal."

Mother graciously handed him his cloak and helped him put it on.

"We'll see you again next eight-mark," Mother said warmly. "And if you need something before then, don't be afraid to ask."

Rike tipped his head. "Miss Annira. Children. Good evening," he said in a husky voice.

He pulled his hood tightly over his head, and with it, a stern demeanor. He gave a stiff bow as he turned in the doorway and went off into the night. Whatever words he was composing in his head as he strode towards home remained locked inside. He had become a blank page once more.

Though Rike was not there to hear it, Tiryn played that night all the same. She usually played her lute, but that night she brought out her wood pipes. She was a skilled musician, though Kion never bothered to tell her. He didn't want her to become overly prideful about her talents.

Her pipes filled the cottage with windy melodies of popular Inrisian songs. Mother hummed softly, but Kion's mind drifted. The music reminded him of Father, who was even more gifted at music than Tiryn, though of course she was still young and learning. A part of Kion envied her talent. For in her music she had a connection to their father that Kion did not.

The notes of the song floated by, vessels on a sea of memory that felt more like a whirlpool. At the bottom of that pool lay sorrow and emptiness. It was a pit that only the presence of Kion's father could fill.

The music shifted, drawing Kion out of his grim thoughts. His sister was playing a song he had never heard before. It must have been one of those she made up from time to time. They were usually full of energy and flair, but this one was quieter, almost mournful. As she finished, she gave him a tender look, as if to say that she, too, knew what it was like to go swirling down to the bottom of the whirlpool.

"What was that last one called?" Mother asked.

"'If Dreams Came True,'" Tiryn said softly.

"It was beautiful, like something your father would have written. Are there words to it?"

Tiryn fiddled with her pipes and glanced toward the chest where she kept her diary. "Maybe."

"Well, if you ever decide to share, I would very much like to hear them," Mother said.

Tiryn bit her lip and stared at the hearth. The flames had faded along with the music. Only faint embers remained.

"All right, dear ones. That's enough for tonight. You both need your sleep." Mother touched Tiryn's nose. "You need time to dream up some new songs."

Tiryn went to one of the chests and returned her pipes with a click of the latch.

Mother nudged Kion. "And you need your rest for the tournament."

"I suppose." Kion looked at the door. Beyond it, out in the dark, his sword sat in the shed. He knew his mother meant well, but what he really needed was more practice; either that or to grow about twenty pounds of muscle. "I bet Dougan Shaw doesn't need to go to bed this early," he said.

"Well then, perhaps you'll have an advantage."

"I don't think so. No one's ever beaten him."

"But no one's ever won the tournament three years in a row either," Tiryn put in. "So I'd say the odds are in your favor."

"As if you knew anything about sword fighting." Kion gave her a blank look. She came to watch his matches, but she'd never shown any real interest in swordplay. If only he had a brother to practice with instead of flighty little Tiryn.

Despite himself, he let out a huge yawn. He was more tired than he wanted to admit. He shuffled over to his hammock but stopped. Tired as he was, there was something besides his lack of practice and Dougan Shaw's size that was bothering him.

"Mother, why didn't Rike want to talk about Father? Did the two of them have a falling out?"

"Oh, no," she said. "But he was with your father in the war. Only, Rike didn't come home when it was over."

Kion's tiredness vanished. "Rike was in the war? How come you never told me before?"

"He doesn't like to talk about it. It stirs up terrible memories."

"Do you know what happened to him?"

Tiryn climbed into her hammock, but she kept one ear cocked to hear the answer to Kion's question.

"He was taken prisoner by the haukmarn," Mother said. "I don't know what they did to him, but he was never the same after he came back."

The old, sinking dread welled up inside Kion at the mention of his father's killers. Kion had never been to the Marred Wastes where the haukmarn dwelt, but it was said that few who went into those lands ever returned. The very air there was said to induce madness.

"How did he escape?" Kion asked, gaining a newfound respect for Rike.

"No one knows. He came back two years after the war. Mae had all but given him up for dead, so I helped her tend their flock. One day he wandered back from the village, wild-looking and with hardly any flesh on his bones. I helped Mae nurse him back to health. She was so happy to have him again. Without her, he might not have recovered. Now that she's gone, he's retreating back inside those walls of fear and torment. We have to do all we can to draw him out."

Kion regretted asking Rike about the war, even indirectly. If only he had known.

"Do you think the haukmarn will ever be defeated?" Kion asked.

"In my father's time, there was peace," Mother said. "Even now, they say the attacks are small and will never amount to much. It's been nothing like the last war. I would like to think they suffered such losses that they will never recover." She kissed him on the cheek.

"I hope you're right."

"Good night, Kion," Tiryn said. Her troubled expression mirrored the doubts in his own heart. Still, he wished she didn't have to hear everything. She worried far too much.

"Good night, Tiryn."

He crawled into his hammock as Mother kissed Tiryn good night. His sadness melted into anger as he thought about what the war had done to his father and Rike. One had lost his life, and the other might as well have. Kion had faced threats to his flock many times, but what had it been like to stand against such vicious warriors, such cruel hate? He drifted off to sleep, thoughts of becoming a soldier burning like a brand in his mind. Maybe one day he'd get the chance to repay those haukmar monsters for what they'd done.

Chapter 4

LADY OF THE TORS

Tiryn's diary lay open to the picture she had drawn of Lina. It was not as good as she was capable of. The lines were too thick, for one thing. Usually she did much better, but somehow it was harder for her to draw things she knew. She had a much easier time sketching from her imagination. The sketch was further marred by the dried tear-stains that had gone into the paper when she drew it.

She didn't need the picture to remember the face of her friend, though. She could still see it perfectly in the warm, protective fastness of memory.

Below the drawing, Tiryn had written these words:

Lina Erlin, dearest friend
16th of Laneld, 822-5th of Longmel, 837
Taken too soon.

"I miss her, too," Mother said.

Tiryn closed the book as her mother finished braiding her hair.

"Do you think it's safe yet to visit her grave?" Tiryn asked.

"I should think so, but Rike still hasn't visited Mae's, so I don't know. I'll ask Mistress Shona, just to be sure. Maybe we can visit it during Seven Fires."

"I would like that." Tiryn ran her hands along the thick braid that fell over her shoulder and down her front. She could have done it herself—she was fifteen, after all—but she liked the way her mother did it better.

"You are so lovely, my little karinna," Mother said. Tiryn blushed. At least there was no one around to hear the compliment. "Karinna" was what her father had called her, but her mother used it sometimes, too, and more of late. The word meant "lady" in some distant land, as far as Tiryn remembered. "My Karinna of the Tors," was the way her father used to say it.

"Kion says I look like Gertrina Slattery," Tiryn said. She didn't know why she always had to explain away Mother's compliments. A bad habit, she supposed.

"Oh, don't be silly. You know he's only teasing. Now, when do I get to hear the words to this wonderful new song of yours?" Mother asked. It had been a four-mark since Tiryn had foolishly played that song after dinner.

Tiryn brought the end of the braid up and stuck it in her mouth. Another habit she'd been trying to break, but she never noticed when she did it.

"It's not ready." No, that wasn't true. But she didn't want her mother to hear the words yet. She didn't want anyone to hear them. They were too sad. If Mother heard them, maybe she'd think Tiryn was sad, too. She was, but she didn't want her mother worrying about her. "At least, I'm not ready to share it," she corrected herself.

"Is it about Father?"

Tiryn was a glass box when it came to keeping things hidden from her mother, who saw straight through to her heart.

"What makes you say that?" Tiryn asked.

"'If Dreams Came True.' What other dream would my daughter have than to wish that her father could hold her in his arms again?" Mother came around front and bent down to look her in the eye. "Don't ever be afraid of your dreams, Tiryn. Hold on to the good ones and let the bad ones go."

"Yes, it's about him," Tiryn said. "The words are a little sad. But it's a good kind of sad, I think."

Mother wrapped her arms around her. "You can tell me the words when you're ready, karinna."

Tiryn leaned into her embrace. She wanted to say something, to tell her mother how wonderful she was, to ask her if the ache of missing Father would ever go away. It had been ten years. If anything, the sorrow was stronger than ever. But Tiryn's words caught in the emotions webbing up her throat.

The two of them held each other in the stillness of the cottage. Outside, the wind sang its own mournful song across the Tors, fanning the struggling grass and rustling against the weary rocks.

"Thank you, Mother," Tiryn said.

Her mother let go, and they both stood.

"You know, I've been thinking about how much Mr. Rike enjoyed that honey bread you made," Mother said. "What do you say we bake some more and have Kion take it over to him?"

Tiryn's heart warmed at the suggestion. Rike seemed so lonely and lost. "That's a wonderful idea. Oh, but we're out of honey. I'll need to get some more."

"Well, it's a little windy today, but I think you should be all right. Just make sure you're home before dinner."

"I will, Mother." Tiryn gave her a contented smile. There were few things Tiryn liked better than a walk across the Tors.

"All right then, here's your cloak and the basket. You might want to go a little farther into the woods today to get out of this wind, but don't go too far." She handed Tiryn her things. The empty clay jar inside the basket gave it a good heft, but Tiryn was used to the weight. It would be even heavier on the return journey.

"I'll be careful, Mother. Don't worry."

Tiryn pulled her cloak tight and kissed her mother in the doorway.

Mother spun her around and whispered in her ear. "It's my dream too," she said.

With the warmth of those words and her mother's beautiful

smile glowing inside, Tiryn set out with her basket for a journey across the Tors.

Tiryn went all the way out to Cloven Brook that afternoon. She had not been out that far all spring, but there was plenty of time for a longer walk, and she had a lot to think about.

Mostly it had to do with her father. She didn't know why she had been thinking so much about him lately. Sometimes she could let her worries fade by writing a song, but the new one only made her think about him more. She hummed it softly on her way to the brook, not daring to sing the words until she got deeper into the woods.

Mother said she had a beautiful voice, but then Mother loved everything Tiryn did. Kion was more honest. He had let her know on more than one occasion how little appreciation he had for her singing. But she loved music too much not to sing. Yet another reason she loved stealing off into the woods.

Not only did she love to sing, she loved to dance. Oddly, dancing did not embarrass her like singing. It was just that in the cottage, there was never any room. And when she was working in the garden, or with the sheep, there was no time for such indulgences. In the woods, she was free. The heath and the roots and the rocks made it less than ideal, but she didn't mind. She would dance in a snow storm if she had to, as long as there was open space.

Sometimes she fancied the creatures of the Tors enjoyed her little performances. The rabbits, the squirrels, the heath mice, the sparrows, the finches, and the crossbills all had been privy to her sylvan prancing. The birds seemed the most pleased. Perhaps because they loved music as much as she did. Or perhaps because they were higher up and safely out of the way of her twirling gyrations.

Lina had told her that she'd once seen a golden songbird

flash through the trees in the early morning. It wasn't gold like yellow, but gold like metal, shining in the midday sun.

"It wasn't a bird at all, you see. It was a forest wisp," Lina had said in a reverent hush.

Some people, like Mistress Shona, the village herbalist, said that these golden creatures could talk and turn themselves into humans and beguile folk, or grant them wishes if they chose. Ever since Lina told her about the wisp, Tiryn had been looking for one, but she'd never seen any. Lina said most people only ever saw one in their whole life, two if they were lucky.

There were certainly no golden creatures to observe her dancing today. Only a handful of flitting birds and the ever-skittering squirrels.

Humming and capering and thinking of her father, she came at last to the brook. It was in a good, healthy spring flow. Dark blue waters poured over the many tumble-down rocks that peppered the stream. A nice-sized beehive hovered on the opposite side, nestled in the bosom of one of the rare, grand old hawthorn trees. It might have been the largest one she'd ever seen. Bees buzzed lazily in and out of the hive. Honey at last!

Six strides, stepping from rock to rock, would take her across the stream, but the wind beat against her, making every step on the slick stones a test of balance. She stepped carefully past one rock, then two. But covering a large gap in the middle, she slipped. She went down in the knee-deep water, drenching her skirt, her shoe, and clean through to her breeches on one side.

Her wool coat resisted the soaking, but her other clothes absorbed every bit of the stream they could hold. Between the icy bath and the cutting wind, she was shivering like a newborn lamb by the time she reached the far bank.

"Clumsy girl," she muttered to herself. Oh, well, she was going to have to make a fire to smoke out the bees anyway. Now she'd just have to make it last a bit longer so she could dry out her clothes.

It didn't take long to gather a sizable heap of fallen branches for the fire, but most of it was still wet from last night's rain. The fierce winds didn't help either. If only she had Kion's knack for fire, she'd have lit it right away. But what she could not do through skill, she achieved through persistence. After several minutes of fiercely striking her flint with her knife, one of the sparks finally took. By then, her teeth were bouncing around in her mouth uncontrollably.

The scent of smoke mingled with the aroma of fresh spring flowers in the cold, clear air. She decided to keep moving to stay warm while the fire grew. And what better way to do that than to dance? There was a nice big open space around the fire. With the Seven Fires Festival coming later that month, she'd been longing to practice the *fiddlewise*, a lively country dance performed at the end of the four-mark-long festival. Mistress Shona was in charge of it, and each year she chose a different set of girls to perform: the candle maidens, they were called. Not only did they get to perform the dance at the closing ceremony, they got to light the candles at the end of each day of the festival. This year, Tiryn had been among the girls picked, probably because Mistress Shona took pity on her on account of Lina's death. Mistress Shona was one of the few people who didn't care that the Brays were shepherds. Tiryn was thrilled and nervous all at once. If she stumbled, or worse, fell, she would never be able to show her face in Furrow again.

She traipsed about the fire, twirling and curtsying and clapping her hands, humming the tune she'd written for her father. It had the same rhythm as the *fiddlewise*, only slower. She let the music move her limbs, like a willow in the breeze.

What an odd picture she must make, stripped down to her breeches and barefoot, like some forest wisp leading her pursuers on a merry chase. She laughed at the absurdity of it, but also for joy, pure joy, which came from lithe movements and the great, swirling melody that played inside her. Let the wind buffet and the river drench her. She was a young girl caught up

in the rapture of music. Nothing could disturb her in these
woods she knew so well.

In times like these, when the old joy came back, she felt closer
than ever to her father. His music filled her sails and sent her out
in a ship of dreams across a gleaming sea of hope and possibility.
Though she could no longer see him, she felt his memory come
alive again inside her.

She burst into song, full-throated and free, the song she had
written for her father. The movements of her dance shifted to
match the somber tone, but her voice rose high and clear and
beautiful above the wind.

If dreams came true
If time rolled back before you left
I would still have you
If dreams came true

If dreams were real
If your voice sang beyond my sleep
I'd know what to feel
If dreams were real

If dreams could stay
If you'd be there when I awake
Night would turn to day
If dreams could stay

The image of her father seemed to float above the fire as she
sang the last few strains. His dark hair and noble features gave
him a regal air. In her eyes, he looked less like a shepherd and
more like royalty. Of course, she had never seen the fane or any
of the council that served him in far-away Gilding, but she could
not imagine they looked any higher or more dignified than her
father.

She closed her eyes, holding on to the vision. But the precious picture lasted only a moment. Her eyes flew open.

Something was watching her.

She didn't know how she knew, but she felt it as strong and sudden as her icy dip in the river. The next moment, the distinct snapping of branches confirmed her intuition. There was something in the woods.

She hurried over to the fire where she'd left her knife. Dark clouds had moved in since she'd crossed the brook. She saw now how foolish she'd been, dancing out in the open like this. Though predators usually avoided people, especially when there was a fire, she knew enough from Kion's misadventures to be on her guard. She had never been attacked like he had, but that was no surety of protection. She spun slowly about the fire, eyeing every bush and clump of tall grass for signs of a threat.

The wind surged, masking the buzzing of the bees and other nearby sounds. She turned this way and that, but no matter which way she faced, she was left exposed in front of the fire. Could it be a beast that even Kion had not encountered? A wolf, perhaps, or a bear?

A low growl sounded from the shadow-ridden brush surrounding the honey tree. It was so faint, she could barely hear it over the wind. She waved her knife threateningly in that direction. She wished she had picked up her walking stick with her other hand, but it lay on the ground several steps away, and she was too frightened now to go back for it. She gripped the knife tighter and took a tentative step towards the bushes. Maybe if she could surprise whatever it was and strike first, she would have a chance. Or maybe her show of aggression would scare the beast off.

Slowly, with a dozen frantic heartbeats between every step, she advanced. Another growl, more threatening than before, came from inside the brush. The branches shook in a way that certainly wasn't from the wind. There was something in there.

She was almost on top of the bushes now.

With a growl ten times the strength of the others, something erupted from the brush. It was huge and brown and...it was laughing at her.

Kion!

He stood in the middle of the thicket, sides shaking and face contorted with delight.

Tiryn's heart turned to water, and her cheeks flushed boiling hot all in one exasperating moment.

"You awful, terrible, naughty scoundrel! You're incorrigible!" she said, waving her knife at him. "You're lucky I didn't run you through."

It took him a moment before he could even respond. "Oh, I would have suffered any wound just to see the look on your face! It was utterly magnificent!"

Tiryn spun around. She couldn't look at him. Not because she was furious. Her fury passed in a moment. It was because she knew that if she looked at him she would burst out laughing herself. She had not seen him this tickled in a long time.

But even turned around, she couldn't escape his cackling, which rang throughout the woods. In the end, unable to resist any longer, she spun back around and gave in to his infectious mirth.

"Oh, Tiryn, I didn't think it would actually work, but I am so glad it did. I may die in peace now, for I have known true joy," Kion said, clutching his belly.

Their laughter resounded through the hills. If there were any predators nearby, they might have thought a pack of wild dogs was racing through the Tors.

"What in the Four Wards are you doing out here?" Tiryn asked when at last they had recovered, holding their aching sides in front of the fire.

"Well, I never got you on the Day of Innocents, so I thought you were due." He gave her a dark-eyed, twinkling stare. Kion always looked people in the eye, whether he was happy or upset. That was one of the things she appreciated about him. And he always told the truth, whether someone liked it or not. But she doubted, with all the work he had to do around the farm, that he came all the way out to Cloven Brook just to scare her out of her wits.

"No, tell me the real reason," she said.

"Mother sent me. Storm clouds are coming, and she was worried you might have wandered too far out. Which, I see, turns out to have been the case."

"I can handle a little rain." She surveyed the sky. Enormous charcoal clouds were rushing in, growing darker by the minute. She touched her skirt lying by the fire. It was only half dry. It looked like she'd have to put it back on as it was.

"From the looks of things, the rain already got you." He pointed at her castoff clothes. "What happened? Did you fall in the water again?"

"That's none of your business."

He stood, handing her the clothes. "Well, as fun as this has been, we do need to get back." He kicked dirt on the fire.

"Wait, what about the honey?"

"No time. Besides, the smoke won't work in the rain."

He finished putting out the fire while she went behind the tree, fastened her skirt, and slipped on her shoes. The sudden shock from the wet clothes was like falling in the stream all over again.

Marking in her mind the terrain surrounding the beehive for when she returned, she and Kion headed for home.

Kion let her cross the brook first. Halfway across, as she stepped on the same stone she'd slipped on before, Kion said, "I heard you singing."

She almost slipped again but caught herself. Mustering every bit of concentration she could, she unfroze her limbs and kept going.

"Was it about Father?" he continued.

She didn't answer. Her heart was beating fast enough with

the brook crossing. She didn't need the embarrassment of being caught singing on top of that.

She bounded over the last few rocks in a graceless flurry. Once across, she worked up the courage to answer him with a quiet, "Yes."

Kion's eyes turned up to the clouds. The first drops of rain began to fall. She shivered from the cold, wondering what he would say.

"Thought so." His face took on a serious look. He bounded across the river stones, crossing quick as a deer.

"Please don't tell Mother," she said.

Kion gave no reply, pulling up his hood against the rain and setting off for home. Tiryn followed, feeling just as exposed as if she'd left her skirt and coat back at the clearing.

"Well," she thought, "at least for once he didn't make fun of my singing."

That night, Tiryn couldn't seem to get warm, no matter how long she sat by the fire. The rain and the wind and the river had taken their toll. Mother took pity on her and made Kion help with dinner.

The soup was plain old potato, but the steamy spoonfuls did her good. She took her time, savoring every bit of its warmth as it slid down her throat.

"No music tonight, I think," Mother said as the meal wound down. "You look a touch pink. Are you feeling all right?"

"I'll be fine. I just have a bit of a chill," Tiryn said.

"It's all right, Mother," Kion said. "I already got to hear her music out on the Tors. It was one of her new songs, in fact."

Oh, please, Kion, she pleaded silently.

"Is that so, Tiryn?" Mother said.

Now she really was sick. "Yes, Mother, but please don't make me sing it. You said it yourself: no music tonight."

"It was about Father," Kion said. He truly was a slug. And he had been so nice to her out in the woods.

"The one about your dreams? Oh, Tiryn, why does Kion get to hear it and not me?"

Tiryn took refuge in a fit of coughing.

Mother touched her forehead. "Ah, my sweet karinna, you have a fever coming on for certain. But I do want to hear it as soon you feel up to it. You have such a beautiful voice."

"I think I might be sick for a long time," Tiryn said.

"Now don't talk like that." Mother frowned, one of the few expressions which managed to diminish her beauty.

"You'll be fine in the morning, Tiryn," Kion said.

"Yes, now just sit still and rest while Kion cleans up," Mother said, pulling a blanket around Tiryn's shoulders.

Kion set about gathering the bowls and cups with uncharacteristic eagerness.

"Thank you, dear," Mother said. "I'm going to make you some ginger tea, karinna."

Tiryn's lips stretched into the best smile she could manage, but her eyes went to Kion. He raised a mischievous eyebrow when Mother wasn't looking. Watching him hurriedly wipe off and put away the dishes, she wanted to stew in her anger over the song, but it was already beginning to fade. Try as she might, she had never been able to stay angry with him for long. She was forgiving by nature, but especially when it came to her brother. He looked far too much like Father for her to hold a grudge. His dark hair and keen eyes were the very mirror of the man she missed most in all the world. Staying angry at Kion felt like pouring water on the last flames of a dying fire.

Tiryn laid her head on the table and waited for her tea, swallowing against the slow-building ache in her throat. Kion got the looks in the family. And what did she get? Right now, the only thing she could think of was a throbbing headache and a steady burning inside that made her feel like she had steam escaping from her forehead and the tips of her ears.

Chapter 5

MIDNIGHT CONVERSATION

Kion stayed up long after his mother and sister went to sleep. It was that song Tiryn sang in the woods. He couldn't get it out of his head. Though he had no musical ability of his own, he was cursed with the useless talent of remembering the words to every song he ever heard.

> If dreams came true
> If time rolled back before you left
> I would still have you
> If dreams came true

Those words were exactly the way he would have put it if he had written a song about their father. Tiryn had an uncanny ability to know what he was thinking sometimes, probably because she was so quiet. She noticed things. Too many things. Kion preferred to keep his thoughts to himself. Especially when it came to Father. He worked hard to hold those thoughts in, to stay strong for his mother and sister.

Moonlight glowed through the gap between the shutters of the northern window. Kion slid quietly out of his hammock. Icy needles prickled his bare feet on the packed dirt floor. He crept silently to where his satchel hung on a nail in the wall.

It was time for another conversation. He had one every few months, when thoughts of his father became especially strong and he needed to hear his words. He pulled out a sheet of vellum from the satchel and unfolded it as he went over to the window. He set the letter on the sill so that it lay in the ribbon of light that snuck in through the crack, and silently read the words written there:

Dear Kion,

My name has been drawn. My path has been set. I cannot help but think it was marked out long ago. I am heading off to war. The Four Wards are calling.

The dream of the Four Wards restored, united and true, first stirred my heart long before you were born—the dream of seeing the old order restored and a new age of peace settle upon the land. But I go now not to fight for fane or Ward or dreams from long ago. It is for you and your mother and your sister that I fight now. Were it given me to choose, I would sing another song, one of pleasant years and gentle days, of summer suns and winter moons with laughter ringing in hearth and hill. It may be that I shall return to such bright days, that my misgivings shall prove no more than the shadow of some great bird, passing overhead in the morning. But for now, the shadow deepens.

Though I go with heavy heart, whatever hardships come I shall bear them willingly, knowing that my three stars still shine beneath a cloudless sky. And I will fight with all that is in me to keep the clouds from you. I will not falter, however black the storms, nor must you.

To be sure, your own storms will come. But take heart. You have greatness in you, my son. Not the greatness of scepters or of flowing coffers or of a mind with answers to every riddle. Your greatness sparks from the fire that burns within, from that steady strength which says, "I will do the right thing even if it is the hard thing." I do not know what deeds you will achieve in life, but I hope I am there when that fire blazes as the noonday sun. If it is not granted me to see it, if fortune should strike me down on some distant field, know that your father loved you to the end, even to the giving of his own life. Wait patiently for my return, or, should I fail to come home, do honor to my memory and protect your mother and sister with all that is in you.

I am, and shall remain, in life or in death,

Your loving father

Kion knew the words by heart, but there was something about the reading of them that made his father's voice come alive. As always, he struggled to hold in his tears. After his father's death, he had made a vow never to shed them again. He had kept that vow for ten years, but it was not always easy.

"Thank you, Father. Your courage and your sacrifice give me strength even now," he whispered. "They say you were a coward, that you fled in the end. In my weaker moments, I confess, I sometimes believe them. I doubt your courage. But I know that these words come from the pen of a warrior. One day the people of Furrow will know that, too. That is my promise. I will fight for our family. I will fight to the end and never give up—just like you."

He could say no more without risking tears. He folded the letter and held it against his face. Long ago it had lost his father's scent. But it had become part of the ritual. He could no more abandon the practice now than he could stop reading the letter itself.

Tiryn tossed restlessly in her hammock. Her breathing sounded like wind trapped inside a bag, trying to get out. He hoped she wasn't getting sick. If she took ill, he might have to help his mother milk the sheep tomorrow. And that would mean no sword practice. Tiryn had her songs to honor Father. All Kion had was the tournament. This was his last year to compete. He didn't know what he would do if he lost. It would be almost as bad as losing his father all over again.

Dust flew up from Kion's cloak as he tossed it on top of a crate beside the shed. He hadn't bothered to tell his mother he was back from another long day out on the Tors. Tiryn had taken an ill turn during the night. If he was going to get in any sword practice, it would have to be now, before he started in on the milking. He wasn't exactly shirking his duties, since he fully intended to do them—just not right away.

He retrieved his sword and unsheathed it as quietly as possible. Outside, behind the shed and safely out of view of the cottage, he assumed one of the Fiorin guard stances, left leg forward, right leg back. It was Zinder who had told him about the Fiorin Batal. Though Zinder wasn't much of a swordsman himself, he had loaned Kion a folio with pictures and instructions on this ancient method of sword fighting. The Fiorin Batal was said to be the same style used by the fanewardens themselves, the warriors charged with the personal defense of the fane, the greatest order of swordsmen in the land.

Kion began his forms, practicing his back edge slices first, his weakest area. The whipping winds, the musky smell of sheep, even the weariness in his limbs all faded as he went through the rhythmic motions. This was what he was meant to do. In that moment, he was no longer a shepherd. He was a warrior. He closed his eyes and imagined his father standing off to the side, watching him, pleased with his progress, the fluidity of his movements, the swiftness of his strikes.

Kion delighted in the hum and the *swoosh* of the blade as it parted the air. If he had the time, he could practice for hours.

His mother's voice came like a slap to his ears. "Kion! Come here, please. I need to speak with you." Oh, no…He had barely finished the first form.

He kicked at the dirt. Taking a deep breath, he sheathed his sword and returned it to the shed. Donning his cloak, he ran back to the cottage.

His mother stood in the doorway, clutching her coin purse.

"Yes, Mother?"

"I need you to run into the village. Tiryn grew worse while

you were away." The frailty in her voice told him she was even more worried than usual.

"The village? But I thought you'd want me to help with the milking."

"Someone needs to go and buy medicine from Mistress Shona, and I'd rather not leave your sister right now. The milking can wait."

"You mean I'll have to help you with it tomorrow, then?"

Mother handed him the purse and gently placed her hand over his. "I need you to do this for me, Kion. I—I need you to go and come back as quickly as possible."

Normally Kion would have jumped at the chance for a trip to Furrow. Though the villagers were cold to him at best, there were all sorts of interesting things to see and do, not the least of which was visiting Zinder's smithy. But he certainly would have no time for such things tonight. Worse, he'd lost his chance at practice. And if Tiryn was as sick as Mother made it sound, it might be days before he got to practice again.

The time for lambing was fast approaching. That meant not only helping the ewes give birth, but looking after the newborns. That usually fell to Tiryn. If she was sick, those duties would fall to him and his mother.

Hopefully Mother was overreacting. She tended to do that whenever her children showed the slightest sign of sickness.

"I'm sure Tiryn's not as sick as she looks," Kion said, trying to sound convincing.

"She needs that medicine as quickly as possible." Mother squeezed his hand. "Please hurry, son."

Her eyes echoed the urgency of her words. The fierce resolve there startled him, but he brushed it off. Everything would be fine in a four-mark.

But what if it wasn't? What if Tiryn's illness cost him the tournament? With the first match only ten days away, he needed to practice now more than ever. It wasn't Tiryn's fault for getting sick, but he couldn't help stewing over the awful timing. Why did swordsmen have to have sisters? Strom Glyre wasn't hampered by one, that much was certain. He went and fought where he pleased. Dougan Shaw didn't have a sister either, for that matter.

Kion let out a sigh long enough to have come from the soles of his feet. There was nothing for it but to get this trip over with as soon as possible. He tied the purse onto his belt, kissed his mother good-bye, and strode off with quick but heavy footfalls.

Chapter 6

TROUBLE WITH PIGS

K ion made the mile-and-a-half journey to the outskirts of Furrow in half the usual time. It was still a good hour before dark when he reached Scuttleback Road. The farms on the outskirts spread before him like upturned blankets with knotted sprouts in the pillowed loam. Tender oat shoots hemmed the road, brimming with the eager green of new life. The farmhouses sat a good distance away, at the back of the acreages. They were made from the same wattle and daub used in Kion's cottage, but were a good deal larger and more colorful. Most were coated in either an eggshell- or straw-colored wash, depending on whether they'd gotten the lime from the surrounding hills or bought it from a traveling merchant. The yellow was the more expensive of the two, and preferred by the wealthier farmers. Kion's cottage had no wash at all. It was just a plain, natural gray. But his family couldn't have sealed the walls even if they wanted to. Like the rest of the shepherds, they didn't own the cottage or the land on which it sat. Their house and farm belonged to Mr. Jeslan, who owned many of the sheep farms in the Tors. Most of the others belonged to Mr. Shaw, Dougan's father.

Kion slowed to catch his breath as the road leveled. Thankfully, it was dinnertime, and the fields were empty. With any luck, he would avoid the stares and murmurings of the villagers.

The second farm he passed was one of Jeslan's. Its powerful stench hit Kion right about the same time it came into view.

One of the larger farms of Furrow, Jeslan's place spanned

both sides of the road. The southern side was strictly hay fields, but the northern side held a pig farm covered in a labyrinth of fence. Six different pens ringed a slaughterhouse five times the size of Kion's cottage. Jeslan didn't actually run the farm himself. Various hired hands took care of the pigs and cut and baled the hay. Jeslan lived in Madrigal, and this was one of many farms he owned throughout Inris.

Kion didn't come into town often enough to grow accustomed to the pungent, sense-assaulting odor of the farm. It hung like an invisible cloud over the road. Some people said sheep stank, but it had to be twice as bad working with pigs.

He picked up his pace, but bursts of raucous laughter checked his momentum, alerting him to the presence of people ahead. The laughter lacked any actual joy, but rang out across the field in mocking notes.

Lounging on the planked fence up ahead was a small group of boys about Kion's age. They had their backs to the road. Their laughter and shouting was inspired by some antics in one of the pigsties. As Kion drew near, it became obvious what those antics were.

Shaun Snetch was riding a pig. At least, he was trying to. The moment Kion saw him, Snetch slipped off the barrel back of a hog and fell face-down in the muck. A fresh round of laughter, pointing, and jeers followed. Snetch ignored their mean-spirited enjoyment at his expense. He was too busy scrambling to his feet to avoid the hog coming up behind him. The hog was only curious, but it was a rough sort of curiosity. It scampered into him from behind, bouncing the red-haired, freckle-faced Snetch onto his rear. The onlookers roared with laughter, some nearly falling off the fence. Snetch became one with the mud, a creature of brown slime and slop. It was hard to tell where the poor boy's body ended and the mud began.

One of the spectators clapped his hands together in a heavy rhythm. "Nice try, Snetch. That was funny! But you've had three goes, and you never stayed on for the full ten seconds. It's

time to pay up." The large boy hopped off the fence and into
the sty.

Kion couldn't see the face, but he knew the voice: Dougan
Shaw. That arrogant baritone could sour fresh milk. Kion picked
up his pace again. Between the stench and Dougan, he had
double reason to get past Jeslan's farm as quickly as possible.
Nothing good would come out of getting noticed by Dougan
Shaw. The Shaws despised shepherds even more than most
villagers, and that was saying something.

Snetch looked up from the ground. His eyes were like two
slivers of butter on a roast mutton. But he sure didn't smell
like one!

"One more try, Dougan, please," Snetch said, wiping his nose
with a muddy sleeve that did nothing but spread the mud
around. "I almost had it that time." He scrambled to his feet,
keeping his eyes fixed on Dougan. He was two years younger
and a good six inches shorter than his tormentor. His buck teeth
and nasally voice didn't help. And he was groveling, which was
exactly what Dougan wanted.

"A bet's a bet, souie," Dougan said. "Pay up or I'll have to
box it out of ya." He cracked his knuckles.

"But I don't have the money." Snetch backpedaled and
bumped into a large pig.

Kion took in a deep breath and got a strong whiff of pig
stench. Snetch was hardly a friend. They had said no more than a
dozen words to each other over the years, but Kion couldn't
stand there and watch Dougan lay into him. Dougan was from
one of the richest families in the village. Snetch was a runaway
from nobody-knew-where.

"That's not my problem," Dougan said. "You made the bet,
fair and square."

"Mr. Jeslan will pay me at the end of Avring. I'll give you the
coin then. I promise!" Snetch got down on his knees in the muck.
The boys on the fence snickered, and Dougan turned back to
flash them a wicked grin.

That was when he noticed Kion.

"Well, I'll be jiggered," Dougan said. "Look who showed up late for the party. Hey, boys, looks like Jeslan let one of his pigs get out."

Kion stood his ground. Inside, he tried every reason he could think of to turn and walk away, but he couldn't do it. Snetch didn't deserve to be treated like this. No one did.

"I doubt Mr. Jeslan would approve of what you're doing here, Dougan. Do you have permission to be on his farm?" Kion said.

"That's none of your business, Bray. This is between me and Snetch, unless you're here to watch. We're fine with that, aren't we, boys?"

The gaggle on the fence nodded on cue. They were all younger than Dougan except Harvin, one of the boys Kion had beaten in last year's tournament.

"He doesn't have the money. Beating him up won't prove anything. Why don't you leave him alone? I'd hate to have to tell Fielder Lorris you're disturbing the peace again."

Dougan scowled. He had narrowly escaped punishment when his cart had run over another farmer's mule during last year's Hidewind Festival. The mule had wandered out into the road where Dougan was racing his cart against one of his friends. He hadn't seen the animal until it was too late. His horses trampled the poor beast in a cloud of dust and squeals. The mule was lamed, but Dougan refused to pay. When he got into a fight with the mule's owner and knocked him out cold, no one in the crowd would say anything because of his family's status—no one except Kion and Zinder. They were the only people willing to tell Fielder Lorris the truth. Lorris made Dougan pay for the animal and warned him that the next time he caught him fighting, he'd put him overnight in the stocks.

The Shaw family started having all their smithing done over in Windstern ever since that day, even though it cost them a good deal more. Dougan had tried to provoke Kion into a fight a couple of times since then, but Kion had managed to wiggle his way out. He preferred to settle their differences in the tournament. Looking at the fire in Dougan's eyes, he wasn't so sure he'd be getting away this time.

"Kion Bray. You sure talk tough for a coward's son," Dougan said.

Now it was Kion's turn to scowl. As many times as he'd heard his father put down, it shouldn't still hurt, but it did.

"Here's what I think of you and that puny little scamp you hang around with." Quick as a snake, Dougan spun and smacked Snetch square in the nose. The unsuspecting boy went down like a dollop of mashed potatoes. He rolled around in the mud, wailing and covering his nose with his hands.

"Now, if you want some of that, woolly, there's plenty to go around." A haughty sneer slithered across Dougan's face.

The boys on the fence whispered and nudged each other in anticipation.

Kion stared down the road into the village. His sister was sick. His mother had given him clear instructions to hurry on to the herbalist and get back as soon as he could. He didn't have time for this.

But he couldn't stand seeing people plowed over like that, just to show off in front of a bunch of hayseed boys. He wished he could just move on, but he couldn't. Somebody had to stand up for Snetch. It might as well be him. Besides, he was a shepherd; he couldn't be any more despised than he already was.

He threw off his cloak and vaulted over the fence and into the muck.

Several boys gasped. One even whistled. Dougan's sneer grew even more jagged and inhuman. If wolves were crossed with men, the result might have produced a smile like that.

Mud seeped through the cracks in Kion's shoes. He liked his odds a lot better at sword fighting with the taller, heavier Dougan. He wasn't entirely sure what he meant to do when he got within striking distance.

Dougan rolled up his sleeves. "So, the chicken has a spine, after all."

"All chickens have spines. You really need to work on your insults."

Kion's retort brought an awkward silence as Dougan and his crew struggled to digest the words. More importantly, it bought Kion time. He stopped a few paces from Dougan and allowed a pair of large pigs to wander between them.

Snetch got to his feet, more to avoid the pigs nosing around him than because he was over the pain of Dougan's blow. He still clutched his nose. Red streaks flowed from it, mingling with the mud on his lips and chin.

Dougan spat into the muck. "Shep here thinks he's smart, boys. We'll see how smart he is after I bash his head in a few times."

"I don't want to hurt you," Kion bluffed, circling to keep the pigs between him and Dougan. "Just leave Snetch alone."

"I can take care of myself, woolly," Snetch said, his voice twice as nasally as before. "Don't worry, Dougan, I'll pay you back at the end of the month."

Dougan turned. "You want to see me lay your protector in the mud, Snetch?"

"He's not my protector. He's a woolhead."

Kion grumbled to himself. He was sticking his neck out for this boy, and this was the thanks he got?

"Well, then." Dougan spun backward and slugged Snetch in the gut. "Why don't you watch it from the ground with the other pigs?"

Snetch's eyes went wide. He crumpled back into the mud.

The boys didn't laugh. There was nothing funny about Dougan's vicious attack. In spite of Snetch's comments, Kion's temples throbbed to an angry rhythm. He almost charged Dougan right there. With great effort, he held his emotions in check. That was exactly what Dougan wanted.

"Dougan, you yellow-blooded scat. You're lower than the mud under a pig's hoof."

That got to Dougan. His ears and cheeks went scarlet, and he rushed at Kion in the same way he had Snetch. But he was much farther away from Kion and he had to maneuver around the pigs. By the time Dougan reached him, Kion had positioned himself so that Dougan had to come at him from the side. Kion leaned away, grabbing Dougan's arm and kicking against Dougan's shins. The maneuver swept Dougan's feet out from under him. The towering oaf joined Snetch face-down in the mud. A dirty trick if Kion had been sword fighting, but in the pigsty, everything was fair game.

A few of the boys on the fence snickered, but they went silent when Dougan shot them a look.

Kion could have landed a few kicks to Dougan's side, but he backed away and moved behind some of the pigs. As much as Dougan deserved it, Kion had no desire to hurt him.

Dougan roared to his feet. His face and clothes were slathered with mud. He howled and charged after Kion with great, squelching strides. "You cheapshot woolly!"

The pigs didn't appreciate Dougan's yelling. They scampered about, turning Dougan's charge and Kion's evasion into an impromptu swine dance with ever-shifting partners. All that was missing was a fiddler and skirts for the pigs. Kion was normally a terrible dancer, but he was holding his own in this muddy jig. If only Tiryn could see him now.

Tiryn! He suddenly remembered his errand. He had to find a way out of this pigsty. Maybe if he could lure Dougan in for another leg sweep, he could knock him down again and take off running. Snetch didn't want his help anyway. This fight was pointless.

But Kion doubted the maneuver would work a second time. Dougan was pursuing him more warily now. His ability to adapt was what made him such a formidable swordsman. He may have had the intelligence of a hollowed-out pumpkin when it came to most things, but not fighting. Dougan had enough cunning in a fight to match his massive frame. He couldn't outlast the quicker, nimbler Kion in a chase around an open field like this; he had to force Kion into a corner.

Dougan plodded forward methodically. The pigs settled down. Most went off to the feeding troughs, having had enough of these human shenanigans.

Kion was either going to have to make a run for the fence and hope he didn't get caught, or stand his ground and hope the leg trick worked a second time.

He had just about decided to make a run for it when he spotted something out of the corner of his eye. On impulse, he kicked at a large mound of mud in front of him. By some miracle, a big glob of it hit Dougan in the eyes.

Kion took off. If he could make it to the road, he'd be safe. Dougan's screams were the only thing that could reach him there. Kion was only a few strides short of the fence when Dougan recovered his sight.

"Get him, boys!" Dougan shouted. "Don't let that woolly get away!"

The boys hesitated. Kion was bigger than all of them, but a few looks from Dougan's blazing eyes reminded them that a thrashing from him would be far worse than anything they'd get from Kion. And though Kion's size and speed gave him the advantage over any of them individually, he wasn't bigger than all of them put together.

Because of their hesitation, Kion managed to make it over the fence, but they pounced on him the moment he landed. They knocked him down and piled on top with whoops and triumphant cries. The combined weight flattened him like a tuft of wool. He struggled to breathe beneath the writhing mass.

"What's all the uproar?" a deep, adult voice bellowed from the road. Everyone who lived within ten miles of Furrow knew that voice: Fielder Lorris. He was the closest thing Furrow had to a ruler. He stood tall and broad-shouldered at the edge of the road. A straw hat, so old and faded it looked like it might disintegrate any moment, drooped almost to his shoulders. A rugged-looking steel mace hung from his belt. "You boys are acting like you caught some vicious haukmar invader."

The weight lifted. A rush of fresh air filled Kion's lungs. Pig stench had never smelled so sweet. The boys stared at the ground and refused to look at the fielder. They shuffled away.

"Kion Bray. I thought that looked like you. And Dougan Shaw, I'm guessing you've got something to do with this."

Dougan came over to the fence, wiping his face and doing his best to look presentable. Kion had a hard time not smiling. Dougan's family may have been one of the wealthiest in the village, but when it came to the fielder, they were just like everyone else. Fielder Lorris wasn't exactly well-liked, but he was respected. In cities and larger towns, fielders organized the local militia and the watch under the authority of a daysman, but Furrow wasn't big enough for that. As a result, Lorris answered directly to the margrave in Madrigal. And that was a power even the Shaw family had to obey.

"We were just horsing around. Weren't we, boys?" Dougan said.

The boys nodded, still refusing to look Fielder Lorris in the eye or even speak. During the exchange, Snetch had gotten up and was quietly slinking off to the slaughterhouse.

"Ho there! Snetch," Lorris called. "Were you in on this, too? Is Dougan telling the truth?"

Dougan gave Snetch a hard stare. Snetch's shoulders slumped. "Yes, sir. Just horsing around."

"Snetch, why don't you tell the truth?" Kion said. "Sir, Snetch lost a bet with Dougan, and Dougan knocked him down when he couldn't pay."

Fielder Lorris scratched the back of his head, pushing his hat forward. "That may be, but I can't go on just one witness. Any of you other boys care to speak up and support Bray's story?"

Harvin, the oldest, spoke. "He's a shepherd. He doesn't know what he's talking about."

Kion started to protest, but Fielder Lorris motioned him to silence. After waiting a few more moments, he said, "So what happened to your nose, there, Snetch?"

"I fell," Snetch said.

"Hmm, I see."

Dougan gave Kion a proud look. He was clever enough not to grin openly, but his gloating eyes said more than enough.

"Well, you should go take care of that nose, boy," Lorris said. "And have a care to who you horse around with. You've only been working Jeslan's farm for a four-mark. I don't think Mr. Jeslan would take too well to you letting this lot run around with his pigs."

Snetch grunted in acknowledgment.

"Now you all better run off home. It's dinnertime, anyway," Lorris said.

Dougan and the boys ran off like they'd suddenly remembered how very hungry they were, but not before Dougan snuck in a venomous smirk at Kion when Lorris wasn't looking.

"I've got an errand to run to Mistress Shona," Kion said.

"Good, I'll walk you into town," Lorris said.

Kion picked up his cloak from the dirt. He'd had more than enough pig stench for today.

Chapter 7

THE SMITHY

Tiryn grew worse over the next five days. Mistress Shona's medicine helped her sleep, but the fever and shivers only intensified. They were especially terrible at night, when the chill air seeped in through the earthen walls of the cottage. Mother tried every remedy she could think of: herbs, tea, hot rags, wet rags, and vinegar on a sponge, but to no avail. Tiryn lay in bed, hollow-eyed, a shell of her once bright and thoughtful self. Sometimes she mumbled strange, unsettling things. "The fire is coming, I can feel it," she'd say. "It's coming for all of us. Watch out—don't stay here—you'll get burned!"

At first Kion thought she was worried about him and Mother getting sick, but whenever they asked about her ramblings, she had no memory of them, or worse, did not acknowledge their questions at all. This happened more and more as the days went on.

Mother said it was the wistering, the same sickness that had taken Tiryn's friend Lina and Rike's wife, Mae. The wistering. Hearing his mother speak the word for the first time had caused a clammy fear to rise in his throat. The disease had killed more people in Furrow than even the war. Few who contracted it survived. It affected mostly younger people, especially girls, but Mae had been in her thirties, and Mother spent nearly every moment at Tiryn's side.

As Tiryn's condition worsened, Mother began to say that the only hope would be to get her to someplace warmer. The houses in Furrow were generally less drafty and exposed than those on the Tors, but no one there would take her in, especially if they thought she had the wistering. None of the villagers cared a fig about the shepherds except for Zinder and Mistress Shona. Zinder would have happily taken Tiryn in, but he lived next to his smithy, and the smoke and the ash and the hammering would only make things worse. Beyond that, if people found out someone with the wistering was staying there, they'd stop coming to Zinder for work. With Mistress Shona, the problem was not that she wouldn't have taken Tiryn in—she had a special fondness for her—but as the village healer, she couldn't play favorites. If she took in one sick person she would have to take them all, and her house was barely larger than the Brays'.

Mother grew more and more convinced that Tiryn would not last another four-mark if they didn't get her out of the cottage. Fear and shadows clung to the walls of their home. The very light from the hearth and candles seemed less than before. Kion and his mother spoke little, only what was necessary for the care of Tiryn and the sheep. Memories of the day Lina died kept running through his mind. Tiryn had cried three days straight when she lost her friend. He half wondered if Lina had given her the sickness, but no, she had died months ago.

"A few girls survived," he kept telling himself. "Tiryn won't die." He repeated this often as the days dragged on, for denial is a ready shield against the arrows of doubt.

In the midst of the sickness, the lambing came. In the best of times, such days were a tense and messy affair. Life hung in the balance for the little creatures that slid or had to be coaxed from their mother's wombs. These tender gifts always came with a measure of anxiety and uncertainty, for they were the lifeblood of the flock, and the future of the farm depended on them.

Sometimes they got the mothers to the shed in time to give birth in a warmer place, but the lambs came when they came and many times the mother would not suffer herself to be moved once the birthing began. Without Tiryn to check on the newborns or help with difficult births, the tasks fell to Kion and his mother.

There had been five births in the last four-mark, one of them breached, which went into the night and early morning. Kion was worn out with checking on the newborns and making sure they took the right herbs to keep from getting sick. Between the lambing and having to run into town for Tiryn's medicines, he had no time for sword practice. With each passing day, his hopes of winning the tournament dwindled.

But Kion was determined not to give up. He had to find time to practice. When only two ewes were left to deliver, and it looked like their lambs would not come for a few days, he decided to take advantage of a rare hour before dark after he'd finished all his other chores to get in some sword work. It would be just the thing to take his mind off his sister and the dark shroud hanging over their home.

He opened the shed and reached into the corner. He had done it so many times he didn't bother looking. But this time his hand closed around open air. His eyes flicked to the place where he had reached.

The sword was gone.

He shoved aside crates and tools to see if it had been misplaced, but a thorough and tumultuous search showed it wasn't there. Mother must have moved it. She'd never done so before, but that had to be it. He rushed back to the cottage and threw open the door. "Mother, have you seen the sword?"

"Shh," she said, nodding toward where Tiryn lay asleep in her hammock. It was rare for her to be asleep at this hour, with the night chill coming on.

"I'm sorry, Mother. I forgot," he said, lowering his voice. "Have you seen Father's sword?"

She brushed aside the stray locks of hair dangling across her face. The dark, wavy strands were not pulled back as they typically were and her usual beauty and calm had been replaced by a haggard and harried mask. She got even less sleep than Tiryn did. She was too worried to rest, even when she had the chance.

"The sword? No, I haven't seen it. Isn't it in the shed?"

"No." The word sucked what little warmth was left from the room.

He could read it in his mother's eyes: it was gone. Oh, he would look for it, probably all night long, but he knew deep down he would never find it. He wanted to scream but held it in for Tiryn's sake. Instead, he collapsed against the doorframe and sank to the floor.

"Kion, please. Close the door. You're letting in the cold," Mother said.

He jumped to his feet and fled into the sheep yard, letting the door bang shut behind him.

She didn't understand. All she saw these days was a sick daughter. She may as well not even have a son. Everything was going wrong. The tournament, the farm, his family—all of it hung on the edge of a cliff. The merest breeze would send it toppling into a crevice of destruction.

He wandered over to the sheep pen and looked out over the flock. Several sheep stared back at him with dark, unthinking eyes.

"It's gone," he said. "My father's sword is gone, and so is my chance at winning the tournament."

Urly, one of Roony's offspring, who thankfully was nothing like his father, came up and licked his hand. But Kion couldn't feel it. He couldn't feel anything at all.

⁂

Smoke and ash drifted slowly through the smithy, carrying with it a dusty, well-cured scent. Zinder hammered away at a sword on an anvil low enough to accommodate his height. He wore a neat leather apron over a dark linen tunic. His white beard was sprinkled with soot. Along the near wall hung tools of sundry sizes and shapes: punches, drifts, hammers, and tongs. Smoky windows ran the length of the wall facing the street. They were all propped open to let out the billowing heat. Below the windows, a long workbench held scattered chisels, pieces of armor in various states of finish, and a few small molds. More molds lay stacked beneath the workbench. In one corner sat a round basin full of water for quenching. In another corner was the grindstone for sharpening, a large stone disk set in a wooden frame with a foot pedal to make it spin. Above it, a small metal cylinder sat on a shelf in the wall. A spigot dripped water onto the wheel when it was in use. On the far wall hung examples of Zinder's work: swords of various sizes and styles, axes, maces, and even a pair of crossbows, one larger and another smaller, with an ingenious tray for housing several bolts at a time. In the far corner loomed the forge itself, a mortared half-circle with an eye of fire. From within that sweltering chamber came the molten forms which Zinder's genius would fashion into tools, weapons, and knickknacks both varied and wondrous.

The heat from the forge stamped beads of sweat across Zinder's brow, but the smithy was cold as winter to Kion. It had been a day since his sword had gone missing. He had been wandering in a daze ever since, only half aware of his surroundings. He was fortunate one of the sheep hadn't wandered off a cliff or into a dangerous ravine.

Contrary to Kion's foolish thought the day before, his mother did know what the sword meant to him, and for once she had let him stop by the smithy on his way to Mistress Shona's. Normally, such a visit would have been a happy occasion, the highlight of the four-mark, but even Zinder and the enchanting hum and glow of the smithy could not pull Kion's spirits out of the dark valley where they now wandered.

"Stolen, you say? Are you sure?" Zinder paused in his hammering to study Kion. A large drop of sweat rolled off his pointy nose.

"Yes, what other explanation is there?" Kion said. "Mother

barely leaves the house, and I've gone to town most nights for medicine. Someone could have easily snuck in and swiped it from the shed. I hadn't touched it for days."

"Curious. Most curious." Zinder held up the blade he was working on. The tip glowed brighter than a sunset.

"What?" Kion said.

"This steel has some other metal mixed in, or I'm a widow's husband." Zinder tapped the blade on the anvil, and it bent.

"Zinder, are you listening to me? It's gone. My father's sword is gone. And the tournament is in seven days!"

Zinder regarded him, but the faraway look in his eyes kept going farther away.

"Zinder!"

"Oh, horn toads, lad, I'm not deaf!" He cleared his throat and teased out the end of his mustache, as he often did when thinking. "Now, go on."

Kion paused a moment to let his frustration foam. He thought the world of Zinder, but today he had no patience for the nyn's frivolities. When at last he calmed down, he spoke with great care, over-enunciating each word. "My—father's—sword—has—been—stolen."

Zinder slammed the blade onto the anvil, bending it even more. "Yes, you said that. What I want to know is, who's the lout that took it? I'll drag him in here and make a suit of armor out of his skin!"

"I don't know who did it, but I have my suspicions." Kion wrung the shaft of his cudgel a few times. Normally he didn't bring such an obvious reminder of his profession on visits to the village. But he wanted to be ready in case he ran into a certain someone.

Zinder stuck the blade in the forge and pulled the chain beside it to pump the bellows. It was an elaborate contraption that was the wonder of the village. If he pulled the chain down, the bellows would go on pumping for however long it took the chain to slowly rise back up. No one had the slightest idea how it worked, but had Zinder been half the blacksmith he was, he would have gotten business on the ingeniousness of this contraption alone.

"Dougan the Dunderhead," Zinder said. "It's him or the wind."

"I don't know of anyone else who would have done it. The rest of the village may hate me, but they're not thieves."

"You're sure about this? You didn't lose your grip and send it sailing over to Rike's place?" Zinder cracked a grin, trying to take the edge off Kion's despair.

"If I was that strong, I could win the tournament with a blade of grass."

Zinder stroked his mustache to an ever-finer point. "Well, I don't suppose we'll ever catch the filcher."

"And I won't be fighting in the tournament. Dougan bested me before we ever got to cross swords."

Zinder's eyes glinted. "Not if I have anything to say about it. When trouble comes, you don't have to just sit there and take what it gives you. How would you like to fight with a nynnian blade at your side?"

"Oh, Zinder, you know I can't. I don't have the money."

"Who said anything about money?"

"But you can't just give me a sword. They're worth far too much, especially one made by you. It would be practically stealing."

"Now, now, now, before you flood me with your noble protestations, there are two things I know that you don't." He motioned Kion down to his level in the way he did when he meant to share some delicious secret. "Firstly, you see that blade over there in the fire? The metal's much too flimsy for actual battle, so it's useless for me to sell. But it will last a few matches in a tournament. I can put it in your hands day after tomorrow, and you'll save me the trouble of having it clutter up my shop."

"But—"

"Ah, now, just let me finish. Secondly, you may not know it, but you are standing in the shop of the richest smith in northern Inris, maybe all of Inris itself! You see, the day after the day after the Day of Innocents, a man came into the smithy. He had an enormously beautiful hat and equally fine and frilly clothes. And the hat had a golden feather—not gold like yellow, but gold like metal. It was the oddest thing; he looked like a regular parade on two feet. Such a smartly dressed fellow. He could have been my cousin, only he was too tall. Anyway, he put in an order for twelve swords—twelve—*and* a suit of armor! He wanted it done by the end of the month, which, I don't have to tell you, has put more than a few kinks in my mustache. Fortunately, he was willing to take some of my stock swords. I've been hammering like a rabid woodpecker ever since!"

For a moment Kion forgot all about the lost sword and the tournament. He was too thrilled for his friend.

"Fire and ice, Zinder, what a stroke! But can he really afford to pay for all that? In one month? Is he an amber merchant? A relation of the fane?"

"There's the wonder. He's a scribe! At least, that's what he claimed to be."

"A scribe? He must work for the fane, then, or the margrave at least."

"He didn't say. All I know is that he gave me ten gold rounds with the promise of fifty more on completion. Not only that, he also promised to deliver an extremely rare and valuable poem!"

"Zinder, sixty gold isn't that much for all that." Kion gave him a reproving look.

"And a poem!"

"How many times do I have to tell you not to let people take advantage of you when it comes to things like this?" Kion said. Zinder had a horrendous weakness for two things: poetry and hats. If that were more widely known, he would probably have had to sell his smithy long ago. At least his ridiculous collection of hats had *some* value. But his musty old chest of poetry was about as worthless as Kion's worn down shoes.

Zinder paid him no mind. "Not just any poem: *The Lay of the Glaives*. I've heard about it ever since I was a beardless dewdrop at my mother's knee. It's been lost for centuries. Now, he only has a fragment, mind you, but still! When he told me, I thought it must be the Day of Innocents all over again! Now, don't you worry, lad, old Zinder hasn't lost all sense. I've got the down payment, and even if the poem turns out to be a hoax, I'll still turn a profit. The poem would just be a feather in my cap—a huge feather, mind you, a big, giant poofy one, with rainbow stripes!"

"So this poem is actually worth something?"

"In gold? Only to a very few, all of whom are holed up in Gilding, but to a lore hound like myself, it's worth all the swords in Casting Selvedge!"

"And I suppose he'll give you this marvelous, mystical poem when he comes back for the goods?"

"Oh, no, that's the other odd bit. The goods aren't for him, you see. They're to be delivered to the Fortress of the Clefts up at Roving. He'll have the poem waiting for me there along with the remainder of the coin."

Kion stared at Zinder in open-mouthed wonder.

"Roving? The very place where Strom and his men are garrisoned? Zinder, don't tell me this is another prank."

Zinder's laughter rang throughout the smithy. "It's true, lad, it's all true! I've never had an order up that way before. The fortress has its own smiths, but I guess they can't keep up. Must be arming for a big offensive. Whatever the reason, I plan on heading up to Roving at the end of Seven Fires. After I watch you beat that rogue Dougan in the tournament!"

Excitement bubbled up inside Kion. "Zinder, you lucky spark! I wonder if you'll get to hand the blades to Strom in person? And the armor—is it for him or for one of his swordswains? Are you going to make it in the full nynnian style? Or do you have enough time for that?"

"Stop, stop, stop! Too many questions!" Zinder waved his hands as if to swat them away.

"It's all right, you don't have to tell me. I won't get to go anyway, so what does it matter?"

"That does chafe a bit, doesn't it? But I promise to tell you all about it. You'll be the first to hear, lad, smith's honor."

Kion turned to the blades lining the walls. How he envied his friend. He was able to do what he loved. He was well paid. And he was respected, which was the most important thing. And now this, the trip of a lifetime, to see a real army and visit a massive fortress. Kion would probably never get ten miles outside of the Tors. But maybe he could still reach Strom another way.

"Would you take my father's helmet?" Kion said. "It might be my last chance to have it blademarked."

"Of course I'll take it. If there's any chance of getting it marked, you can bet your best sheep I'll see it done." Zinder eyed the forge. "Now you'd best hurry along, lad. I've got smithing to do, and you've got medicine to buy. I do hope Tiryn takes a turn for the better soon."

Tiryn. In all the whirlwind of news and emotions, he had utterly forgotten about his errand. "Oh, you're right. Thanks for reminding me. You're sure you'll have time to finish the order and my sword?"

Zinder patted him on the arm. "Lad, I'm a nyn. I can smith in my sleep. You can pick up your sword day after tomorrow. Give my best to your mother. And keep my worst for yourself!" he said with an angular grin.

Chapter 8

CHARRING ROAD

A fire raged in Tiryn's bones, slowly burning the life out of her. Sometimes her body fought back, and she'd shake uncontrollably, and a terrible chill would quench the fire, but in the end, the fire always returned. And yet for all it blazed, it brought all the pain of fire and none of the warmth.

She lapsed in and out of consciousness, rolling down the hill of time until she no longer knew what day it was. Any rhythm and routine to life was gone. All she had were fragments, glimpses of moments: a wet rag on her forehead, whispered words of worry, a candle flame sputtering in melted wax. Her mother's gentle face and Kion's stern one were the only constants. And the visions. Or rather, the same vision over and over again.

The vision always happened in the same place: a large house. She sat in a chair in one of the rooms, bundled up in front of the fireplace. The fire leapt and danced to invisible music. It warmed her cheeks. She felt safe. Then came a knock at the door. The next part was always hazy. Shouts rang out and metal clashed against metal. It sounded like a battle. She ran through the house, looking for a way out, but she couldn't find a door. In the windows, great walls of flame advanced toward the house as if possessing a will of their own. She didn't know which would overtake her first, the flames or the battle.

Tiryn would cry out, but she could never remember what she said. Then the vision would fade, and she would lapse into a fitful, fevered sleep.

As the sickness consumed her, she grew more and more convinced the vision was real, that it was something that would happen unless she found a way to stop it.

"Tiryn, my sweet, can you hear me?" Mother's voice broke through her delirium. "Please, karinna, tell me if you can hear my voice." With great effort, Tiryn opened her eyes the barest sliver.

Mother was pressing a rag against her forehead. The moisture coaxed Tiryn's eyes open a little more. The look on her mother's face made Tiryn want to cry. "You look so tired, Mother. And your hair—" She forced the words out through her brittle, cracked throat. "It's all messy."

Her mother dabbed the corners of her own eyes with the edge of her sleeve. "Oh, Tiryn, you're awake, thank goodness."

"But I'm so tired. Can I sleep some more?" Even now, it took all her energy and focus to keep from drifting back to sleep.

"In a moment. First, I need you to listen to me. I'm taking you away. We're going to a place where you can get better."

Going away? But she didn't want to go anywhere. "Why can't I stay here?"

"Because you're too sick. If we don't get you someplace warmer, you may, well, it's best for your health, that's all."

Tiryn didn't like the sound of this, but she trusted her mother. "Can I say good-bye to Lina first?"

Her mother covered her mouth with her hand and turned away. Another figure moved up beside her. After a moment, she recognized Kion's face. "It's all right, Mother. She doesn't remember. Let me talk to her."

Something in the tone of his voice stirred her further awake. She took a good look at him. For the first time since Father's death, he seemed genuinely frightened, but the expression soon passed and the old, confident Kion returned.

The door creaked, and a burst of cold air rushed straight for her head. It swirled inside her, all the way down to her feet. She shrank back into the safety of her wool blanket.

"Mother is taking you to Charring, to Aunt Lizard's house," Kion said. "It's warmer there, and they have better medicines. Do you understand?"

She latched onto the strength in his voice, allowing it to tether her to the moment.

"Yes, I understand. But why Aunt Liz? I thought she didn't like you?"

"I'm not going. I have to stay and take care of the sheep. But Aunt Lizard thinks you're made of gold, and that's all that matters."

A journey overland hardly felt safe, especially without Kion to protect them. And it would be so awfully cold at night.

"We packed your wood pipes for when you get better," Kion continued. "After you get well again, I want you to practice that song you wrote about Father so you can play it for me." The fear in his eyes came back now. His voice lost its edge. It was soft and tinged with regret.

"You really want to hear one of my songs?"

"I would love nothing better."

What was happening? Was this part of her delirium? Kion never wanted to hear her music.

"And my diary? Did you pack that as well?"

"Yes, and Zinder sent some charcoal drawing sticks for you. I packed those too."

Mother returned and brought another swirl of cold with her. "Rike was kind enough to loan us his mule and cart," Mother said. "Everything is ready. Kion, let's carry her out."

Invisible arms wrapped around her. Tiryn barely felt them. She seemed to float through the doorway. Her heart ached for the home she was leaving. Somehow, she felt she would never see it again.

The chill air swallowed her, smothering her melancholy. She had no time to wallow in self-pity. She was dying. This she also knew.

It was dark outside. A pale green light menaced the land off in the distance. Mr. Rike stood close by, beside his mule, whispering to it. When he saw her he stepped back, but she knew it wasn't her sickness he was afraid of. That was just the way he was. Scared. Scared of everyone and everything outside of his sheep and his farm. The world was a cruel and perilous place. Mr. Rike was right to be afraid.

"I'm sorry I couldn't make you more honey bread," she said.

A deep thankfulness radiated from his eyes, and she knew her words had been more sweet to him than any bread she could have made. He dropped his eyes and stepped away.

Her mother and brother set her on a bed of hay in the back of the cart. The starchy smell was familiar and comforting. They added a second blanket and pulled it snug around her.

"Good-bye, Tiryn," Kion said. He made an effort to appear brave and fearless again, but the truth came out through his eyes.

"Kion." Strength flowed out of her and into the frigid night with each passing moment. She wanted to stay awake, to hold onto the image of his face, so much like Father, to keep that picture before her eyes as long as possible, but even now it began to fade.

"Yes, Tiryn?"

"I want to see that silver medallion around your neck when I come home. Win the tournament for me, for your Lady of the Tors." She had never cared for his "fencing," as she called it, but now, on the edge of so much uncertainty, this was the one parting gift she could give him.

Kion kissed her on the forehead and gazed steadily into her eyes. The old confidence, the old fire, returned. "I will," he said. "If you promise to come back and see it."

"I...I will try." That was all she could manage before she collapsed into her blankets and the fever pulled her down inside itself and claimed her once more. It was her master, and she could do naught but obey.

Though the road to Charring was well-traveled, the cart itself was not made for comfort. The wheels wobbled and the wood creaked, and the jostling shook Tiryn every waking moment. Often she escaped into sleep, but while awake, she felt every knot, every gap, every warp in the floorboards. Even the sky, so often her friend in days past, looked down on her with an ashen face, a mirror of her misery writ large. How she longed to see the sun. Perhaps it could bring her the life-giving warmth she so desperately needed.

She passed most of the morning of the first day shivering and despondent. The blankets were her only protection, but even they could not keep the chill from seeping into her bones. Eventually, exhausted and unable to endure the pain any longer, she surrendered to sleep.

She awoke to find that they had stopped. The sky was still gray, though the air had warmed by a small but precious measure.

"Mother," Tiryn said in a hoarse whisper. She repeated it several times before her mother responded.

"Oh, what is it, my karinna?" Mother said, turning back.

"Why are we stopped?"

"Jeppers needs to eat."

Jeppers. Was that the name of Rike's mule? She couldn't remember. Tiryn listened hard and thought she heard the munching and mashing of some beast, but her senses were muddled in a feverish fog.

"Would you like something?" Mother asked. She stepped into the back of the cart, setting a small bag beside Tiryn.

"No, I'm not hungry."

Mother touched her forehead. "Oh, Tiryn, your skin is burning. Please, have some water at least."

Tiryn took a little. It did make her feel better, but not much.

The relief evaporated as quickly as it came, like a drizzle on a bonfire.

"What day is it?" Tiryn asked.

"It's the 12th of Avring," came Mother's voice.

"And when did we leave?" She forced the words through her throbbing throat. She did not know whether she would have the strength to say them again.

"Last night."

"I thought maybe it had been longer. How long does it take to get to where we're going?"

Mother cast her tired eyes to some distant point. She needed sleep, but Tiryn knew it would do no good to tell her. "Three days. We should get going," Mother said.

A barrage of coughing racked her chest. "Mother?"

"Yes, karinna?"

"What about the haukmarn? Kion says their harriers have attacked many farmers and travelers. Will we be safe?"

Mother's face grew even more troubled, if that were possible. "We are two poor women; we have nothing of value to attract the attention of harriers."

"Kion says the haukmarn attack for blood and sport."

Mother turned away. "The haukmarn live in the north. We travel farther from their lands with each passing hour. We will reach Charring soon, my karinna. I promise. Now rest if you can."

Mother took her seat up front and shook the reins. A creature snorted, and the cart groaned into motion.

The jostling resumed, bringing fresh agony along with it, but sleep came mercifully to Tiryn's rescue.

She did not wake until the following morning. When she did, she found her mother at her side, her arms wrapped around her, but they gave no warmth. The sun had returned, setting alight the grass of the plains, but it glimmered cold and cruel and did nothing to banish the shaking and the chills.

Mother stirred the moment Tiryn awoke. She made her eat some oat cakes, but Tiryn could only manage a few bites. The second day passed in sleep and sorrow. Though the sound of pursuing footsteps plagued her dreams, no harriers came to assail them.

If they met anyone along the road, it must have been during Tiryn's sleep. Still, she feared the haukmarn and what they might do to her mother. Despite what Mother said about moving farther from the haukmar lands, the long shadow of those menacing giants fell more heavily upon Tiryn with each fevered mile, and the noise of battle grew ever louder in her tumultuous dreams.

The second night, a low, incessant wind beat against the sides of the cart. It dragged her out of precious sleep the few brief times she managed to take refuge in its embrace.

On the third day, she awoke more miserable than ever. She could no longer feel her arms or legs. Though the sun shone brighter and the clouds had fled the sky, the light was powerless to melt the icy grip of sickness slowly consuming her body.

Tiryn longed for release from the pain. She longed to surrender, to cease from the struggle, but every time she looked up to see the bent form of her mother clinging doggedly to the reins, she regained the will to fight. Her mother had sacrificed everything for her and Kion. She was beautiful, intelligent, kind, and confident, everything Tiryn wished to be. She could have remarried some well-off farmer, or even a merchant. Aunt Lizet had sent letters urging her to do just that many times since Father's death, but Mother always said she had only one heart to give, and it had been given to Father. Tiryn loved her all the more for that.

Tiryn had to hold on. She could not break her mother's heart. Father fought the haukmarn. Her battle was against this sickness, against the constant, deadly song which sought to lull her into an eternal sleep. Her only weapon was her will, and she would not lay it down as long as she had strength to fight.

As the sun fell in a fiery cascade over the horizon on the third day, the cart slowed. A great black iron gate swung open before them. The cart rumbled into a wide courtyard, and there it stopped. A large tree, straight and towering, rose before her. It had an odd shape, like an upside-down pear. But the next moment she forgot all about the tree. For looming beyond it was an enormous house, the largest Tiryn had ever seen. She had heard Mother describe the place where she had grown up many times—Marlibrim Mansion—but seeing it now, Tiryn realized Mother's descriptions had not done it justice. The fane's own residence could scarcely have been larger. Beyond the sheer size of it, the stonework, the wrought-iron windows, and the steep slate roofs had a severe beauty to them.

As she gazed up at the home of her aunt, a different sort of chill seized her.

It was a large house. A very large house. Just like the one from her vision.

Chapter 9

A DASH OF COLD WATER

Rike came over every day to visit Kion. He didn't say much, though Kion became more adept at reading the unspoken words knotted on his brow. A hesitant bond began to form between the taciturn shepherd and his young neighbor that grew with each visit. There is a side of friendship which needs no words and may at times be marred by them. Kion wasn't sure Rike thought the same way about him, but for his part Rike became more than just an enigmatic neighbor during these days. Rike helped milk the sheep and finish the lambing. He helped weed the garden. Once, he even came over for dinner. Kion's awful, overcooked porridge was hardly a fitting payment for all of Rike's help, but he scooped it down without so much as a grimace or grumble.

Kion thought often of Tiryn. He had always hoped to win the tournament for his father, but now he had another reason to fight. Winning the medallion would not cure her, but keeping his promise was his way of taking care of her. "Just win the tournament," he told himself. "That's all you can do for her now."

He practiced the forms with his wooden sword the first night they were gone. He stayed up late, hoping to make up for all the time lost to Tiryn's illness. The next day, and every day after, he awoke sore, and not just from his sword work. On top of practice, he now had to do the work of three people. The garden sprouted weeds every time he turned his back. One of the newborn lambs came down with the hairy shakes and had to be given extra medi-

cine. Urly started limping. He had a large thorn in his leg that had
to be taken out, and the wound had to be cleaned and dressed twice
a day. He must have wandered off into a bush when Kion wasn't
looking. Sheep were always doing dimwitted things like that.

Cooking was the worst of all. Kion had no skill whatsoever
when it came to judging the heat of the oven. The porridge came
out like soup or like cinder. He missed his mother more and
more with each passing meal. How did Rike do it? He'd worked
by himself for months since his wife died and never once asked
for a meal. If Kion had to keep cooking for himself, he was not
likely to live out the spring.

On the second night, after finishing the chores early, Kion
rushed over to Rike's cottage and asked him to keep an eye on
the farm while he ran into Furrow. After the stolen sword, he no
longer felt entirely safe leaving the sheep alone.

As he drew near the commons at the center of town, prepara-
tions were well underway for the Seven Fires Festival, set to
begin in five days. White ribbons ran between tall poles staked
along the main road.

A group of men were pounding in posts for the temporary
fence surrounding Memory Lawn, creating what would become
the sparring grounds. There, the Tournament of Mettle would
play out. Kion's pulse quickened as he imagined the upcoming
battles. It would not be long until he clashed swords inside that
fence.

On the far side of the Lawn stood Fielder's House, which
served as everything from the offices of Fielder Lorris to the
court room, the barracks, and even the jail. It was a wide, square
building, the third largest in Furrow. Only the Jeslan and Shaw
houses were bigger.

Behind the House, some stonework and a newly raised
embankment marked Fielder Lorris's fledgling stronghold. It
was little more than a long rectangular foundation at this point,
but Zinder was right: it hardly looked like it would be any real

defense against the haukmarn once it was finished. It wasn't even as big as Fielder's House.

A short distance from the sparring grounds stood a pillared wooden pavilion. Its roof was nothing more than thick beams open to the sky. Carvings in the form of daisy garlands lined the arches between the pillars. The flowers burst with bright yellow paint set against a field of dark green leaves.

Women buzzed about the pavilion, wrapping actual garlands around the poles. Others set potted daisies along the paths leading across the commons to Memory Lawn. Still others sewed dried daisies into white ribbons draped along the streets.

A quartet of musicians was rehearsing inside the pavilion. At the moment they were practicing the song "Seven Fires," which would be played every night of the festival. The women working around the commons hummed along to the familiar melody.

One of the musicians played the wood pipes, a favorite of both Tiryn and Father. The airy notes turned heavy and sullen in Kion's ears. The song was sad enough by itself, but the thought that his father, and perhaps his sister, would never play the pipes again drained the life from the otherwise happy scene.

Kion shuffled on toward the smithy. As he cut across the commons to save time, the song finished, and one of the musicians startled him by waving him over. It was then he realized he had seen these musicians before. They'd played at other festivals. They were a traveling troupe, so they did not come every year, but he must have seen them two or three times.

"Ho there! You're Dorn Bray's son, aren't you?" the man asked as Kion drew near. He had a gray beard and a kind face.

Kion wasn't sure how to respond. His natural reaction was defensiveness. Usually bad things happened when his father's name came up. This man, though, seemed mostly just curious. He sounded like he might have even known Kion's father. That thought kept Kion from pulling away. He gave a tentative nod.

"Your father was a good man." His accent was southern,

from Madrigal perhaps, or even as far away as Verisward. "And a gifted musician—the best I ever played with."

Kion forgot his wariness. "You played with my father?"

"Yes, we all did." He gestured toward the other three. Two of them were the same age as the man, but the fourth was perhaps ten to fifteen years younger. The one addressing him held a flute. The older two played the gemshorn and the bassoon. The youngest had the wood pipes. "All of us except Neril." He indicated the younger man. "He joined us after your father got married and moved to Furrow. We're the Driftwood Winds. Your father is the one who started this quartet many years ago."

Kion stared in wonder. In his mind, his father's life began when he married Mother. The time before that was opaque and mysterious at best, like the back of a painting that hung in his mind.

"My father was a great musician, but he died in the war," Kion said.

"So we heard." The man laid a hand on Kion's shoulder. "It's a shame he had to go off to fight, your father. War is grim business. I don't fault him for sounding the retreat. I'd have done the same."

The wonder of the previous moment vanished, replaced by hot, glowing anger. "My father did not call the retreat. And at least he fought for his people. Did you?"

The man pulled back in shock. Clearly he'd meant no ill with his remark, but Kion could not forgive him. "I was too old to fight, son."

"Cowards have no right to curse the brave," Kion said. He took off without so much as a backward glance. The man said something after him, but Kion was too furious to hear. He was tired of defending his father's name. He had heard these accusations all his life, but he knew the truth: his father had not fled. He may not have been a great soldier like Strom, but he was no coward like that flute player. He was the bravest man in Inris, in all the Four Wards for that matter. And Kion was going to prove it at the tournament.

All he needed was a sword. He quickened his step and hurried past Fielder's House to Zinder's smithy.

A wave of brutal cold shocked Kion awake. He sat up with a shout. His hair and most of his tunic, not to mention his hammock, were dripping with ice water.

Zinder stood next to him with an empty bucket and a full smile. "Well, it's about time!" he said.

Kion shook his head, spraying Zinder with a dose of his own medicine. Zinder just laughed.

"Zinder, you little—time? Oh no! What time is it?" Kion asked, an awful realization dawning on him.

"A quarter 'til nine."

"The tournament!" Kion leapt from his hammock and rushed about the cottage. How could he oversleep? And today of all days!

"Of course, the tournament, you dunderhead! You should be glad I came when I did."

Kion was only half listening. He yanked on his boots and ripped his sword belt off a hook.

Zinder kept jabbering. "I had an inkling you might sleep in when I saw you yesterday at the market. Your eyes were so droopy they almost fell off your face. I'm surprised you made it home standing up."

Kion strapped on his new sword and flailed his way into his cloak. His upper half was still soaked, and he was shivering, but he could hardly blame Zinder. Kion was a notoriously sound sleeper.

"Come on, lad," Zinder said, skipping out the door ahead of him. "I gave Crusty *two* carrots for breakfast this morning. He'll get you to the tournament on time. Fastest mule in Inris, aren't you, old fellow?"

Crusty gave him a look of utter indifference, but the cart seemed ready enough. The morning mist had all but cleared from the Tors. Kion had been too busy to notice before, but Zinder was dressed in a smart, striped tunic of red and white. His thick black belt had a silver buckle the size of a tea saucer. His red, pleated pants puffed out over the tops of a pair of black boots so shiny and stiff they might have been carved from polished stone. A large hat with an enormous red feather over-shadowed his head like a portable awning.

Kion gave the ostentatious outfit barely a passing glance. He tossed his finely tailored friend up and into the driver's bench with all the courtesy and care he'd have given a sheep at shearing time.

"*Eeee*! Careful with my pin cushions!" Zinder said as he landed on his bottom.

Kion landed beside him, shoving the reins into Zinder's gloved hands. Zinder tossed his enormous hat into the back of the cart and flicked the reins. He let out a few high-pitched shouts at Crusty, and the cart lurched into motion.

Zinder wasn't joking when he promised a timely arrival. Once Crusty got going, he ran like a young colt. Of course, it was mostly downhill, and at some point Crusty was outrunning the cart as much as anything, but the wild, galloping mule was a sight to behold. Two carrots, indeed!

With all the bouncing over the rocky turf, it was a wonder Kion or Zinder didn't fly out of the cart. Zinder whooped and laughed the whole way, even more whenever a vicious dip or bump threw him in the air. White-haired though he was, Zinder had a child's spirit. That left Kion to do all the worrying. About halfway there, he began to seriously doubt they would make it to the tournament in one piece. Every tree that hurtled past seemed to lean into the path to smash the cart into kindling, but by some special grace, they kept missing them. Soon, even Kion's fears gave way to the sheer exhilaration of racing through the Tors with a freezing wind in his face and a wild, cackling nyn at his side.

As they careened onto the main road into Furrow, Zinder reined in the thundering mule at last. The poor beast was huffing louder than Zinder's bellows, but it whinnied in triumph, announcing their arrival to the many folk wandering the street.

"Didn't know Crusty was a racing mule, did you?" Zinder said.

Kion slapped Zinder on the back. "Zinder, that was a ride for the ages. I'm almost glad I slept in!"

A few villagers eyed the two breathless arrivals with mild disdain and no small amount of alarm. Most were too busy navigating the crowded street to bother with them, however. Every inch of the main road was lined with vendors hawking their wares. Meat pies, sweet pies, jam-basted pheasant legs, glazed apples, corn cakes, beef skewers, bacon-wrapped cheeseballs, and all manner of sugar cookies filled the air with sunny aromas that made Kion's stomach grumble in lament for his missed breakfast. Many stalls had food grilling or baking on an open fire.

Stitched jackets, fine wool trousers, flowing shawls, and feather-tipped caps (which Zinder eyed with magnetic fascination) were laid out for all to see. One booth was even selling colored flags for cheering on combatants in the tournament. Zinder eyed those as well, but when he saw the merchant wanted a full two silver squares for them, he didn't give them a second look. Carved wooden figures, painted pots, cloth dolls, and dangling glass ornaments were surrounded by children and mothers swatting away their hands to keep them from touching. The Seven Fires Festival had begun.

But Kion had no time to meander and gawk at all the wonders brought in by traveling merchants and visitors from as far away as Madrigal, Quelling, and Seabrim. He sprang from the cart and pushed through the crowd.

"You go on ahead," Zinder said. "I can't bring the cart any farther anyway. I'll find a place to hitch old Crusty and catch up to you."

"See you at the Lawn, then," Kion said with a wave.

The closer he got to the center of the village, the more crowded it became. He had been to the Seven Fires Festival every year since it started, but never had it drawn this many people. It was ten years since the Battle of Fane's Falling, which the festival commemorated, so this was an extra-special occasion.

At last he came within sight of the Lawn. A shrill brass bell tinkled dreadfully over the milling crowds.

"Last call for entrants to the Tournament of Mettle! Last call!" rang out the voice of Etran Squigsworth, the judge who presided over the tournament. He was one of only half a dozen survivors from Furrow at the Battle of Fane's Falling, and the only soldier in the village to have achieved anything higher than the rank of glinthelm in the army of the fane. Most said he'd succeed Fielder Lorris whenever he stepped down.

Etran had no love for Kion's father. He was the one who claimed his father had sounded the retreat. He'd never said this to Kion directly, but Furrow was not a large village, and rumors are like rain clouds; they start in one place, but by the time they pass through, everyone gets wet. As far as Kion was concerned, this particular rumor was deep enough to drown in.

"He won't be calling the Brays cowards when he puts that medallion around my neck," Kion muttered.

He pushed on through the crowd. More and more people refused to give way, afraid he would take their spot on the Lawn.

"Going once!" Etran shouted.

Kion accidentally stepped on a fellow's toes. "Sorry," he said, not waiting for a reply.

He nudged a rotund fellow to the side.

"Watch it!" the man growled.

"Sorry, just trying to get to the ring before it's too late," Kion said.

"Not my fault, you lazy shepherd." The man grunted and turned away.

"Going twice!"

Kion bowled over the last poor fellow in front of him. He didn't mean to, but the figure shifted at the last moment and went down on the grass with a thud.

"Terribly sorry—oh, Snetch, I didn't know it was you!"

Snetch's face went lemon sour. He rattled some spittle around in the back of his throat, as if he meant to pay Kion back in the crassest way possible, but Etran's shout interrupted him.

"And—"

"Here I am, sir." Kion burst through the gate and staggered forward into the middle of Memory Lawn. Two lines of boys stood on either side of Etran. Kion squeezed in beside Harvin, Dougan's friend.

"I see," Etran said. His weathered face was as cold as the water Zinder had splashed on Kion that morning.

"You'd have been better off staying home, woolly." Harvin gave Kion a sharp elbow to the ribs, but Kion didn't care.

The tournament was about to begin.

Chapter 10

THE TRIALS

The blast of a ram's horn silenced all the chatter and commotion on Memory Lawn.

Fielder Lorris, dressed in a full suit of plate armor, save the helm, strode into the center of the sparring grounds. There he joined Etran who stood next to a small table. The fielder's armor had seen better days. It was full of nicks and dents, and a few bits were missing altogether, but that didn't matter; it was only for show. Older men were not allowed to compete in the tournament.

On the table between Etran and Lorris rested a large plaque that served to showcase the silver medallion to be given to the winner of this year's Tournament of Mettle. The medallion hung on two pegs, gleaming warmly in the early morning sun. It was the size of Kion's palm and had a beautiful, bas-relief sword carved in the center with seven stylized flames ringing the edge. Just a few short matches and it would be his, and with it, redemption for his father.

When the horn blast died away, Fielder Lorris cleared his throat and shouted, "People of Furrow and sundry parts of Inris, welcome to the Seven Fires Festival!"

Cheers broke out across the commons. Hundreds of people crowded around the fenced off area where the twenty-four entrants waited. The boys stood inside the sparring grounds, each decked out in half plate armor. Compared to what the entrants had been outfitted with, Fielder Lorris's suit might have been of nynnian craftsmanship. The boys' suits had all been salvaged from defeated fanewardens and swordswains at the Battle of Fane's Falling. None of the helmets matched the breast-plates. Nor did any of the pauldrons match the vambraces. Like-wise when it came to the helms, gauntlets, cuirasses, and tassets. The boys were lucky if they fit even reasonably well. The smaller boys had to wear extra padding in addition to their gambesons to fill out the barrel-like suits. That would put them at a disad-vantage as far as mobility, but it couldn't be helped.

The one exception to the hodgepodge armor was Dougan. His well-fitted, fluted plate made him seem a man among boys. Like the others, he wore no leg armor, but aside from that, he could have passed for any swordswain in the fane's host. The armor had even been presumptuously engraved on the breast-plate with the same design featured on the tournament's silver medallion. Zinder said Dougan's father had ordered it from that new smith they were using in Windstern.

Across from the entrants stood a line of seven girls wearing yellow smocks over white dresses, the candle maidens for this year's festival. As with the armor, the smocks and dresses were mostly worn down, patched up affairs, though a couple of the older girls wore brand new ones. The maidens ranged in age from about nine or ten to fifteen, the oldest age at which a girl could be chosen. Each one held several garlands of daisies, ready to present to the aspirants. A heaviness rose inside Kion at the sight of them, knowing that Tiryn should have been standing among them. For the first time he realized how much she must have been looking forward to dancing in the festival. In her own way, it was probably as important to her as the tournament was to Kion. All the more reason for him to win the medallion for her.

Fielder Lorris continued, "As most of you know, this festival was founded by royal charter in the year 828 to commemorate the bravery, grit, and sacrifice of fifty-seven sons of Furrow in the

Battle of Fane's Falling. The fine food, good homes, and abundant fields we enjoy today, we owe in large measure to their willingness to fight and die to stop the haukmar hordes from sweeping through our lands. This lawn, Memory Lawn, was so named that we might guard their memory as they guarded our lives. May we never forget, Inris. May we never forget."

Subdued applause dribbled through the assembly. It was still hard for the people of Inris to accept the loss of so many of their husbands and fathers. Over half the men of Furrow had died in the War of the Claws, the majority of them in the final battle, the bloodiest of all: the Battle of Fane's Falling. They were so close to surviving the war and coming home. Instead, they lay buried in the fields of Roving, a day's journey north, entombed forever in the land they died to defend.

The girls stepped forward at a gesture from Lorris. Kion, along with the other entrants, took a knee. The girl presenting her garland to Kion was one of the younger ones, still too innocent to fully realize how shameful it was to have to place a garland around the neck of a shepherd. She had brown hair and smiling eyes, though she did her best to stay solemn, as befitting the occasion. Each girl passed out garlands to several aspirants. As they presented the garlands, the maids broke into song:

Winter roared through the valley, and her claws scarred the land
As she hunted for daisies, leaving none left to stand

And the wind froze our teardrops as the last daisies fell
Never more shall we see them, those we once knew so well

Under ice they are buried in the ground far below
Cold and hard as the daisies trapped beneath all the snow

Through the long winter twilight hold your memories dear
Let the memory of daisies linger on through the year

For with every winter there must then come a spring
  And a new field of daisies will fresh memories bring

When the maids gather daisies in the folds of their skirts
  Let the sun melt your sorrows, and the rain heal your hurts

We will hang them from ribbons on a nail in the door
  As if bright golden medals that they won in the war

Not a few of the ladies in the crowd, and even a few of the men, dabbed the corners of their eyes with kerchiefs.

"They would want us to be merry on this occasion," Lorris resumed his speech. "Let us hold fast to the days we had with them and not lament the days that are lost. And to that end, by the authority of Fane Sathe and Margrave Berrintall, I hereby commence this, the tenth annual Festival of Seven Fires!"

Real applause came this time, mixed with shouts of "hear, hear!" "so be it!" "heigh-ho!", and "here's to our men!"

Smokecrackers boomed from the four corners of the commons, provoking laughs and squeals from the younger members of the audience. Puffs of gray clouds roiled across the grass. Pandemonium reigned as people flung handfuls of colored corn, showering everyone with kernels of yellow, red, and blue.

Kion did not cheer. He had no room in his heart for the frivolous merriment that had overtaken the commons. He stood in the corn rain and stared at the silver medallion. He had to win. Nothing else mattered.

Etran Squigsworth paced before the two lines of aspirants. Behind him stood a target dummy encased in battered armor and stuffed with hay. Like the aspirants, the armor extended only to the figure's "waist." A stout pole formed its single "leg."

On one side of the dummy stood a tall stump with an over-ripe squash on top. On the other side was a wooden panel, supported by perpendicular slats that served as footers to keep it standing. The panel was about the size of a door.

Etran was dressed in a solemn black tunic with white sleeves. An array of silver ribbons hung from his belt, as did a sheathed short sword.

"Aspirants of the Tournament of Mettle," Etran addressed the twenty-four boys before him. Villagers leaned on the surrounding fence, listening in. Among them, directly across from Kion, was Zinder. He sported his wide-brimmed black hat with a bright red feather the size of a windmill. It certainly was catching enough wind to make it seem like one. That made it hard for him to keep his balance. He clung to his hat with one hand and the fence with the other, like a sailor tossed at sea.

"The Tournament of Mettle follows the same format as most Inrisian tournaments," Etran continued, "but as this may be the first tournament for some of you, I will go over the rules."

The shorter boys, who stood in the foremost of the two lines, straightened up, as if Etran were about to give valuable insights on how to handle a blade.

"The tournament consists of a qualification round in which you will compete in three trials. This will be followed by five rounds of sparring, with those scoring highest in the challenges advancing automatically to the second round."

Etran unsheathed his sword. It was a solid blade, identical to the one that had belonged to Kion's father. Many of the youths would be fighting with similar weapons, passed on to them by their own fathers.

"The first trial consists of the blind strike. You will begin with your back to the table and must execute a strike in the following manner."

Etran spun around and sliced the squash in half, though it was not a clean cut. He frowned as he watched the jagged halves fall to the ground. "You get three strikes. Points will be given for the cleanness of the strike and the proportion of the two slices. Points will be deducted for hitting the table, and of course, no points will be awarded for a complete miss."

He moved on to the target dummy. "The second challenge consists of seven strikes in combination. Two of the six target areas will be called out in rapid succession. The six areas are"— and here he tapped each in succession on the target as he said them—"high left, high right"—hitting the shoulders—"mid left, mid right"—striking the torso—"and lower left, lower right"— hitting the waist. "Points will be given for speed and accuracy. Points will be deducted for blows to the wrong mark."

Kion adjusted his sword belt. He knew these rules by heart. Watching Etran review them was like having an itch he couldn't scratch.

"And finally," Etran said, "the most difficult test of all: the guarding trial." That was its official name. Kion, along with the other veteran aspirants, simply called it the egg toss.

Etran went behind the wooden screen and pulled out a large basket of eggs. "Now, these have been hollowed out and filled with colored powder. An attendant will stand behind the screen and toss an egg at the aspirant from either the top, left, or right, one every second for seven seconds. The aspirant must deflect or dodge each as it comes. Any that hit the aspirant will leave a mark like so." He tossed an egg at the target dummy. It burst into a puff of blue powder, leaving a large spot in the middle of the breastplate. "Each egg deflected grants two points, and each one dodged will grant a single point. A perfect score is thus fourteen points. Any questions?"

"Do we get to eat the eggs that miss?" asked one of the boys from the front row. He was the smallest and probably the skinniest of the aspirants.

Several of the boys laughed, but Etran flashed the boy a sharp look. "They're filled with powder. You're welcome to eat as many as you like. Perhaps it would help tame your tongue. Any other questions?"

Dougan puffed out his chest. "I've got a question. When can we start? I want to see which one of these blighters gets second place." A few boys laughed at that, but Kion knew it wasn't meant to be funny. Dougan had the sense of humor of a brick wall. Unfortunately, he struck like one too.

At that moment, a violent wind whipped up and blew across the sparring grounds. It knocked Zinder's enormous red feather clean off his hat. The plume smacked Etran Squigsworth full in the face, transforming him from stern tournament judge into someone fighting with a bird costume gone awry.

The boys broke out in howling laughter, even Kion. Etran flailed about, trying to swat the feather away, but whether from some caprice of the wind or his own lack of coordination, it kept flying back in his face.

"We already had the masquerade this year!" Kion shouted.

"Shoddy haberdashery!" Zinder called out. "Oh, my. Terribly sorry, Squigsworth!" He vaulted over the fence and ran to the aid of the hapless judge, doing his best not to laugh.

"There you are." Zinder failed miserably at containing his laughter, but he jumped up and snatched the unruly feather, quick as a flea. "Saved from the attack of the vicious feather!" He held it up triumphantly.

Etran's face turned as red as the feather. He swiped the offending plumage from Zinder and cast it to the ground. Before Zinder knew what was happening, the furious judge squashed it beneath his boot. The loud snapping noise signaled the end of Zinder's magnificent feather, as well as his mischievous grin, but the rest of the crowd went on laughing for a good while.

"Mid left. High right." *Thwack, thwack.* "Mid left. Lower left." *Thwack, thwack.* "High left. Lower right." *Thwack, thwack.*

Kion finished the last three combinations of his second challenge perfectly, just as he had the first four. Zinder's sword was nearly identical in heft and feel to his old one, and the grip was more sure. The metal was darker, though, far darker than the swords of any of the other aspirants.

"Kion Bray receives a mark of fourteen in combinations," Etran pronounced in a monotone voice. He had recovered his composure from the incident with the feather and was back to his usual, somber ways.

A round of tepid applause came in answer to the score. It was the first perfect of the day. Had it been scored by anyone other than a shepherd, there would have been cheers along with the applause, but Kion would take any appreciation he could get.

The second trial was his best event. It was really just an exercise in the Fiorin Batal without the proper names. Mid left was a gerlin twist, high right was a forte swing, lower left was a revil sweep, and so forth.

He had scored third in the first trial, the blind strike. Strictly speaking, it didn't matter who got the high scores in these challenges. They were only for seeding in the tournament. But Dougan, as last year's winner, was automatically seeded first and exempt from the trials. If Kion wanted to avoid meeting him before the final, he would have to come in at the top of qualifications.

Kion saluted Etran with his sword and retired into the crowd. He chatted with Zinder as they watched the rest of the combination trials.

Zinder had already replaced the feather in his hat. The new one was a relatively inconspicuous black feather with a white tip, much smaller than the previous one. The wind had died down as well, but he wasn't taking any chances. He had the feather set at such a low angle, it was practically perpendicular to the rim. Even still, he felt for it every so often to make sure it hadn't flown away.

Going into the third and final trial, the egg toss, Kion was in second place behind a boy named Provian. Provian had scored first in the blind strike and second in combinations. He had never competed in this tournament before. According to Zinder, he was from a merchant family in Madrigal and had been traveling about, attending all the local tournaments. He was a year younger than Kion, and a few inches shorter, but stockier. He looked like a smaller version of Dougan but moved more fluidly. That was easy enough in the trials. It would be no guarantee of success when the matches began.

Provian went first in the egg toss and did miserably. He only managed to block two of the seven eggs and dodge one other. His armor looked like a jester's tunic when he was finished. Kion was called to go next.

He missed the first egg, but connected with five in a row after that. He got a little overconfident and missed the last one, but still managed to dodge it. His new sword sang through the air. Eleven points. He was in the top spot by a wide margin.

Another boy went after him and did almost as bad as Provian. Then came Harvin. With a perfect score he could claim the lead, but no one had ever gotten a perfect score at the egg toss. As it turned out, neither did Harvin. He did get eight points, though, enough to move into second behind Kion, granting him the third seed. Kion didn't bother staying to watch the rest of the trials. None of the other aspirants had a chance to pass him or Harvin. He knew the lay of his bracket. He and Harvin would most likely meet in the semifinals. Kion had beaten him last year, so he was confident about his chances of facing Dougan in the final.

Kion and Zinder went over to the food stands, where Zinder brought him to a big plate of cornbread, white beans, and a fat sausage.

"Fire and ice, Zinder, I didn't give you enough coin for a meal like this."

Zinder ignored him and thrust the plate into his hands.

"Now, Kion, my dear lad, this is a celebration of your first-place qualification in the trials. You deserve no less! Besides—I wanted to do it. Here's your coin back." Zinder sat down with an identical plate of food. It was not apparent by looking at him, but Zinder was a complete gobbledown. He was half Kion's size, but ate twice as much. He claimed it all went to his brain.

"Well, I suppose, since you already bought it, I'll have to eat it. Thank you, Zinder, you're a gem," Kion said. In truth, it was all he could do not to drool on his plate. He only ever got to eat food like this at festivals, and even then, never this much. The awful fare he'd been cooking for himself over the last few days combined with his missing breakfast made this food look and smell better than anything he'd ever eaten in his entire life.

"No need to flap about it. I finished the scribe's order yestereve. After I make that delivery to Strom's men, I'll be able to afford sausage every day for a year. Even at festival prices!" Zinder bit into his sausage with zeal. Hot oil squirted into his beard, but he dabbed it away so quickly and deftly it never marred his flawless grooming.

Kion lit into his plate with all the relish of a bear fresh from a winter nap. Very rarely in life does experience exceed anticipation, but it did that day. The cornbread melted into the beans, which infused their juices into the sausage, which seasoned the bread, and so it went in a delicious circle.

To top it off, Zinder's quips and comments kept him laughing the whole time. They had an especially long laugh about the incident with Etran and the feather all over again. No one could make Kion laugh like Zinder.

When the meal ended, Kion had to return to look in on his sheep. Zinder offered to give him a ride back to the farm, but Kion declined.

"Walking's not too good for a shepherd, you know. Stay and enjoy the festival. And try not to spend all your money!"

"All right, lad. Off with you, then. And get a good night's sleep this time. You don't want me to have to douse you two days in a row!"

"I don't intend to give you that pleasure. I'll see you tomorrow at the tournament," Kion said, and waved good-bye to his friend.

The day was almost here. And Kion was ready.

Chapter 11

HAMMER AND TONG

Kion pulled away to catch his breath. This was his first match; he should have bested his opponent by now. This was not how he had pictured his start to the tournament.

A smattering of people stood watching along three sides of the ring. The northern section, which faced the main road, Meadow's Way, was bordered by a raised platform. Only the wealthy were allowed to spectate from there in one of eight high-backed chairs. Today, the chairs were empty. No one was interested in a first round match between a shepherd and an out-of-towner.

Of those present, most were against him, even though his opponent was from Windstern and almost all of the spectators were from Furrow. This was mostly due to the efforts of Dougan, who yelled things like, "Sheepstink can't fight!" and "Try your staff, maybe you'd fight better!" and similar jeers, making sure everyone knew that if they rooted for Kion, they'd be rooting for a worthless, uncouth shepherd.

As loud as Dougan was, Snetch was louder.

"Woolly's getting tired!" he shouted. "Finish him off, whoever you are!" His freckled face sneered at Kion from just outside the fence.

Brodin, for that was his opponent's name, heeded the advice of his newly acquired admirer and rushed Kion with a series of whirling strikes. Kion met them with guarded counterstrikes but barely missed on one, and Brodin landed a glancing blow on

Kion's shoulder. The scraping sound of metal on metal rang out across the ring.

Etran Squigsworth raised his white scoring flag.

"Point for the green," he said.

Etran's assistant planted a green flag in a slot on the right-most scoring placard. Brodin wore a matching green sash, denoting him as the lower seed in this match.

"That's it! I knew he could do it!" Snetch said. "How about that, woolly? Give up while you still can!"

"Baa-aaa! I hear your sheep calling!" Dougan added.

Kion still had three red flags on his board to Brodin's one, but he was tired of listening to the abuse. It was time to stop playing at swords and start fighting with them.

"Don't worry, lad." Zinder's high-pitched voice rose above the jeers. "You only need two more flags to win. Two more to shut the door!"

Kion bounced around the edge of the ring, shaking off the momentary setback. He was still learning the forms; he couldn't count on pulling them off perfectly every time. But he was still quicker and stronger than his opponent. He just needed to shift his tactics a bit.

When Etran gave the signal to resume the match, Kion decided to see if Brodin could handle a bit of his own medicine. Kion abandoned the strict use of the forms and swung his sword in wild, erratic strokes. This left him exposed, but Brodin didn't know how to take advantage or counter. Kion landed an easy strike on the right side.

"That's the Blade of the North, my friends! He strikes like the wind," Zinder shouted, waving his fancy red hat. "You never know where he'll hit next!" But when Kion caught his eye, Zinder flashed him a troubled look.

"Point for the red," Etran said and a fourth red flag was added to Kion's placard.

Zinder's look puzzled Kion, but he had no time to unravel it. He now saw his opponent's weakness. Brodin was raw. He knew none of the forms. He had been getting by on sheer nerve and instinct, swinging his sword in unconventional ways, but with such unrelenting swiftness he had managed to keep Kion guessing.

When the fighting resumed, Kion repeated the same tactic, launching another undisciplined flurry. Brodin blocked the first few this time, but he couldn't keep up. Kion was older, stronger, and quicker. He scored a hit to the left side.

Etran raised his flag. "Point for the red. Kion Bray is the winner."

There was respectful applause. Snetch mumbled and whined something incoherent, but for the most part, even he was silenced. Dougan gave Kion a threatening look before wandering off into the small crowd.

Kion removed a gauntlet and undid his helmet. When he reached the outside of the ring, Zinder was there to congratulate him.

"I knew you'd come out on top, lad," Zinder said, but he wasn't quite his usual enthusiastic self.

"You don't seem all that excited."

"Well, I won't say I'm not happy you won, but what was there at the end?" Zinder made some flapping motions with his hands.

"He was too wild. The forms weren't working. So I adjusted."

"That may have worked against an untrained fellow like that, but don't count on it next time. You need to stick to your train- ing. Trust in the forms. The Fiorin Batal's been developed over centuries. I know you're just learning, but it's your best shot at winning this tournament. A sword fight is won through disci- pline, not reckless thrashing and blind luck."

When Zinder gave him that earnest look, Kion had learned it was best not to contradict him. He was probably right anyway. Even if Zinder wasn't a great swordsman himself, he knew blades, and he knew swordplay.

"Fair enough. I'll be more disciplined in the next match. Now, help me get out of this armor. It's blazing like the sun in here."

In Kion's second match, he faced Nevil, a boy from one of the poorer farming families of Furrow. Kion had watched one of his matches last year. He was a year younger, but tall for his age and quick with a blade.

This time, Kion stuck to the forms, swinging in familiar patterns and combinations. Nevil countered a few of his strokes with mere reflexes, but he had no experience with the Fiorin Batal. And why should he? He was a farm boy, like most of them.

The crowd was larger and louder than before—and even more against him, since he was fighting a local. Kion bested him after five minutes, but Nevil's speed allowed him to score two hits, much to Snetch's delight. Kion wondered how defending him from Dougan had earned him Snetch's special ire, but apparently it had. Next time he would mind his own business and stay out of other peoples' battles.

Dougan was watching as well, cheering Nevil and jeering Kion as before, but once, after Kion had scored a hit, he caught a more calculated look in Dougan's eyes. That was even more troubling than the jeers. Dougan was sizing him up, looking for weaknesses in his style. And Kion gave him plenty to work with in that match.

Kion yanked off his helmet after he finished and grunted in frustration.

"Now, don't be a poor winner, lad," Zinder said. "You fought well. You stuck to the forms."

"But he got two hits on me. I'll never beat Dougan if I fight like this."

"No one's perfect. You can't expect to be a master in a day. I only stumbled across that folio last year. Fiorin himself took a lifetime to learn what's inside it."

Kion wiped the sweat from his brow with his sleeve. He wasn't sure what was more troubling: his lack of mastery with the blade, or the knowledge that Dougan was studying his every move. Of course, Kion couldn't return the favor. He had too much to do back at the farm.

"Yes, yes, you're right, as usual," Kion said. "I'll try to take things in stride, but only if you promise not to look so smug when I agree with you."

Zinder scrubbed his lips, but it didn't work. That smug look apparently did not come off so easily.

"Look, lad, whatever happens from here on out, you've nothing to be ashamed of. You've held your head up when all were against you and shown yourself to be a person of quality. And that's worth more than winning or losing."

Good old Zinder. If only Furrow were filled with people like him.

"I suppose," Kion said. "But I still want to win."

"Of course you do. Now, why don't you let me take that blade overnight and grind the nicks out. You'll want it looking your best tomorrow when you win the tournament!"

Good old Zinder indeed.

For once Kion went to bed early. The armor and the gambeson had protected him from the blows, but he was still wiped out. His muscles longed for rest. Moving and fighting in armor against actual opponents was not as simple as practicing forms against air. He wasn't used to all the extra heat, for one thing; he'd forgotten how tiring it could be. And he had overworked himself leading up to the tournament. It all caught up to him now, and he sank into his hammock in utter exhaustion.

The third day of the festival dawned a blanket of gray. A spitting drizzle glazed the Tors. It brought with it a curious tingling, a sense of expectation, as if all of nature strained not to miss what would unfold that day.

Kion had enjoyed a lovely dream during the night in which he'd won the tournament and Dougan had been forced to present the award. But instead of hanging the medallion around Kion's neck, Dougan had to melt down the previous medallions he'd won and forge them into an actual full-sized sword made of silver. Kion was a little sad when he woke to find that no such sword in the cottage. Still, he took it for a good omen.

He stretched and let out a terrific yawn. He had slept late again, but he didn't mind. His matches were not until the afternoon, and he needed the rest.

"No pail of water today," he said.

Kion dressed quickly and skipped breakfast. He rushed through his chores with little awareness of what he was doing, one thought repeating itself over and over again in his mind.

"Today's the day."

By noon, hunger forced him to stop and cook something. Like all his culinary misadventures, it turned out awful, but it went down too fast to leave a lasting impression. He shoved the last bite in his mouth and headed out the door. The dishes could wait. He didn't even bother stopping by Rike's farm. He trusted him to remember to come by and check on the sheep.

Kion had to push his way through the crowds on his way to the smithy. He did his best to ignore the gurglings of his stomach as he walked past the scrumptious smells. The crowds and, more mercifully, the food disappeared once he got past the commons. Long before he reached the door of the smithy, Zinder's bright, unmistakable tenor came ringing out through the dusty street.

Hammer and Tong
Ringing along
Singing the song
Of hammer and tong

We will rise with the daybreak
And we'll stoke up the fire
As we'll pile on the charcoal
'Til the flames flicker higher

Hammer and Tong
Ringing along
Singing our song
Of hammer and tong

And we'll pound on the sword tang
And we'll strike on the blade
As the blows sound the rhythm
For the song we have made

Hammer and Tong
Ringing along
Singing this song
Of hammer and tong

Oh, we'll work 'til the sundown
'Til the sword's finally formed
Then we'll sleep 'til the dawning
With our hearts full and warmed

Hammer and Tong
Ringing along
Singing the song
Of hammer and tong

Kion poked his head through the top half of the smithy door. Several of the shops had half-and-half doors like that. Zinder finished hammering on the glowing stake in his tongs. Kion couldn't tell if it would end up as a dagger or some tool, but Zinder made a low whistle as he looked it up and down. His face glowed with more than the reflection from the hot metal. It shone with the pride of a master craftsman, delighting in the act of creating.

"That's good work, that is," Zinder said to himself.

Kion imitated his whistle, and Zinder gave a quick turn, noticing him for the first time. "Good work indeed, but I hope that's not my sword," Kion said.

"Well, you've been winning so easy, I thought I might whittle it down a bit, give the other lads a chance!" Zinder said. "Now, let me see, where did I put yours? Ah, yes, right over there. Here you are, lad. All shined up and ready to swing you to victory. This is going to be a fabulous day, I say. I can feel my nynnian blood tingling. When they sling that medallion around your neck, be sure to tell them who made the sword of the champion!"

"I will." Kion examined the polished blade. The edges were smooth and perfect. It had a vaguely yellow sheen that came from the particular oil Zinder used on his blades.

"You're all ready, then?" Zinder said.

Kion sheathed the blade. "Yes. Though I do wish Tiryn and Mother could be here. I was half hoping they might have made it back by now."

Zinder patted his arm. "I'm sure they'll be back as soon as dear, sweet Tiryn recovers."

"I suppose so," Kion said. His family's absence was the one doubt hanging over the day. Winning wouldn't be the same without them present. "I should be off now. Are you coming?"

"Is the sky full of sparks? Course I'm coming! I don't want to miss the look on that thieving stoat's face when you slap him sideways to Seabrim. I just have to clean up here, and I'll catch up with you as quick as my nynnian sticks can waddle over to the commons."

"I had a dream last night, Zinder. I dreamed I won the tournament and Dougan had to proclaim me the champion. Only, instead of a medallion, he gave me a full-sized sword made out of silver."

"A sword of silver, eh?" Zinder said. "Well, it's your dream, I suppose, but let's hope you never have to use that sword in battle! Silver's far too soft for something like that. Still, I do hope the part about winning comes true!"

Chapter 12

TOURNAMENT OF METTLE

The rain cleared well before Kion's mid-afternoon match, and the sparring ring had enough fresh sand and gravel laid over it to ensure good footing. A fair-sized crowd was on hand by the time he arrived.

Kion stood across the ring from Harvin. Harvin and Dougan were roughly the same age, but Harvin acted more like a little brother around Dougan. He was shorter than Kion, but only just. His thicker chest and arms more than made up for the slight disadvantage of his height, but like most of the farm boys, he was raw and self-trained with a blade.

While Harvin's father helped him strap on the last of his armor, Harvin kept his sour gaze trained on Kion, his left eye twitching occasionally.

"The shame of losing to you has been eating him up all year," Zinder said, noting Harvin's expression. "That look on his face would almost be intimidating if it wasn't so silly. I imagine he has to practice to look that ridiculous."

Kion tried to keep a straight face while Zinder finished fastening his armor. He wanted Harvin to think he was getting to him.

Near Harvin's corner were Dougan and Snetch. Snetch waved a green flag and chanted, "Harvin, Harvin, Harvin!" while glancing at Dougan out of the corner of his eye.

Dougan barely noticed Snetch's antics. He had already won his earlier semifinal match, so he'd be facing the winner of this one. He leaned his large frame against the fence and spoke in relaxed fashion with Harvin. Kion couldn't hear his words over the chattering of the crowd, but he made several striking gestures, to which Harvin nodded.

"I wonder how Snetch got that flag?" Kion said. "Did that fellow selling them finally lower his price?"

"Not a nick. I tried to bargain with him, but he wouldn't budge." Zinder was on tiptoe atop a small stool, straining to fasten Kion's shoulder armor. "Like as not Snetch stole it. He just lost his job at Jeslan's. Old Jeslan said he was shaving off from what he sold at the market. He's lucky Lorris didn't put him in the stocks or run him into the hills."

Zinder finished tightening the straps and tied off the red sash around Kion's waist.

Etran stepped into the ring, his white flag hanging at his side.

Kion slapped down his visor and signaled he was ready. Harvin, wearing the green sash, did the same. A stray fit of nerves rippled through Kion's stomach.

"Kion Bray, in the red," Etran said.

Zinder let out a high-pitched whoop, and a few others mustered some polite applause.

"Harvin Poulter, in the green."

The crowd cheered for him like the fane's own cousin. Kion should have been used to it by now, but it still stung to be so despised.

"Just win the match," he said to himself. "That'll quiet them up."

He drew his sword and hummed *Hammer and Tong* to try to take his mind off the noise.

"Touch swords," Etran said.

The two boys took their stances and crossed swords. Harvin pressed hard against Kion's blade. That meant he would likely open with an immediate attack.

"And...fight!" Etran shouted.

A rumbling cheer shook the commons. Harvin lunged forward, going immediately for the throat. Even if Kion hadn't been expecting it, it was a clumsy attack. Kion countered and stepped to the side, slapping his blade against Harvin's backside as he passed.

"Point for the red," Etran said, placing a scoring flag beneath Kion's name.

The crowd went silent, stunned by the quickness of the hit. It even took a moment to register with Zinder.

Harvin growled and slapped his helmet.

"Bravo, lad! Well struck," Zinder said when he found his voice at last.

Dougan was the only one who didn't seem surprised. He kept his eyes trained on Kion, and for once he wasn't cheering or jeering. He just watched Kion intently, studying his every move. It was far more disturbing than Harvin's fits of rage, but Kion couldn't afford to think about Dougan now. He had to beat Harvin first.

They crossed swords again and Harvin immediately executed a wild swipe, selling all his sheep, as the saying went. Kion's blade shivered on the counter, but he side-stepped as before and clanked Harvin on the shoulder.

"Agh!" Harvin cried.

"Point for the red."

If Harvin didn't rein himself in, this was going to be over before Kion broke a sweat.

Zinder cheered. Scattered applause drifted through the rest of the crowd. Most stood in stunned silence.

"Come on, Harvin!" Snetch shouted. "You're better than that woolly. Give him what for!" He started a chant of "Green, green, green!" but no one joined him.

Harvin paced back and forth, stamping the ground. He took his time coming in to cross swords.

There was no pressure on Kion's blade. Harvin wasn't looking to attack this time.

Kion batted Harvin's sword away and circled to the left. Harvin stepped back, dropping into a fool's guard. Kion wondered if Harvin knew the guard or if he was just resting, taking a moment to rethink his strategy. In their match the previous year, Harvin had only lost three to five. He fought on instinct, but his instincts were good. He showed no sign, though, that he knew the Fiorin Batal, or any other fighting style. Maybe that was why he'd been taken off guard. He was expecting Kion to fight in the same undisciplined way as last year.

The lowered blade was tempting. Kion rehearsed in his mind the sequence for attacking it. He doubted Harvin knew the correct counter. He decided to advance with that assumption. He feinted and then lunged for the chest. Harvin blocked it, but Kion slid out of the bind and easily reversed the stroke, hitting Harvin with the weak edge of his blade.

"No!" Snetch shouted. "He must be cheating!"

"Point for the red."

Zinder leapt onto the lower rail of the fence and did a little dance. "Brilliant! Sublime! That's swordplay with style, I say! With flair!"

Harvin looked down, jarred by the suddenness with which he'd fallen into a three-nil hole.

"Chin up, Harv! You'll turn it around. They were lucky hits. Pure luck!" Snetch called out. Harvin's head stayed down. Dougan was ominously quiet, keeping his eyes trained on Kion.

Harvin gave up after that. He made a few counters, but they were half-hearted at best. He didn't bother hazarding a single offensive strike. Kion scored two more hits almost as quickly as the others. In the end, he actually felt bad for how easily he bested his opponent.

Etran lifted Kion's hand. "Winner, and moving on to the final, Kion Bray."

The crowd gave a measured acknowledgment of the victory.

"You're a better fighter than that, Harvin. I'm sure you'll have better luck in the consolation match," Kion said amidst the weak applause.

"What do you know, woolhead?" Harvin huffed over to the gate.

"Don't worry, Harv," Dougan said after him. "I'll send him crying back to his little lambies." But Harvin stormed off without a glance Dougan's way.

Dougan gave Kion a self-satisfied look, as if he'd been the one who'd just beaten Harvin five-nil. Kion didn't care. For the first time, his training was paying off. He'd stuck to the forms and blanked a skilled opponent. Let Dougan boast and smirk all he wanted. Kion was one match away from his dream.

"Now remember," Zinder said, tightening Kion's fittings. "He's got the advantage over you when it comes to reach and strength. And frankly, with that custom-made armor, he's got better movement, too. Not to mention his focus was sharper than a nynnian throwing knife in his last match. He went down two to one, but he didn't fluster or flinch—"

"Are you trying to inspire me or get me to surrender before the match even starts?" Kion said.

"I'm just saying that that armor of his isn't the only thing new about him. You've gotten better, but so has he. I'm just giving you fair warning. But don't worry too much. You've got something he'll never have." Zinder pounded Kion on the chest. "You've got fire beating in that heart of yours. I can see it sure as forge light. You were born to fight. It takes more courage to face down a hungry wolf than it does this lout. He's just another beast threatening your flock. Now go into that ring and don't let that lumbering fool steal your dreams!"

Kion drew in a long, deep breath, letting Zinder's words wash over him.

"I beat Harvin five-nil," Kion said. "I don't care if Dougan's twice as good as last year, he's not going to get his third medallion today." With a nod to his friend, he headed for the gate and entered the ring.

Zinder clapped and hollered as Kion took his place beside Etran. "Kion the brave, everyone! Look at him. He's got arms like oaks and thunder in his strokes! He's a paragon of prowess! A matchless master of maneuverability! Behold your champion!" He got a few eye rolls for his efforts, but he paid them no attention.

Dougan's father sat in one of the eight chairs on the prestigious platform on the northern side of the ring. All the chairs were full today. He was laughing and joking with members of the wealthier families of Furrow but stopped at Zinder's proclamation.

"You've the same eye for swordsmen that you do for smithing," Mr. Shaw shouted. "Make yourself some spectacles, nyn! Dougan will take the championship, same as all the other years!"

Zinder shrugged, turned up his nose, and went on cheering.

A rousing wave of applause and shouts of affirmation drowned out his voice. Dougan had entered the ring. He looked a foot taller than Kion in that armor. For a brief moment the thought crossed Kion's mind that he was a boy fighting a giant.

The commons were filled to bursting. Dozens of children watched from their parents' shoulders. The air on Memory Lawn was still as a stone. It smelled of sweat and oil and all the pungent odor of packed humanity. This was the last day of the festival and the biggest event of the entire four-mark: the final for the Tournament of Mettle.

"Dougan Shaw in the red," Etran said.

Snetch didn't have to incite the crowd to cheers this time. The words, "Dougan, Dougan, Dougan," rang out across the commons. Fielder Lorris, who stood near the scoring placards, surveyed the crowd. He had four stronghands from the local militia posted at the corners to keep order.

Opposite Dougan's father, Snetch shouted along with the others as he whipped his red flag about in ecstatic gyrations.

When the cheering died down, Etran said, "Kion Bray in the green."

Zinder did his best to cheer over the boos and jeers, but it was one voice against hundreds. Though the noise did not eclipse the volume of the cheering moments ago, it was far too much even for the gamely, energetic hurrahs of the nyn. The crowd was roughly double the size of last year. Every face flushed hot with anger and curses, as if they would have trampled Kion underfoot had the fences not held them back. Was this what his father felt when the haukmarn charged across the Claywash at Roving? Kion's armor weighed twenty pounds heavier in the face of such open animosity.

Dougan's father roared over the rest, "You're a shepherd, Bray. You don't deserve to be here!" The people around him echoed his remark.

Kion closed his eyes. The roar of insults could not drown out his own inner voice. "No matter how many stand against me, I will fight on. For Father. For Tiryn." Maybe, just maybe, a victory today would quiet these people and earn his family the respect they deserved.

"Touch swords," Etran said once he could make himself heard above the crowd.

Kion raised his sword defiantly towards the masses before crossing his blade with Dougan's.

The noise spiked again, a mixture of taunts and cheers. Kion felt out his opponent's pressure on the blade. It wasn't strong enough that an immediate attack seemed likely. Dougan moved his blade up and down Kion's, toying with him, not giving anything away.

Etran raised his hands, calling for quiet. The crowd obeyed in fits and starts, with Snetch's calls to "bash the woolly" particularly defiant against the order.

"And...fight," Etran said at last.

Stillness. Quiet. Then a cataract of noise as Dougan slapped Kion's blade away. It jarred his sword all the way down through the hilt. The sudden power generated in that stroke served as a warning. Dougan was stronger than Kion remembered.

Kion backed away. He could sense Dougan's sneer inside his helmet coming through his eyes. He had to put him in his place, quiet the crowd. On impulse, he took a risk. Kion set his feet and lowered his sword into the fool's guard.

"Let's see how much you've improved," he muttered.

Dougan waved his sword in front of Kion, shifting left and right. He was still toying with him. He wasn't taking the bait.

Kion shifted into the ox stance, angling his sword down at his opponent from above. This was a more aggressive position. Maybe Dougan would be drawn in by it.

Dougan held his blade steady, taking the basic Fiorin guard stance.

Had he studied the Fiorin Batal? This sent a shiver though Kion that was equal parts excitement and fear. It was time to test all that he had studied. He would either rise to the occasion or go home in disgrace.

"Nice sword you got there, Bray," Dougan said. "Not near as nice as your old one, though."

The pompous cur! Dougan was practically admitting he stole the sword to Kion's face. Kion's poise vanished in an instant. He lunged forward, unleashing a furious barrage of wild swings. His footwork and the forms flew from his mind. All he cared about was bashing this gutterswill out of the ring.

Dougan parried the attacks, giving ground. Then he shifted unexpectedly to the left and Kion's momentum and unbalanced footwork sent him sailing into the fence. Dougan's jarring strike on the back of his armor blared like a warning bell across the commons.

"Point for the red!" Etran said with uncharacteristic excitement.

The crowd roared.

Dougan rose out of his stance to soak in the adulation.

Kion took a swipe at the dirt, carving out a sheep-length divot. Dougan had baited him, and he'd stepped right in up to the knee.

"You're better than this," he told himself. "Put it past you." He turned, settled into the basic stance, and waited out the cheers. It was only one hit. He could still win.

"Touch swords!" Etran yelled over the raucous crowd.

Dougan barely touched Kion's blade before going on the offensive. The energy of the crowd quickened his strokes.

Kion used his footwork to counter and dodge, counter and dodge. Dougan was the sloppy one now. Most of his swings weren't part of the Batal. Kion waited for an opening.

As strong as Dougan was, he couldn't keep up an offensive like that forever. The velocity of his strokes was diminishing.

Kion counterattacked with a triple strike to Dougan's left, his weaker side. Dougan was too overextended to block them all. The third strike hit home.

The clanking noise fell on the commons like a gavel. Looks of astonishment spread across wilted faces. Their champion was not invincible. Only Snetch had the gall to complain in the time-honored words of the spoilsport: "Not fair!"

"Evens!" Zinder cried. "Keep it up, lad! Let the bruiser beat himself!" A few children and outsiders who didn't know better clapped in the distance.

"Touch swords!" Etran said.

The two fighters took their stances, and the battle now began in earnest. Dougan had learned his lesson. He wasn't going to be able to ride the roar of the crowd to victory. His attacks came now in short bursts. He didn't exactly execute textbook Fiorin Batal, but his strikes were tighter, more concentrated, though they still came with tremendous force.

Kion struggled to parry his opponent's swings. A few times he managed a counter, but couldn't connect. Dougan's reach meant Kion's strikes usually hit open air.

Once, he got in close enough to land a hit, but Dougan executed a swift reverse that sent Kion's blade flying wide. Dougan seized the opportunity to twist back into a thrust, which landed solidly on Kion's stomach.

The crowd burst into uproarious applause. They were louder than before, but Kion wasn't listening. He was talking to his father.

"Father, please. I want to win this match. I want to make you proud—and Mother and Tiryn. Oh, I want it so badly! Help me to be strong. Help me to strike true."

Etran ordered them to touch swords, and the battle resumed.

Dougan pressed the attack again. Kion used his footwork to dodge most of the strikes. The ones he couldn't, he parried.

Though Dougan's attacks were hardly reckless, he was putting out more effort than his opponent. Kion sensed Dougan's frustration after a sustained series of attacks failed to land. Seeing an opening, Kion launched his own attack in response. Dougan put up an awkward defense, but his counters were too slow. Kion landed a hit on his waist.

"Twos are better than boos!" Zinder lectured the crowd as they let their displeasure be known. "Keep to it, lad. Almost halfway!"

Back and forth they went, back and forth, and the pattern repeated itself. Dougan got the next hit, and the crowd went wild, ever louder than before. But then he got impatient, and Kion used his quickness and skill for a sudden strike to even the match. So it went, point, counterpoint, for the next few minutes, until, breathless and in a rush of exhilaration, Etran called out Kion's fourth hit.

The match was even.

There was no shouting when Etran called for swords to touch this time. Even Snetch was silent. It was four to four. Whoever landed the next strike would win the match.

If things followed the same pattern, the match would go to

Dougan. He had managed to go up each time Kion scored the equalizer.

Both boys were slow to take their positions. They were winded. This match had gone on twice as long as last year's. Kion's armor felt like a forge, his throat like a chimney. His body oozed with sweat. His gauntlets squished in slimy uncertainty.

"One last time, Father," Kion whispered. "Let me be equal to the challenge. One last time. Don't let me fail."

The words fell upon him like a frosty blast. The furnace inside his armor quenched, replaced by a cool breeze, the kind he sometimes felt on the Tors when he hunkered down with the sheep after a long journey back from pasture. The ache in his arms fled. His armor grew lighter. He raised his sword, eager to resume the fray.

He and Dougan touched swords for the final time. As Kion looked at him, memories of last year's award ceremony came rushing back. He remembered the medallion dangling from Dougan's neck, glistening in the sun, Dougan's self-satisfied expression, the adoration of the village.

Not this time. This time the medallion belonged to Kion. One strike was all it would take.

Dougan staggered back. His size, which had allowed him to push Kion around the ring throughout the match, had come to bite him in the end. He was spent. In contrast, Kion drew upon some mysterious hidden strength.

He set his feet and raised his sword above his head in the wrath stance, ready to strike.

The aggressive pose stirred something inside Dougan. He took the plow stance, sword in front, raised slightly. He shuffled forward, offering a pair of feints that Kion didn't take. But the feints made Kion question his strategy. Dougan hadn't thrown two feints in a row the whole match. Was he perhaps not as tired as he looked? Had he been holding something back as well? Or was he just too exhausted to mount another attack?

Kion took a tentative step forward. In that moment Dougan

pounced. His sword shot forward. Kion twisted his blade to parry. Dougan's sword circled out of the block for a weak side strike. Kion met it with his blade, but Dougan's sword wasn't there. A third feint. Dougan had never done that before. It wasn't his style. Was it even in the Fiorin Batal? Kion couldn't remember. His training fled from him. His mind went blank. All he was aware of was a single sound: the shuddering crash of sword on armor. Dougan's blade landed square in his chest.

The crowd erupted in a thunderous frenzy. Etran's "point for the red" was utterly lost. Snetch's face turned redder than the flag he was waving. He jumped and stomped and screamed like he was on fire. Fielder Lorris and his stronghands tried to urge restraint, tried to keep order, but it was of no use. The commons exploded in jubilation.

Kion sank to the ground. His sword fell from his grasp.

As bedlam conquered the world around him, his whispered words were heard by no one at all. "I'm sorry, Father...I failed you..."

Chapter 13

SEVEN FIRES

The chairs on the raised platform next to the sparring ring had been replaced by the musicians from Driftwood Winds. The quartet was finishing up their last piece, a lofty, stirring melody, which Kion had never heard before. The beauty of the song registered vaguely in his mind but failed to move him. It sounded like something his father would have played, but he wanted no more reminders of his father on this day. The award ceremony was reminder enough that Kion had failed him. He shut out the music and turned his eyes from the torchlit commons to the night sky. He often stared at the spark trails flickering above when he was out on the Tors with the sheep at night. Sometimes the streaks of light crossed and formed letters or other simple patterns. When he was younger he often imagined they were writing a message for him to read, trying to tell him something important, if only he could understand their language. But the sparks were fainter than usual this evening. Furrow was not usually this bright. No matter. The sparks could go cold for all he cared. Darkness would better suit his mood.

Kion was standing off to the side with Mistress Shona, Fielder Lorris, Etran Squigsworth, and the other three tournament semifinalists, waiting to take the stage. Mistress Shona was in charge of the closing ceremony every year, and it was her duty to announce the various entertainers who graced the platform during the festival: the jugglers, magicians, animal trainers, and knife throwers who delighted the crowds throughout the four-mark festival. Her wavy gray hair flowed freely in the breeze, and her head bobbed to the music.

Zinder tapped his foot and clapped his hands where he sat on the grass in the crowd. Seeing his friend so oblivious to his own misery felt like an insult, though Kion knew Zinder couldn't help himself. He loved music almost as much as Tiryn did. If it wouldn't block the view of those behind him, he'd have gotten up and danced a jig. A few people swayed here and there to the songs, but most stared blissfully at the musicians as the amber twilight crept across the crowded commons.

Kion's chest tightened as he thought back to past tournaments. Two years ago, he'd been thrilled just to make it into the final four. Last year he'd been bitter about his loss, but that bitterness had fired him to train even harder. Now, a numb disbelief settled inside him like a stone dropped to the bottom of a lake. He had come so close, but the closer the defeat, the more devastating the loss.

"I'm never coming back here," he told himself. He gazed longingly at Meadow's Way, which led toward home. It was choked with people, the same people who had cackled and jeered at him all throughout the tournament. "I don't care what Mother says. Tiryn can be the one to come into the village from now on. She's old enough. I'll stay out on the Tors with the sheep. They're more human than these people." Of course, that depended on Tiryn pulling through. Again, the pang of regret that came at the moment of defeat pierced his heart. Winning the medallion was supposed to give his sister something to come home to. With his loss, all he had to offer her was the shame of a brother who didn't measure up, who had failed when it mattered most.

The music ended. Cheerful applause filled the commons. Mistress Shona stepped onto the center of the platform.

"The Driftwood Winds!" She waved her arms in a flourish.

The musicians bowed numerous times before the applause finally dwindled. The lead musician, the man Kion had talked to a few days before, spotted him and gave a kindly wave. Kion pretended not to notice. He rattled his sword in its sheath. How he loathed the thing. Whatever happened after today, he knew one thing for certain. He would never wield a sword again. Zinder could have his sword back, and that foolish folio too. All it was good for was forge kindling.

Mistress Shona gestured toward the opposite side of the stage. "And now, please welcome this year's candle maidens for the dance of the *fiddlewise*," she said. She gave a dignified bow and departed the stage.

The same seven girls who had presented the garlands at the beginning of the tournament entered the large, corded-off semicircle in front of the stage. To Kion's unfocused eyes, they all looked like Tiryn. She should have been there. This would have been her last chance to participate in the dance, but the wistering had stolen that from her. Was that all it had stolen?

The girls formed a circle and struck the same pose, one leg forward, torso bent, one arm above their heads, the other held gracefully out to the side.

The Driftwood Winds breathed their song into the silence. It floated and fluttered from their instruments. The pleasant, lilting notes drifted in, around, and through the dancers, causing them to spring alive. They whirled in a circle, going left, then right, dipping and leaping in unison. One of the girls danced into the center as the others whirled in a circle around her. Then they alternated in their willowy movements, half following the dancer in the center in her leaping, the other half bending or twirling around her. As the song rose and fell, different girls took turns in the center. Sometimes two of them crossed, leaping, and took each others' places on the opposite side. It was one giant wheel of melody and motion. The musicians moved that wheel with their instruments, the wood pipes lamenting, the flute consoling, the gemshorn sighing, the bassoon brooding, and yet they all blended together in an aural tapestry to tell the same story. Higher and louder the notes went until, in a dramatic crescendo, the dancers struck their final poses and the music stopped. The crowd rose to their feet in a swell of grateful noise. The girls bowed and danced back the way they came, but their grace and gentleness lingered. A contemplative mood fell over the crowd like an enchantment.

Fielder Lorris, wearing the forest-green jacket of his office, strode onto the stage and broke the spell.

"Thank you, girls. Thank you, Mistress Shona. That was truly wonderful." His voice boomed over the commons. He paused, as if reluctant to end the festival that had brought so much life and gaiety to his small village. "And now, my friends, we come to the close of this momentous festival. It has been a time of sober remembrance, but also of new joys and fresh promise, of thankfulness for the days of peace we have enjoyed these past ten years. I'd be remiss if I did not thank the fane once again for granting us permission to hold this festival."

Reluctant applause trickled through the crowd. The fane's taxes made him about as popular as the Inrisian shepherds were with the farmers.

"But before the final lighting of the candles, we shall present the finalists of this year's Tournament of Mettle. These young men are the hope of our village, the future warriors who will take up arms and defend our homes should the haukmarn rise against us once more in open battle."

Etran, holding a dark, finely carved, wooden box, led the four young men onstage. Dougan brought up the rear. Kion walked in front of him. When Dougan came out, he received so much applause Kion wanted to cover his ears. Snetch's voice rang out above the tumult.

"Dougan Shaw! Dougan Shaw! Stand in awe of Dougan Shaw!"

Kion couldn't spot Snetch in the crowd, but it was just as well. If he never saw the little blighter again, it would be a mercy.

"And now," Lorris said, "let's give a rousing, Northern cheer for each of these fine young swordsmen."

After the applause, he proceeded to announce the fourth-place winner, a boy of barely fifteen years. He had yellow hair and was a good half a foot shorter than Kion. His face lit up as if he'd won the whole tournament when Etran pinned a white ribbon on his chest. The ribbon had the numbers of the year, 838, stitched on it. He was one of the boys who had been at the pig farm that day, cheering on Dougan while he humiliated Snetch. Most likely he would take Dougan's place in next year's tournament, since Kion, Dougan, and Harvin had all aged out.

Harvin's face stayed sour from the moment he stepped onstage. Receiving his green ribbon did nothing to change it. So much spite poured from his puffed, pinkish eyes, Kion couldn't tell who Harvin hated more, him or Dougan.

"And in second place, winner of the red ribbon: Kion Bray," Lorris announced.

The response on the commons was generous compared to how it had been during the tournament, but the scattered applause ended the moment the ribbon was placed in his hands.

Kion ground his teeth. It took great effort to keep his face from slipping into an open scowl. He could only bear the shame knowing he would never have to see these people again.

"There's a swordsman for you! Fought the best you could, lad!" Zinder shouted. His bright, lively eyes were impossible to miss. At least Kion had one true friend in this wretched crowd.

"And finally, this year's champion, for a remarkable three years in a row: Dougan Shaw," Lorris said.

The commons trembled from the noise that followed. The Shaw family and the vast contingent around them shouted and chanted Dougan's name with boisterous glee. Mothers kissed their young children and pointed at Furrow's favored son and future protector. Snetch climbed above everyone, propped up on some crate or some poor fellow's shoulders. He flapped his green and red flags like a bird, as if they were wings keeping him aloft.

Etran placed the silver medallion around Dougan's thick neck. Dougan pulled out his other two medallions from inside his vest and held them aloft. He basked in the warmth of Furrow's praise. If it had been any louder, it might have scared up the sun.

Lorris had to raise his hands for the crowd to quiet down. Even then, it took some time.

Dougan stepped forward. "Thank you, Fielder Lorris, and everyone who came to watch me fight. Three years in a row. Well, that's something, isn't it? I only wish I could do it a fourth!" His chest swelled, but a hint of regret clouded his eyes, making Kion wonder if his victory wasn't as sweet as he'd expected. What would Dougan do now that he'd beaten all comers and had no one left to fight? Find some poor soul like Snetch to torment, most likely. What did it matter? This would be the last time Kion ever saw the conceited fool.

The people might never have left off cheering if not for a shout from someone in the crowd.

"Hey, you, freckle face! Those are my flags. You stole 'em from my booth! Give 'em over, you thief!"

A commotion broke out near Snetch. He disappeared into the churning mass around him. Shouts of "There he is!" "The little pig!" and "He's over there!" followed his escape. At a gesture from Fielder Lorris, a couple of stronghand militia waded into the crowd. This only made matters worse, as people everywhere began to move, straining for a look at the flag thief and the sight of his imminent capture. But Snetch's smallness and the general confusion played into his favor. The only glimpse anyone got was of the top of his head, glowing rosy in the twilight, scuttling off past the edge of the commons into the village proper. The stronghands gave chase, but it took them a good minute to free themselves from the crowd. It was doubtful they would catch him in the dark with a lead like that.

"If you're going to steal something, don't go waving it around for the whole world to see," Kion thought to himself.

"It's all right, everyone," Lorris said. "The men will see that he is dealt with." Once the commons settled back down, Mistress Shona returned to the stage, this time holding a glowing lantern that swayed as she walked.

"And now, one last time, we light the seven fires," she said, raising a slender arm toward the left side of the stage. The candle maidens returned, each holding a long white candle.

Mistress Shona spoke these words:

Four Wards forged beneath the nascent sun
Four Lords watched and ruled the land as one
Until the day tears rained on high
Though none knew how and none knew why

Though what has past may never be
More than echoes of memory
Yet hope shall stir and bind us when
We look unto what once has been

She spoke the ancient words with great conviction. Kion knew them well, for they were recited at the close of every Seven Fires. They stirred a longing too deep for understanding, as if, in that moment, the veil of time slipped back, and he could almost see the world as it once was, a place without heartbreak and sorrow, a place of golden beginnings and faithful fellowship, when the Four Lords sat together in harmony upon their majestic thrones. They ruled, it was said, for hundreds, if not thousands of years, in perfect peace, before the first histories were ever written, for without suffering and strife, what need was there for writing, when every day was better and more beautiful and full of blessings than the one before? It was a time without death, without war, a time when brave men did not die and leave their children all alone. The Four Wards. If only they would return to what they had once been, and all would be made right again. Even now, in Kion's shame and grief, the vision almost burned away the numbing coldness that clenched his heart, but failure was a winter whose frost would not relent, and the dream of the Four Wards died anew in his heart, dismissed as an idle fable not worth hoping for. The world had been broken beyond redemption. It would never heal. That world was gone forever and those who hoped for its return hoped in vain.

The maidens lit their candles in turn from Mistress Shona's lantern. As they did so, the torches around the commons winked out. Then they sang the song of the Seven Fires one last time, the voices of the gathered masses rising along with them.

And seven fires I will light upon these candlesticks
Seven fires to fill these dark and lonely days
Seven fires for the warmth of all your memories
Seven fires to cheer and guide you on the way

And seven times I cried the morning into breaking
Seven times I woke to find that you were gone
Seven times I lost all hope of your returning
But seven times the night was vanquished by the dawn

No one spoke. That was the way it always was. All the laughter and swordplay and noise and cheer and feasts and music of the festival faded into swiftly darkening memory. The people gazed into the flames many long moments, remembering a father, a husband, a brother, or an uncle who had fallen in the war.

One by one, the candle maidens blew out their flames until darkness ruled the commons. Only Mistress Shona's feeble lantern stood against it. The sun had fallen and the moon not yet risen. Light clung faintly to the clothes of the people as they floated, ghost-like, out into the village. They dispersed silent as ghosts as well. It was a sacred moment.

But not for Kion. For him, the spell of the music and the flames and the longing of the ancient words held no power. The disappearing people might as well have been ghosts, for all he cared. This was no longer his home. He marched out to the Tors, not even bothering to look for Zinder, but turning his back on Furrow in bitterness and shame.

Chapter 14

AUNT LIZARD

The bells tolled four times. Four deep, solemn notes hummed from somewhere across the city, as if waking Charring from an afternoon nap.

"Will I be able to leave my bed today?" Tiryn asked weakly.

"Aunt Lizet is afraid you'll contaminate the rest of the house," Mother said.

Tiryn coughed, an awful, brittle sound like dead leaves crunching, but there was no blood. There hadn't been for two days now. "But my fever's gone. I'm getting better. You said so yourself." She coughed again.

"I know, karinna, but we must respect her wishes." Mother sat at the end of the bed in the big rose velvet chair, the same one she'd sat and slept in for the past six days. "But even if Aunt Lizet would allow you to move about the house, you're still not strong enough. If you push yourself too much, it might take even longer to recover. A few more days and I think you'll be well enough to get up."

The bells faded, but their absence brought forth a longing in Tiryn. The light of memory filled her mind, and for a moment she was back home, in a time when she had a body that did not scream from every movement, a time when she played music and wrote songs and danced in the woods. And further still, another memory came, even more precious. She saw her father, walking away along the path toward Furrow, playing the song of Seven Fires on his pipes. All too quickly he disappeared around the bend, but long after, the song lingered above the Tors. Tiryn and Kion and Mother sat outside and cried on the stoop. It was the last time she ever saw him. This same memory returned to her every time the bells tolled at four o'clock. Four o'clock was the hour of remembrance. Tiryn, along with her mother and hundreds of others around the city, stopped and spoke the words:

Veris, Koris, Inris, Bey
As in light of dawn's first ray
So shall it be again one day.

Veris, of course, referred to Verisward, the lush land to the south beyond the mountains, and Inris was her own homeland, whose full name was Inrisward. Koris and Bey were a mystery. They must be the names of the other two wards, but no one she knew had ever been to those lands, or even knew where they lay. She suspected Zinder knew, for he had seen many places and read many books, but he did not often speak of his travels outside of Inris.

"Father, I miss you," she whispered into the endless fluff of pillows and blankets surrounding her. Though her father had left for the war when she was only five, she had vivid memories of him playing mud dolls with her and chasing her through the heather. He was always singing, either a song they both knew, in which case she would sing along, or a new one he had just written, which she would soon learn. Laughter and joy were all she knew in those days. But all too soon, the frost choked the heather, dark clouds covered the sun, and war took her father away.

"I will sing to you every day, my Karinna of the Tors," he had promised, kissing her forehead the day he found out his name had been called.

And then came the day they delivered his sword, the day before he left. Her father lifted it with both hands. Tiryn thought it must weigh more than all the world, but her father was strong enough to bear it.

After that came the days of endless waiting. So many hours she sat at the window, staring at the candle...Its flame was both a comfort and a curse. It kept the hope of her father's return alive. As long as it burned through the night, she had hope that he might one day see it and find her waiting faithfully at the end of the long road home. The light was her way of protecting him, of helping him in the war. But the light also reminded her of her loss, and she yearned for the day when she could extinguish it once and for all.

"But you didn't come back, did you? Why didn't you come? I waited for you," she thought to herself.

She and Mother sat together in silence, but they were not alone. They had their memories to fill the long, lonely hours.

The sound of creaking footsteps brought Tiryn out of sleep. Someone was coming up the stairs. No, two people. She rubbed her face and did her best to tame her wild mane of hair.

Mother came through the door, followed unexpectedly by Aunt Lizet. Tiryn had not seen her since she first arrived.

The tall, wide-boned woman clacked into the room with all the grace of an oak tree walking on its roots. She was not fat, but she was "solid," as mother liked to put it, as thick of bone as she was thick of will. She owned the massive mansion and every-thing in it, and she carried herself as if the title deed went down to the very air in the room. She acted that way no matter what building or location she happened to be in. Every step into an unvisited place was the conquest of new lands, and every visit to a familiar place the reassertion of her sovereignty. Her manner in this regard ensured that she remained unmarried, for no man had ever consented to being reduced to another item on her ledger. For this, and many other reasons, Tiryn felt sorry for her.

"Oh, Annira, it's far too stuffy up here," Aunt Lizet said, fanning herself with her hand. The room had its own hearth. A handful of logs smoldered in the grate. Even so, it was barely warm to Tiryn. "The girl will never recover if you keep it like an oven up here."

"The healer said the heat would help her recover more quickly," Mother said.

"More likely it'll turn her into a loaf of bread," Aunt Lizet said in combative tones. She remained in the doorway. "Healers. Not worth the coin you pay them. I swear they make up half of what they say on the spot."

Mother moved in front of the hearth to shield Lizet from the heat. "But she has gotten better, Lizet. You remember what she was like when she first came."

Aunt Lizet eyed Tiryn like she might when buying a piece of questionable furniture.

"She still looks unnaturally pale. Then again, as I recall, she always looked rather unhealthy. She has your beauty, Annira, but unfortunately not your constitution. It's a wonder she's even survived this long, living out in that wilderness hut you've chosen to hide yourself away in. It's little better than a stable."

"Lizet, please," Mother said. "Let us not go over that now. I do not wish to upset Tiryn."

"It's fine, Mother," Tiryn said in a small voice, which Aunt Lizet didn't hear.

"Upset her? But can't you see, Annira, that it's only out of familial love and affection that I say such things? Would she not have died if you'd left her in that windswept hovel? Was that not the very reason you brought her here, to save her from that glorified sheep pen you've consigned yourself to? Can't you see that I am only looking out for your own good?" She peered down upon Mother with patronizing pity.

"Well, of course, Lizet. I'm sorry. And of course, I'm deeply grateful. It's just that the healer said—"

"She's the only good thing to come out of your marriage to

that troubadour." Aunt Lizet's piteous gaze turned to Tiryn. The expression on her face was somewhere between biting on a lemon and burying a pet. "It was bad enough that you married him, but to leave Charring where you had everything, dear—everything—and choose the life of a shepherd, of all things. Had he no sense? Why, it strains the mind to conceive of a better way to ruin your life than what that man did to you. I shall never forgive him."

Mother said nothing to defend Father. Tiryn guessed Aunt Lizet had said worse things than these.

Aunt Lizet peered down on them in small-eyed silence. At length, convinced of her conquest of the conversation, she straightened and said, "Well, at least you're talking sensibly, Tiryn. Your babbling was scaring the servants half to death. Even I found it a bit unsettling."

"I'm sorry," Tiryn said. "But I'm glad you came to visit me, even though I don't remember it."

"Of course. I may be many things, but I do take care of my own." Aunt Lizet's lips pulled back into something almost like a smile. "I can see you are improving despite being in this cauldron. I shall check on you again as soon as my schedule allows." She lifted her skirts and turned to go.

"Aunt Lizet, if I might ask. What did I say?" For some reason Mother always evaded Tiryn when she asked this question, which was not like her.

"Pardon, dear?"

"When I was babbling, what did I say?" Tiryn sat up on her pillow, curious to hear what her aunt might tell her.

"Oh, nonsense really. You kept screaming 'Fire, the house is on fire,' and the first few times, of course, we believed you."

Tiryn pulled the covers up around her neck. She felt a chill coming on. "Oh, was that all?" she said, trying to make light of it.

"No, there were other things. A few times the servants said you went on about a sword or a battle or some such hysterics.

And your brother, you were warning him about something. Oh, I'm sure they must have been frightful nightmares, dear."

It sounded very much like her vision. Was Kion a part of it now?

"I'm sure they were, Aunt Lizet. But I'm getting better. I don't think I'll have any more nightmares."

But inwardly she worried that Kion was in some terrible danger.

That night Tiryn had another vision. Only this one wasn't feverish. It felt frighteningly real. Voices clamored outside the house, men shouting and pounding and trying to force their way in.

"We must flee," came an old man's voice in the dark. Someone gripped her arm. "Come, child, we must hide."

Where was she? Was she still in the manor? If so, why was it so dark?

She bumped her head and cried out, but a hand clamped over her mouth immediately.

"Shh! If they hear us, we've no chance!" said the voice in a hissing whisper.

A draft of cold air rushed over Tiryn's skin. It came with an awful smell, a rotting, unnatural smell, the smell of death. They began descending what must have been stairs. Each step seemed to screech an octave higher than the one before, and the fear of her foot slipping dogged her every movement.

"I don't want to go down here. Please don't make me," she wanted to scream, but she bit her lip and kept on. If she made a noise, she knew they would find her, though she still had no idea who *they* were.

The stench of decay grew worse. Air became her foe. She wanted to gag back every breath like poisoned food. Her feet touched hard-packed dirt.

"This way," said the voice. He wasn't whispering anymore.

And the shouts and voices died away. Maybe it was safe to speak.

"Please, tell me where we are. Where's my mother?"

"Gone, child. Gone. We're all that's left."

The stench was not half so sickening as those stomach-turning words. "Gone? And my brother? Where is he? Is he here?" Something told her he was. He had to be. He was coming for her. She was sure of it.

But the vision ended before the voice could answer.

Chapter 15

THE WIMWISSLE SWATH

The day after the festival, the rumble of a cart came in through the cottage window. Kion shoved a loaf of bread inside a bulging satchel and strained to fasten it shut. Normal bread would have crumbled, but this loaf was stiff as stone. It was probably not even edible.

"Maybe I can use it to fight off bandits," Kion muttered. The clopping hooves and straining snorts of a mule echoed closer and closer. For the hundredth time, Kion doubted his decision. Thoughts of his mother and sister rushed in. What if Tiryn was already dead? Would what he was planning even matter if she didn't come back? He scuttled the thought off into a dark corner of his mind. No—he had to put his failure behind him; it was burning him up inside. He had barely slept for two nights. If he didn't do this now, he'd never get the chance.

He shoved his father's helmet onto his head and slid the satchel over his shoulder. He tucked his father's letter under his shirt and tied off his coin pouch on his belt. This was what he had to do.

Now he just had to convince Zinder.

Kion burst into the morning light. Stiff grass crunched beneath his feet. The sun was just poking through the trees, glowing cold and white through a swiftly brightening sky. Crusty's scruffy head came up behind a cloud of foggy breath as Zinder's cart rounded the shed. The nyn's sparkling face bobbed into view a moment later. For once his face was the most colorful thing about him. He wore a drab gray coat and a flimsy black scarf. The cap atop his head was small, brown, and brimless.

"Where are you off to, a funeral?" Kion asked, striding up to the cart. He gave Crusty a hearty pat on the neck.

"These are my traveling clothes, lad. For every occasion an outfit, and an outfit for every occasion. First rule of fashion. I can't have ruffians thinking I'm some flashy merchant jingling with coins, now can I?" He looked Kion up and down, his eyes lingering on the helmet. "I might ask you about your choice of attire as well. You look a bit over-prepared for tending your sheep."

"Perhaps I did pack too much." Kion hefted his satchel so it didn't ride so low on his back. "I'm not sure. I've never been on an overland journey before."

Zinder bounced up in his seat. "Excuse me? I think my hearing's starting to go. First the taste in friends, then the hearing, that's how it usually works with nyn. Did you say 'overland journey'?"

"I did. You're headed off to see Strom, aren't you? Well, I'm coming with you. That is, if you'll have me." Kion clutched his satchel. Everything depended on Zinder now.

Zinder puffed out a blast of frosty air. "Are you trying to pull my white beard down to the grave? You can't leave the farm. Your mother would spit rocks if she found out. And if she found out you went with me, several of those rocks would be aimed in my direction! I love this finely groomed head of mine far too much to risk the wrath of such a dear, sweet lady. And with her having to swallow her pride and grovel before that vulture of an aunt of yours! And what about Tiryn? Fighting for her very breath! It's all wrong—as wrong as could be. I admit, I did think better of you, lad."

Kion looked off to the east, past Old Slick Rock, toward Rike's place. He hadn't expected this was going to be easy. "I've already made arrangements with Rike. He even agreed to let me pay him. We'll only be gone a few days."

"Pay him? With what, your belly lint? It's not enough abandoning the farm? You plan on spending the few nicks your mother's saved as well?"

"I've got my own money." Kion rattled the pouch at his waist. It tinkled and clinked. "I sold your sword. I don't have any use for it now. I will pay you back someday, though—however long it takes."

"It was a gift. You don't owe me one nick. Still..." Zinder lectured him with his eyes. "You could certainly use that money for better purposes."

"Please, Zinder, I've dreamt of seeing Strom for years, ever since I found out he fought in the same battle as my father. Sometimes I have the wild hope—I know it's foolish, but I can't help but think it—that he might have seen my father on that last day, or spoken with him, or maybe even fought at his side. I don't know why, but somehow seeing him would be...well, it would be the next best thing to seeing my father again." Kion's voice cracked involuntarily. This was going even worse than he'd hoped.

"And your mother? Do you think she'd see it your way?"

Kion let the satchel slide to the ground. He pulled off his helmet. "Zinder, I lost the tournament. That was my one hope of honoring my father, of proving that my family isn't a pack of cowards. Blademarking his helm isn't the same as winning the tournament, but it's all I have left. Strom's blademark would tell everyone my father wasn't a coward, that he died an honorable death. Mother would understand that. At least...I think she would." She would worry, yes, but she knew the heart of her son. Meeting Strom was the only thing that could salvage the disaster of the tournament.

Zinder crossed his arms and shook his head. His gaze went back and forth between Kion and the helm a dozen times. "Ah, scoomdiggers! You've put me in a spot, lad. My good sense is telling me 'no,' but then you go and say that part about your father...Well, Crusty, what are we to do with such a fellow?

Should we take on a vagabond of such questionable morals and character?" Crusty was apparently too busy munching on clumps of grass to give an answer, so Zinder had to make the difficult decision on his own. "You'll at least let your mother know where you're going, won't you?"

Good old Zinder! Kion jingled the coins excitedly. "I was going to hire a messenger when we passed back through Furrow."

Zinder tugged his beard. "I stop by to pick up your father's helm and this is how you repay me? You certainly were prepared, I'll give you that."

"I even took a bath!" Kion said, sniffing under his arm.

"Oh, well, in that case…" Zinder rolled not just his eyes, but his entire head. "Throw your satchel in the back and hop in before I come to my senses—and mind the swords!"

Kion tossed in his satchel amongst the other bundles in the back and vaulted into the seat with a single leap. With all the pent-up dreams coursing inside him—dreams so close to finally coming true—he was lucky he didn't overshoot the cart completely.

As Furrow disappeared over a craggy hill, a flutter went through Kion's chest. The air hung heavy with mysteries waiting to unravel; he could almost smell the possibilities. He had never left the southern Tors in his entire life. All that he now saw brimmed with a wondrous enchantment. He marveled at every rock, every clump of grass, every gnarled tree. He barely heard Zinder's endless chatter, nodding dumbly to whatever was said, too enthralled by the expanding vistas to respond. Birds wheeled high and noble in the clear, unfettered sky or flitted from branch to branch in far off copses of curious trees. Farther still, great sloping plains unfurled, dusted in a powdery white, as enigmatic as it was beautiful.

The miles floated by like a gentle stream. The bundle of swords, the armor crate, a metal box of tools (a nyn was never without them), and the two passengers and their traveling gear were little trouble for Crusty's stout frame. Other than a few snorts, some foul-smelling winds, and the occasional halt to feast on clumps of grass or take water, the mule caused few problems.

By mid-morning they had left the Tors behind. They now traveled through a rolling sea of glassy white grass, dotted with islands of rocks and dirt. The blanched landscape was puzzling. The sun was out and shining, but the grass appeared as if it was still caught in the moonlight.

"Is that snow?" Kion pointed toward the vast whiteness blanketing the ground.

"No, lad. It's grass. This is the Wimwissle Swath," Zinder said.

"Grass? But it's white. Is it some new kind I've never heard of?"

"No. There's something in the ground up here. It makes the grass lose its color. It looks white from far away, but it actually has no color at all. Some say the land is cursed. They won't even eat the plants that grow here, but that's just spinster's talk. In one of the volumes of *Nain's Enchiridions,* it says the grass lost its color due to the wanstones of the haukmarn and the fact that Roving is so close to their lands."

"Wanstones? What are those? And why haven't you ever told me about this place?" Kion asked, trying to imagine how stones could change the color of grass.

"I've never been up this way either, remember. I've only read about it. As far as the wanstones, I've never seen them myself, but they say the stones give the haukmarn extra strength and endurance—as if they needed it! Nothing but good luck charms, if you ask me, but they give off an awful stench, from what I've heard."

Indeed, there was a faint, unpleasant odor, now that Kion thought about it. He had assumed it was from Crusty, but his odors were much more natural—odors you could get used to, even though they were bad. This smell felt like it would burn his nostrils if it were stronger.

By late afternoon, the swathes of white grass grew smaller and less frequent. The rubble-strewn dirt that replaced it had a sallow cast. The strangeness of it all and the immense, open spaces made it look as if they had wandered into some foreign land, but this was still Casting Selvedge, only a few short hours from home. Not many but soldiers ever came this way, and now he saw why.

The odd landscape didn't have much of an effect on Zinder. He continued to talk incessantly. Sometimes he let Kion take the reins so he could read from a weathered book called *The Book of Pearls*, which had poems and stories, mostly about places and people Kion had never heard of and only some of which had any chance of being true. Zinder also told stories about his travels up and down the Tors selling his wares. Kion had heard most of these before, but somehow, each time Zinder told them, they became a little more dramatic. He wasn't chased by three bandits; it was five. He didn't suffer out in the rain for six days, but eight, and so on.

He did tell Kion a few new stories, though, one about a baker he made three pans for in Windstern. The fellow was famous for his pastries.

"They were so light and fluffy you started to float after you'd eaten two or three. Just thinking about it sets my tongue to tingling," Zinder said.

"Well, if you're hungry, you're welcome to some of my bread," Kion said, as seriously as he could manage.

"Your bread? Your…" Zinder's chuckling kept him from finishing.

"It's not *that* bad," Kion said, but that only made it worse.

Zinder laughed so hard he almost lost the reins. "Oh, lad, if we could sell it for doorstops we'd make a fortune, but I'm afraid that's all it's good for."

The absurdity of the image struck Kion. He imagined his brick-like loaves being put to good use in homes all over Furrow.

"You might be onto something." Kion joined in his friend's merriment. "We could go into business together, 'Blacksmithing and Bread Stops'!"

"Profits would be on the rise!" Zinder said, tears squirting from his eyes.

"But careful not to stub your toe on the dough!"

"Yes—'Dough Stops'! That's an even better name!"

"Oh, Zinder, please. Quit before my sides burst open."

The giggling, cackling, and howling went on for some time. It finally ended when Zinder actually did lose the reins and they had to stop the wagon to retrieve them.

It was good to laugh again. Maybe the world was just as cruel and unfair as ever, but laughter chased away the chill winds and dark clouds, at least for the moment. Kion was reassured that he'd made the right decision in leaving the farm to Rike. This journey had already done him good and it was barely underway.

Around midday, they stopped for a meal. As usual, when it came to eating, Zinder's loquaciousness only increased, if that were possible. Reflecting on their imaginary business venture, he said, "But one thing I've learned—or better said, a lesson I'm *trying* to learn—is that in business you can never make riches your goal. It will only end in misery, like with old Avrix the Avaricious, Ruler of Plenty. He was so greedy, s-o-o-o greedy, that if someone passed in front of a mirror, he would tax them twice! You've heard of him, haven't you?"

"Of course, what child hasn't?" Kion said.

"But did you know how he became so greedy? He wasn't always that way, you see."

"Do tell."

"Well, it all started with crumpets."

"Crumpets?"

"Yes, crumpets. As a boy, he loved the tasty little things.

Gobbled them up whenever his mother would make them. Couldn't say no to them. Would do any chore happily if she promised him one. But soon one wasn't enough. She had to promise him two or three or ten or twenty!"

"Twenty! He must have been a pretty big boy."

"You don't know the half of it! Soon his mother couldn't keep up with the demand. Fortunately, about that time, he was old enough to discover a new fancy—girls. So he set about a-courtin'. But no sooner had he won the heart of his first true love (a fine lass named Bruniful) than he grew tired of her and sought the hand of another. But that one couldn't hold onto his heart either. And so on with the third, and the fourth, and on and on he went, wooing and winning and flinging them aside, like plates of empty crumpets."

"So you're saying he was greedy for more than just money?"

"You don't know the tenth of it! After girls it was horses. After horses it was jewels, after jewels it was paintings, after paintings, violins—don't ask," Zinder said, seeing the rise of Kion's eyebrow. "They can be quite expensive—but when all was said and done, and after a hundred other things had gripped his greedy heart, he eventually bought and acquired and finagled his way into owning the entire country of Plenty. And still he was not satisfied."

"So you're saying maybe we shouldn't go into business together?" Kion said jokingly. "I should be satisfied with staying a sheep farmer? Yes, yes, I see your point—"

"That's not the point at all. The point isn't that he wasn't satisfied." Zinder turned a serious eye on his young friend. "The point is that he did not know how to deny his own desires. Neither did his poor mother, for that matter. Satisfaction is a state that may or may not come. It certainly never did for Avrix. It's the learning to be *unsatisfied* that matters: taking one dumpling when you really want two, maybe even need two. Not all desires are meant to be fulfilled. That's what Avrix, and most of the rest of the world, for that matter, never figures out. And that's why men do terrible things to each other. That's what drives the haukmarn to raid and pillage, and forces men like Strom and your father to leave their homes and take up arms against them."

Zinder's tone had a sobering effect on Kion. "Hmm...to be unsatisfied and still go on as if you weren't. I suppose that does make some sense. Zinder, you might have actually told a story worth telling for once."

Zinder cracked a grin. "Why, Kion, my boy, are you saying that you're *satisfied* with my tale?"

Kion whacked Zinder on the shoulder with the back of his hand. "Oh, Zinder, you're hopeless."

Not long after they resumed their journey, a sudden rain washed the sun away, turning the strange wimwissle grass to gray. But the sun did not give up so easily. It transformed the rain into an incandescent curtain and flung it back over the impertinent clouds. After a long struggle, the rain gave up and scattered to mist. The clouds dispersed and the blanched grass was almost florescent in the brilliance of the victorious sun.

Kion fidgeted in his seat. If all went well, he would see Roving by nightfall. If all went well after that, he would have his helm blademarked by Strom Glyre by this time tomorrow. His father had told him countless stories of the great warriors of the past, but that was long ago. There was only one warrior now living who deserved to walk in their company, and he resided but half a day's journey away.

Despite the cautious anticipation building inside him, Kion labored beneath a growing heaviness. Soon they would pass into the lands where his father had fallen, never to rise again. Would sorrow overtake him once he reached those cruel plains? Would he regret having come all this way? He wondered if he was fleeing from one defeat to another.

The road melted into an outbreak of hills and the land grew more and more rugged the farther they went. The grassy patches disappeared altogether, flooded in a sea of yellow dirt. The land settled into one great murky mirror of the sun. Kion had heard of deserts in far distant lands but of course had never seen one. He asked Zinder if this was what they looked like.

"Nothing of the sort. Deserts are all sand and sift. And there's nothing alive there except scorpions and snakes and spiked plants. Or, so I've read. I've never actually seen one either."

As he said this, something small darted up a hill and off to the side of the road. A flash of gold caught the sun. It was not the lemon color of the dirt, but genuine gold, as bright and shiny as the fane's own crown. It moved so fast Kion couldn't tell what it was at first. It looked too big to be a rabbit, but it ran like one. It must have been a hare, but if so, it was the biggest and the fastest one he'd ever seen.

Zinder had his crossbow out in a flash. Not the small one that shot multiple bolts, but the large one, with more range and power. It was fashioned from coalwood, a kind of hardwood mixed with a nynnian resin that both preserved it and made it fire farther and with greater force. But Zinder did not shoot.

"That pelt would fetch a fine price," Kion said, watching the singular creature bound up the hillside. "What are you waiting for?"

Zinder lowered his weapon. "I'm sure it would, but that's a prize not worth winning. Any animal with a golden pelt is forbidden to slay."

The hare disappeared into a valley between two hills so fast Kion was left to wonder whether he had seen it at all. "Is that some decree of the margrave? I've never known you to pass on a chance for a good meal. I thought you said you were hungry?"

"No, it's an Old Rule, something everyone used to know, but something we still remember in Lowerwyn."

"Ah, yes, the mysterious Lowerwyn. Well, if you ever take me there—or even tell me anything helpful about it—maybe I'll learn some of these obscure rules as well," Kion said. Zinder claimed Lowerwyn was the homeland of all nyn, but would never say where it was.

"You'll get there with no help from me, I can assure you. Now, let's get this cart moving again."

As usual when the subject of Lowerwyn came up, Zinder's expression soured. He clamped his jaw shut and said no more.

The silent day dwindled away until at last Roving drew near. The mood in the cart quickened. Kion, tapping his foot excitedly, asked Zinder for the hundredth time about their business at the fortress. How long would they be staying? What chance did they have to actually see Strom? Did Zinder know anyone who lived there? What was the village like? And what about the fortress?

As Zinder had never been to Roving, he couldn't help Kion with most of his questions. He did share what he knew about the business side of things, though.

"The scribe told me to deliver the goods at the fortress and then pick up the rest of the payment at an inn called *The Wandering Spark*. Let's hope it has decent food!"

Kion thought back to the enormous golden hare. It would have provided more than enough for a meal for the two of them. But the more he thought about Zinder's "Old Rule," the more he found himself agreeing with it. It didn't seem right to kill a creature so spectacularly beautiful just for a meal. For all Kion knew, it was the only one of its kind.

The sun grew weary and slipped beneath the smooth, unburnished sky. A chill wind brushed Kion's ears and nose. The hills grew steeper and rockier. The stones vacillated between bleached and brown, mostly some mixture of both.

Crusty had a long, hard pull up the last bit of road. The rise, though gradual, was steady and unforgiving. Unconquerable cliffs closed off the land to the east and the west, affording a single way of approaching the town from the south. About half a mile from their destination, the road leveled off, and Crusty's puffing and straining diminished by measure. A wide bluff rose before them in the middle of a valley. Along the top of it, rigid towers stood at attention, ready to defend the town of Roving and the lands around it. Walls ringed the base of the bluff like the exposed spine of some great dragon. Their crenellations captured the reddening rays of the sun. White banners, long and thin, beckoned in the breeze. A golden diamond blazed in the center of them. This fortress, though part of the land of Inris, flew the fane's flags, for only the fane had the men and the will to defend it during these uncertain times.

A wide ditch ran around the base of the walls. An open drawbridge and a raised, double portcullis welcomed travelers into the protected village beyond. Two much larger and taller towers stood on either side of the gate. Beyond this, rising above the walls to an unthinkable height, loomed the Fortress of the Clefts. Its two southern towers were twice the height of those at the gate, and its outer walls were almost as tall. The northern towers climbed higher still, peering down at the surrounding village from such a height it seemed as if they must topple at any moment.

Waving torches dotted the sand-colored walls, lit in anticipation of the coming night. At this distance, no men could be seen patrolling the walls, but Kion knew they were there. But even if the walls were empty and bare and the whole place as still and dead as the stone it was made of, the structures radiated with such intimidating presence, Kion didn't see how any army, haukmar or no, could ever assail such a massive stronghold.

And then he saw it. A low, wide mound covered with thin blades of grass. The grass of the surrounding fields waved with supple splendor, but that which grew on the mound held stiff, resisting the wind. The unnatural swell of land was too large and out of place on the flat plain to be anything other than a mass grave. At last Kion knew the place of his father's rest, a place he'd tried to imagine a thousand times, yet somehow he'd never thought it would be as plain and forlorn as this. His head dropped. All went silent. He patted his father's letter inside his cloak, remembering their many midnight conversations.

"If fortune should strike me down on some distant field, know that your father loved you to the end, even to the giving of his own life."

Had his father seen this place in some vision? Had he come here knowing death awaited, that he would end his days in that cruel mound of dirt and grass?

"How I wish Tiryn and Mother were here..." Kion thought. But no, if they could see this lonely hill, unmarked by any stone or sign, they would fall to weeping, and Kion would come to tears himself. Better to look away and to the fortress beyond. There was hope. There was honor. There was redemption for his father's sacrifice.

He clutched his father's helm and passed into the shadow of the majestic walls and mighty towers of the Fortress of the Clefts. Strom Glyre awaited within. And with him, his father's redemption.

Chapter 16

HORNSWOGGLE

They passed through the gatehouse after some questioning from the guards. Zinder was made to pay a full silver square for a "security tax."

"They invent a new tax every day," Zinder mumbled as the cart rolled away, but Kion was too overwhelmed by the guards' armor and fine, white tabards to pay much attention to his friend's concerns. The gatehouse and its stately-looking guards was for him like a portal to another world. He was passing into the land of true warriors, of men who lived by honor and trained with discipline, whose strength and skill at arms was beyond that of anyone in Furrow. And yet, the other side of that portal proved to be not at all what he had imagined.

The gates opened onto a cramped and dirty village. It looked much smaller on the inside than it had from the outside. The streets, though covered in cobblestone, were even narrower than those of Furrow, and the buildings went right up to the edge of them. The steady stream of people wandering past wore distant looks and dreary faces. They walked by without so much as a glance. Heavy shadows covered most everything as the surrounding walls hastened the sunset.

The cart rolled through the central street, which the guards said would take them to the fortress. After following it for a time, it wrapped around a large stable. A few boys around Kion's age worked there repairing harnesses, cleaning out stalls, and wheeling around bags of oats or loads of hay. Kion had only ever seen a handful of horses in his life, but there looked to be twenty or more stabled here. He stared in awe at these enormous beasts, which dwarfed poor, common Crusty. A great black one, sleek and towering, stamped and whinnied in its stall as though it longed to ride forth into battle.

"That must be Strom's steed," Kion thought.

Beyond the stable, the fortress rose imperiously. Kion had to crane his neck to see the top of it. If anything, he had misjudged its height from afar. It was a mountain of stonework whose sheer walls and rounded towers clawed their way into the sky. The strength and power emanating from the structure grew with each step. Kion had never conceived of anything so large. It was like wandering into the land of giants.

He glanced down at his father's helm, polished and bright so that Strom's blademark would stand out all the more. Had his father entered this great fortress before he died? Kion knew so little of what had happened in that final battle, but every stone stared down at him in silent witness to those last, terrible moments. Sorrow welled up inside of him, but he fought against it. This was to be a moment of triumph. Soon his father would have the honor he deserved.

At the entrance to the fortress, a contingent of eight guards milled about, chatting. The double portcullis hung open, just as at the outer wall. The guards ceased speaking at the cart's approach and eyed Zinder and Kion in standoffish fashion.

"Greetings." Zinder addressed the two men who stood before them as the cart clattered to a stop. They wore padded gambesons with chain shirts and skirts and white livery trimmed in gold with a gold diamond in the center.

"Well, now, a nyn at the Clefts. Don't see one of your kind every day," one of the guards said, nodding to his companions. "State your name and your business." Whatever curiosity he may have had about Zinder's race was lost in the cold concerns of executing his duty. The man had a haughty look about him, as if he'd already sized them up and found them wanting. The expression was unsettlingly reminiscent of Dougan Shaw.

Zinder removed his hat with a flourish. He had swapped out his drab traveling cap for a smart-looking gray one with a raven's feather. "Zinder Hamryn, smith of Furrow and forger of all things worthy and illustrious, specializing in weapons and armor of the finest quality, two-time winner of the prestigious—"

"Are all nyn this long-winded?" the guard said. "Get to the point. What business do you have at the Clefts?"

Zinder returned his hat and cleared his throat. "Forgive me, I am new to these lands. This is my first visit to—"

"Your business?"

"Yes, well," Zinder said and muttered under his breath, "typical military courtesy," before continuing on. "I'm here to deliver instruments of war. Twelve of the finest longswords made in Inris this year, as well as a full suit of plate armor." He pointed to the bundles behind him.

Kion thrust his father's helm forward. "And I was hoping to have my father's helmet blademarked. He fought here in the Battle of—"

"I've had no notice a shipment was coming," the guard said, failing even to acknowledge Kion's presence. He looked to the others. "Was there anything in the manifest?"

"Nothing, sir," said one of the men.

"I can't think why we'd need them. The armory's full up. We don't have enough soldiers for what we've already got."

The soldier sent one of the others inside to check with the quartermaster. A tense silence ensued. Kion squeezed the helm nervously. Perhaps now the man would have time to entertain his request.

"Please, sir," he said. "I just want—"

"Do you always let your servants speak out of turn like this?" the guard said, giving Kion a warning glare. He was looking more and more like Dougan by the moment.

"I'm sorry," Zinder said. He leaned over and told Kion in a low voice, "Perhaps it's best if I do the talking, but don't worry, I won't forget about the helm."

The other soldier returned a minute later, shaking his head.

"No record of an order," he said.

"There must be some mistake. I was hired by a scribe, a very well-dressed scribe, who offered a fair price. He's already paid the down payment, in fact." Zinder produced a receipt from his purse listing the terms of the agreement and signed in a flowery script.

"Hmm, it just says 'The Scribe' for the signature?" The guard snorted. "I've been here a year and never seen any scribe come through. Did he give you a name?"

Zinder scrutinized the document. "Um, no, I'm afraid not."

"Well, I can't do a thing for you. You'll have to hash it out with this mysterious fellow on your own."

"But I have no idea where to find him. I don't know a thing about him," Zinder said.

"That's your problem, not mine. You should be more careful who you do business with. I thought you nyn were supposed to be smart." This drew a few hard grins from the soldiers and turned Zinder's ears pink. He was at the point of bursting out in some show of righteous indignation when a laborer manning a wheelbarrow with a bag of grain rolled up behind them.

"Ho there, Wardmark," the newcomer said to the guard.

"What about my father's helm?" Kion nudged Zinder, seeing the guard was about to dismiss them.

"Sir, if I may." Zinder quickly adjusted his hat and regained his composure. "This boy's father fought in the Battle of Fane's Falling, and it would mean the world to him if Strom Glyre could blademark his helm."

"Sorry, the bladewarden's not got time for that sort of thing," the guard said. "Especially not for riffraff from the hills. Go back to your farm, boy."

"But, sir, we've come all this way—" Zinder said.

The wardmark waved them off, and the other soldiers stepped forward to ensure that the cart was promptly turned around.

Crusty led them away, barely above a trot, as if he shared in his master's disappointment.

"If I ever get hold of that scribe, I'll teach him a few new words to write in his books. Let's see if he can make a rhyme with hornswoggle!" Zinder said.

Kion remained silent. The memory of his final match swept over him once more. He watched the unexpected feint fly away from him and heard the devastating return stroke clanking against his armor. The weight of his defeat pressed down on him heavier than ever. Now he was twice a failure. No medallion and no blademark. And Tiryn...what did he have to show her? Nothing. Again, thoughts of her death returned. Why had he come here? Why had he abandoned the farm and his family? They needed him to be steady, to stay the course. And what had he done? Run off after some foolish dream.

He sank into his seat as the wagon rattled over the pavement, rocking him back and forth. Everything he did, everything he tried, was a failure. No matter how hard he worked, there would always be a Dougan Shaw who was better, stronger, richer, and more well-liked to put him in his place.

"There's still *The Wandering Spark*," Zinder said. "That's where that scoundrel of a scribe said he'd leave the balance. If we've any hope of finding answers—and salvaging this venture —we'll find it there."

The cart rolled on. Zinder was too livid to notice his friend's silence. Kion cradled the helmet and poured all his strength into keeping himself from giving in to tears.

The Wandering Spark could be heard from several streets away, a muffled rumbling, like mayhem with a lid on top. The windows glowed like beacons, attracting patrons from all directions. A great, brick-encrusted chimney piped out smoke so thick it could have been fog. As the cart rolled up, the two-story structure seemed to lean over them, as if inspecting their clothes and wares to see if they were worthy of entrance to the carnival of food and drink and song pulsing within.

Zinder left Kion with the cart and popped inside to see about getting a room and stabling his weary beast. A large stable, also two stories, stood next to the *Spark*, brooding darkly in contrast to its more lively counterpart.

Kion failed to hear the music, the laughter, or the hearty banter that spilled out into the street. His father's helmet was the only thing his mind could lay hold of, the only thing he had left. It was his burden now, his medallion of shame. Without the blademark, his father would always be the coward who had sounded the retreat at the Battle of Fane's Falling. His family would always be a grubby lot of no-good shepherds whose only purpose was to be the subject of insults and to give the farmers someone to look down upon.

"Come along now," Zinder said. He had re-emerged from the inn with a boy about Tiryn's height. "This lad'll take care of Crusty. Be sure he gets extra hay." Zinder flicked the boy a silver nick.

"Yes, sir." The boy pocketed the coin and grabbed the reins with a spring in his step. "Those are some fine swords. I'll make sure they get locked away tight."

"That's a good lad," Zinder said as the boy headed off. "Now." He turned to Kion. "I know things haven't gone as planned, and I'm awfully sorry about what happened with the helm, but there's nothing we can do about that just now. Maybe we can take another crack at it in the morning. In the meantime, though, I did manage to get us a room. Even better, I got this." For the first time, Kion noticed the leather scroll case in Zinder's hand. He had a dim recollection that he should know what was inside, but his mind was too clouded over with grief.

"What is it?"

"It's—" Several patrons pushed past, opening the door to the inn. The noise, the warm light, and the enticing smells caught

Zinder's attention. His gaze lingered on the open door as the others passed inside. "I'll tell you later. For now, let's just go inside."

Kion roused his deadened limbs into motion and followed Zinder through the door. Inside, boisterous voices and over-wrought strains of music assaulted his ears. Smoke from the hearth, along with spices and the smell of roast meats and simmering vegetables rankled his nose. He was in no mood to eat.

"Where's our room?" Kion asked, avoiding eye contact with the many patrons inside. There didn't look to be an empty chair, much less an empty table, in the place. Lanterns stood on little shelves in the corners. A large wooden chandelier hung in the middle of the room with four miniature lanterns resting on its rim. A few pictures hung on the walls, mostly of night scenes made impossibly bright by sparkling yellow bursts. The frames swayed or bounced as people knocked into them or stamped the floor nearby with their excessive jigs. The dancing was constrained mostly to a tiny stage in one corner, but it erupted at inconvenient spots whenever a musician would step up to play or when one of the tables burst into song. It was like the entire Seven Fires festival all crammed into a space not much larger than Zinder's smithy.

"Ah, yes, the room. Upstairs," Zinder said. "Our friend the scribe at least had the decency to reserve us the nicest one in the inn, it seems. If only he'd had the courtesy to tell the quarter-master or Strom we were coming."

Zinder weaved his way through the tangle of people with a great many "pardon-mes" sand "if-I-may-just-pass-throughs" and "please-watch-where-you're-goings" as he went mostly unnoticed until he was right on top of someone.

At last they reached the stairs, and up they went. The room was certainly nice. It had plastered walls painted sunflower yellow. A lantern hung from the ceiling on a brass chain, casting a warm glow about the room. Two beds were nestled in the corners. A trunk butted up against each one, and a small table stood between them. A clay wash basin rested on top of it.

Kion set the helmet next to the basin and splashed his face. The cold water shook him out of his haze.

"Did you say someone reserved this room for us?" Kion said.

"Yes, and a good thing, too. The inn's full up."

"Who was it, again?"

"The scribe, or should I call him *The* Scribe, with a capital S. That's how he signed his name. The very same charlatan who sent me on this madcap expedition in the first place." Zinder hung his hat on a bed post and doused his face with water as well. Then he let out a long "ahhhhhh" as he flopped on his back and spread his limbs across the bed.

"The Scribe. Right," Kion said. "So, does that scroll case hold the poem he promised you?"

"Ah, yes, the poem!" Zinder popped up and pulled the case from his satchel. It was made from dark leather and had a symbol stamped on the lid of two triangles overlapping at the tips, one large and one small. It looked quite new. "At least he wasn't misleading me on this account. The innkeep had this locked away for me. And The Scribe even left the coin to pay for the rest of the balance! Odd fellow. Infuriatingly odd. But enough of him. Now that we're safe from prying eyes, would you like to see what our mysterious malefactor has left us?"

Kion gave the slightest of shrugs. "I suppose so." He sat down across from Zinder on the other bed.

Zinder unscrewed the lid to the case. A rich, woody smell rushed out.

"Ah...knowledge. The best smell in the world." Zinder drew out a single golden-white piece of vellum with the greatest of care. It had a few nicks around the edges but was otherwise in excellent condition. The paper had a shine to it, as if it had been lacquered. It was twice as thick as any paper Kion had ever seen. The writing was extremely ornate, full of stylized letters with superfluous flourishes.

Zinder sat there staring and studying it for the longest time.

"Aren't you going to read it to me?" Kion asked.

"Sorry, I got lost in the letters and forgot myself!" Zinder licked his lips and scooted to the edge of the bed. He lifted the scroll and held it reverently to the light so that the letters and glossy vellum shone like silver.

In elder days the Mastersmith
Before men's hearts grew cold
Through craft of thought, in wisdom wrought
The mighty glaives of old

With silver true and tempered fold
In secret fire unseen
He spoke the names and bound the flames
Into a blinding sheen

The reaping blade and hatchet keen
Twin gifts he gave to men
To tend the land and guide their hand
In forest, plain, and glen

And with these gifts, through wit and ken
Fair gilded halls arose
But golden day could not allay
The doom that one man chose

They sat in silence for the longest time as the spell of the words worked itself upon their minds. The poem called Kion out from the dim, lonely landscapes where he had been wandering ever since the tournament, a world made only darker by his failure to blademark his father's helm. The verses came like a sunrise upon that desolate land, shedding the first rays of nurturing light upon the cracked and broken terrain. He saw just how small his own struggles were in the grand sweep of time, how ancient the world was, and how mysterious and unknown —and marvelous.

This was more than just a poem. How he knew this, he couldn't say, but from the look on Zinder's face, he felt the same.

"Now that's something, isn't it, lad?" Zinder broke the silence with hushed wonder. *"The Lay of the Glaives."*

Kion stared into the lantern, lost in smoky thoughts. For a long time, it was hard to find any words. "I can see why you, especially, should be drawn to this," he said at last. "It's about forging and smithcraft. But it sounds almost real, as if it were describing something that actually happened."

"Of course it actually happened. Anyone can see that. But it's something so old and so long ago, I don't even know what it's describing. Isn't it a delicious mystery? I love old forgotten shards of the past like this. A fellow could spend days upon days just imagining what it all means." Zinder gazed dreamily at the shiny vellum.

"That's not how I see it," Kion said, pulling off his traveling cloak and tossing it on one of the trunks. "I can't stand not knowing the answers. Why is it called the *Lay of the Glaives*? What does the word 'glaive' even mean?"

"It's another word for sword. An older word, not much used these days."

"A sword? But all it talks about is a hatchet and a reaping blade—whatever that is. Is it a scythe? A plowshare? And who is this Mastersmith? Is he the fane's smith? You must at least know that part, right?"

"Not a clue! Maybe he was the father of all blacksmiths, the first one to discover the craft and teach it to others. Or maybe he was the head of a guild of smiths—think of it! A guild of smiths! It's been ages since such a thing existed." Zinder returned to scanning the lines, as if the poem's secrets were sure to reveal themselves upon further examination.

"A guild of smiths? What a load of rubbish. You're just making that up to suit your fancy."

"And why shouldn't I? That's what imagination is for, and it's just about the loveliest gift ever given to man. Besides, even if it isn't true, maybe it will inspire me to found my own guild. And then *I'll* be the master smith, and I can write a poem of my own! Think of that!"

"How can you be satisfied with 'what if,' Zinder? Don't you want to know the truth?"

"Of course I do, but I'm not about to let a little ignorance get in the way of my delusions of grandeur. It's dreams that keep the world spinning, lad. That and fine meals at regular intervals. Speaking of which, all this poetry's gone straight to my stomach. What do you say we sally forth to conquer the common room and win us some hearty victuals?"

Kion still wasn't hungry. The mystery of the poem was all he could think about just now. But he didn't feel he would have much luck figuring it out on his own, and Zinder was already halfway out the door, so he rose and followed after his friend.

Chapter 17

SCRUM AT THE SPARK

The buttons on Zinder's coat strained at the seams. The mysterious scribe who had sent them to Roving had told the innkeep he would pick up the bill for any meals Zinder ate, and the nyn, with his out-sized appetite, was taking full advantage, just finishing off his third plate of meat and vegetables. Kion was still picking at his first, his mind wandering everywhere but the room in which he found himself.

"So how much more of the poem is missing?" Kion said, half shouting. The common room was so packed, it was impossible to have a normal conversation. The noise and cramped quarters had all the charm and subtlety of a heated argument. The only reason Zinder and Kion had a table at all was because the innkeep had forced two other patrons out of theirs, another benefit of staying in the *Wandering Spark's* "private room."

"Ah, yes, the *Lay*. I was enjoying this food so much, I forgot all about it." Zinder dabbed his mouth with his kerchief. "According to a book of lore written by Nimrain the Wanderer, the poem has six parts, each being four quatrain stanzas. It's hard to know for certain, but I would hazard a guess that the one we have is the first. Those opening lines about 'in olden days' and so forth sound like a beginning."

"Five parts are still missing? Then we'll never find out what it means."

"I wonder if that scoundrel of a scribe doesn't have the rest stashed away in some vault. There's more to him, I'd wager, than you or I will ever know. What purpose could he possibly have in sending us to deliver these weapons without telling Strom? You don't drop sixty gold rounds on a joke. If you do, it had better be a lot funnier."

"At least you got paid. And I haven't heard you complain about all the food he provided."

"That does soften the blow a bit, doesn't it?" Zinder laughed and accidentally flung the pheasant bone in his hand over his shoulder, hitting a mountainous patron in the back. Fortunately, the man didn't feel it, but the bone got stuck in his wool shirt.

Zinder turned around and tapped the man on the side. "Excuse me, sir." The stranger was so intent on his meal and the conversation blaring at his table that he failed to notice. Five other people crowded around him, all talking at once.

Kion hoped Zinder would leave it be. The man had a grimy, unpleasant face and logs for arms. He was not likely to appreciate the interruption.

Zinder got out of his chair. "Excuse me, sir." Zinder pulled at his elbow. "You've got a bone on your shirt."

The man turned a lizard-like eye toward him. He grunted something rough, but his mouth was so full of food it was incomprehensible.

"I said, you've got a bone sticking in your shirt," Zinder said, practically yelling.

The man pointed at him with the leg of mutton he was chewing on. "Do I know you? Go pick your own bone."

Kion set down his fork. He didn't like where this was going. Zinder's impeccable manners and this man's utter lack of them did not look to end well.

"But it's in your shirt. If you'll just allow me to—" Zinder reached up, and the man swatted his hand away. His elbow knocked a goblet over. A dark purple lake formed in the middle of one plate, with similar puddles sprinkled on several others.

"Now you've done it." The man rose to his full height, which seemed to take an awfully long time. He would have grabbed Zinder by the collar, but Zinder leapt back, quick as a wink.

"I'm terribly sorry, terribly, terribly sorry," Zinder said. "Please, no need for tempers to flare. I'll clean the mess and pay for any food that was ruined."

"You little nit!" The man let out a growl. "You better believe you'll pay!" His face turned purple, and he lunged at Zinder.

Several arms shot out to hold him back.

"Calm down, Scubrut," said the man's companions. "It's just a little food."

"I'll be back in a moment with something for the mess," Zinder said, easing farther away.

"Awfully kind of you, shortbread," said one of Scubrut's companions. "And no need to pay for the food. We were almost finished."

Zinder bristled at the "short" remark (he was rather sensitive about his height) but bowed abruptly. "It is the least I can do. It was my fiddly fingers that caused the mess...albeit indirectly."

"I'll help," Kion said, rising.

Zinder waved him away. "No need, lad. I'll have this taken care of in a snap. Besides, it's easier for shortbreads like me to get around in a place like this. You finish your meal." He weaseled away through the maze of tables.

Kion considered following him, but the musicians in the corner had just launched into a rousing tune. The two closest tables unloaded onto the little stage and proceeded to whirl about, knocking into the musicians, who didn't seem to care. The musicians capered and bounced right along with the dancing patrons. Shifting his gaze from the ungraceful gyrations, Kion's attention was drawn to the one person at the table who did not rise with the others. He had red hair and a small frame. Kion thought he looked awfully familiar, but the fellow had his back turned, so he couldn't be sure.

Kion rose and headed over, squeezing between the intervening tables with great effort and many an apology. He tapped the fellow on the shoulder, who turned and looked up.

"Snetch! Fire and ice, what are you doing here?"

Snetch grabbed a satchel from the floor and started to rise. Kion grabbed him by the shoulders and kept him in his chair.

"I'm not here to hurt you, or turn you in," Kion said. "Though I don't know why I shouldn't." He sat down next to the pinch-faced boy.

"I didn't steal those flags!" Snetch said. "Dougan gave 'em to me. Honest!"

Kion didn't believe him but decided not to press the point, at least not yet. He was curious to find out what Snetch was doing in Roving.

"So is this your new home? You've found work here?"

Snetch stuck out his chest. "Sure have. Started yesterday, as a matter of fact—as a porter. I carry things for the soldiers; sometimes I even run messages for them."

"Is that so?"

"You see, they trust me here in Roving. Not like those riffraff in Furrow. In fact, yesterday I delivered something extremely important—to the bladewarden's quarters no less."

Kion studied Snetch more closely. He couldn't tell if he was lying or not.

"What did you deliver?"

Snetch's face soured. "That's private information. Do you think Strom wants his business proclaimed to every wool-eared bumpkin that wanders into town?"

Kion brushed off the insult. He'd heard plenty worse. His eyes went to Snetch's satchel. The leather was worn but freshly oiled, and despite its age, the thick rivets and tight stitching showed its quality.

"Is that what you were supposed to deliver?" he asked.

Snetch shoved the satchel behind him. "Don't get cheeky with me, woolly. I already told you, I delivered Strom's things to him, just like I was ordered."

"So that's your satchel, then?"

"Well—so what if it is? Can't I have a nice satchel if I want to? You think I'm not good enough for one like this?"

"May I take a look, then? I've never seen one that nice before."

Snetch pushed his chair farther away. "When the moon turns red, you will. This is *my* bag."

An idea formed in Kion's head. What if it really was Strom's satchel?

"Two nicks says it's not yours. I bet you stole it," he said.

The color drained from Snetch's face. Kion's guess had hit the mark. For one panicked moment, Snetch sat there, his eyes shifting to every place in the room except Kion, his nose twitching like he was about to sneeze. Without warning, he swung the satchel and smashed Kion in the face. It felt like a brick. It almost knocked him out of his chair, but the tables were packed too tightly and his momentum was checked by the nearest patron.

"Hey!" the man yelled, but Kion had no time for him. He shook off the blow and launched himself after Snetch. The little coward had already taken off, but he only got as far as the next table before he tripped over someone's leg. Kion swooped in and pounced before Snetch could regain his feet.

"Give me Strom's bag, you shameless thief!" Kion laid hands on the satchel.

Snetch was stronger than he looked. He wrestled and squirmed with the ferocity of a wet badger. Every time Kion thought he had him pinned, he wriggled his way out. Meanwhile, he was giving as good as he got, pounding Kion in the side and chest and face. They careened against chairs and other patrons. In the midst of all the thrashing, a chair slammed down on top of Kion's back, almost knocking the wind out of him.

"You ratfink!" shouted the patron who had fallen out of his chair. He spun around and lunged at Kion, who now found himself fighting off a grown man and Snetch at the same time.

"Somebody corral those rascals!" a voice shouted.

Men rushed in to help. But the room was so crowded, the rescuers knocked over another patron on the way.

"Hey, that's my brother!" yelled another man.

A thud and a crash followed. Plates shattered. Shouts for order were drowned by bellowed challenges. The music screeched to a discordant end, but the noise in the room went from a waterfall to a hurricane.

More people fell or got knocked down all around Kion. The man grappling him was swept aside by someone even bigger. Snetch kicked Kion in the stomach and broke free. Kion leapt up to go after him, but two men crashed in front of him and started pummeling each other, cutting him off.

Everyone was out of their seats. Half of them were caught up in the raging brawl, the other half in trying to stop it or in scrambling for the exit. Snetch squeezed and dodged his way through the melee, heading not for the exit, but the nearest window.

"Help, lad!" Zinder's high-pitched voice shrieked above the din.

Zinder was dangling from the chandelier by his arms, swinging round and round like a dog chasing its tail. Scubrut, the mountainous man with the bone in his shirt, flailed his arms, trying to catch hold of the whirling nyn.

Snetch was almost to the window. Kion didn't think he could save Zinder and still catch him.

"Oh, bother!" he said. He took off toward Zinder, ducking fists and darting past writhing patrons. He was almost there when the big man grabbed hold of one of Zinder's legs, and the nyn lost his grip. Zinder kicked the man in the face as he fell, breaking free. Kion launched forward, catching his friend in midair. The two of them crashed onto the table and rolled off. Instead of the floor, they bounced off three or four men rolling around in a scrum between the tables, ending on top of the next table over. Scubrut lunged at them, but slipped and was sucked down into the human whirlpool.

"Thanks for the ride, lad." Zinder sat up, rubbing his head.

Kion rose to his hands and knees. His eyes leapt to the

window. Snetch was gone. A smashed window pane revealed his means of escape.

"I'll be right back," Kion said.

"Wait, where—?"

Kion went flying across the tables. He was not the only one. Two men were chasing each other over the tabletops as well. They nearly knocked him off as they hurtled past. He kept his balance and bounded across the rest of the tables until he leapt off and landed in front of the broken window.

The shattered glass and splintered frame were far too dangerous for someone Kion's size to fit through.

"The sneak got away," he said, but then he spotted something. A leather strap was caught in the broken glass. It belonged to the fancy satchel. The strap had snapped off on one side, but the bag dangled just outside the frame. Kion tried pulling it free, but it wouldn't budge. It must have gotten caught when Snetch crashed through and he'd been forced to leave it behind.

Kion pulled the satchel carefully inside and, with a bit of wiggling, it broke loose. The chaos around him seemed to die away as he knelt to open the coveted satchel. Out tumbled a well-worn shirt, a pair of pants, and a thick, leather-bound book. He carefully picked them up and stood staring at them. A weighty sense of responsibility came over him. Did these things belong to Strom?

There was only one way to find out.

Kion laid the book on his bed. Downstairs, the arrival of guards from the fortress had quelled the brawl. Kion and Zinder had managed to escape to their room before they arrived.

"I need to give this to Strom," Kion said.

Zinder lay spread-eagle on his bed, as if he wished to take up as much of it as possible. He had changed out of his traveling clothes and into a gray woolen nightgown. "The guards are right downstairs," Zinder said. "I'm sure they'd be more than happy to take it off your hands."

"No. I want to give it to him personally."

"You think the guards at the gatehouse will let you in?"

"I have to at least try. It's the last chance I have to get Strom to blademark my father's helm. I'll take it to the fortress first thing in the morning." Kion patted the book. Out of respect for Strom, he had only read the first page, but he'd flipped through the others just to get a sense of what kind of book it was.

The first page read simply, "Property of Strom Glyre, soldier of the fane," in faded ink. The other pages all had dated entries, with the last ones quite recent. It was a journal of some sort, or perhaps a log book. Kion was dying to read it, but if they were personal accounts, he dared not violate Strom's privacy, and if it was an official record, he might get in trouble.

"That book falling into your lap certainly is an encouraging turn," Zinder said. "And after we try our luck with Strom, I was thinking about going to see if I can sell off these swords. It's a shame I didn't set up shop in the brawl down there. I'm sure I could have sold a weapon or two!"

"Perhaps tomorrow will bring a change in fortune for the both of us." Kion picked up Strom's book and returned it to the satchel, which he placed gently within the chest at the end of the bed. If that journal got him in to see Strom, it would be worth all the swords in Roving.

It took him a long time to finally drift off to sleep. Thoughts of Strom kept pulling him back from the edge of dreams. He tried picturing what his father's helm would look like with its new blademark and where he would display it in the cottage once he got back home.

When at last his mind and body gave in to sleep, his dreams carried him to a dark place. He was climbing a cliff, trying to reach the Fortress of the Clefts, which stood at the top. It was a moonless night. His fingers ached from the strain. He could barely see. A vicious wind threatened to cast him into the dark chasm below. He had managed to climb about halfway up when he realized he did not have the strength to finish. His arms began shaking. Any moment now and he would lose his grip.

When he thought he could not hold on a moment longer, a voice sounded in his ear.

"I am near, glaivebond...Come...Restore me to what I once was... Make haste, while yet you can hear my voice..."

"Who are you?" Kion said. But in that moment, he lost his grip and fell into the waiting dark.

Chapter 18

BURDEN OF THE BLADEWARDEN

A cheerless light reached through the bailey window into Strom's quarters, but he needed no light to finish dressing. His leather jerkin fell easily over his arming jacket, and his legs sank into his boots with familiar smoothness. He draped his white tabard over his shoulders, where it settled like a second skin. Last came his belt and his sword, Verisguard, the one part of his dress which, he had to confess, had never grown comfortable. He wore the symbol of the bladewardens more as a burden than a mantle of authority. Though grateful for the honor of defending the fane as his chosen champion and the commander of his armies, the weight of leadership grew heavier with each passing day.

As a symbol, Verisguard may have grown burdensome, but it served its other, more primal purpose as well as ever. Though dim with age and possessing the plainest, most unadorned of hilts, it had never failed him in battle.

A knock on the door pulled Strom from his thoughts.

"Yes?"

"My lord, the messenger from Madrigal arrived in the night. You asked to be informed of it first thing in the morning," said the voice at the door.

"Very good. I shall meet with him in the great hall."

"Yes, sir." The man's footsteps on the flagstones faded into the bowels of the fortress.

Strom rattled the sword in its sheath. Perhaps it was some

good news at last. Perhaps it would soon be time to unsheathe Verisguard once more.

He rose and made his way through the drafty corridors of the keep. The cold, solemn stones were the only things that observed his passing. Old memories followed him as he walked. The face of Antirith, bladewarden before him, loomed cold and marble-white in his thoughts. He had died at Roving in the Battle of Fane's Falling along with so many others, but none more noble.

"I should have been the one," Strom thought. "But my doom shall come another day."

At last he reached the western guardroom. Roardin stood waiting for him, his promptness as unfailing as the sun.

"Swordswain." Strom returned the soldier's salute, arms crossed over the chest.

"Bladewarden, I trust you slept well," Roardin said. His short black beard was streaked with gray, but his cold blue eyes glittered keenly. The mail beneath his white tabard was dull and in need of repair, but he was too often on patrol to attend to it. He and Strom had spent most of yesterday riding the western Clefts, scouting for haukmar harriers.

"I do sleep," Strom said. "But never well. Not while the fane shackles my hands and refuses to unleash the full power of his army to vanquish the haukmar threat."

"Perhaps the messenger brings good tidings." Roardin's voice was hopeful, though his face betrayed him. "Shall we see what news from Madrigal?"

"Yes, Roardin, let us see. Lead the way." Strom motioned toward the door. Four glinthelms, the lowest rank in the Verisian army, accompanied them, bearing spears.

The great hall opened before them. The vaulted ceiling echoed with the booted rhythm of their entry. Strom and his men strode across the dais to the great table, where lanterns shone across a map of northern Inris and southern Haukmarn with marble tokens marking the locations of enemy sightings as well as all their most recent raids. There had been few of late, but this only worried Strom all the more. The haukmarn were like a blister that needed to be drained by the release of battle or it would burst forth in one sudden and painful rupture.

The messenger from Madrigal saluted at the base of the dais. The gesture came off stiff and tentative. Not a good sign.

Two glinthelms accompanied the messenger, himself a glinthelm as well. Behind them stretched row upon row of stout oak tables, only about a third of which would be used when meals were served here.

"Messenger, what news have you for the bladewarden?" Roardin asked.

Strom motioned for silence before he could answer. "First, your name, soldier."

The messenger relaxed, but only slightly. "Glinthelm Endrith, sir."

"Good. What does the fane have to say in response to my request, Glinthelm Endrith?"

Endrith looked him in the eye as duty demanded, but his chin dropped involuntarily. "He sent word that he is pleased with your recent progress in halting the haukmar raids. And that, in light of your success, he does not believe an augmentation of the northern forces is necessary at this time."

Strom's fist landed on the table, but not nearly so hard as it might have. He had to maintain discipline before the men. And Endrith would be reporting on Strom's response, so there was that to consider as well.

"And the margrave? Has he any men to spare for the defense of his lands?" Strom labored to keep bitterness from his voice.

"The margrave says he will send a battalion in early summer," Endrith said, vainly attempting to infuse his words with a note of hope.

Roardin crossed his arms. The swordswain's teeth made a faint grinding sound.

"A single battalion? And not until summer?" Strom said. "And did he give a reason for this delay?"

"Funds, sir," Endrith said. "It was a lean winter."

"Indeed it was. But not so lean that the haukmarn will not find much to feast upon should they attack us in force. Go. You have done your duty. Send my gratitude to the fane for the faith he has placed in me to hold these lands, and for his kind words. Tell the margrave I await with anticipation the reinforcements he has promised."

Endrith saluted with crossed arms, and the two glinthelms escorted him from the hall.

Strom waited until the large, double oaken doors had closed before pounding the table again. This time the lanterns jumped. One nearly fell over, but Roardin caught it in time. "They are slitting our throats, Roardin."

"They are slitting their own throats, sir. We are merely pall-bearers at the funeral."

Strom bowed his head in thought, then dismissed the glinthelms attending them. "Come, Swordswain, let us walk."

They exited through the open doors at the back of the dais. Well-placed shafts allowed for air and light in the enclosed space. Four glinthelms stood at attention along the hallway. Strom acknowledged their salutes. They ascended the stairs of the northwest tower and exited the walkway, crossing to the northern battlements. Voices carried in the keep. It was safer to discuss important matters in the open air.

From this height, even in the weak morning sun they had a good view of the outer walls and the Claywash below. The wide, tawny blanket of loam narrowed on either side as that smooth swath of land swept south and upward and wrapped itself around the fortress, isolating Roving from the rugged crags known as the Clefts. The fortress sat atop a high butte, with parts of its walls built into the very bedrock. The Winding Rise, a steep and treacherous road, ran from the northern gatehouse down into the Claywash. This was the side that was the most easily defended. An army would be foolish to attack from that direction, and in fact, no enemy ever had, except during the Battle of Fane's Falling.

Strom leaned on the crenellations.

"I will not order it, because it would not make sense from a tactical point of view, but as your friend, I give you leave to return home to Nivilwane and await a new post. You have your wife and son to think of. To stay here would only mean your death, or worse, being taken prisoner by the haukmarn."

Roardin was quick to respond. "My heart may belong to my family, but my body is not my own. It belongs to the fane, to do with as he wills. Though these past few months have shown that he places little value on the men who would die for him, it is never right to repay a lack of honor by betraying one's own."

"If his soldiers were made of gold and not flesh, he might esteem them otherwise," Strom said. "I miss Galbraith more with each passing day. It is hard to believe that Sathe could ever be his son. They are as unalike as a hole and a rock."

"True enough. Have you any ideas, sir? The host we observed moving through the Clefts may pass us by for Windstern or even Quelling, but they are bound to strike within an eight-mark at most."

"They should have struck already. I do not know why they tarry."

"The only answer must be that they are gathering even more harriers to swell their ranks."

"With the haukmarn, there is never any sense. Their minds are rotted, though their bodies are strong. Still, we should at least send for more supplies to replace those we lost from the mold."

"They will not come in time. The margrave's coffers are bare. The messenger said as much."

Strom turned his back on the Claywash and faced the village of Roving, though little of it was visible from this side of the fortress. "Our numbers are perilously thin. Are there any new arrivals within the past eight-mark we might press into service?"

"A few. Six boys, three men, and a nyn, according to the ledger. I do not believe word has yet gotten out of how dire the threat is, but four families left recently, abandoning their homes. It is only a matter of time before word spreads through the rest of Inris."

"A nyn?" Strom stroked his short beard. "Odd. But unless he brought us a dozen war machines, he will do no good. Send for the others. Arm them with spears and mail."

"Mail, sir? Do you think we should waste it on green recruits?"

"Who else are we going to put it on?" Strom snapped uncharacteristically. "Forgive me. But the armory is no good to us if we are overrun. We can at least make the haukmarn have to work to gather it all up instead of leaving it conveniently in one place."

A long pause followed. The still morning air hung bitterly between the two soldiers.

"Sir, this is the end, isn't it?" Roardin said.

Strom looked into the eyes of his friend. "It has been an honor to serve alongside you these many years."

Roardin saluted. "The honor has been mine. We have known many marvelous victories, not all of which we deserved. But it does seem a cruel turn that upon the field where you had your greatest victory should come your final defeat."

"When strength fades, the will grows stronger," Strom said, repeating the battle cry of the fanewardens, the greatest order of warriors in the land, of whom he was chief.

Off in the distance, a horn blast, long and dour, shivered the air.

The haukmarn had come at last.

The haukmar host swelled Roving Field before the southern gates, a sea of black flecked with white, the black from the long hair and dark armor of the harriers, and the white from the mosaic of glowing wanstones embedded in their armor. The haukmarn claimed the stones were the source of their great strength and endurance. Indeed, they could march for days without rest when needed, as Strom knew all too well. But no one in the Four Wards dared use them. Prolonged exposure to the stones clouded the mind and ate away at one's sanity. For this reason, Warding soldiers always burned them after a battle. This seemed to purge the stones of their strange smoke and fumes, turning them into colorless baubles.

Shouts of challenge rippled through the host, cavernous cries of blind rage that sought to shatter whatever stood in its way. Axes cleaved the air in violent strokes. At the back, the slavering, snarling dreadwulfs, almost as tall as the haukmarn themselves, with eyes that glowed with maddening white light, joined their howling fury to that of their masters. Beyond the dreadwulfs, teams of oversized muskoxen stamped before massive lashtail siege engines, catapult-like contraptions that would rain down searing slivers of metal upon the town of Roving.

"This is twenty-fold the host we faced at Fane's Falling," Roardin said.

He and Strom stood atop the southern gatehouse battlements, surveying the ranks assembled just out of bowshot. Roving's defenders lined the walls on either side of the bladewarden, clad in mail, bows at the ready, waiting for the hopeless onslaught to begin. Down in Roving proper, all those devoted to the running of the town and the daily operation of the keep gathered in the streets before the gate to hear what transpired.

"How they have gathered an army of this size is beyond my ken," Strom said. "It appears as if all of Haukmarn stands before us."

"Never before have all ten Claws been assembled," Roardin said. "Surely we look upon the doom of the Four Wards."

Strom gripped the hilt of Verisguard. "They will have to reckon with the bladewarden of Verisward ere that day comes."

Roardin gazed at the fane's champion with an admiration

born of many battles fought side by side, each saving the life of the other many times over. "That they will, my lord. We will make them pay dearly for every stone of this fortress that they take."

Strom turned to the east, where the white sun hung as if caught in a web of gray clouds. The haukmarn had taken more than half an hour to march from the northern pass around to the southern gate. There they had remained in ragged, restless formations for the better part of another hour. The haukmarn were not a subtle race given to thought or clever tactics in battle. They struck fast and hard, and therein lay their greatest strength and their greatest weakness. This delay now was troubling. The haukmarn had surprised them at Fane's Falling and nearly won the day. Were they planning something on this day as well?

The cruel, snaggled mouths of the haukmar thundered on. When at last their war chants died away, a group of ten harriers strode forth, bearing the white banner of parley. The shortest among them, a figure still passing seven feet in height, lifted his voice and addressed the forces assembled along the walls.

"Cravens of Roving, I, Vayd Mokán, Faneslayer and Zaron of Haukmarn, come to declare an end to the fane's rule over the lands of Warding. The haukmarn claim the throne of Gilding by right and by might. Our blood claim cannot be denied, for we are descended from Terroc the Chosen, rightful heir to the throne. I challenge the champion of the fane, or whichever fool leader of yours holds sway over the usurpers within these walls, to meet me before this gate under the terms of the ancient oaths of battle. The winner will gain control of this fortress. The loser will gain for his people safe passage from these lands, wherever his army should choose to go, to wallow in humiliation at their champion's defeat, and to await death on some other day. For death now comes to these lands, and I am its messenger. Now, give me your answer!"

A chill silence swept the walls and fields of Roving. It was as if all of Warding turned its eyes upon the rugged walls of the

Clefts, suspecting that their fate rested with the answer to this challenge. Strom's body thrummed with a swirl of conflicting emotions: anger at the affront of this brazen haukmar, fear at the realization that this was Vayd Mokán, the villain who had slain Fane Galbraith ten years ago before these very walls, and doubt at the nobility of Vayd's words, so unlike the haukmarn, but finally, and above all, hope. For he saw clearly that, apart from this unlooked-for challenge, his men had no hope of holding these walls, nor of living to see another spring. But a single battle against a single warrior gave them a chance. Strom had bested dozens of haukmarn in battle over the years. They were slow and clumsy and did not fight with their heads, but with the frenzied madness raging inside their chests. But Vayd had beaten Fane Galbraith, and that was not to be taken lightly. Galbraith had been in the twilight of his strength and Vayd a young harrier, but the fane was not an unskilled swordsman. And now, with ten years of raiding and battle to whet the edge of his axe, this new leader of the haukmarn might prove to be Strom's death as well.

Roardin placed his hand over Strom's wrist. "You must refuse. We will hold out until reinforcements come."

"Well, vermin, I grow impatient," Vayd bellowed from below. "If your champion is too cowardly to accept my challenge, I will crush whatever miserable runt you choose to send in his place."

A low murmur arose along the walls. The men were talking. They knew Strom held their future in his hands.

The question for Strom was whether Vayd would honor the battle oath and let his men go free if he was slain. A single combat had not been fought between a Verisian and a haukmar in Strom's lifetime. Would they honor the ancient codes? Strom looked up and down the walls, marking the soldiers he cared for so deeply. The look of proud defiance in their faces told him that they looked to him for victory. They believed he could defeat this brutish warrior, believed Vayd had no place on the same battlefield with the most celebrated champion of this generation. They saw the challenge as an opportunity, a gift to those who still held fast to the dream of a reunited Four Wards. That dream had long lain dormant inside him. He had fought so many petty battles and fended off so many raids, he had all but forgotten what Warding had once been and what it might be again one day. But the spark of that vision gave him courage now. If he could defeat the haukmarn here, perhaps war could be avoided. Perhaps a time of peace would come at last, and the fane and his people could rebuild what was lost.

In the end, the choice was clear. Reinforcements would not come. His men would die the long death of the siege if he did not take this chance, for surrender to the haukmarn was worse than death. This was their only hope for victory, the only hope for Inris, and even, should he fall, the only hope of saving his men and the people within these walls.

Strom unsheathed Verisguard and held it high. "I, Strom Glyre, Bladewarden of Fane Sathe, thorn of the haukmar harriers since their inglorious defeat at my hand in the War of the Claws, accept this challenge with a glad will. In accordance with the laws of the ancient oaths of battle, by swift sword and sure stroke, I will avenge the death of Fane Galbraith, prove the might of my people against this loathsome rabble, and send your foul brood of beastmen despairing back to their filthy hovels in the Marred Wastes!"

Cheers shook the air upon the walls and echoed in the streets of Roving. Everywhere a voice could be sounded, the news went forth. The Bladewarden of Verisward would fight for the people of Roving. His feats and prowess in battle were repeated over and over. He had vanquished hundreds, never lost a battle since the War of the Claws. Could he not defeat a single haukmar harrier, brutish and brash, before the gates of the fane's own keep? The shouts and cries at this joyous news left little doubt as to the answer.

Chapter 19

BEFORE THE GATES

I n the same moment Strom stood upon the battlements and heard the echoing blasts of the haukmar host, those same blasts shook Kion and Zinder awake. Neither of them had ever been in a battle, much less a war, yet they knew at once what the sound meant.

"The haukmarn? In Roving?" Kion cast off his blanket. The chill air assaulted his senses.

"Oh, lad, I should never have brought you here," Zinder said in the dark.

The horn echoed in Kion's mind. But the longer he listened to the memory of the sound, the less sense it made.

"They wouldn't dare attack the Clefts," he said, attempting to dismiss the threat of those echoing notes. "They'd never take it."

"If there were enough of them they might. We've got to get dressed—get outside and discover what's happening."

Kion stirred, as if waking a second time, and fumbled for his boots. There wasn't time to light the lantern. As loud as that horn was, the haukmarn might be at the gates at any moment. He wasn't sure what he would do once they got outside, but they still had Zinder's swords. No—better not to think about that yet. Move first and think later.

Kion yanked on his shoes and his cloak.

"Zinder, are you ready?"

"I'm right behind you. Or in front of you. I can't tell in the dark." The whole inn rumbled with noise. Feet stampeded down the hallway. Panicked cries penetrated the walls.

Kion banged his foot against the corner of the trunk and bit back a yell. At least he'd found it. He tottered around, toes throbbing, and emptied the trunk. He slung his satchel over his shoulder and tucked Strom's bag under one arm.

"I'll never get to give it to him now," he thought. As if that mattered. As if any of his hopes and dreams mattered now.

"I have no idea if these clothes match," Zinder said in a fret.

"If it's a haukmar invasion, I'm sure they'll kill you just as easily if you're out of fashion," Kion said, hurrying to the door and out into the hallway. A dark shape clambered by, but from the sound of things, most everyone on the upper floor was already downstairs or out in the streets.

They met a log jam of bodies at the base of the stairs. Thirty people were talking at once. Their endless gibbering kept on as they pressed out the front door. Some spoke in terror, as if the fall of the fortress had already happened; others bristled with anticipation at the thought of the hated haukmarn, daring to come out of hiding, being dealt with once and for all by Strom Glyre and his men.

Kion and Zinder squeezed their way outside and into the street. The sun had yet to climb above the fortress walls, but there was enough light to see people and carts crammed into the bloated pathways of the town. No one could make any progress. Though the actual number of people was not great, Roving's streets were not designed to hold so many at once.

Along the outer walls, soldiers rushed from tower to tower. Bowmen took positions. Mailed warriors shouted orders. The air rippled with the worst kind of anticipation.

Mutterings about the invading warhost fluttered through the masses. Though everyone had an opinion as to the size and nature of the force beyond the gates, as far as Kion could tell, it was all guesswork. No one had actually been atop the outer walls, and the front gates were locked and barred.

"I'm going to see if I can hitch up old Crusty and get us into our cart," Zinder said.

"We're going to try to flee before the haukmarn attack?"

"No, and I doubt they would let us out if we tried. But we'll at least be able to see better. And I'd just as soon have everything packed and ready, should we need it."

Zinder ducked his way through the crowds. His size and quick feet allowed him to pass where no human could. By the time he got back twenty minutes later, the crowd had thinned a little. A few had gone into the inn to wait, others to find better vantage points throughout the town. By now Kion also had some idea as to the nature of the haukmar threat. Two soldiers had passed by and confirmed that a large haukmar army with siege engines was arrayed before the southern gates. The *Wandering Spark* was located right up against the wall, very near those gates. The line of mailed soldiers manning the eastern and western battlements steadied Kion's confidence in the strength of their defenses. Surely such fell-looking warriors would be able to repel the haukmarn, and more were arriving by the minute. Yet he could not shake the mounting dread inside him.

Zinder returned wearing a saffron shirt with purple pants and a red cap with a green feather. Kion hadn't noticed the garish outfit before, but he didn't say anything. They had enough to worry about without dragging Zinder's wardrobe into things.

From Kion's new perch in the cart, he could see a contingent of a dozen or so soldiers in white uniform and mail pressing through an intersection. Two of them got into a scuffle with a commoner who demanded the gates be opened for himself and his family. He was quickly put in his place, which was flat on the pavement.

Shortly after, another, smaller group of soldiers came by asking everyone to return to their dwellings or shops. Only a few listened, and there were not enough soldiers to enforce the order. Not long after that, an enterprising merchant passed through, hawking old biscuits for the outrageous price of a full silver square. A few desperate souls took him up on the offer, unwilling to go back to the inn or their own homes for fear of missing out on news of what was to come.

The waiting dragged on for what seemed like hours, but it was probably only a few minutes later when a hush fell over the crowd. A lonely wind whisked through the streets. A low murmur broke out, everyone passing along the same news: "Strom's on his way to the battlements."

Kion stood so he could see better, but the inn and the nearest gate tower blocked much of his view. Even on his toes, he only caught sight of a small band of soldiers entering the far guard tower.

"Did you see him?" Kion asked, his face and hands clammy with the thought that he'd missed Strom.

"Me? How would you expect a stubby little tick like me to see when a towering oak like you can't?"

"I thought perhaps with your sharp eyes…" Kion said, but at the moment Zinder wasn't even looking at the gates. His gaze lingered on the merchant's biscuits as he passed by for the third time. If the man came again, Kion doubted Zinder would be able to resist. How could he be thinking of food at a time like this? Kion had no appetite whatsoever.

The crowd remained hushed a few more moments longer, then broke into cheers.

"Hail, Strom!" went the cries. Other phrases came with them: "There goes the hero of Fane's Falling," "There's a soldier for you," and "He has the look of one of the Four Lords, he does."

The shouts and exclamations only made Kion all the more dismayed he couldn't see what everyone was talking about. He jumped out of the cart.

"Now see here, lad. Don't you go running off!" Zinder sprang to his feet, scolding his young friend with a flapping finger.

"I'll be back in a snap!" Kion said, pushing his way into the maze of bodies.

"You'll get lost is what you'll do. Don't be a mutton brain. Get back here!"

But Kion was past the first wave of humanity before Zinder could jump down after him. Zinder would forgive him—eventually. Besides, it wasn't as if he could go outside the fortress.

He waded through the press of the crowd. The streets had grown more packed since Strom's arrival. They reeked like a human trash heap. He had to squeeze past stale bodies oozing sweat and spewing forth all manner of questionable odors.

"Kion Bray, if you don't get back here, I'll tell your mother to fry your toes and feed them to the sheep!" Poor Zinder was beside himself, but he couldn't leave his cart and goods. For a prankster, he didn't have much stomach for surprises.

While Kion pushed and squeezed his way to a spot where he could clearly see the ramparts, the sound of thousands of marching boots spilled over the walls, growing ominously with each passing moment, like a great surge of water about to break over a dike. Primal howls punctuated the surging rhythm. They were far too beast-like even for the haukmarn. The howls were akin to those of wolves, only deeper and more savage. An unnatural hunger for flesh and blood echoed at the back of them. Kion had heard the word "dreadwulf" before, and, like his experience with the word "war", he recognized it now that it was here because he had lived so long in its shadow. He had faced many predators to his flock over the years, but none had ever instilled in him such unnatural fear.

No one upon the walls or down in the village spoke. The pounding boots grew louder and louder and the howls more horrifying. A horn blast crashed over the walls, and the haukmarn broke into chants so loud, they overshadowed even the dreadwulf howling. The noise went on and on. The longer it went, the more jittery the crowd became.

But not Kion. As the chanting droned on, it began to have a very different effect upon him. It lit a fire inside him. These were the beasts that had killed his father. These were the savages who wanted to ransack his homeland and seize what little his family had. The voices were monstrous, bellowing with rage and violence. And they had to be answered. Hearing them awakened a deep, slow-burning anger inside, consuming all his fears.

"This fortress will stand. I don't care if they fill the fields from here to Furrow. They'll never be able to take the Clefts before reinforcements arrive." Kion's vow to leave off sword fighting crumbled in the clamor and fury of the haukmar challenge. His fingers itched for a blade. He was ready to rush through the gates and fight them that very moment.

When the noise of the haukmarn ceased, a single, deep voice, rough and haughty, arose in its place.

But Kion did not hear the words. For another voice, noble and yet strange, with words of crackling fire, drowned out all other sounds.

"At last you come in open day. The darkness lifts. My will flows back. I am myself again. And because myself, at last I may be yours. You must come to me now. Do not tarry in fear. I know you have questions, doubts. Do not allow them to overmaster you. The foes of Gilding draw near. Long have I slept. To what purpose I am now called, I know not. But this I know: I was sent for you. Sent to serve as well as to guide. I will show you the art of the swift stroke, the cold calm at the center of the fire, the quiet truth of the everlasting moment. Only speak to me, tell me who you are, that I may know the one to whom my Master sends me."

The words ripped through Kion's mind in a quickening heat that both terrified and exhausted him all at once. He reeled, blundering into a short man with scraggly hair.

"Get off, will you?" the man said.

"Sorry," Kion said. He regained his feet. The voice of the haukmar challenger before the gates had died away. The unmistakable scrape of a sword sliding from its sheath cleaved the silence in twain. Kion felt, more than saw—he could not explain how—a shaft of light pierce the gray morning, blazing across the top of the gatehouse. From above the gates came a new voice, brave and fell. It was not like the words of fire that throbbed in Kion's mind, yet in its own way, it had a fire all its own, the fire of courage and grim resolve. Kion knew it at once. It was the voice of dignity and greatness, the voice of the best of men. It was the voice of Strom Glyre, accepting the challenge of the foolish enemy who dared hazard himself before the gates of the Fortress of the Clefts.

The streets of Roving swarmed with people. No one had the power to remain still after the news of the challenge broke. Kion groped through the writhing currents of men and women, at last clawing his way back to Zinder's cart.

"What's wrong with you, lad? You look paler than a haukmar miner," Zinder said. He grabbed Kion's arm and helped him up.

Kion's head still thrummed with the mysterious heat, but it was not a physical sensation. He wasn't sweating. His cheeks and ears were not flushed. In fact, they were cold as stone. But his mind was shrouded in fiery thoughts. He could sense the voice pushing in at the edge of his awareness, but he resisted. He had to. There was danger in that voice. Something told him that if he gave in to it, he would never again be master of his own destiny.

Was this what Tiryn felt? In those last few days, she had often raved in her dreams of a coming fire and the fear of a nameless threat. Had he taken sick like her?

"Just a little shaken, that's all," Kion said. "I may be coming down with something."

Zinder touched his forehead. "Well, you picked a terrible time to boil your brain. You heard the challenge, didn't you?"

The haze made it hard for Kion to recall. "Yes, I think so. One of the haukmarn challenged Strom. What exactly did he say? My mind's a little foggy."

"You don't remember? You really must be coming down with

something," Zinder said. "There's to be a duel. Do you think you can hold out, or do we need to get you back to the inn? From the way everyone's rushing about, it looks as if it's to happen right away."

Kion cradled his head in his hands. This wasn't a fever. He felt no ill effects in any part of his body. The fire inside wasn't even painful, just unsettling, like his vision had shifted and he could no longer see things as they once were. Whatever it was, it was wholly unnatural, and he wished it would go away.

"I—I'll be fine," Kion said.

"You're sure? Because if we're to have any sort of view of the fight, we'd best get moving. All the best places will fill in a hurry."

Kion nodded, and the cart rumbled forward. Zinder couldn't go very fast, because of all the people dashing up and down the street.

"It's like everyone's a packet of smokecrackers and they all went off at the same time," Zinder said.

The rocking motion of the cart helped quiet the fire in Kion's head. His awareness of the strange voice faded. Slowly, it receded until it ceased to press in on him.

The townsfolk had formed a half-circle in the broad court-yard around the gates. Soldiers stood every few feet to keep them back. As Zinder had feared, all the good spots were taken. He and Kion found a place about five rows back. However, the cart gave them a fair enough view.

Other carts were scattered about the crowd, and folk began piling into them. Several people asked if they could climb into Zinder's, but he eyed his swords and armor nervously and told them he was sorry, but no. He had a mortal fear of thieves when it came to his wares.

After a short time, a soldier passed into the center of the clearing and announced the nature of the duel. It would be a fight to the death, with the winner gaining access to the keep. In the event Strom was defeated, the Warding forces would be granted one hour to pack their things and vacate Roving. If Vayd, the haukmar leader, lost, the invading army would return to their lands by the Clefts Road to the north.

"Do you think they'll honor their word?" Kion said.

"Oh, they'll honor it, all right," Zinder said. "That's the thing about haukmarn: they need a strongman, a leader, who can bully them into submission and keep them together. Without this Vayd character, there probably wouldn't even be an army outside the gates. The haukmarn risk far more than we do. If we lose, we just surrender Roving, which is little more than an outpost for keeping the haukmarn at bay. If they lose, the horde is scattered and they go back to their miserable hovels to howl over their defeat."

Kion felt almost normal by now. He was beginning to think it had just been the excitement of almost seeing Strom that had gotten to him. But that voice; where had it come from? Was it Vayd, somehow, the haukmar leader? No, the voice may have been forceful, but it did not sound evil, just dangerous.

"But why risk everything on a battle like this?" Kion said. "I heard some men say they've got ten thousand harriers out there, besides the dreadwulfs and lashtails, whatever those are."

"I'm no expert on the haukmarn, but if I had to hazard a guess, I'd say it's two things. First, Roving was the place of their last major defeat. Strom's victory here ended the war. And they don't forget a grudge. But more importantly, if they can take Roving in one fell swoop, that means they'll have access to the heart of Inris that much quicker, and they can begin conquering Inris in late spring instead of mid-summer. With an army that size, they're not here to raid. They mean to march on Madrigal, and Roving will be a thorn in their backside until they can take it. The last thing they want is a long, drawn-out siege."

"I thought you'd never been in a war. You sure sound like you know what you're talking about."

Zinder tapped his temple. "Books, lad, books. Paper swords have won more battles than steel."

"Well, maybe you're in the wrong business, then. Start making paper swords and see how you fare," Kion said.

"It's just—it's just an expression!" Zinder said, pretending to be more exasperated than he was.

A low drum beat broke up their conversation. The proud call of a trumpet joined the rhythm. Then a piccolo, high and free, floated above it all. The song brought to mind Kion's father. It sounded like something he might have written. Noble. Hopeful. Brave.

Marching feet joined the drums as a group of eight soldiers advanced toward the gates. The crowd parted as the troop, mail glittering and swords held rigid at their sides, marshaled themselves in a circle before the gates.

Two more soldiers came behind them. One had a short beard and wore a white uniform with yellow bars on each shoulder, marking him as a swordswain ascendant. The other was a man of high bearing, clean of face and grave in aspect. He alone wore no armor, only the white, gold-trimmed uniform of a commander in the fane's army. His shoulder bars and the four gold diamonds stitched upon his breast matched the trim. Though he marched to the same rhythm as the others, he moved with a grace and ease they lacked, as if he alone, of all those present, was at peace with what was about to transpire.

This was Strom Glyre at last. The Bladewarden. The Fane's Champion. The greatest warrior of the age.

Seeing him in the flesh was more telling than a thousand pages in the folio of the Fiorin Batal. This was a true warrior. The forms and the exercises could teach someone how to fight, but they could not teach the bravery, prowess, and confidence that radiated from Strom's countenance. Only hardened battle could do that. If ever there was a soldier made for fighting, this was he.

Behind him trailed a troop of three musicians. They played a few more bars and then their music, along with their march, stopped. Reverent silence fell like a gentle rain across the keep.

In the midst of the silence, the fiery presence sparked in Kion once again. He swayed uncertainly, but the sight of Strom galvanized him. He would not let the fire master him, not when the champion of Verisward stood near. He strained hard against it, putting all his energy and thought into the scene before him.

Strom stepped forward and addressed the gathered crowd.

"People of Roving. I stand before you in the name of our great and noble fane. Although we have not sought war, war beckons at our gates. Such is the manner of life. Where evil stalks, those of good will must gather to oppose it. But those who least seek battle may be the better to meet it. For they fight not for riches or power, but for love of those they hold dear, for those who guard the hearth and keep its fires burning until their return. The haukmarn are a blight upon the land, but do not let their violence and spite overmaster you. Ever we must go to the battle, not out of malice, or despair, or a spirit of vengeance, but in solemn duty. And so now, for the fane, for his people, and for the honor and hope that binds the Four Wards together, may I be worthy of this hour."

No cheers came at these words, but no small sum of tears fell to the pavement.

The musicians roused their instruments, sounding a stirring melody that rose to the sky. It was a song Kion knew well, as did all those gathered, who lifted their voices and sang the words.

When the Four Wards stand
And the oaths that were broken will once more be spoken

Fear will flee this land
And the curse will not bind us, the darkness behind us

Let our cry ring forth
From the sand and the mountain the field and the fountain

East, west, south, and north
The Four Wards united, and all wrongs are righted

When the Four Wards stand

The song ended with the blast of a horn from beyond the walls, but the dreadful sound could not dim the hope that the song inspired. Seeing Strom, hearing his voice, and now this ancient song—all these worked powerfully upon Kion, and the dream of the Four Wards, which he had thought buried at the festival of Seven Fires, rose anew from the ashes of his heart. Where that light would take him he knew not, but at that moment he was sure that all the old tales were true and that new tales must be written to carry on those dreams that had been so long forgotten.

The gates opened, and the double portcullis rose. Beyond, a contingent of thirty haukmarn advanced from among the massed host.

The haukmar horns blared forth again, in random, tuneless notes so loud it pained the ears. They made their way to the gates and passed inside the fortress walls. The soldiers and musicians around Strom retired, going back the way they came, all but the swordswain, who stood resolutely at his lord's side.

The haukmarn stopped just inside the gate. Ashen-faced and stout, they bore no arms, though they were outfitted in angular-looking armor. Their legs and the lower half of their torsos were covered with ill-fitting plates, the metal dark, dented, and rusted. What the armor lacked in craftsmanship it made up for in thickness and heft. Their upper bodies and upper arms were covered in leather studded with white stones, which gave off a strong, acidic stench, even at a distance, and emitted a wispy, lingering smoke. Their skin was gray and bloodless. Long faces, flat noses, small eyes, and almost lipless mouths made them appear animal-like, but a devious cunning simmered just beneath the surface of their savage expressions. It struck Kion that if men could be divested of all that was good and noble, if they passed beyond all hope and wisdom and reason, they might look something like this. With that thought, it was as if some jar of innocence broke deep inside him, and he shivered in revulsion.

The least massive of the haukmarn stepped forward. Though smaller than the others, he stood at least a foot taller than Kion. His muscular frame did not move with the sluggish lumbering of the others. He moved with unnatural quickness for someone his size.

He wore no armor save a pair of thick leather gauntlets. His tunic was kettle black and matched his shoulder-length hair. His boots had been sewn together from scraps of thick hide. An oversized battle axe rested on his shoulder. The notched blade and worn hickory haft told of the many battles Vayd had fought with this very weapon. Kion would have struggled to wield it even with two hands, but the haukmar held it easily in one. Scars on his face made him appear older than he was. Vayd had been a young harrier when he killed Fane Galbraith. He was perhaps now only about ten years older than Kion, if haukmarn matured at roughly the same rate as men. But Kion would never grow to that size and strength, not if he practiced swordplay every day for the rest of his life.

Vayd eyed the surrounding crowd with contempt, silently challenging each of them with a wrinkled lip and arrogant gaze.

The bearded swordswain who had marched in with Strom stepped between them.

"Will you, Vayd Mokán, Zaron of Haukmarn, agree to fight this duel according to the ancient rites of challenge?"

"I will!" Vayd said. His harriers howled like wolves on the hunt, causing some in the crowd to shrink back.

The swordswain, undaunted by the savage haukmarn, continued, "And will you, Strom Glyre, bladewarden of the fane, agree to fight according to the ancient rites of challenge?"

"I will," Strom said quietly. A collective inrush of breath was the only response from the surrounding crowd.

The swordswain hesitated a moment and said, "Let the challenge begin."

A rustling murmur floated through the courtyard.

"Do you think Strom will win?" Kion asked in a whisper as the two fighters approached one another.

"Oh, he'll win, all right," Zinder said. "He's never lost a battle since he became bladewarden, and a challenge is far easier than a fight on the battlefield. You only have to worry about one enemy in a duel."

Kion turned his gaze to the two combatants as they readied their weapons. Sword against axe. It was not an even match on that score. The axe was the slower weapon, and terrible for defense, but Vayd had the advantage in physical prowess, especially in reach. Kion wondered how many battles the haukmar had lost. From the way Vayd carried himself, it did not look like any. But every fighter had his weakness, and Strom would find Vayd's. For the second time in ten years he would send the haukmar army home in defeat. And with this second victory, his legend would only grow.

Chapter 20

KION'S CALL

The two combatants circled one another, Strom shifting, Vayd plodding.

"I take a great risk in fighting you here," Vayd said in cavernous tones, far deeper than the voice of any man. "You could easily shoot me down in the midst of battle." He gestured at the archers lining the walls on either side of the gatehouse. "And if I win, you could simply slay me and overwhelm my harriers."

Strom answered back, sure and steady. "We would not be so dishonorable. Is it not I who take the greater risk, wagering the fate of the keep on the outcome of a duel when we could have held out for reinforcements?"

Vayd wagged his head mockingly. "No reinforcements will come. Your fane is a coward and a fool." He took a step toward Strom.

Mutterings of "haukmar lies" trickled through the crowd. One bold man cried out, "Never trust a haukmar. Give him a good thrashing!" But he quailed when Vayd leveled his gaze at him.

Kion gripped the seat of the cart, wondering who would take the first swing. Zinder kept up a low whistle through his teeth, his way of releasing the tension building inside him.

"Don't be so sure you know the mind of the fane. Or the resolve of his people." Strom came out of his stance, kissed his blade, and said, "May you ever strike true." The dull gray sword was unimpressive, but it was not called a longsword for nothing.

Its length was enough to erase the advantage of Vayd's reach. The blade rose swiftly, and Strom shuffled forward so fast, Kion almost missed the move. Strom closed the gap and struck, first high, then low.

Vayd blocked the high stroke with the haft of his axe, and his legs shot back to avoid the second strike, which sliced through a ragged cloth that hung from his belt. Kion didn't see how Vayd could have possibly escaped both attacks when he had been plodding about so methodically. But that was not all. He countered with a great lateral swipe at Strom's neck. It came with too much velocity to parry. Strom dove to the ground and rolled to the side, back on his feet in a blink, his sword at the ready.

Vayd grinned, displaying rows of cracked, stone-like teeth. "It seems we have a fight."

The gathered haukmarn bellowed and stomped and waved their club-like fists in the air. Despite their booming voices and intimidating presence, the townsfolk and soldiers were far greater in number and would not be drowned out by these unwelcome invaders.

Chants of "Strom, Strom, Strom!" thundered through the streets. Kion and Zinder joined in, competing with each other to see who could shout the loudest.

Strom was unmoved by the display. He nodded to his foe and waited.

Vayd's eyes flicked hotly over the crowd. "Your champion will fall as Galbraith fell, just another worm beneath my boot!" A battle cry tore from his throat. He rushed Strom, eyes wide, nostrils flaring. His axe whirled side to side, alternating hands. The *whoosh* of it sounded even above the din.

Strom gave ground, darting left and right, leading Vayd on a wild chase. He was careful not to get too close to the crowd lest one of Vayd's swings slice a helpless spectator.

Vayd could not sustain the whirling strikes forever and at last held his ground. He settled back into a defensive stance, holding his axe in two hands with the haft protecting his body.

Strom raised his sword in the wrath stance and swept in. He unleashed bursts of three, four, and five swings at a time. He was not looking to strike home with any of them, but waiting for Vayd to make a mistake. Short rests between each flurry allowed him to sustain the attacks at an incredible pace.

Vayd ricocheted the axe haft back and forth, careening from one attack to the next. He was quick, but he was tiring. Strom sensed this, his strikes growing bolder. He risked an extended swipe at his enemy's legs. Vayd again dodged backward, bending at the waist so that his legs hopped out of reach. Instead of countering as he had before with a massive swing, he brought the end of the haft full on Strom's face. Blood shot from the bladewarden's nose and streamed from his forehead across his eyes.

The shouting of the townsfolk gave way to a collective gasp.

In the midst of the silence, the fiery voice breathed to life in Kion's ears.

"You must take me up and fight this battle. It is not his to fight."

Kion had been so intent on the battle, his resistance to the voice had weakened. It came roaring back, stronger than ever.

"Do not delay. To resist will only bring sorrow. Once the gift of hearing is granted, you cannot but hear."

Cheers filled the crowd, mercifully pulling Kion's attention away from the voice. Strom was dodging another onslaught of spinning strikes. Vayd hounded him at every step, looming, like a tower about to fall on top of him.

Strom evaded the rain of blows on instinct alone. With so much blood streaming into his eyes, it seemed impossible he could see the attacks coming, but he escaped time and time again.

"Now, glaivebond—take up your sword, before all is lost!" Kion had feared the power of the voice before, but it had spoken gently until now. The words pummeled his will like hammer strokes. Where was it coming from? Was no one else hearing it? Was he going mad?

"The time has come!" stormed the voice.

Kion shouted, "Stop!" but his voice was lost in the crowd. He doubled over and covered his ears. The noise of the crowd was even louder than it had been at the tournament, but still the voice came through.

"Be brave. You know what you must do!" it urged.

But Kion did not feel brave; he was lost, confused, frightened, and weaker than he had ever been before. His awareness of the duel slipped away. He had to get away from the voice, but the people were packed in too tight. But he had to do something. He threw himself over the side of the cart. He fell on top of some unsuspecting fellow, knocking him down.

"What in the fane's britches?" The man's voice was muffled under Kion's bulk. The man squirmed beneath him. Kion rolled off and staggered to his feet, bumbling into three more people. One of them shoved back and told him to watch where he was going.

"Yes, come. There is little time left." said the voice, hotter than forge fire, searing as the sun. It was a blaze of thought and emotions and will and it spread throughout his being, threatening to engulf him.

"I don't understand. Why are you doing this to me?" Kion said.

Cries of "Strom!" and "Bladewarden!" drowned out his voice. Down amongst the gyrating spectators, and bent over in confusion and fear, all he saw were glimpses. One moment Vayd's axe flashed; the next, the back of Strom's head staggered past. All the while, the fire, that unquenchable fire, overpowered the voices around him so that they were no more than a distant echo.

"When you lay hold of me, you will understand. This I promise." The voice was somehow unaffected by the noise. It was like a voice that comes from the waking world into a dream. The words have nothing to do with the dream itself and yet they somehow become part of it. These words now sought to lead

him back to the waking world, to lead him out of the dream. He did not want to wake, but if the voice persisted, he feared he could not help it.

He flailed through the mass of people toward the duel, drawn as if lashed by invisible chains.

"Hurry. There is little time left if you wish to save the one called Strom."

"Strom? Strom is in trouble? What have you done to him?"

The crowd jostled and jerked, but Kion kept pushing. He was almost to the front now. Strom dodged a whirlwind of blows. Vayd was wounded in many places, but mostly on his arms, and nothing that looked serious.

Strom was limping. He no longer fought with his sword in two hands, but one. The other was pressed against his side, the arm covered in blood.

"You must take me up now, or this fortress is lost!"

"Who are you?" Kion asked, bursting through into the first row.

Vayd was breathing heavily, Strom even heavier. They had both spent themselves, given all they had to the fight. But Vayd yet had some strength left. It was clear to everyone that Strom was beaten. All it would take was one more cut from the axe. What honor or will held Strom upright, it was impossible to say. Yet even in defeat, it was a wonder to behold.

"Kneel before me and I will make your death painless and swift," Vayd said.

Strom staggered, then rose to his full height. He held his sword with both hands above his head in the wrath stance. Blood flowed freely from his side.

"I will not yield. I will not relent. My honor is my blood, and my duty is my heart." His face was streaked with blood, his appearance no longer noble or high, but his words brought silence upon the keep. Even the harriers paused in their mocking.

"Here I am. Take me and fight! Fight and win!" said the voice.

And for the first time, Kion knew where the voice came from. It came from Strom's sword.

But how? How could an old gray piece of metal speak? It was impossible. And why was no one else hearing this voice? He surveyed the crowd. Surely someone must have heard it, but all eyes were focused on the duel.

"I'm not thinking straight. I must have come down with Tiryn's fever. It's overtaken my mind," Kion said.

"*No. You have never been more sane. This is what you were born to. You are a swordspeaker. Now take me up and win this battle!*"

Kion took a step forward, then stopped. Vayd was a giant, ten times the warrior Kion was. He had bested Strom Glyre, the greatest swordsman in the Four Wards.

"This is folly," he muttered.

Vayd also lifted his weapon high. The axehead gleamed, wet with blood. It loomed so large it seemed to blot out the sun.

"If honor is your blood, then prepare to spill the last of your honor on these stones."

"*Now, swordspeaker! Now!*"

Kion froze. He knew he should obey, but his heart failed. He could not accept certain death.

Strom let forth a cry. Vayd answered with a louder one. The two rushed headlong toward each other. Strom's blade came down at the same time as Vayd's. The axe brushed it aside like chaff in the wind. The sword flew from Strom's hands. The axe fell in murderous descent. It plunged into Strom's shoulder, separating sinew from bone.

Strom Glyre, Bladewarden and hero of the Four Wards, fell.

Vayd shouted in triumph, louder than a trumpet blast, but never had a trumpet sounded so cruel. His harriers blew their horns. Out on the plains, the waiting army sounded its reply. Each note rang out like a dirge throughout the keep. Each note pierced Kion's heart deeper and deeper. Strom, the best of men, had fallen, and Kion had done nothing but stand there and watch him die.

The soldiers lining the walls and those at the edge of the crowd crossed their arms in reverent salute.

Vayd's wicked grin proclaimed what everyone was thinking. The war seemed, at that moment, over before it began. The haukmarn had won it with one fell stroke. Vayd paraded haughtily around the edge of the crowd.

"I have beaten your champion! The best your pathetic race has to offer. You are nothing but chattel to me. The Fortress of the Clefts is mine!"

The harriers shouted guttural words in reply, too wild and incoherent to be understood.

"You have failed, but not utterly." The voice of the sword came back, still hot as a scorching summer wind. *"If the ancient rites hold true, a commoner may make a second challenge when a champion of noble blood falls."*

Kion was too devastated at that point to resist. The dream was over. He was awake now, cold and shivering in a bed bereft of comfort.

"Challenge Vayd?" Kion said. It had seemed unthinkable only a moment before. But Strom's death made Kion desperate to atone for his mistake. He saw that there might still be some virtue in doing late what ought to have been done before. Failure once was no reason for failure twice.

Only half aware of what he was doing, Kion stepped into the open space.

"I claim the right of the commoner to defend the fallen. He who can defeat a champion must also stand ready to prove himself against the lowliest citizen of a realm, according to the ancient rites...Or so I believe it says, though I may not have the words quite right."

Vayd's momentary shock gave way to a mocking sneer. "You? A red-faced whelp? Are you his ill-gotten son?"

"Will you face me, or be marked as a coward?" Kion wasn't sure where the words, much less his boldness, came from. Terror bristled up and down his spine. His throat turned to rust.

Sunstroke could not have made him any weaker. And yet he stood there, staring at Vayd defiantly.

"You have no weapon. A challenger, even a commoner, must have a weapon."

Kion pointed to Strom's sword. "I will fight with his." He started toward the blade.

Vayd shook his head and let out a brutal laugh. He brought his foot down on top of Strom's sword just as Kion knelt to pick it up. Kion's hands tingled with anticipation. As much as he had resisted the sword's voice before, he longed for it now more than breath itself. He had to have it. He had to face this enemy, though he had no hope of winning.

"No," Vayd said. "You must fight with your own weapon. And as you have none, your claim to the challenge is invalidated." He kicked Kion in the gut with his massive boot. It hit like a charging ram. He doubled over beside Strom's body.

Vayd lifted his arms in triumph as he paced before the crowd. "Would anyone else—with a weapon—care to throw his life away? I am more than willing to spill the blood of those who wish to die."

No answer came, but in the silence, Kion heard a whisper.

"Have you come back to save me one last time?"

It took Kion a moment to recognize where it came from, until he saw Strom staring at him with eyes open wide.

"You're alive?" Kion said, sliding over, forgetting his own pain.

"I never knew your name. But I never forgot you," Strom said. Blood spat from his lips with each word.

"What? I don't understand," Kion said, certain Strom must be delirious in his final moments.

"You played the song...the song that rallied my men at Fane's Falling...the song that won the war. I can hear it even now..."

At that moment the ten-year-old wall surrounding Kion's

heart cracked in two, and tears welled up in his eyes. Was Strom delirious? Or was it...could it be?

"You mean Dorn? Are you talking about Dorn, my father?" Kion asked.

Strom struggled to speak. There was commotion amongst the crowd now. Soldiers were moving in. Vayd was bellowing commands in a voice of iron.

"You look so much like him. I thought it must be..." Strom whispered through bloody lips. "Thank your father for me. Thank him for his song. It gave me strength, when the tides of battle grew grim. Into the hope of that song I now go...though strength fades, the will grows stronger."

Then he shut his eyes and spoke no more.

Chapter 21

TRUESILVER

our soldiers lifted Strom's body from the ground. A fifth knelt and lifted Kion. It was the bearded swordswain who had officiated the duel. His bright eyes glistened with tears.

"That was foolish of you, my son," he said. "But also one of the bravest things I have ever seen."

"I am sorry," Kion said. "I failed him."

The crowd was breaking up. Some stayed to watch Strom's body carried away; others rushed to their homes. They had but one hour to clear out their things. Vayd left with half his harriers while the other half went to occupy the gatehouse.

"There was nothing you could have done. Strom knew the risk. All warriors taste defeat one day, whether by an enemy's blade or time's withering hand," the swordswain said. "I am just glad that today was not your day. We will need courage like yours in times ahead. May it never fail you." He gave Kion a cross-armed salute.

A stillness washed over Kion. He didn't know why he found the soldier's words so comforting. It was not so much the man's praise, but a peace that came from knowing he had answered the call he had been given, even if he had answered it too late. And yet, that peace was not complete. For Strom was dead, and nothing could change that. If only Kion had taken up the sword when it had called. He cast his eyes about the courtyard, searching for the blade, but it was nowhere to be seen. The absence of its voice left a cold emptiness in his mind.

"Sir," Kion said, catching the man as he turned to follow the soldiers carrying away Strom's body. "Where is Strom's sword? I didn't see who picked it up."

The man surveyed the square with a puzzled expression. "That is a good question. I do not believe any of my men picked it up. And I know Vayd did not carry it off. Odd. I hate to think one of the commoners might have taken it. We will have to organize a search for it. It is the sword of the bladewardens, after all. Thank you for reminding me. In my grief, it slipped my mind."

As the swordswain disappeared into the milling crowds that lingered to see off their champion, Zinder's cart came clacking over the pavement.

"Are you all right, lad? Shar's Dome, you had me scared out of my wits. I crushed a perfectly good hat on your account," Zinder said. Indeed, the poor hat he clutched looked like it would never recover. The near-battle with Vayd had left Zinder's face almost as pale as his beard.

"Why didn't you try to stop me, then?" Kion asked.

"It is forbidden by the laws of the challenge to interfere. How did you know about the commoner challenge, anyway? It doesn't seem the sort of thing Dorn would have taught you."

"Zinder, I have to tell you something," Kion said, lowering his voice, though the gatehouse road grew more deserted by the moment. "Strom spoke to me before he died. He said he knew my father. He talked about the song that rallied the soldiers at Fane's Falling. He said my father's song won the war."

Zinder looked off to the side with faraway wonder. "That sounds about right, lad. I never did put any faith in that talk about him calling a retreat. Well, that must have been something special. What a gift for you. Even in death Strom defended the innocent. If you live a hundred years, you'll not see his like again. You can mark that."

A cart came racing past and nearly sideswiped them. Off in the distance, the discordant horns of the haukmarn sounded, and the low thunder of their army on the move sent everyone scurrying even faster.

"Come now, lad," Zinder said. "We must be off at once. I expect we'll have to vacate Furrow as well. We'll need to get there before the haukmarn and gather what things we can."

Kion stared at the people and carts rushing all around them, still in too much shock to grasp what was happening. "But where will we go?"

"Charring. They'll be able to put up a token defense, maybe slow the haukmarn down, at least. And your mother and sister are likely still there. Once we find them, we can decide what to do next."

As the cart pulled away from Roving, Kion stared long at the magnificent towers that rose above the town. Only yesterday, the sight had swelled his heart with pride and awe at the majesty of Inris and the strength of its defenses. His only hope had been to see Strom and restore his father's honor. In the end, he was granted both, but in a way both far worse and far better than he had ever hoped. Even if no one else ever believed it, Kion now knew that his father had been a hero at Fane's Falling, a hero whose song had inspired the great Strom Glyre to victory. Yet that knowledge had come as the dying gift from the man Kion looked up to more than any other apart from his father.

Kion scanned the field for his father's burial mound. Throngs of haukmarn stood upon it now, desecrating it by their very presence. They did not belong here. They did not deserve to stand within a hundred miles of that hallowed hill. The fire he'd felt before the duel flared up again inside him. "I'll drive them from this place, Father," Kion promised. "I'll finish what you came here to do, and this time I'll make sure they never come back."

The cart rolled on through the endless ranks of the haukmar

host. The two friends, along with a growing stream of refugees, hurried past the watching harriers along either side of the road. Yesterday the haukmarn had been nothing more than a byword, a whisper blowing somewhere far away on the wind. Now, they surrounded Kion on every side. They leered and jeered as he passed. The acrid stench from the stones in their armor battered his senses until he had to hold his sleeve over his nose to keep from gagging. Not all of them wore armor, though. The ones who didn't pulled carts loaded with heaps of scrap metal or open sacks of pickled fish or other slimy victuals. Some labored under huge packs, towering two to three feet above their heads. These burden bearers had scars and lashings stamped on their skin. Without their armor, the haukmarn looked even more freakish. Their heads were tall and narrow, and sat atop thick, squat necks. Oversized hands and arms, and hunched shoulders, gave the impression of creatures ill-suited to their own bodies, as if they'd been made from fleshly scraps and castoffs. Vayd and his personal guard, by contrast, were far more well-proportioned.

The haukmar siege engines were even more ugly and misshapen than their masters. Built from dozens of ill-fitting planks and just enough nails to keep them from flying apart, they looked more like scaffolding on wheels than engines of war. Wider than they were tall, they could not have been easy to maneuver, especially with teams of three muskoxen pulling them. Each engine had five wooden arms on top, bent back like a catapult. Each arm ended in a pouch-like container made of metal mesh.

"Those are the lashtails," Zinder said.

"What do they put in the buckets?"

"Scrap metal, mostly. Though in the last war, they fired balls of flaming pitch in a few battles."

"Why aren't more of the haukmarn going to occupy the keep?" Kion said. Though Roving could not have held anything close to the full haukmar army, only about two hundred were marching toward the gates. Thousands more remained standing on the battlefield.

"It does not take many to hold a fortress like the Clefts. The rest of the army will be sent elsewhere," Zinder said.

A few snarling dreadwulfs strained against their handlers' chains at the back of the haukmar ranks. They were enormous, even taller than Kion. Their eyes glowed white. Wisps of blanched smoke issued from them, as if they had wanstones instead of eyes to see. Their wicked-looking fangs snapped, and their ragged claws scraped the ground, pawing to be loosed. It took two haukmarn to restrain each one. From the looks on their handlers' faces, they would have liked nothing more than to release their beasts on the defenseless refugees.

Zinder slid away from the edge of the cart and the terrible creatures. He snapped the reins to quicken Crusty's pace.

The haukmar ranks began to thin. Kion and Zinder, along with a cavalcade of refugees, left the army behind and passed through the lowlands and up the far slope, which led into the valley of Roving. As they crested the hill, they had their last view of the fortress. The white banners had fallen. An air of doom rose in their place. The fortress stood cold and lifeless and dour, a massive gravestone signifying Strom's defeat.

Kion turned bitterly and did not look back. He rode on in silence, his heart turned to ash. He longed for things to go back to the way they had been, longed for his mother's embrace, or Tiryn's songs, but the road he now traveled offered only hollow regrets and tuneless memories. The world of only one short day ago was ground to dust beneath the boots of the haukmar army. What would happen to Furrow? To the flock? The haukmar invasion changed everything. He could no longer be responsible for the fate of his sheep. At least not until he found his family again. And yet, even if he did find them, how would they survive with no wool or milk to sell?

An uncertain, trackless path lay before him. The way seemed strewn with thorns and choked with bramble. Who would protect them from the haukmarn? The margrave would surely send his soldiers, but without the bladewarden, how could they hope to push back such an innumerable host? Warding's protector was gone, his life snuffed out, leaving all of Inris shuddering in darkness. But though his light had dwindled, the memory of Strom's final words made the darkened, briar-choked road possible for Kion to bear. For Strom had given Kion's father back his honor, and that would bring comfort even on the blackest nights.

Kion gripped Strom's journal on his knees, stroking the thick leather cover. The bladewarden's deeds, his great victories, would live on in the hearts of the people and the great books of history, but his thoughts, the words that told of Strom the man, lived now only here, in this journal.

"Well, are you going to read it or not?" Zinder asked.

"I don't know. I want to. Would it be disrespectful?"

"I don't think so. Unless you think it's too soon."

"Maybe it would be all right to read just a little." Kion slid his finger inside the cover, flipped past the page identifying the book as Strom's property, and began to read:

Avring 1, 822

My first day at the Avelar Batal. It is an honor to be training at the finest battle school in all of Warding. So many of the great heroes of the past have come through this place. I wonder if any of the men here now will be worthy of that tradition? I met a fellow aspirant named Ivers Kendsford. Odd fellow. He seems a bit out of place, as if he knows he doesn't quite belong here but makes up for it with a sort of brash confidence. We'll see how he fares tomorrow at the drills. And how will I fare? Do I belong here? I suppose I'll find out soon enough. If only—

Zinder interrupted with a hoarse cough. "Sorry, lad. Would

you be so kind as to fetch the waterskin? My throat's still parched from all that screaming I did during the duel."

Kion slid the journal back into its satchel and rummaged through the supplies behind them, unable to find the waterskin at first. At length he spotted Zinder's traveling bag at the very back. "Why did you put it all the way back there?" Kion asked.

"Sorry, lad. I was in a bit of a rush, if you remember."

Kion crawled over the other supplies: his own satchel, their bedrolls, the sack of food, and the bundle of swords. The bundle had been retied, but not as neatly as before. Another sword, with a good deal of pitting on its lusterless blade, lay at the bottom of the cart, wedged beneath the bundle so it wouldn't shift about on the journey.

"What's this? Did you offer to restore some poor fool's sword?" Kion asked.

"Eh, what's that?" Zinder turned, and Kion pointed. "Oh, that rusted old thing. Yes, well, after Strom's death, a fellow came up to me who wanted to buy one of the others. I was in no mood to do business after a tragedy like that, but he was desperate. He couldn't afford the full price, so he offered to trade me his old sword plus a few silvers. The oddest thing was, he was fantastically dressed. Had a fancy hat I'd rather have taken than that sword, but the sword was all he would trade. Strange fellow. He looked oddly familiar, but he had a scarf covering half his face, so I couldn't see exactly what he looked like."

Kion retrieved the waterskin and handed it to him. But something about that rusted sword stuck in his mind. He felt as though he had to inspect it; whether from curiosity or to make fun of Zinder for trading for it, or some other reason, he couldn't say.

"Mind if I have a look?" Kion asked.

"I don't see why not. I can tell by your eyes you've taken a fancy to it. But it'll make a poor substitute for the one I made you, I can tell you that," Zinder said, puzzled at Kion's sudden interest.

"Wait." It was the fiery voice. It flared to life like a red-hot brand in the darkness.

"What—no. It can't be. It's you, isn't it?" Kion said.

"Yes, but now is not the time. Wait until you get farther away from the fortress."

Zinder turned back around. "What's that, lad? What's that gibberish you're talking?"

Kion had been talking out loud, he realized. It felt more like a thought.

"You didn't hear that, Zinder?" Kion asked.

"I heard you blabbing, that's what I heard."

"You didn't hear the voice telling me to wait?"

"He can't hear me. He's not a swordspeaker," the voice said.

"Wait? What are you talking about?" Zinder said. "We're the only folk within half a mile. And unless mules can talk, I'd say you're hearing things." Zinder scowled, studied Kion's face, then scowled some more. "You're serious, aren't you?" He guided Crusty off the road and stopped the cart. "All right, now. Time to set things square. You've been discombobulated ever since the duel. I thought maybe it was Strom's death, or you were worried about your family, but it's something else, isn't it?"

Kion's hands began to sweat. He glanced back at the sword. "How do I tell him?"

Zinder looked at the back of the cart. "Do we have a stowaway? Is there someone back there? He'd have to be smaller than a newborn nyn to hide in that, but I wouldn't put it past one. We're born crafty."

"Zinder," Kion said.

"All right. Maybe not *that* crafty. What's going on?"

"Tell him the truth. You are a swordspeaker and I am your glaive," the voice said. It was still a voice of fire, almost too intense for his ears, but after what happened with Strom, he sensed he could trust it.

"I don't understand what's happening." Kion wasn't even

sure who the words were addressed to: Zinder, himself, or the voice from the sword.

"*The direct approach is usually preferable.*"

"Calm down, lad. You're worried. Anyone can see that. The day dawned hard for all of us. But we'll pull through."

"It's not that, Zinder. It's that sword, the rusty one. It's... it's..."

"It's what?"

"*The truth, glaivebond.*"

"It's talking to me."

Zinder's mouth hung open. He didn't blink for the longest time. "It's talking to you? That sword?" He moved toward it.

Kion grabbed him by the arm. "I don't think you should touch it. It told me to wait."

"Wickets and crickets, you're talking nonsense!" Zinder shook him off and reached down to pick up the sword. Kion tried to grab hold of him again, but Zinder was too quick. He unwedged the sword from beneath the others and hefted it aloft. Kion cringed, waiting for repercussions, but Zinder was perfectly fine. "So this old ruster is what all the fuss is about? I should never have traded for it. What a nuisance. I've half a mind to throw it in the ditch."

"No—don't. I know it sounds crazy, but I have to be honest with you. I heard a voice in Roving and I'm hearing it now. And it's telling me not to touch it, at least not until we get farther away from the fortress."

Zinder let out a squirrelly whistle, utterly unconvinced. "Listen, lad. You've been through an awful lot. I'll tell you what. Why don't you pull out one of the bedrolls and take a rest in the back of the cart while I get us back on the road?" He returned the sword to where he'd found it.

"*That is fine. I will tell you when it is time to take me up,*" said the sword.

"Why were you silent until now? And what happened to you after the battle? How did you turn into this?" The questions tumbled from Kion's lips. He couldn't help himself. This was all so impossibly strange.

"Lad, you really need to give up on this prank or delirium or whatever it is. Take a rest now. I'm ordering you, as your Mother's official...nyn."

"You see how your friend is reacting? That is why I've remained silent. He will not understand. Not until after the bonding, and perhaps not even then."

The bonding? This was more confusing than ever. But he had to calm Zinder down. "Mother never gave you any authority over me, Zinder. I'd like to point that out. But I'll lie down if it will make you feel better."

Kion crawled into the back and made a place for himself.

"Yes, lad, just rest. You'll wake up in a few short hours and we'll forget all about this talking sword nonsense." It took a few flicks of the reins and some cajoling, but the cart got moving again.

They rumbled on for a few miles after that without a word. Kion tried his best to actually sleep, but he could no more sleep than jump the moon. He kept his eyes closed to calm Zinder's doubts, but restless thoughts spun inside him. What did the sword mean about bonding? How would he ever make Zinder believe he wasn't crazy? Or what if he *was* crazy?

By midday, the gray clouds had passed. The sun sparkled upon the rock-strewn plains, but it shone with a cheerless light. The refugees who had left Roving with them had by now either forged ahead or fallen behind. Their cart was all alone. They stopped to give Crusty a rest and take a quick meal. The moment the wheels stopped moving, the fiery voice returned.

"It is time."

Kion sat up like a smokecracker had just gone off in the cart.

Zinder, obliviously humming away, grabbed the rations and waterskins.

"Now?" Kion asked.

Zinder narrowed his eyes, and the humming stopped. He

held a package of rations hovering in the air between himself and Kion.

"*Yes, now. It is time for you to know the truth,*" the voice said. A wave of heat rose from deep inside Kion's chest.

"Yes, now," Zinder said. "You just told me how hungry you were."

The voice returned. "*Do not answer him. Answers will come easier once he has witnessed the bonding. For now, let him step away from the cart, lest he be frightened.*"

A trickle of sweat streaked down the side of Kion's face. Fear of what the sword intended spread like wildfire inside him. He took the rations and stayed in the cart as Zinder hopped down.

Zinder eyed him with a look of worry that only deepened when Kion did not follow him down.

"I'll be right there, Zinder," Kion said. "There's something I need to do first."

Not a drop of moisture remained in Kion's throat. It had all seeped out in a sudden flash of sweat around his face. With a will and resolve not his own, he stepped into the back of the cart and shoved the bundle of swords aside.

"Lad, you're starting to worry me," Zinder said, not taking his eyes off Kion.

Kion did not hesitate. Something in him knew he had to hold this weapon. He reached down and grabbed hold of the blade.

Fire flashed through his body. It burned with real heat this time, not merely an inner sensation. The blade hummed with otherworldly energy. It was like a heart that had yet to beat but brimmed with life. Without knowing what he was doing, Kion held the blade aloft and let forth a visceral cry. The sound echoed off the hills. From the distant, smoldering sun, or perhaps beyond it, shot an amber beam of quickening light. Its brightness should have blinded him, but Kion saw all this with something more than his eyes, and so endured it.

The shining ray burned through the sky, a smoldering streak across the clouds. It lanced into Kion's upheld blade, scattering into a thousand glittering fragments. The light burst over his body, the swords, the supplies, the cart, and all. The pitted metal and rust of the blade boiled and simmered beneath this cleansing radiance. The outer metal curdled and peeled and disappeared altogether in a volcanic flash.

As quickly as it had come, the blazing light engulfing Kion and the cart died away. Kion, along with everything else, was as before, but not the sword. It had been utterly transformed.

The sword's voice returned, but for the first time, it was no longer fiery. It was gentle and wise and somehow like the voice Kion had always longed to hear, but had been too afraid to listen for. He marveled that he could ever have found it threatening.

"I am Kithian the True, first of the Mastersmith's glaives. But to those not gifted in the swordspeaker's ways, I have another name. To the wider world, I am known as Truesilver."

Chapter 22

AFLAME

Zinder's rations and waterskin rolled out of his limp hands and onto the dirt. Lunch was entirely forgotten.

"Wha—wha—wha...?" he stammered. They were the only sounds he could make for some time.

Kion jumped down from the cart. Zinder backpedaled away so fast he slipped and fell.

"Wha—what just happened, lad?" Zinder finally managed.

Kion still knew almost nothing, but the mysterious connection he felt with the sword told him that he would not stay ignorant for long. But there was one thing he understood, even now.

"I am a swordspeaker. And this is my glaive."

The blade was the most exquisite creation he had ever seen. It shone in the high sun with a warm, silvery sheen, nothing like the cold steel glint of an ordinary blade. The surface was clean and pure; no mark or nick blemished the metal. Zinder could not have polished it any brighter if he'd gone at it for forty days. The hilt was fitted with a blazing citrine, perfectly round. The gem sat in the center of the guard, rimmed by golden triangles. A smaller citrine adorned each end of the cross-guard. Metal prongs projected from the ends, formed and etched to look like metal flames. The pommel was the plainest thing about it. It was fashioned in the form of two triangles, one large, one small, inverted towards each other and overlapping at the tips. Warmth radiated from the grip, as if the sword had sat out all morning in the sun.

"A swordspeaker? What does that mean?" Zinder said, dusting himself off and getting to his feet. "And this marvelous work of singular beauty, where in the Four Wards did you get it? Did it come down with the light?"

"The sword's name is Kithian, but it is also known as Truesilver. And it speaks to me, somehow, though you don't seem to be able to hear it. It says it came from the Mastersmith. I suppose the same one mentioned in your poem, the *Lay of the Glaives*."

"*You've read the* Lay?" Kithian asked, intensely curious.

"Only part of it. I have no idea what it means."

"Wait." Zinder waved his arms. "Are you talking to it again?"

"Yes, sorry," Kion said. "It was asking about the *Lay*." He turned back to the blade. "So is there more than one glaive, then? The part I read only mentioned two weapons."

"*There are many. Though it has been so long since I have been awake, it may be that the others are lost.*"

"And are they all like you? Can the other swords think and talk, too?" Kion asked.

"*Yes, though not all are swords.*"

"Now you listen here, lad," Zinder said. "I'm not going to just sit here drooling while you carry on these private conversations with that thing in your hand—if it really talks, which I am still not entirely sure I'm ready to sign off on. But if it does talk, the least you could do is fill me in on the conversation!"

"Right, sorry. Kithian—Truesilver—the sword—was telling me that it is one of the glaives written about in the *Lay of the Glaives*. There are others as well, weapons that can talk and think, though I suppose talking isn't the right word, since no one else can hear its voice. Those of us who can are called swordspeakers."

Zinder stared at the blade with hesitant wonder. Whatever his opinion of Kion's claims, as a blacksmith he could not hide his sheer delight at gazing upon a work of such supreme craftsmanship. "You say there are others? So did this Mastersmith make them as well? And if he's still alive, would he teach me, I wonder?" Zinder moved closer, asking with his eyes if he could touch the blade.

Kion knew, though he couldn't say how, that Truesilver was no danger to a friend. He lowered the blade so Zinder could get a better look. For the first time Kion realized how light it was. It was like holding a dried stick, yet it had a sturdiness to it that made it feel stronger than any other blade he had ever held.

"You see again why I love poetry and stories? It's because they aren't just words on a page, they're about real, actual things, things with a history and a past—like this!" Zinder's eyes sparkled as he gingerly reached out and touched the blade. "But the *Lay* didn't say anything about talking swords, or rather talking swords that nobody can understand except 'swordspeakers.' And this Mastersmith—who is he, after all? He's no doubt the greatest smith I've ever heard of. I can't even tell what material this is."

Kion addressed the blade. "Yes, who is the Mastersmith?"

"You have not heard of him? That is indeed troubling. Once all knew his name and revered him. These must be dark days if you have now forgotten him. Without his will and sustaining power, nothing would or could exist. It is he who makes life and all matter with the hammer of his thought. He can fashion it from any material he wishes, or from nothing at all, for he is one with the Spark, which is a great mystery that even the glaives do not fully comprehend."

"I'm still not sure I understand. Where is he now? Does he know you found me? What does he want me to do with you?" Kion knew without asking that Kithian was meant for him and he for the sword. The bonding had left no question about that in his mind, though beyond that, all was cloaked in mystery.

"Ah-ah-ah, don't forget!" Zinder reminded him. Kion quickly summarized what Kithian had just told him.

When Kion finished, Truesilver continued, *"The Mastersmith is at his forge, where he ever is and always shall be. But as for what his plans are, I do not know. But of this you can be sure: they are good and shall be made known in the fullness of time. I am sure he has some mighty work for us to do. And we shall begin this battle as we begin all battles, by fighting the foe in front of us."*

"And who is that, the haukmarn?" Kion asked, after informing Zinder what Kithian had said.

"Are they before you now? No, the haukmarn will have to wait. The first battle is the open road. You and your friend spoke of your home and your family. Wisdom tells me that haste is of the essence. We have tarried here long enough. Let us ride forth while we still have light, and we shall speak more along the way."

Kion learned much as they traveled, always relaying what Kithian said to Zinder, though sometimes he got so carried away that Zinder had to remind him with an elbow to the ribs.

"From your questions, I can see that I have slept long," Kithian said. *"And from the times of old, it seems that much has changed."*

"Did you fight in any wars? Zinder says the haukmarn have sought to conquer our lands for hundreds of years."

"I have no memory of the haukmarn. Those giants who took the fortress did not exist in my time."

Strange. How old could this blade be if it was from before the time of the haukmarn? They had dwelt in the lands north of Inris for as long as anyone knew.

Zinder chimed in at that point. He seemed to be warming to the idea that the sword could actually talk, though he had yet to admit it openly. "Ask it about why it looked so different before— you know, all rusty and so forth. Can it turn itself into anything it wants? Because a massive stallion would come in quite handy right about now. No offense, Crusty."

"Tell him that no, I can only change my appearance in subtle ways. I will always be a sword as long as the Mastersmith wills."

"Why did you hide your true form from Strom?" Kion said. "Why didn't you call out to him the way you called out to me?"

"The call goes out only to those for whom it is meant. You are a swordspeaker. He was not."

The idea that Kion had some ability that Strom lacked was hard to imagine. Then again, nothing about a talking sword was natural.

"You were the voice in my dreams, weren't you? I remember now. But the first time was a month ago, or more. Why didn't you speak to me again until I came to Roving?"

"The distance was too great. Strom passed through your village that night. That is the night I awoke. Since then, I have been calling out to you when I had the strength—calling, always calling, hoping to find you once more."

If only Kion had listened to Truesilver's call in time, he might have saved Strom. Watching him die had been the most terrible ordeal he had suffered since the death of his father. Heroes were not supposed to die. Not like that. Strom should have been the swordspeaker. He certainly would have defeated Vayd if Truesilver had been in his present form. The blade's heft and balance, its masterful lines, and, most importantly, the strange living energy that pulsed inside it gave Kion the belief that he could hold his ground against almost any foe. He could only imagine what it could have done in the hands of a master like Strom.

Kion kept the sword on his lap as they traveled, for they had no sheaths for the swords Zinder had brought. A pleasant warmth radiated from the blade. Zinder was right. It was unlike any metal either of them had ever seen. Even when the sun passed behind the clouds, it glowed softly, as if in memory of the light. And when the sun shone forth, it dazzled like light on the water.

They passed a few travelers on foot headed to Charring, but there was no need to ask for news. The haukmarn were abroad, and by now all Casting Selvedge knew. The very air hung thick and close with the threat of battle.

As the trail passed on through the white grasses of the Wimwissle Swath, Kion found that Kithian had just as many questions as he did. He wanted to know about the state of Inrisward and Verisward, about the fane, about Gilding, about the War of the Claws, and whatever else Kion could think to relay regarding recent events. Kion had to defer to Zinder on most things, because he himself had only ever heard snatches of what went on outside of Furrow.

What Kion could tell him about most was his family. Kithian was particularly interested to hear about them. He wanted to know not only about Kion's mother and sister, but about his father. Usually, Kion avoided speaking about him. It was too painful. But he found himself telling Kithian everything he could think of—about the wonderful father he had been and how talented and kind he was, and how he had died a hero in the Battle of Fane's Falling.

"Strom said his song won the war," Kion said proudly.

The hard thing now was to speak of his mother and Tiryn. Guilt that he had snuck off to Roving haunted him. His decision seemed a childish lark in light of everything that had happened since, not to mention that he would be a day closer to Charring right now if he didn't have to travel from Roving.

He told Kithian about Tiryn's illness but assured him she must have recovered by now. Inwardly, his doubts festered. He remembered her feverish ramblings and the vacant look in her eyes, and he could not erase those images for all that he tried.

As the sun set, a faint rumbling drifted across the plains. Zinder stopped the cart, and they looked off into the distance. Far behind them, a whitish glow crept over the horizon, like an ill-born sunrise from the north. Minutes later, the glowstone-studded ranks of the haukmar army seeped over the hills.

"Shar's Dome, they've come," Zinder said. He snapped the reins and steered Crusty toward the grass and bushes beside the road. With great reluctance, Crusty turned from the well-trav-eled road onto the turf beside it. Zinder showed no mercy to the mule as he pushed him on with angry shouts and snapping reins until they reached the top of a small hill. As they crested it, a glimmering river of haukmar harriers appeared to the north, closing toward them.

"*Tell me what you see,*" Kithian said.

"The haukmarn are marching south along the road, a thousand strong, maybe more."

"*You told me more than ten thousand stood outside the gates at Roving. They are dividing their forces, then.*"

"That leader of theirs is cunning," Zinder said.

"Do you think they saw us?" Kion said. Though Truesilver no longer shone as brightly as he did during the day, Kion covered it with his cloak to avoid the blade reflecting the moonlight.

"I doubt it. We are one tiny tuft in all this wide land. They are hunting far bigger game." Even so, they covered the rest of the swords in the back as well.

The cart rolled quickly down the other side of the hill, out of view of the road.

"We'll have to travel overland for now," Zinder said.

"Will the cart be able to handle it?" They were still at least three hours from Furrow, and rocks and divots filled the land.

"I don't know." Zinder's grim answer matched his expression. His eyes scanned the ground ahead, searching out the smoothest stretches. Kion would never have been able to spy out a safe route in the moonlight, but Zinder's nynnian eyes were far keener than his.

"Maybe they'll stop and make camp," Kion said. If not, there was no way he and Zinder could reach Furrow before the haukmarn.

"And maybe we'll make popcorn on ice! Haukmarn can march faster and longer than any man. On a war march, they sometimes go two or three days without rest. When those feeble minds of theirs are set on a task, naught that lives and breathes will hinder them."

"Mother and Tiryn…" Kion said. What if they had already returned to Furrow and the haukmarn reached there first?

"Steady yourself, swordspeaker. Remember, we may only fight the battle before us. The fate of your family has not yet been made clear. We will fight for them when the hour comes."

Warmth from the blade filled Kion's lap, but as the echoes of the marching armies grew from a murmur to a growl to a roar, the image of his mother and sister lying dead in the fields grew harder and harder to shake. Though he could no longer see the road or the relentless hordes, judging by the sounds of their rumbling advance, the haukmarn overtook them within the hour. As Crusty gamely pulled them on through the dark, scraggly plains, the rumble of the marching army dwindled further and further. By the second hour it was gone altogether. The sparks appeared overhead, drawing their golden hatchings across the ebony blue sky. The patterns looked even more chaotic and indecipherable than usual. If only Kion could fly as fast as they did and see as far.

Slowed miserably by the terrain, the cart trundled through the night.

"How close are we to Furrow?" Kion asked at length. A waning moon shed precious little light on the land around them. The knobby rocks and sparse trees told him they were back in the Tors, but nothing looked familiar.

"Close, lad, close," Zinder said. He leaned forward in his seat, as if he could make the mule go faster by doing so. A few moments later he let out a gasp. "Oh, no…"

"What?" Kion saw what Zinder saw, but his mind failed to grasp it. "What is that light on the horizon? It's not white, so it couldn't be the haukmarn."

Zinder's mouth gaped, his voice choked in silence, but Kithian answered for him.

"Fire," he said.

"Are you sure? Can you see that far?" Kion asked, disbelieving.

"No, but I can feel it," Kithian answered. Never before had the blade's words robbed Kion of warmth. They did so now.

As the cart creaked up to the top of the next hill, Zinder found his voice.

"Furrow is in flames."

Chapter 23

SHEEP WITHOUT A SHEPHERD

Zinder armed his crossbow, then hooked a case of bolts onto his belt.

Kion gripped Truesilver. His muscles tingled with anticipation and fear. He did not want to fight the haukmarn. Two against a thousand was madness, no matter how perfect the blade. And yet, he yearned to find out how the sword would handle in battle. Like a caged bird, Kion longed to see it fly.

They left Crusty tethered to a hawthorn tree in a sheltered valley, half a mile north of town.

"It's not likely any of the haukmarn would linger in a place like Furrow, but if we do need to hide, we'd best be on foot," Zinder said.

"Why put it to the flame? Why didn't they just capture it like Roving?" Kion said. The glow from the other side of the hill ran like a tear through the fabric of his mind. Never had he seen a more malevolent light.

"For sport, I imagine, and out of the cruelty that rages in their hearts. They wouldn't waste time capturing a place like this. They've got bigger conquests in mind. But that didn't stop them from sacking Furrow just to watch it burn—the monsters."

"The desire for power and destruction are bound together. I am deeply sorry about your home," Kithian said.

Furrow. Yes, it was home, after all. The only one Kion had ever known. He realized at that moment that he did love his village, and its people, however little love they may have shown for him. What did those petty disagreements and insults matter now? He would have suffered a mountain of insults, if it meant that they were still alive. What he wouldn't give to see the people who, only a few days ago, he'd vowed never to see again.

The blazing fire awaited. Would there be anything left? His mind wandered through the streets of his village, past Memory Lawn, the Fielder's House, Mistress Shona's shop, and… "Oh, Zinder, your smithy," Kion said. "Do you think there's any chance it survived?"

Zinder gazed steadily at the ember horizon.

"No, I don't suppose it did," he said, his voice uncharacteristically deep. "All my work, all those years sweating over the anvil…all gone in a moment, vanished in a breath." He hung his head. Kion did not know what to say. Zinder's work meant everything to him. Not to mention his collection of books and rare parchments.

"I'm sorry," was all Kion could think to say.

Zinder's head rose, and the old gleam sparked in his eyes. "It's nothing compared to your mother and sister. Come now, we must reach your cottage and see if by chance they've returned. And if we come upon any haukmar looters straggling behind, I've got a barb or two to sting 'em with!" He hefted his crossbow and hurried up the hill. Kion took off after him, going at a half run so as not to outdistance his friend.

The town was still ablaze when they arrived. The fires lit up rolling smoke clouds above the houses. The eerie, crackling glow wafted embers up to the sky. Not a home remained that was not aflame or already burned to the ground. They did not enter the town—the fires were too widespread and dangerous—but they caught glimpses of the Fielder's House. It rose above the other buildings, consumed by a great pillar of flame. The commons were a smoldering carpet of desolation. No sounds other than the cracking and popping of wood and the low hum of fire could be heard. No one moved. No one cried out for help. Furrow, the village that had caused Kion so much suffering and sorrow, was no more.

It was all too much. Each moment he stared at the blaze brought another memory of his times in the village: his visits to Zinder's shop, the market days haggling over the price of wool, the festivals, the dances, the music, even his failures at the tournament. They were all gone now, all gone, carried away on smoke into the night.

"The tales of the haukmar atrocities do not come close to the truth," Kion said. "They're savages."

"Less than that in my book. And this is only the beginning. Charring is next," Zinder said. "Furrow just happened to be along the way, but Charring is what they're after. If that city falls, they'll have another well-defended place from which to launch assaults. From there, they'll most likely head west to Quelling or east to Dunskein. They'll want to bottle up the north before assaulting Madrigal."

"And if they take Madrigal?" Kion went numb at the thought of Charring and the rest of Inris under the tyranny of the haukmarn.

"They'll push south, quick as they can. Inrisward is just the gatekeeper. The real prize is Verisward."

"The nyn speaks wisely," Kithian said. *"Ages may pass, but the rules of war do not change. Strike swiftly and give your enemy as little time as possible to marshal his defenses."*

"Very well," Kion said. "Furrow may be destroyed, but that doesn't mean they razed the outlying settlements. If Mother and Tiryn made it back, they may be safe inside the cottage." The words sounded hollow in his ears, but a frail hope is better than none at all.

With leaden feet, they followed the path northwest to Kion's cottage. When they arrived, the house stood lonely and silent. Though untouched by the flames, it appeared deserted. But his family could still be hiding inside. He had to go in and see.

Kion flung the door open. Cold emptiness stared back at him. Everything was just as he had left it, and yet it was as if he were looking at the house of a stranger.

"Could they have taken refuge with Rike?" Zinder asked.

"I don't know. But we should see if he knows anything." It was a slim chance, but he dared not head on to Charring until he was sure.

Zinder picked up an empty sack hanging above the wash basin. "I'll stay here and gather what food I can for the journey. Is there anything special you'd like to keep?"

Kion cast a quick glance around the cottage, the only house he had ever known, and yet without his mother and sister, it was no longer his home. "No. I have my father's letter. That's the only thing that matters. I'll go see if I can find Rike."

He flew up the hill as though running headlong down it. But Rike's small cottage was as dark and lifeless as his own.

Kion returned and stopped near the sheep pen to catch his breath. The pen was empty, the gate left open. The moon came out from behind the clouds and shone a clear light on fresh sheep tracks headed toward the woods. Could his family have taken the sheep there for safety?

Kion popped his head in through the doorway of the cottage. Zinder was still mucking about, throwing some potatoes into a sack.

"They weren't there. Neither was Rike. I hope he made it. Are you about finished?"

"Almost. This is my second sack. Your mother kept quite the larder." Zinder pointed to some dried meat hanging on the wall. "I'll get the meat and fill up our waterskins at the well, and we can be off."

"The sheep are gone as well. I wonder if Rike went with Mother and Tiryn and the sheep. While you finish packing, I think I'll go into the forest a little way to see if I can spot them. The flock will be easy enough to track, and I doubt they'll have gone far. I won't be long."

"All right. I suppose we do have to check. It would be awful if we somehow missed them. Go, but hurry back."

Kion sped off into the woods, following the sheep trail in the moonlight. When clouds or trees crowded out the moon, True-silver lit the way, glowing like a flameless candle floating through the woods.

"Ro-de-da," he called out quietly to his sheep as he went. He'd seen no sign of the haukmarn, but he kept his voice down just in case. Though he had wandered these woods a thousand times, they had never felt so unfamiliar. Shadows jumped out at him, and a threat menaced behind every rustle of the wind. Every step deepened the uncertainty. Fear seeped in from the corners of his vision. Where were his mother and sister? Were they still alive? And even if they were, and if he did manage to find them, how could things ever be set right after a day like this?

A bleating sheep stopped his heart in his chest. He set off at a run. The sound came again, closer this time.

He came upon the flock in a clearing. Most lay asleep, but a handful wandered about. The clearing was one the flock came to often. It had been well picked over, but the flock had not come here for food. In hard times, sheep, like men, find comfort in the familiar.

The animals showed no sign they were aware of the blazing village a mile and a half away. They stared at him for a moment before first one, then another, trotted over. Soon, half a dozen pressed in around him. Rike's sheep were there too, but they stayed back while his own animals bumbled about, nudging him in the dark. He leaned Truesilver against a tree and knelt and rubbed their fleeces and took in their smell. How long had he been gone? Two days felt like as many years. A peace settled over him. It would not last, but this moment was a breath of cool, clean air amidst the smoke and ash blowing across his homeland. His flock was safe.

Urly, who was among those surrounding him, drew near and licked his hand. His leg had healed nicely, and he shuffled about with the pep and spring of a yearling.

"You made it, boy, you made it!" Kion said. "Old Roony

would be proud." Old Roony. Kion shook his head at the memory of that dead sheep lying in the grass, his legs stiff and straight up in the air.

He had found his flock, and Rike's was here too, but there was no sign of his family or of Rike.

"They're not here," Kion said.

"What will you do with your flock?" Kithian asked in a somber tone.

"I hadn't really thought about that," Kion said. "But even if Mother and Tiryn weren't here, I expected to find Rike, but I don't see him."

"There is a man asleep nearby," Kithian said. *"Perhaps that is him."*

Kion picked up the sword and looked around. Truesilver's light did not travel far, and the rest of the woods were a patchwork of moonlight and shadow. Rike certainly wasn't anywhere that Kion could see.

"How do you know someone's nearby? I can't see anyone."

"I can. He's in those bushes over to your left."

The bushes were not fifty feet away, but they were covered in deep shadow.

"Are you sure? How do you see, anyway, and how far?" Kion started toward the bushes.

"While I am in your hand, I can see through your eyes. But I also have a sight of my own. There are many things in the world that cannot be seen with the eye. If you wish, I can share my vision with you," Kithian said warmly. The sword's eagerness mirrored Kion's own.

"Yes, show me," Kion said.

A blur washed over him. One moment he was walking, the next he had left his body. It was like falling up. At first, he was so disoriented, he couldn't tell what he was seeing. Then, slowly, his senses adjusted. He found himself looking down from directly overhead, perhaps sixty feet in the air. His body had stopped moving, but he still held the sword upright. The sheep, looking like rounded tufts of wool, wandered about him, rubbing against his legs. Occasionally their noses would pop out as they nuzzled him. Around him loomed the clearing and the trees, but of course he was looking down at them from the top, so they looked more like giant brambles or piles of leafy debris. But the most curious thing of all was the light. It was not like normal light at all. Instead, everything, from sheep to rocks to trees, even his own body, glowed so that the outlines of things were more prominent and the inner parts semi-transparent. The unusual nature of Truesilver's vision allowed him to see straight through the bushes and trees, even through the sheep and his own body to the ground below. The experience was eerie and beautiful and ghostlike.

Inside one of the bushes, he could now discern the outline of a man lying on the ground. It was almost certainly Rike.

After adjusting to the sword sight, Kion found he could still walk and see himself from above at the same time. The floating window of translucent things moved with him. It was odd, but with each step it became more natural.

When he arrived at the bushes, he paused. "This is astonishing, Kithian, but I think I need to go back to my own eyes now."

"*Of course,*" Kithian said.

The world blurred back to normal, and his own vision returned. The soft light of the blade shone upon the dark form of Rike, sprawled out in the underbrush. Kion pushed the branches aside and touched him lightly on the shoulder.

"Rike," he said.

Rike jumped back with a cry. "No! Don't take me back!" His eyes shot this way and that. He rolled away, not even looking at Kion, but only succeeded in entangling himself in the undergrowth.

"It's me, Rike. It's Kion. Don't be afraid." Kion held Truesilver close to his face so Rike could see him better.

Rike struggled a while longer, but at last recognition sparked in his eyes.

"Kion? Kion Bray? Is that you?" Rike asked. His hair was damp and his face even dirtier than usual, but a grim hope flickered there.

"Yes, it's me. Are you all right?" Kion reached down and, after a brief hesitation, Rike took his hand, and Kion pulled him up.

"I—I..." Rike gazed about the clearing in confusion. "I don't know." His eyes caught sight of the sword and stayed there. "What is that?"

"It's a sword I found. Or maybe you could say it found me," Kion said. Rike searched his eyes, looking to understand, but his confusion only deepened. "It doesn't matter. You saved the sheep and you're alive. That's the most important thing. Rike, did Mother or Tiryn make it back before the harriers came? Do you know anything about them?"

Rike's eyes came briefly into focus. "No, nothing. They're safe, aren't they? They weren't in Furrow when it...when it..." His face darkened, and his mouth contorted as if he were about to gag or scream. He rushed forward and threw his arms around Kion, squeezing him tight while shaking uncontrollably.

"They wouldn't have gone to Furrow, Rike. They must still be in Charring."

"Oh, good, oh, good! But—but will they be safe, even there?" He let go of Kion but stuck close, his hunted eyes locked on Kion's face.

"I don't know. That's why I have to go there," Kion said.

"No, don't go—don't do it. What if they capture you? Oh, Kion, don't let them capture you! You don't know what horrible things they do to their prisoners. They—they—"

No, Kion didn't know. But the terror in Rike's eyes was enough to send a throb of panic shooting through him. He had to get to his mother and sister. He'd wasted enough time already.

"Rike, it's not safe here. You must leave these lands. And I must go to Charring, however dangerous the road may be."

"But it won't be safe in the cities and towns anymore. We should go—take the sheep to a cave or someplace safe—someplace far away."

Kion thought for a moment, looking over his flock.

"Yes, take them someplace safe. You must watch over the sheep, Rike—both flocks now."

Rike's face broke out in alarm. "But I can't, I can't take your—"

Kion was quick to interrupt before the hysterics took hold of him. "I have to go to Charring, Rike. Mother and Tiryn are there. I have to find them. We both have a responsibility now. Yours is the sheep. Mine is my family. I can't take the sheep where I'm going, and I can't run to safety while my family is in danger. You understand what I'm saying, Rike, don't you?"

"Yes…I suppose they need you. I just wish…It doesn't seem right for me to take your flock."

"Do you know anyone in Madrigal or Quelling?" Kion asked, seizing upon an idea.

Rike grimaced, struggling to master his fears and think clearly. "I—I have a sister in Madrigal. But that's an awfully long way."

"And yet it may be the last safe haven in the north. The haukmarn are sweeping across our lands. If you can get to Madrigal, the sheep should be safe there for a while," Kion said. "And when I've found Mother and Tiryn, I'll come find you. Would you do that for me, Rike?"

For the first time, Rike's shaking faded completely. He pinned back his shoulders and looked Kion square in the eye. "Your mother took care of my flock when I was—when I was gone. If this will help you and your family, I will do it."

Kion looked over the flock one last time. Most of them were still asleep. Despite his promise to Rike, he doubted he would ever see them again, not unless the fortunes of war turned quickly in their favor. He would miss his troubled neighbor who had become a friend. And he would miss his flock. For all the troubles and toil they caused him, he loved them after all. But his family meant more than anything.

"Thank, you, Rike. I am in your debt." Kion embraced him and, after a brief resistance, Rike returned the gesture. "Goodbye, my friend," Kion said, pulling away. "I'm off to Charring."

Amidst all the confusion and doubt upon Rike's face, the knots in his brow eased, and there dawned a look of quiet admiration.

Chapter 24

A DIFFERENT KIND OF NIGHTMARE

The crow of an overzealous rooster battered Tiryn's ears for what felt like the hundredth time. Though she clung to the sweetness of sleep as long as she could, in the end she surrendered to the rooster's insufferable persistence and opened her eyes. For the first time she could remember since arriving at Aunt Lizet's, sleep had brought no nightmares. The simple joy of a peaceful night's rest was all the more precious for its long absence.

"I can see now why Mother never wanted chickens," Tiryn said to herself. The thought stirred up a remembrance. Her sleep may have gone undisturbed, but Tiryn had another nightmare now to haunt her, one that occurred during the day. Mother had left Marlibrim.

Kion's message had arrived the day before. Her brother had done some foolish things in his life, but abandoning the farm for a chance to have some old warrior scratch a helmet had to be his crowning achievement. He had probably done the right thing by sending the messenger, but he ought to have known it would make Mother worry.

"I have to go," Mother had said after agonizing over the news for several hours. "You understand, don't you, my karinna?"

"Of course, Mother. I'm almost better anyway. I just wish Kion would have more sense."

"So do I, Tiryn. So do I. But he lost the tournament. And when we lose a dream, sometimes we cling even tighter to the ones that remain. I expect to have a few words with Zinder when I get home, though. He at least should have known better."

"I just hope you'll be safe."

"I'll be fine. I traveled the road from Furrow to Charring many times in my youth. I know it well. Don't you worry and let yourself get sick again over me. I've told Lizet to send you on as soon as you are well."

But now, a day later, worrying was about all Tiryn found herself capable of.

After the crowing ceased, she lay in bed for some time, wishing in vain for sleep to return. But worries scurried about in her head, amplifying every distraction. The sounds of the servants stirring away in pots and clinking dishes rustled through the mansion walls, and the flapping of the shingles on the roof clattered like stones pelting down from the sky.

She rolled over and stretched. The aches in her chest, arms, and legs warbled in a woeful chorus. But strength trickled through her frame as well. Once she had breakfast, she would feel better. Aunt Lizet had even promised to take her on a walk outside today. Up until now, Tiryn still had not been let out of the house, though she had been allowed to explore certain rooms.

The parlor, with its enormous fireplace, was her favorite. Like all the rooms, it had lofty ceilings and crown molding. The fireplace was large enough to fit a full-grown sheep and had a lovely mantel over it with a collection of crystal bells. Two simply enormous padded chairs sat in front of it, together with a divan that seemed a mile long. Once she asked if Aunt Lizet would let her play her instruments or sing before the fire, but Lizet said it would send "noxious airs" through the house. Whether that was because she feared Tiryn was still contagious, or because she simply didn't like her music, Tiryn preferred not to hazard a guess. It was enough that Aunt Lizet had looked after her for so long. Tiryn was content with that and (though she felt a touch guilty about it) the thought that she would soon be leaving. "A day or two more," Aunt Lizet had said yesterday evening, "just to be sure."

Tiryn pushed back the avalanche of blankets. With grit and effort, she put her feet on the chilly floor and rose to dress herself and make the bed. Moving about helped not only with the aches, but also kept her mind off her mother—mostly. By the time she was ready to go downstairs, her aches were barely noticeable, but the worries had returned in full force. Why hadn't she'd begged Mother to let her go with her? No woman should travel the open road alone. Every bandit, wolf, and accident story Tiryn had ever heard rattled around in her mind over and over again.

She had to stop thinking about this. She forced herself out the door and onto the stairs. Though she descended slowly, by the time she reached the bottom she was forced to pause and catch her breath.

Amalia, the senior maid, passed by on her way to the kitchen. "Morning, Miss Tiryn," she said. She was a short, thin lady, old enough to be Tiryn's grandmother, but she moved spryly and had a sharp eye.

"Good morning, Amalia," Tiryn said.

"You've got a bit more color in your face today. That's a good sign."

Tiryn nodded, her heart warmed by Amalia's kindness. She had not been able to speak more than a few words to her during her stay, but Amalia had brought her several meals, and Tiryn remembered her fondly for that. "If only there weren't so many stairs in this house," Tiryn said, taking another deep breath. "I don't know how you and the other servants manage."

"Oh, we're too busy to be tired, m'lady. Now, if you'll excuse me, I've still a dozen things to get done before breakfast is ready."

"Of course. Sorry for keeping you." The mention of breakfast sent a few unseemly rumblings up from her stomach. "Oh, my," Tiryn said, her face flushing.

Amalia chuckled. "That's a good sign, m'lady. It means you've got your appetite back."

The laugh eased Tiryn's embarrassment enough for her to reply, "And also that I thoroughly enjoy your cooking."

"M'lady is too kind," Amalia said, curtsying. "By your leave."

With a nod from Tiryn, Amalia disappeared through the swinging doors to the kitchen. Tiryn would never get used to being waited on like she'd been at Marlibrim. No one in Furrow would ever dream of waiting upon a shepherdess.

Tiryn sat down on a bench near one of the large windows. The curtains were drawn back. The bright melodies of a green-breasted bird piped from a nearby tree, a large oak that grew next to the house. Birdsong had often cheered her in her loneliest moments at Marlibrim. She fancied it may have even sped her recovery, for music, more than anything else, was the delight of her soul, and Mistress Shona said the body could not grow strong where the soul languished.

Beyond the tree stood the stables. A groomsman opened the gate and passed inside. She had watched the horses going out to pasture for the past few mornings and fallen in love with them, particularly a black one with dappled gray flanks. Only two families in Furrow, the Shaws and the Jeslans, had horses. The thought of riding one felt almost criminal, something reserved for only the richest merchants or highest of lords, and yet she so longed to try. How lovely to be carried along at such heights, practically floating by with your head in the clouds.

"Good morning, Tiryn." Aunt Lizet's cool greeting scattered Tiryn's musings.

"Good morning, Aunt Lizet." Tiryn rose as quickly as she could and gave a little bow. But she stepped on the hem of her dress and pitched to the side. She only just caught herself on an end table.

"Oh, my dear Tiryn." Aunt Lizet shook her head. "Are you faint? I dare say you're looking paler than yesterday."

"Am I?" Tiryn asked. She thought about Amalia's comment but dared not contradict her aunt, who placed little stock in the thoughts and opinions of her servants. "Perhaps after I've had a walk about the grounds, I'll gain a little color."

"Yes, perhaps. You can't stay ill forever. I've never seen a sickness go on this long." Aunt Lizet cast a concerned look at the crystal chandelier hanging from the parlor ceiling. It glittered wistfully in the dim chamber, but she was unmoved by its beauty. She seemed rather to be inspecting it for dust. "Still, I hope you will not think me too selfish in being glad for it, in a way. You and your mother never would have visited me otherwise."

Her aunt's wounded expression had the desired effect upon Tiryn, who found herself regretting her earlier excitement about leaving. Poor Aunt Lizet *was* all alone, while Tiryn had Mother and Kion. Though after the shenanigans Kion had pulled, perhaps living alone was not as terrible as it seemed. At least she wouldn't have to contend with morose brothers running off on mad quests and leaving her mother to pick up the pieces.

"I wish I could stay, but Mother needs me," Tiryn said.

"I dare say she does. From the sounds of things, I'd wager you'll be left to tend the sheep from now on. I should not be the least surprised if that bothersome brother of yours never returns. He's probably run off and joined the fane's army, if you ask me." Aunt Lizet harrumphed.

In the face of Aunt Lizet's barbs, sympathy for her brother, and perhaps a little family pride, stirred in Tiryn. "He'll be back," she said. "He just made a mistake."

Aunt Lizet's eyebrows quivered. Tiryn bit her lip. Perhaps it would have been best to just keep quiet.

"Tiryn, listen to yourself. The way you two coddle that boy, it's no wonder he's just as empty-headed as his father. If your mother had any sense, she'd give him a good lashing and make him sleep out with the beasts for an eight-mark. Trust me. Discipline, hard discipline, is the only remedy for people like him."

Tiryn clenched her lips and swallowed the words that came to mind, hoping to quell the dark clouds brewing on her aunt's horizon before they erupted into a full-blown storm. Thankfully, Amalia's appearance at the kitchen door saved her from a good drenching.

"Morning tea is on the table," Amalia said. "Breakfast shall be served shortly."

Aunt Lizet dismissed her with a terse wave.

Tiryn breathed a sigh of relief. Aunt Lizet was always much more pleasant after tea.

The walk outside had to wait. Aunt Lizet was not more pleasant either during or after tea, or even after breakfast. Riled by their talk about Tiryn's brother, she launched into a lengthy exposition of how Mother had taken advantage of her kindness in looking after Tiryn, only to run off and leave her the moment "that Bray boy" got into trouble. It was "just like what happened with your father."

As Tiryn quietly endured her aunt's tirade, Lizet droned on and on about the great affront that Mother's marriage had been to the honor and fortunes of their family. The scandal Lizet had had to endure was sure to drive her to an early grave. She warned Tiryn not to be taken in by such brazen, gold-mining, sweet-singing dreamers like her father. She got so incensed as she rehearsed his infamous deeds that at one point, she set her tea cup down with altogether too much force and chipped it. She blamed the damage on Tiryn for "stirring her up," though Tiryn had said nothing for a full five minutes prior.

After the tragedy that was breakfast, Tiryn retired to her bedroom while Aunt Lizet went on a walk by herself, "to clear her head." Even though the prospect of spending more time with her aunt was sure to bring a fresh round of diatribes, Tiryn would have endured an eight-mark of speeches if only she could have gone outside for a little while.

Once again she had to watch the horses through the window. Dwelling on her dashed hopes made it far less enjoyable than usual. She had so wanted to see their great size and beauty up close, perhaps even pet one or feed it from her hand. But Aunt Lizet didn't come back and didn't come back, and the morning drained itself away without so much as a knock at her door.

When the knock did come, Tiryn rushed to answer it, only to find Amalia before her. She tried not to appear too crestfallen when Amalia announced that lunch would be served in approximately fifteen minutes.

"Thank you, Amalia," Tiryn said. "Has my aunt come back?"

"I'm sorry, m'lady. I haven't seen her. I believe Mistress Lizet got into the carriage and went to the market after her walk. But we'll be setting out a serving for her in case she returns."

"Oh, I see," Tiryn said. Her appetite, which had been steadily growing over the last hour, suddenly dwindled to nothing. "I shall be down shortly."

Tiryn returned to the window, struggling not to resent her aunt. Heat rushed to her cheeks. She doubted Aunt Lizet would have called her pale at that moment.

"It's not fair," she said to the horses grazing in the field below. "You are the beasts, yet I'm the one who's penned up. She could at least let me go outside on my own, but no, here I am once again, just like yesterday, and every other day before that. How I miss my walks in the woods!"

The great dappled stallion looked up toward her window just then. He had never done so before. For a moment she thought he was looking at her, but then all the horses looked up. They were all staring at the mansion as if it were about to collapse. But Tiryn felt nothing. The muffled busyness of the servants preparing lunch was the only sound. The stallion trotted over to the fence. He no longer looked straight at the window, but still looked toward the mansion, along with the others.

The deep note of a bell tolled in the distance. How odd. Four o'clock was still several hours away.

The bell tolled again. And again and again and again. It rang frantically over and over. The horses whinnied in reply. The bustle of the servants below turned into the buzzing of a bee hive. Footsteps peppered the stairs. Tiryn ran to the door and flung it open. Amalia bounded up the last few steps. This time it was she who was breathless. And pale.

"Mistress Tiryn, there's an army marching on Charring!"

Chapter 25

NATURAL SPEECH

T he road unraveled to the south, marred and mangled by the tread of the haukmarn army. Gray sunlight smoked across the horizon, as drear and cheerless as a morning could be. Crusty scampered to avoid the divots, stamping down the dirt clods and dragging the cart like an old plow. The wheels skittered and jumped over the uneven sod, giving the wagon seat lots of play. In the best of times, wagon travel was a bushel of aches and a leaky barrel of endurance, but on this journey, it threatened to jumble their bones and fish out their lunch. If the haukmarn had not mucked up the road so horribly, this might have been another heart-pounding ride like the one on their way to the tournament. As it was, this journey had all of the harrow and none of the thrill of that other ride.

"Are you sure about this?" Kion asked as the cart rolled along at double the normal pace. "This road is little better than going overland."

Zinder, who every few seconds found himself shot several inches into the air, held the reins with one hand and his brown tricorn hat with the other. He gave Kion a rather greenish-looking glance. "The land here has too many rocks. We'd crack a wheel for certain if we went this fast off-road. Here, we might at least last a few miles before we bottom out."

"I almost wish we would. I'd prefer running to this. The haukmarn certainly don't seem to mind it."

"You wouldn't say that after you'd gone a few miles at their pace."

"Zinder is right," Kithian said. *"There is something unnatural about their marching."*

Kion had been forced to put the sword in the back. Holding an unsheathed blade in his lap in the midst of all this jostling was asking to get his nose sliced off.

"We still haven't figured out what we're going to do when we get there," Kion said.

"I don't think it's much good trying to hammer things out on this cart ride. My brain's too rattled to think," Zinder said.

"Ouch!" Kion cried as a sliver gouged the underside of his leg. "Oh, bother," he said, fishing for it. The seesaw motion of the cart made it impossible to pin down. "Fire and ice! I wonder how many splinters I'll get before this is all over?"

"I've got three already," Zinder said, looking greener by the minute.

"Kithian will come up with something," Kion said, wincing. The splinter mercifully sprang free after a hard bump. "I don't think the ride is affecting him the way it does us. One of the many advantages, no doubt, to having a body of solid metal."

"Keep hope, glaivebond. A plan will present itself by the time we arrive at Charring."

The wheel cracked just after sunset. At least the cart had good timing.

As the wagon dipped suddenly, it threw Kion off the side of the road. He thudded to the ground and rolled to a stop in the nettles and grit. He wasn't sure what hurt worse: the fall, or the forest of slivers on his legs and backside he'd accumulated during the ride. While he couldn't do much about his bumps and bruises, he could hunt down the slivers, so that was what he did, not even bothering to rise from where he had fallen.

Zinder had somehow managed to land on Crusty when the cart bottomed out. If it had been anyone else, Crusty would have bucked him off, but he allowed Zinder to slide down without so much as a flick of his tail.

Once he hit the ground, Zinder crawled to the side of the road and joined Kion in hunting for splinters. Zinder had just as many as Kion, but he was far better at fishing them out. With his nynnian eyes and nimble fingers, he removed all his in a few minutes. Then he pulled out his tools and set to work repairing the wheel. Thankfully, the outer wheel remained mostly intact, so it was only a matter of replacing a few spokes, filling in the cracks with shims, and shaving down the rough spots.

Kion never did find all his splinters. A few tiny, pernicious ones evaded his most concerted attempts. After an hour, he gave up and brought out some provisions. Now that his stomach had finally settled down from the ride, he realized how famished he was. He brought some food to Zinder as well. Kion offered to help with the wheel while Zinder ate, but he declined with a chuckle.

"No, thank you, I wish to *repair* the wheel, not break it into a thousand more pieces."

"Fine. I was only being polite," Kion said, tearing off a hunk of jerky. "So, Kithian, do you have a plan yet?"

"*I believe some scouting is in order first. The more we know, the better we may plan. And we are not yet close enough to do that,*" Kithian said.

"Do you think we'll have time to scout? What if the haukmarn have already taken Charring by the time we get there?" Kion said. It seemed unlikely Charring would fall that quickly, but after what had happened at Roving, anything was possible.

"What's it saying?" Zinder asked. He was taking a break at the moment to enjoy some jerky of his own. Kion shared Kithian's words.

"*From what Zinder has said, Charring is a walled town. They may hold out for some time, even against a thousand haukmarn. From the tracks on the road, the haukmarn do not appear to be carrying any siege engines. But whether they take the city in a sudden assault or encamp about it, our task remains the same: to find a way to the place where your family is staying. For that we will need a scout. If we can get close enough to Charring tomorrow, I may be able to convince a bird to scout for us."*

"A bird?" Kion stopped chewing mid-bite. "What good will a bird do us?"

"I will ask it to help us. Most animals will, you know, if you ask in the right way."

"You can speak to birds?" Kion's jerky almost fell out of his mouth.

"It can speak to birds?" Zinder's jerky did fall out of his mouth.

"Yes, all glaives can speak to animals. Once men could too, but the art has been lost."

Kion had to chew the rest of his jerky before this new revelation fully sank in. Zinder cleaned his off with some water and a rag, wondering aloud what this strange sword *couldn't* do.

"Can you speak to any animal, even dangerous ones like wolves and lions?" Kion asked, not bothering with the rest of his food.

"It can speak to *any* animal? Ah, lad, now you're just making things up," Zinder said.

"Yes, I can speak to predators, but there is little chance they will answer. Like men, they listen only to their own kind now. A life of blood drowns out all other voices."

"If only I had known when we went to Furrow. What I wouldn't have given to be able to tell my sheep good-bye," Kion said.

"So we get a bird, send it flapping all over the town, and suddenly we'll know all the haukmarn's secret plans? It's a lovely sentiment and all, but so far, all I've seen this sword do is shine in the dark and look pretty," Zinder said.

"You just wait until tomorrow. If Kithian says he can do it, I believe him. I'm not so much interested in the haukmarn's plans as I am in what happened to Mother and Tiryn. If we can find out that they aren't there, we can bypass Charring altogether."

"Humph." Zinder adjusted his tricorn. "We shall see, lad. We shall see." He grabbed another strip of jerky and went back to work.

They were on pace to reach Charring by morning the third day. Crusty had been able to keep a champion's pace even with the road in such awful shape. But even more amazing—and disheartening—was the fact that they had yet to overtake the haukmarn.

"They're not sleeping," Kion said. "We've seen no sign of them making camp."

"Either that or they've learned to fly," Zinder said, letting out a huff.

Their rambling wreck of a cart barreled on across the plains. The slope of the land was gentler now, the vistas more open, and the land more green, but the road wasn't any better. Kion barely noticed. All he could think about was birds. What would it be like to talk to one? Would it fly away from fright at the first "hello"? Would it ask for a few worms as payment?

Many times, birds wheeled above or came soaring near the road, but they never came close enough for Kithian to speak to them.

"Some animals are able to sense me from farther away and may be drawn to my presence," Kithian said. *"In the meantime, describe to me the place in Charring where your family dwells."*

"Marlibrim Mansion? Well, unfortunately I've never been there. I've only heard descriptions from my mother," Kion said.

"Do the best you can."

Kion told him all he could remember from his mother's stories of growing up in the massive mansion. The one thing he was sure of was that it had three stories. He doubted too many other buildings in the city were that high.

As he answered Kithian's unending questions about Charring and Marlibrim, the miles passed in a wild rhythm. Zinder and Kion continued to bounce around like popcorn in a pot. As flat as the plains were, the cart seemed to find every dip and hardened knot the road had to offer. The Tors had long shrunk from view. Though farms sometimes broke up the tall, feathery grass, none of them looked inhabited. Their chimneys sat square and cold, and the cottage windows showed motionless rooms inside.

"They're abandoned, most likely," Zinder said. "Or the owners are in hiding."

They stopped for the briefest of lunches before rolling on. A pair of ravens came within a hundred yards while they ate but flew away the moment Kion started toward them.

"I think we may need some bait," Kithian said a few miles after they'd resumed their journey. *"We have three hours before sunset. We should be close enough to Charring now to see if we can find our scout."*

"Kithian wants to pull over," Kion said.

Zinder rolled his eyes. "Never thought I'd be taking orders from a sword! I suppose this is payment for all the ones I mangled as an apprentice."

Crusty certainly offered no complaints about the break. He started in on the grass as soon as they got off the road and never once looked their way.

Kion walked away from the cart, Truesilver in hand.

"Set the bait in the middle of the road, a good distance from the cart," Kithian said.

Zinder walked beside Kion, cleaning his face with a damp rag. His dark outfit was caked with dust, making it look several shades lighter. Kion had never seen him so unkempt.

"I hope this bird business is worth the delay," Zinder said.

Kion stopped fifty yards from the cart. He set down a large handful of crumbs from his uneaten loaf of bread.

"How did you get those crumbs, lad, with a chisel?" Zinder chuckled. "I thought you said you were trying to attract the birds, not scare them away."

"They won't know the difference," Kion said.

"Painted rocks would be better than that!"

"Would you like to share one of *your* biscuits?" Kion asked. Zinder usually kept one in his vest.

"Well, not really. Who knows when we'll have a chance to get some more, but since I don't want to spend all this time bird hunting for naught..." He unwrapped a biscuit and crumbled about a quarter of it into another pile beside Kion's.

They stepped back and waited. And waited some more. Birds fluttered around a small copse of trees about a mile away, but none came near.

About half an hour later, a lone speck of green descended from the west.

Zinder recognized it when it came within half a mile. "It's a crossbill," he said.

The bird circled the road several times, chirping in high, lively notes.

"I will wait until it lands and starts eating to begin speaking," Kithian said, as if the landing was a foregone conclusion. *"I don't want to frighten him. It's likely no glaive has spoken to a bird in centuries."*

The bird fluttered a few more times, then dove in.

Zinder stared at Truesilver expectantly. "Well?"

"Take me closer first. I'd rather not have to raise my voice. Most birds prefer a more gentle approach," Kithian said.

Kion started walking. Zinder stayed where he was, hunched over and holding his breath.

"Make no sound. I will do the talking."

Kion took a few steps before stopping, expecting the bird to dart away at any moment. Sunlight glittered off the blade so brightly, Kion was sure it would scare the bird off, but the cross-bill pecked contentedly at Zinder's pile of crumbs. Kion braved a few more steps, paused, and braved a few more.

The bird hopped away from the crumbs and looked up at Kion.

He froze.

"What's wrong?" Kithian asked.

Kion hissed through clenched lips, "You said I wasn't supposed to talk."

"Ah, yes. Keep moving, then. I think he's a brave sort—or very hungry. I don't think he will fly away."

Kion looked back at Zinder, who was biting his knuckles. Kion took another step. The bird hopped back again. He waited. The bird hopped back toward the crumbs. Kion waited again until the bird was back pecking at the bait. Kion took three cautious steps in a row. "This is like playing 'Margrave, May I?'" he thought.

Kithian spoke up at last. "Well met, my green-breasted friend, I am Kithian the True."

The bird cocked its head at Kion, first left, then right. It sounded a series of high fluted chirps.

"Yes, a very fine day indeed. I hope you enjoy our food," Kithian said.

The bird chirped a nearly identical set of notes, though not as many.

"I am glad of it. I wonder, do you know the dwellings of men to the south?" Kithian asked.

The bird's chirps came back in an excited rush, one on top of the other.

"A dangerous place indeed. Tell me, did you see a great gathering of giants pass this way recently?"

This time the bird chirped so rapidly the notes could hardly be told apart. It flapped its wings and even fluttered in the air for a moment.

"It is as you fear," Kithian said. "Hear me now, Nar-vel-lis of the *green breast. I am a servant of the Mastersmith. As you know, the winds of men blow in all breezes. I have urgent need of news from that great roost of men, as you call it, to the south. Many nests will fall if we do not stop the gray giants that came through here. Will you lend us your aid?"*

The bird cocked its head, jerking its beady gaze from the blade, to Kion, and back, several times. Then it hopped forward, spread its wings, and opened its beak to the sky. The notes of its song rang out bright and noble as the sunrise, as gentle and airy as the wind weaving a dance through a field of daisies.

"He will help," Kithian said.

Chapter 26

UNDER A GAUZY MOON

Kithian's voice flickered into Kion's dreamless sleep like fire in the dark. It stirred something in Kion every time he heard it, something half longing, half contentment.

"Do you see the sundered oak yet?"

Kion opened his eyes. Had he been dozing off again? He glanced about. It was almost dark now. Was that gray smudge in the hills ahead Charring?

"No, no oak yet," Kion said.

Zinder grunted. "Ah, so the dreamer returns. Good of you to join us; I was just about to put on supper."

"I'm sorry, Zinder. I won't let it happen again." But Kion had no reason to believe he could keep his promise. He had already nodded off three times, maybe more. They were not going to catch the haukmarn, so they slowed to a normal pace, and the rocking of the cart kept lulling him to sleep. He had barely slept at all since they'd left Roving three days ago.

"Don't you fret." Zinder yawned. It was the first time Kion had ever seen him tired. "I'm just envious, that's all."

"I can take the reins," Kion said.

"No, I'll be fine. We're almost there, and I can sleep then." He let out another terrific yawn.

"Ask him about the oak. His nynnian eyes will see it before yours," Kithian said.

"No, nothing like what you described," Zinder said in response when Kion passed the question along. "No sign of a tree that I was told to look for by a bird who told a sword who told my sleepy-headed friend who probably dreamt the whole thing up. If this entire wild chase doesn't turn out to be the most elaborate, belated Day of Innocents prank, I will be sorely disappointed. At this point I'm only along because I can't wait to see the end of the joke."

"I admit, it is a rather strange road we're on," Kion said. "But if it takes us to Mother and Tiryn, I don't care how strange it gets."

"Lad, about your mother and sister. I don't want to quench your fire, but even if this cuckoo friend of yours finds them, we still have no idea how we're going to get past the haukmarn."

"Kithian says we have to find out where they are first."

Zinder frowned and made some inarticulate noises. "Well... never mind. I suppose we'll find out soon enough who's the real cuckoo."

"Trust me," Kion said, laying hold of his friend's shoulder. Zinder's misgivings were clearly written on his face, but he nodded, and the cart rolled on. Kion understood his doubts, but if Zinder could have heard Kithian's voice, he'd know they were on the right path—the only path to Mother and Tiryn.

They found the sundered oak shortly after sunset. It was near a long, rounded stone, a few hundred wing flaps east of the road. A wing flap, Kithian explained, was about ten feet. That was how Nar-vel-lis reckoned distances.

The stone near the oak was easy enough to spot. It stood out amongst all the rolling grass, as high as Kion's shoulder. They didn't spot the tree Nar-vel-lis had said would be nearby until they were right on top of the stone. The fallen tree lay engulfed by the surrounding grass, rich with rot, riven and blackened by disease or fire.

"Well, the tree's here, all right," Zinder said. "That's a point in the sword's favor. But there's no sign of our Mr. Greenbreast, so at this juncture I'd call it a wash."

"Zinder, you're turning into a royal grump. Give the bird some time. We just got here."

"You drive a mule cart for three days straight and see how pleasant you are." Zinder stretched as wide as his nynnian arms would go and let out a cavernous yawn. "It's your turn to stay vigilant now, lad. I'm not long for nighttime appointments after a journey like that. Even a nyn has to sleep once in a while. Give my regards to your little flying spy. I can't fight off one more wink." With that he toppled into the back of the cart and fell dead asleep. Half his body was draped over the bundle of swords, but he could have slept on a bed of broken glass.

Kion watched him with envy, but he didn't dare miss the crossbill. He took a swig of water and started pacing. A tepid breeze wafted across the plains. The sun died on a flaming, maroon pyre and twilight descended, trampling upon the ashes.

Kion listened intently for the sound of Nar-vel-lis's chirping, but nothing came but the wind.

"Kithian, can you teach me to speak to animals the way you do?" Kion asked.

"Yes, but we have no time for such lessons now."

"I know. But if we ever get back to the farm, that skill would make me the best shepherd in all of Inris. Though I don't suppose I'll be tending my sheep anytime soon. More likely I'll never see my flock again."

"I have not the gift of foresight, but it serves little to dwell on what we have lost. Only hope and strive for what may be."

"Some healers are said to have that gift," Kion said. "I'd give anything to know that Mother and Tiryn will be all right."

"Such gifts are as much a curse as they are a blessing," Kithian said, and Kion sensed a hidden sadness behind the words. It was the first time he had heard anything but confidence and authority in that ageless voice.

The strong, shrill notes of Nar-vel-lis interrupted their

conversation. It was too dark to spot him, but the sounds came from the south. They grew louder and louder until a darting streak of green alighted on the great rock.

Nar-vel-lis chirped a merry greeting.

"He says he has good and bad news," Kithian said. Kion squeezed Truesilver's grip and steeled himself for the worst. *"The gray giants have indeed seized the great stone roost of men. They are putting the men in fetters, and some were taken off along the western trail."*

Kion's heart lurched in his chest. Prisoners. They had been taken prisoner.

"But he said there was good news, didn't he?" Kion said, trying to push away the image of his mother and sister in chains. "They didn't take my family, did they?"

"And what of the tall nest, the one with Kion's flock?" Kithian asked. *"Did you find it?"*

The bird's chirping rose and fell enigmatically, a shower of bright and dark notes.

"He saw many covered nests within the great stone roost, and he flew around each one, looking for the red-crested girl and the dark-crested female that I described to him. He despaired of finding them until he met a young crossbill hen. She lived in a tree beside one of the larger nests near the edge of the roost. She told him she often sang to a red-crested human chick who would sit in one of the topmost holes of the tall nest. Sadly, by the time he arrived, the nest had been seized by the gray giants. Many wandered in, out, and around it, as though it were their own nest now. He saw no men or human chicks about it, or inside the holes. In fact, he saw no men there at all."

"And he calls that good news? That my aunt's house has been seized and is crawling with haukmarn?" Kion held True-silver up near his face. "They're gone. They've been taken prisoner. That's plain as day." He lowered the sword. "Why didn't we push harder? I knew we'd never make it in time. This bird might as well have not come back at all if this is what it brings us!"

"Be patient. Calm yourself and listen. Nar-vel-lis has more to say." The tempered restraint in Kithian's voice lent Kion enough composure to check another outburst.

Nar-vel-lis hopped about the rock animatedly as he resumed his night song. The notes came rapidly, one after the other.

Kithian relayed the words of this new song with mounting excitement. *"He says that the hen saw several gray- and white-crested men being led away in fetters when the giants came, but the red and black-crested females were not among them. The hen believes they are still somewhere inside."*

"Inside?" Kion struggled to master himself. A part of him wanted to hope, but it was impossible to think they still lived if the haukmarn had seized Marlibrim. His mother and sister must surely be dead, or worse.

The bird's chirping ceased. Its head danced from side to side, studying Kion as it hopped about.

"I know what you are thinking, that the haukmarn must have killed them. But we do not know that."

"Do you honestly believe we should risk our lives on that chance? What hope do we have of rescuing them if the mansion is crawling with haukmarn, as the bird says?"

"Firstly, the bird's name is Nar-vel-lis. He has done us a great service, and you must be mindful of that. But that aside, you are forgetting that you have me. And I am no common sword. I do not fear a houseful of haukmarn and neither should you. Take courage, swordspeaker. Noble deeds spent in a just cause are never in vain."

Kion stared at the bird. The two regarded each other for several long moments until Nar-vel-lis leapt onto Kion's sword arm and began to sing, a slow, deliberate, ponderous song, unlike any he had sung before. It was a simple melody, but it stirred Kion from his grim musings. *I can still sing,* it seemed to say. *And while there is song, there is hope.*

Kithian conveyed Nar-vel-lis's actual words as follows: *"Now this is the best news of all. Before he left the great stone roost, he flew one last time around the outside of it. Just as he was about to fly away, he spotted a hole in the stone surrounding it. From this hole a feeble, yet foul stream poured forth. It was just large enough for a single man to enter. He flew inside and, after a wing flap, found it blocked by metal branches, but he flew between the branches. On the other side, the stone hollow sloped gradually upward for many wing flaps and through more metal branches. Beyond that the hollow grew a bit wider.*

"He kept flying, straight ahead for many wing flaps, until he came to the end, where he found a shaft. It had metal branches all the way up the sides. Not knowing what lay above, he hopped upwards from branch to branch until he hit a clay roof of some sort and could go no farther, but he heard the chattering of men above. He believes this hole may be a secret way into the great stone roost."

Kion's hopes stirred, however feebly.

"It's a slim chance," he said. "But it is a chance."

"If we are to try this way, we must leave at once. We dare not risk entering the city during the day."

"Yes, you're right. Give Nar-vel-lis my thanks." He bowed to the bird, which leapt back onto the stone and regarded him with his head cocked to the side. "I still fear Mother and Tiryn are dead, or carried away with the other prisoners, but we have to at least try. I just hope you have a way of dealing with the haukmarn."

"I will show you how to deal with them when the time comes," Kithian said. *"Now go, wake your sleeping friend. Let us hope he approves of our plan. I believe we will need his aid."*

"Oh, he'll like it," Kion said. "He has to."

The two friends stood at the edge of a small pool hidden in the prickly underbrush. The stench of offal assaulted their senses, but Zinder was more bothered by it than Kion. As a shepherd, Kion was accustomed to less-than-pleasant smells. At the other end of the pool, some thirty feet away, rose an almost sheer wall of natural rock, dark and unyielding. The pool let out to either side, running in a thin moat around the edge of Charring. A mortared wall sat atop the natural one, rising fifty feet above the bedrock on which it rested. The Fortress of the Clefts had awed Kion with its power and strength, but now that so much rock stood arrayed against him, he saw that rock could be hard and cruel as well. An assault from this side of the city would be unthinkable, but near the top of the natural wall, some forty feet above the pool, was the opening Nar-vel-lis the crossbill had told them about. A dull gray stream trickled down the cliff with dark stains on either side. This was the one chink in Charring's armor, the one glimmer on this darkened night.

"This is the worst plan in the history of plans. My grandnyn could think of a better plan, and she's dead!" Zinder said in a low whisper. A large figure had walked past on the ramparts five minutes ago, but it had been quiet since then. A soft wind and the gurgling trickle of water masked their voices, but they kept them to a whisper just to be sure.

"You agreed we should at least see if we can get up there," Kion said. "Besides, do you have a better one?"

"Yes. How about we strangle that crossbill and roast it for dinner?"

"You're out of luck, my friend, unless you can fly. He's off to his home in the north. From the sounds of it, he lives somewhere near Windstern."

"I'll be sure to pay him a visit," Zinder said, grumbling. "I suppose this is what I get for sleeping when the plans are made. I'll be sure to stay awake in the future."

"Enough talk. Will the rope reach or not?"

"It certainly looks like it," Kion said. "But hooking it on that metal grate might be another matter."

Kion carried Truesilver wrapped in a blanket. Though the blade was able to mute its glow, it could do nothing to stop stray shafts of moonlight. A crescent moon lay hidden behind a gauzy curtain of clouds, like a bright smudge in a child's painting, but it shed enough light to glint off metal. For that reason, Kion also wore his cloak to cover his armor and his father's helm. Battling the haukmarn was certainly not part of the plan, but it was foolish to think of entering the city unprepared. The armor had not been made for him, so it was tight in spots, loose in others, but Zinder didn't have time to make more than a few adjustments.

Zinder aimed his crossbow at the black opening in the cliff face. The hole was about forty feet off the ground, but they only had fifty feet of rope and the grate was ten feet inside, if Nar-vel-lis's description was accurate. Zinder bound a metal hook to the tip of a crossbow bolt and tied the rope to the other end. The hook had a clever hinge that would make it collapse as it passed through the grate and lock in the open position as the rope was pulled back through.

"We should have enough of an angle for the bolt's momentum to carry it all the way to the grate," Zinder said. With a quick intake of breath, he pulled the trigger and let the bolt fly.

At this distance, hitting the hole wasn't hard. The only question was if the bolt would have enough velocity to make it all the way in and catch. A muffled clink and a click sounded from inside the shaft. The rope held, dangling about ten feet above the water.

Kion wanted to cheer but limited himself to a quiet clap on Zinder's shoulder.

Now came the hard part: getting inside the hole. If a haukmar guard came by while they were climbing and heard them, they'd be done for. Crusty was half a mile away in a little stand of trees, but the haukmarn would easily overtake them if they came out and gave chase. More likely, they'd just shoot them with the great lancing arrows of their bows.

Kion crawled out from the bushes and slipped into the pool. Now that he was in the offal infested water, even he had to make an effort to keep from gagging. The pool was also deeper than expected. With his feet on the bottom, the water came up to his chest.

"It's too deep," he whispered to Zinder. "And the rope's too high to reach."

"Just get me close and I can climb to it," Zinder said. "Here, duck down and let me get on your shoulders. I don't want to get wet."

"Fire and ice, Zinder, now's not the time to be thinking about ruining your precious clothes. Look at me, I'm covered in filth."

"It's for the climb, lad. I don't want to be slipping on the rocks. Humph. Fashion. Do you really think I'm that obsessed with style?"

"Do you really want me to answer that question?"

"Shh, now hurry up and get moving."

Kion carried Zinder across the pool. Zinder made several aborted retching sounds but managed to hold down his supper. As they reached the other side, the sound of boots on stone echoed down the ramparts.

They huddled motionless under the shadow of the cliff, which leaned out a little over the pool so that they couldn't see the guard. More importantly, the guard couldn't see them—but he might still hear. The footsteps grew louder, stopped for an agonizing few moments, then grew softer until they faded away.

Zinder waited a bit and then started up the bare wall toward the end of the rope. What looked to Kion to be sheer rock from a distance had a surprising amount of bumps and knobs up close. Still, it was no easy task reaching the rope. Zinder zig-zagged his way up, finding little irregularities Kion would have missed. Once he grabbed hold of the rope, he scurried the rest of the way up like a squirrel on a tree.

Kion had to wait in the wretched pool until Zinder crawled all the way up to the grate and unfastened the rope. Then he lowered it down far enough for Kion to reach. Kion grabbed it with one hand, then realized he had a problem.

"Kithian, how am I going to carry you? I can't climb with one hand and hold onto you with the other, especially not with you wrapped in this blanket."

"Leave me in the pool and call me to yourself when you reach the opening," Kithian said.

Kion pulled away the blanket so he could take a look at the sword. The blade no longer glowed, but the orange gems in the hilt sparkled with a faint, inner light. Had he heard correctly? All he had to do was call the blade?

"I don't understand. Can you fly?" Kion asked.

"To your hand, yes. If I am close enough to see you, you may always call me to you, and I will come," Kithian said.

Kion felt a yank on the rope.

"What's the hold-up?" Zinder hissed down at him.

Kion didn't answer. He unwrapped the blade and lowered it into the water, casting his blanket into the depths at the same time.

"You're sure about this?"

"I would not have told you if it were not so."

With deep ambivalence, Kion let the blade slip through his fingers. It seemed a tragedy to allow a thing of such beauty to sink beneath these rancid waters, but he had to trust Kithian.

He hoisted himself up. Though the armor did not normally feel heavy, the added weight strained his arms, and his soggy cloak didn't help. But the cloak did mask the clinking and chinking as he scampered up the wall. It took him twice as long as Zinder to reach the top. He only just made it inside the opening when the thudding footsteps of a guard sounded again overhead. The two friends barely breathed until the steps passed.

"Well done, lad," Zinder said once it got quiet again. "Now let's see about cracking that grate."

"Wait, I left the sword," Kion said. "Just let me—"

"Fiddles and riddles! You left the sword?" Zinder said, altogether too loudly.

"Yes, in the pool."

"Tell me you're joking."

"It's all right. It will come to me if I call it."

"It'll what?"

Kion couldn't see Zinder's expression in the dark, but from the sound of his voice, he imagined his eyes were the size of eggs.

"I just need to lower myself back down over the edge a little. It's too tight in here for me to turn around."

"Have you lost your—?"

"Shh. Just do it."

Zinder miraculously held his tongue and failed to offer further disputes, but Kion could feel him thinking in protest in the dark. The bewildered nyn stayed put and steadied the rope as Kion went back over the edge.

"Truesilver, fly to me," Kion said in a loud whisper to the waters below and stretched out his free hand.

A glinting flash came from below, and the warm, solid hilt slapped into his hand. Kion allowed himself a moment to marvel at the wondrous blade before pulling it gently into the shaft and crawling in.

"Oh, my..." came Zinder's barely audible voice in the grimy dark near the back of the shaft. "How did you...?"

"Now do you believe this isn't a common sword?" Kion asked.

"I'm starting to come around, lad," Zinder said. "I'm starting to come around."

Chapter 27

ILK'S TREACHERY

U sing the faintest of glows from Truesilver's blade and his keen nynnian sight, Zinder sized up the bars.

"We're in luck," he said, pulling off his pack, where he kept an assortment of tools. "They're typical human craftsmanship, no thicker than my finger. And rusted from all this moisture besides. I'll have us through in less than an hour."

But it ended up taking longer than that. With Kion listening for footsteps at the lip of the shaft, Zinder had to take small breaks every few minutes, lest the guard overhear them. And then, of course, he couldn't put his full strength into sawing. It would have been far too loud.

As it was, through cautious, clever work, as only a nyn could do, he had enough bars sawed by the end of two hours for him to slip past. Kion was another matter. He ended up having to remove part of his armor to be able to fit through, and then, of course, get back into it on the other side, which was no small matter in the cramped tunnel.

After that, it was a long, slow slither on their bellies, clawing their way gradually upward through the damp and the reek. Zinder half-gagged every few feet, but through sheer force of will kept his insides on the inside. After nearly an hour of scraping, inch by inch, up the chute, they came to the second set of iron bars.

These received no mercy from Zinder. They were far enough inside the tunnel by now for the noise not to be a problem, and he was so rankled and reeling from the stomach-turning odor, he was past caring if anyone heard. He sawed through them in a little over half an hour.

The space beyond was like stepping into a forest meadow on a midsummer's day by comparison. It was almost tall enough for Zinder to stand up in, and there was a small ledge on either side of the tunnel. The water ran past in a groove, leaving the ledge relatively dry. Kion lay down for several minutes, stretching out his poor, cramped muscles. The air was a shade fresher here, too. Not much, but enough to quell Zinder's gagging.

From then on, they went at a much faster pace. Zinder trotted ahead, crouching down. Kion crawled on all fours behind him. It was still a miserable experience, but with every step forward, Kion told himself he was that much closer to finding his family.

"How far exactly did the bird say we had to go?" Kion asked.

"He did not give me a definite indication, only that it was many wing flaps."

"If only I could fly," Kion said.

"Birds must have no sense of smell," Zinder muttered.

"I am sorry for you, glaivebond," Kithian told him. *"But sometimes the hard way is the only way."*

Easy for a sword to say. It didn't have to crawl through this filth.

There were tiny alcoves at the intersections between most of the tunnels. By the time they passed five of them, Kion's hands and knees would have been in shreds if not for his gloves and armor. As it was, both his hands and knees were horribly chafed and starting to throb. But then they came to the sixth alcove, and here at last was the shaft Nar-vel-lis had told them about.

How many hours they'd passed underground, it was hard to say, but all the misery of the journey vanished the moment Kion craned his neck and looked at the opening above. It was slightly wider than the tunnels and cut straight through the rock. Rusted metal rungs showed that from time to time people came down the shaft.

Kion peered up through the opening. The subtle light from Truesilver's blade failed to reach the end of it.

"This is where the real test begins," Kithian said.

Kion straightened and grabbed hold of the first rung. "Right. I'll go up first, in case there are any difficulties."

"No, lad, I'll go first," Zinder said. "I know what you're thinking, but it's not a question of bravery or anything like that. It's just that the bird said the top was covered and whatever's covering it is likely to be as stubborn as that grate. So you'll need me to open it."

Kion tried to think of a reason against it, but couldn't come up with one. "I suppose you're right," he said.

Zinder moved in close, so close that his nose almost touched Kion's. "Now we don't know what's up there, lad, but all sense and reason say this can't end very well for either one of us. Whatever happens, I want you to know something. I'm proud of you, proud to call you a friend, and proud of the man you've become. Oh, you're not there all the way yet, but what you're doing for your mother and sister, well, your father would be proud. His blood runs strong in you. Never forget that you're his son."

Kion couldn't respond for the lump in his throat. Zinder was hardly ever this serious. The thought that neither of them might live through the night loomed like a predator lurking in the darkness.

"Thank you, Zinder. You don't have to go, you know. This isn't your family. I would never forgive myself if something happened to you."

"Not my family? Not my—now don't talk nonsense. Course it's my family. You're too young to remember, but your father was the best friend I ever had. And when he left, I promised him I'd watch over you. And your mother and your sister, too, but especially you, because it's hard for a boy to grow up without a father. A lot of men who turned out bad might have ended up different if only they'd had a man to guide them, to keep them straight when they turned the wrong way. I know I haven't been around as much as I'd like—too busy making a fortune and becoming the greatest blacksmith of the Four Wards—and look where it's got me. All my work gone up in smoke, just like that. But I'm here for you now, lad. And I intend to see this through to the end. Now let's go up and teach those haukmar brutes how clever and sneaky two lads from Furrow with not two squares of sense between them can be!"

With twinkling eyes, Zinder slung his crossbow over his back, laid hold of the first rung, and started to climb.

"You are fortunate to have such a friend," Kithian said.

"Don't I know it," Kion said quietly.

Kion waited until Zinder was a safe distance before coming after him so he didn't nick him with the sword. It wasn't easy climbing with Truesilver in hand, and once again his soggy cloak slowed him down. He was more than ready to be rid of the smelly, sagging thing. Zinder kept having to wait for him and the light from the blade. The nimble nyn would have been up the rungs like a puff of air if he'd been on his own.

At last the light shone on the end of the shaft. A clay slab blocked their way.

When Zinder reached the top, he motioned for Kion to douse the light.

"Kithian, we no longer need your light," Kion whispered. Darkness filled the empty shaft.

The two of them stayed on the rungs, listening for several minutes. Finally, Zinder made a few soft grunts.

"It's shut fast," he said in a low voice. "Probably held by a bolt or some other mechanism. More work for the old nyn."

Zinder's tools clinked once again in the dark as he set to work on the covering.

Kion couldn't see what he was doing, but the amount of racket Zinder made worried him. Zinder started and stopped several times, but no matter what he tried, the grinding, scraping, sawing, and tapping echoed horribly inside the shaft.

Finally he stopped for a long, terrible stretch. Footsteps sounded on the stones above. Whispered voices conferred together in the dark.

"There are men above us," Kithian said.

But Zinder didn't need Kithian's warning. "Down, down— quick," he said in a panicked voice.

Kion fumbled and almost lost the sword in his shock. His foot slipped. He recovered, but the footsteps got louder, and sweat streamed from every part of him. His mind told him to rush down the ladder, but his body stayed where it was, clinging uselessly to the rungs. His hands started to shake. The shaft was pitch black. He was sure he'd fall if he started down. An awful thud and a blast of clean air arrested his senses.

Zinder squealed, and torchlight flickered down the shaft. The suddenness of it dazzled Kion's eyes.

"There he is!" shouted a voice.

"Got you, little fellow!" said another.

Kion could just make out the outline of Zinder disappearing through the top of the shaft.

"Unhand me, you dunderwit!" Zinder said.

More torchlight poured into the shaft. Kion was paralyzed with indecision. He could abandon Zinder, attempt to flee, and come back for him later, or leap up and try to save him and most likely get himself captured or killed. The moment seemed a fathomless forever.

In truth, the decision really only took a second. He had to save his friend. For good or ill, his body lurched into motion, and he clambered up the rungs as fast as he could.

"Careful, they will try to grab you the minute you're out," Kithian said.

The top half of Kion burst out of the shaft. A guard wearing a leather jerkin and looking plenty perplexed himself was backing away from the opening while maintaining a smothering grip on a squirming Zinder.

"Look out, lad. Behind—" Zinder shouted, but Kion didn't

hear the warning in time. He had just put his hands on the floor to pull himself out when someone grabbed him from behind. His arms were jerked and twisted behind his back. Pain shot through them, and he lost his grip on Truesilver. He dropped the blade, and the man in front of him rushed forward and kicked it away.

With a sudden heave, Kion's assailant yanked him clean out of the shaft and pinned him to the floor. Whoever it was, he outweighed Kion by a good measure. Kion flopped helplessly beneath what felt like half a dozen dead sheep on top of him.

"Now stop your struggling," said a man's voice in Kion's ear. "Unless you're working for Ilk, we don't mean you any harm."

"Don't listen to them, lad," Zinder said. "Quick as you like, he'll grab your sword and run us both through."

"Hush, you feisty little nyn," said the man holding Zinder. "Hormgar's not lying. Just tell us if you're on Ilk's side or not. And we'll know if you're lying—so no shenanigans."

"These men speak the truth," Kithian said.

"How can you be sure?" Kion said, though he barely had enough air in his lungs to voice the words.

"'Cause we're...we're astute about such things," Zinder's captor said.

"I am Kithian the True. I can see behind mere words to the designs of the heart, especially amongst simple folk, such as these."

"You heard Orvis," said the man on top of Kion, who apparently was called Hormgar.

"Oh, you're astute, all right," Zinder said. "Regular sages! Now let me go!"

"Ow!" Orvis said. "He bit me, Hormgar. The little gnat bit me!"

"Zinder, it's all right," Kion wheezed. "Let's hear them out." Hormgar let off the pressure a bit. "Please, sir. We're not on Ilk's side. We don't even know who that is."

"And you also swear that you mean no harm?" Hormgar said.

"I give you my word."

"Well, Orvis, what do you say?" A long pause followed, with a lot of breathing, and Hormgar seeming to grow heavier by the moment.

"Yes, yes, let's hear what they have to say. If for no other reason than to save my bloomin' hand. This nyn's half muskrat!"

Hormgar released Kion, and Orvis let go of Zinder.

Zinder gave Orvis a scathing look and snapped his teeth, but otherwise did him no further harm.

Hormgar picked up Truesilver and held the blade, admiring it as Kion rose to his feet.

"This is quite the blade you've got, boy. It tells me you're more than you look." Hormgar was indeed as large as he had felt on Kion's back. Though he was a little shorter than Kion, his leather jerkin struggled to cover his massive middle. His arms and neck were twice as thick as Kion's.

"If you'll please return my sword…" Kion said.

"In due time, in due time. We have your word, but forgive me if we don't exactly feel comfortable letting two armed men into our guardhouse without finding out a little bit more about them first."

Orvis had relieved Zinder of his crossbow, too, and held it in the air, well out of Zinder's reach, like a sweet treat dangled above a surly child.

Zinder took off his hat, which was never a good sign. His cheeks popped out like cherries against his white beard. "I don't trust these two one nick." He pointed with his hat at them. "Looking for a bribe, I'll warrant, or I'm the son of a haukmar. I'll bet you're not even real guards, are you? What sort of guard goes about unarmed in the middle of the night?"

"We already told you," Orvis said. "We're not on Ilk's side, don't you see? He took all our weapons and gave 'em to the haukmarn. Said it was to 'prevent bloodshed,' but he's always had gold rounds for eyes. Sold us for a gaggle of coin, no doubt, to these haukmar brutes. He sent most of the women and children off with a bunch of their harriers yestereve, but he's not ready to deal with us yet, so he locked all the stronghands in the barracks. Orvis and I weren't guarding this room, just up in the middle of the night using the privy, you see."

"He speaks true," Kithian said.

"What Orvis says is the plain truth," Hormgar said. "We figured maybe Ilk had decided to send in some assassins to do his dirty work when we heard someone down in the shaft. No offense, Master Nyn, but aside from your bite, you don't have much of the look of an assassin. And apart from this sword, neither does the boy. Still, we've told you our side, but you haven't given us your end. Why should we trust you? What's your business sneaking in here three winks shy of the crack of dawn?"

Zinder opened his mouth to answer, but Kion cut him off before he said something rash. Normally, it would have been Zinder who was the level-headed one, but nyn (well, Zinder at least, Kion didn't know about the others) had no tolerance for being picked up and bandied about like that. It made Zinder feel like he was being treated like a child or singled out for his height, and it would take him a good while before he forgave the poor guard, who probably didn't know any better.

"Fair enough," Kion said. "We're from Furrow. If you haven't heard, the haukmarn razed our village and left it in flames. I have relatives in Charring, and we followed the haukmar army as it marched south. We'd hoped to beat them here, but they run with a savage purpose. Though we found Charring already in haukmar hands, we decided to risk sneaking into the city to see if there was any hope of saving my family. And so we made our way up through the drains below, and here we stand before you."

"That's ill news about Furrow," Hromgar said.

Orvis's expression turned to one of pity. "Well, I'll give you marks for bravery, but have you gone bloomin' mad, child? There's seven hundred haukmarn outside these barracks. If you plan on heading into the city, you'd just as well fall on your sword right now. At least it would be a quicker death."

"You believe us, then?" Kion said.

"Aye, we do," Hormgar said. "It's too outlandish a tale for anyone to make up."

"Then, will you help us?" Kion asked.

"You heard what Orvis said. We're prisoners in our own barracks. And we're as helpless as you to do anything about it," Hormgar said.

"We're not asking you to go with us, just show us the way out of here and leave us to our own fate. That's all we need," Kion said.

Zinder still scowled, but the flush in his cheeks had diminished.

Hormgar crossed his arms, resting them atop his fat barrel of a belly. He took his time answering. "All right, we'll help," he said at last. "It's against my better judgment—seems like we'll just be sending you to your deaths—but you don't have a sword like this for nothing." He handed Truesilver back to Kion. "So listen here. Your best shot is getting out through one of the windows on the top floor. You've got some rope on you, so that's good. It's too far a drop otherwise. Follow me upstairs and I'll tell you more on the way."

Hormgar headed out of the room with Kion following, but Zinder tapped his foot and cleared his throat. "You're forgetting something, you giant oaf," he said to Orvis.

"Oh, right, here you go." Orvis handed him his crossbow.

Zinder inspected it with near parental doting and, at last satisfied it was unharmed, sauntered away with his nose pointed indignantly to the ceiling.

Chapter 28

OUT THE WINDOW

An eerie stillness filled the barracks as the four figures ascended the wide stairway to the second floor. Kion could not believe they had stumbled into this unexpected help in the midst of a city crawling with haukmarn. He eyed every door they passed, half expecting the haukmarn to burst through. Zinder was even more suspicious, never taking his eyes off the soldiers and constantly fingering his crossbow.

But Hormgar and Orvis, true to their word, led them to a wide hallway at the top of the stairs with no more than the muffed snoring of imprisoned soldiers to disturb the anxious silence.

"Don't worry," Orvis said once they reached the top of the stairs. "There's no haukmarn inside. Our fielder, Hyndric, was at least able to arrange that."

"Small consolation," Hormgar said. "This might be our last night in the land of sense and reason. I've heard frightening tales about the haukmar prison camps."

It looked like Hormgar was leading them to the large rectangular window at the end of the hallway. Many doors lined the passage to either side, all made of dark, stout wood. A thin rug ran down the middle of the passage, muffling the sound of their passing.

"Why don't you try to escape?" Kion asked.

"Don't think we haven't thought about it," Hormgar said. "But there's too many of us to slip past the guards outside. And even if we overwhelmed them, where would we go? Without any weapons, we'd be run down in the streets."

"What about the tunnels?"

"Humph. That might work for two twigs like you. The main tunnels are fine enough, but the ones leading to the drains would squeeze the stuffing out of Orvis and me. We'd never make it to freedom."

When they reached the end of the hall, Hormgar ignored the large window. Instead he opened the door to his right. They entered a room lit only by the moonlight, which streamed in through a pair of large windows in the far wall. Boxes and bags stacked to the ceiling cluttered the room, and the whole place smelled of oil and leather. Shelves full of dark bottles and small boxes lined the walls on either side of the door. Hormgar went to one of the two windows and cracked it open. A fresh breeze brushed against Kion's face. It tasted sweeter than honey after the gut-wrenching reek of the tunnels.

Hormgar pointed down to a walled area at the back of the barracks. Two large sparring rings, several empty weapon racks, and four archery targets ringed the large courtyard.

"That's the Marshaling Grounds," Hormgar said in a low voice. "You see those two brutes over there?" He pointed to his right, where a pair of huge haukmarn stood in front of wide double doors, dead center of the barracks. "They're guarding the only exit out the back. But even if they weren't there, if you went out those doors, you'd still have to climb the ten-foot walls of the grounds. It'd be a tough nut escaping that way. There's loads more guards out front, so it's even worse there. Your best shot is to lower a rope out this window and swing to the top of the outer wall. From there you can drop onto Rain Street, which runs along that side."

Zinder had to stand tiptoe to see out the window. "But won't those guards see us?" he asked in a concerned tone. He had mostly calmed down from the great offense of the "nyn-handling."

"I think not," Orvis said. "You see, if I'm thinking what Hormgar's thinking, we'll go over to the other end of the barracks and make some sort of distraction, right, Hormgar?"

"Just so. Don't start climbing until you hear the noises. Then, both of you shimmy down quick as lightning and be off. And remember, once you're out, don't go 'round to the front. Head to the back and set off from there. By the by, where in the Four Wards are you two headed, anyway?"

"Marlibrim Mansion," Kion said.

Hormgar raised an eyebrow. "If that's your family home, you're awful high stock. No wonder your sword looks like it came from the fane's own closet."

"A lot you know." Zinder's voice took on a note of exasperation. "His aunt lives there, yes, but he didn't get the sword from her. And he's not exactly in her good graces. More like the black sheep of the family, if you take my meaning."

"I'll leave that between you and the Marlibrims," Hormgar said. "But that district's been all cleared out. All the houses are empty. It's all haukmarn now. Are you sure your family's still there?"

"No, but we're going there anyway," Kion said. "We've a rough idea where it is, but if you could tell us the best way to go, that would save us some time."

Hormgar eyed Kion with a mixture of sadness and respect. "Well, you are quite the pair, aren't you? The mansion is straight on, due east of here, near Charring's outer wall. Got it?"

"Yes," Kion said. "Wait for the noises, climb down to the wall, and then head east to find my family."

"This plan can't be any worse than our first one," Zinder mumbled.

"Ask them for some oil. I see some on those shelves over there," Kithian said.

"What? Why?" Kion said without thinking.

"We may need it."

"I know it's risky, but at least it gives you a chance. And these haukmarn are not exactly the brightest lot," Hormgar said, answering Kion's question without knowing it wasn't meant for him.

"Oh, yes, well, we'll just have to see. Say, you don't happen to have any oil, do you?" Kion said.

The two guards and Zinder gave him blank looks.

"What do you want with oil?" Hormgar said.

Kion couldn't think of anything clever to say. After a moment he blurted out, "We may need it. I've found it's helpful in these sorts of...situations." Of course, this response did nothing to dismiss the puzzled expressions around him.

"Is it for a lantern?" Orvis asked.

Kion caught Zinder's eye and nodded toward the sword.

"No, of course not," Zinder said, catching the hint. "But it comes in handy for getting out of tight spots, greasing hinges, springing locks, if you see what I mean. But bother all that—do you have some or don't you?"

"Of course we do. This is a supply room, after all," Hormgar said. He went over to one of the shelves and pulled off a bottle made of dark glass. "Will this do?"

Kion waited awkwardly for Kithian's reply.

"Yes, that should be more than enough," Kithian said.

"Yes, that should be more than enough," Kion repeated, trying hard to speak in a conversational tone.

Zinder took the bottle and put it into his pack with his other tools.

Orvis cleared his throat to break the ensuing silence. "Well, it was nice meeting you fellows," he said. He offered his hand. Zinder pretended not to notice, but Kion shook it, and Hormgar's as well.

"If we can find some way to come back for you, we will," Kion said. "In any case, we shall not forget you."

The two soldiers gave them anxious looks and left the room, shaking their heads.

"We were fortunate to have such help. It is often at our greatest

need that we find a way has already been prepared for us."

"Are you saying you knew those two would be here to help us?"

"No, only that a way always presents itself. Your task is to follow when it comes, however difficult it may seem."

"You're talking to the blade about those two?" Zinder said. "Well, good riddance, I say." He went over to the window Hormgar had opened. He made sure the guards weren't looking and quietly slid the end of the rope through. "Open the other window and take this end."

"They weren't that bad," Kion said. He cracked open the second window and pulled the rope inside, careful not to make a sound. "Would you have treated intruders into your house any better?"

Kion brought the rope inside. While Zinder tied it off, Kion wrung as much water out of his soggy, foul-smelling cloak as he could. It would be much easier to climb without all that extra weight.

"Even a thief is a person," Zinder said, "not a sack of potatoes to be shook until their eyes pop out."

"Shh. We'd better keep quiet. We don't want to miss the signal."

Zinder finished tying the rope, and not a moment too soon. A loud crash came from the other end of the barracks, followed by heated, bickering voices.

"Here we go." Zinder slid the end of the rope down the wall in the best compromise between silence and speed he could manage. "You go first."

"Can you make the climb with me in your hand?" Kithian asked.

"I think so. Climbing down won't be as hard as climbing up. But I really wish you'd come with a scabbard."

Kion glanced outside. One of the haukmarn was heading over to investigate the noises. The other was watching him from in front of the doors. Kion flung one leg out and then the other. He let go of the windowsill and started down. It was only about a fifteen-foot drop to the Marshaling Grounds wall. The sword made it hard to grip with his right hand, but his worries that the guards would suddenly turn and notice him overshadowed his fears of falling. His eyes darted between the dark shapes of the haukmarn to his left and the wall to his right. Hormgar and Orvis kept up a terrific racket, hooting and bellowing about something. About halfway down, the guard who'd gone to investigate started shouting at them to quit their arguing and go back to bed.

Kion swung onto the top of the wall but wobbled when he let go of the rope. After one long, terrifying moment, he regained his balance. He pressed himself against the side of the building and waited for Zinder with a hammering heart.

Zinder slid down like he was floating on air and landed lightly beside Kion.

With one last glance at the irate guards, now shaking their fists and threatening all manner of torture and malice against Hormgar and Orvis, Kion dropped over the edge with a great clank and clatter. But the haukmarn kept shouting and gave no indication they heard it. A moment later, Zinder landed gracefully beside him with no more noise than a whisper.

And then they were off into the dark, narrow, winding streets of Charring. Zinder had been here many times, and though he had never had occasion to travel to Marlibrim Mansion, he had little difficulty directing them away from the barracks so as not to be seen by the guards out front. As they put distance between themselves and the barracks, the sounds of haukmarn carousing the streets drifted in from every direction. For the moment they were more incoherent than threatening, and none seemed close, but Kion's heart quickened. This was it. No turning back now. It was straight through to the end, whether in triumph or disaster.

They turned east and set their faces towards Marlibrim, racing through the empty streets as fast as they dared, stopping to listen at every new cross street. Soon they reached the main thoroughfare, a road wide enough for two carts to travel abreast.

It stretched right up to the edge of the buildings. Most of the structures here were prim, slender, two-storied affairs with shingled roofs. At any other time, Kion would have marveled at the splendidly maintained pavement lined by fine old houses rising toward the central square, but now his only thought was to flee across the open ground as quickly as possible.

This, they could not do. For coming down the street marched a company of armored haukmarn, eight strong, half of them wielding pikes and the other half axes. Zinder and Kion retreated into the shadows and hid behind a pile of refuse. Kion had never been so grateful for the sight of trash in all his life.

The harriers marched down the street at a good pace, scowling at the passing houses, as if their very beauty was an offense. In a matter of moments, they passed Kion and Zinder's side street. One gargoyle-faced brute glanced their way. He sniffed the air and paused a moment before falling back in step with the others.

Kion and Zinder waited until the patrol crested the hill before dashing across to the narrow street on the opposite side.

"The haukmarn may have the eyes of a slug, but their sense of smell is nothing to sniff at," Zinder said. "Thankfully, the citizens of Charring are none too tidy. That trash surely masked our scent."

"How much farther have we to go?" Kithian asked.

As if in answer, Zinder said, "Halfway there," and picked up the pace.

Kion had never seen Zinder run so fast. Though his friend always joked about being old, he was only thirty-five. According to him, that was old for a nyn. He claimed nyn rarely lived past fifty. But he seemed far more youthful than Kion on this night. He bounded down the streets with the grace of a deer in flight. Kion, in contrast, was so hindered by the ill-fitting armor and his efforts to keep the clinking, jangling, and slapping of the plates and mail to a minimum, he found it difficult to keep up.

They skirted the edge of a wide park almost half as big as

Furrow's commons, but far grander. Stone benches and potted flowers dotted the pavement. In the center stood a large statue of a robed figure holding a book aloft.

After that, the streets ran together in Kion's mind. The only variations in the long, dark run came from the sound of the haukmar patrols marching through the city. Occasionally, Zinder would bring them to a halt to listen and, not liking what he heard, would double back down a different route. Soon, glimpses of the city's outer wall poked through between the houses. The great barrier hovered, gray and skeletal some distance away, but the sight of it gave them something to aim for.

They passed through a part of the city where all the houses were one story, small, and dark. The smoke streaking from the chimneys was weak and wispy, as if the buildings were on their last breath. The outer wall was easier to spot here, but it remained a good distance away. They met no sounds of haukmarn in this area and so rushed through it with all the more haste.

Past that, the houses got bigger again and more varied in style. They passed a fountain that surely would have been lovely during the day, but at night looked sterile, grim, and lifeless. Sightings of the outer wall now became more frequent and closer than ever. So did the sounds of the haukmarn. Patrols marched down seemingly every second or third street. The roads were wider here, like the main one they'd passed earlier. Down one of them, in an open square, camped dozens of haukmarn, but most looked asleep. A single pair of guards wandered around the edge. When they had their backs turned, Zinder and Kion rushed past into a cross street.

"We should be close to Marlibrim," Zinder whispered, pointing at the outer wall looming ahead. "Only a few more streets to go."

At the next corner, they paused to catch their breaths. Kion was doubly glad for the sight of the wall. It meant that not only were they close to Marlibrim, but also afforded a much-needed break in the running. Kion's side ached with needling stabs. He rubbed his neck and arms where the ill-fitting armor chafed him the most. But Zinder took off again before he could fully catch his breath.

Kion longed to call for another stop but dared not—not with haukmarn swarming all around them. Boots pounded the pavement, gruff voices rumbled in the night, and vile laughter echoed down the streets. Not for the first time, Kion questioned the wisdom of their decision to come here.

Zinder proved an able infiltrator. His sharp eyes always searched out just the right path to weave through the wandering patrols. But then they came to the very last street before the wall. Here, nothing short of invisibility would get them through. For not only did haukmar sentries dot the walls, which were always in view here, but the street itself had scores of haukmarn camped out farther down. Kion and Zinder would have to pass in plain view of them if they meant to reach the mansion.

The one encouraging thing was the sight of a towering three-story structure not a hundred yards down the street. From everything his mother had told him, Kion knew it had to be Marlibrim.

They pulled back around a corner.

"This may be as far as we go, lad," Zinder said. He was winded like Kion from the long run. "Unless we can turn ourselves into green-breasted crossbills, we'll get no farther."

"Kithian, what are we to do? That's the street to the mansion, but it's crawling with haukmarn. Most of them are sleeping, but there are guards on duty as well." Kion said, trying not to breathe too hard.

"If there are two, there are a hundred," Zinder said.

"Could we not cross farther up and wander through the grounds of the houses until we reach your family's?"

"The houses next to the mansion lie right up against the city wall. There are sentries up there as well and fences and walls run between each estate. Zinder could probably sneak through, but I'd be sure to give us away, especially in this armor."

Kion measured Kithian's silence in beads of sweat. He must have wiped his face ten times before Kithian answered.

"These are wealthy people. They must have stables, yes?"

Kion eased up to the corner and darted his head out for a look. "Yes, they all have stables, from the looks of it."

"Look for one we can get into without being seen."

Kion, as usual, had been telling Zinder what Kithian said. Zinder risked a quick look of his own.

"We can probably get into the one just to the right of us. The gate's been left open there, by some stroke of luck," Zinder said, rushing back to the shadows. "Phew, I ducked away just when that guard turned, but I don't think he saw me."

"Kithian, what good is a stable going to do us?" Kion asked.

"Get me there and you will see."

Zinder shook his head when Kion told him. "Another mad plan, but I suppose we've gotten this far on madness; why change?"

"Whatever you've got in mind, Kithian, I don't see how we'll get there anyway," Kion said.

"Wait until the moon is behind the clouds and sneak across."

"But what about the guards down the street?" Kion asked.

"If we time it just right, I think the sword might actually be onto something," Zinder said. "That haukmar snoring is louder than a sawmill. It should mask the sound of our footsteps, and without the moon, we'll be no more substantial than a pair of passing shadows."

And so they crept up to the corner as close as they dared and waited. This part was the worst of all. The clouds never grew quite thick enough to hide the moon completely. The minutes stacked on top of each other until the weight of them was unbearable. Sunrise would be coming soon, and their chance would be gone forever.

Suddenly, a cool darkness spread over Charring. The moon

sank beneath a thick black mask of clouds.

Zinder looked, waited...and then rushed into the street, hunched down to make himself as small as possible. Kion did his best to imitate him. They shuffled across, their steps making a *pap, pap, clack, clack,* that seemed even louder than the haukmar snoring to Kion's ears, but no alarm was raised. They progressed in quick, agonizing movements, tiptoeing amongst the enormous bodies of the slumbering haukmarn.

Without warning, Zinder went prone. Kion instinctively did the same. They landed next to an enormous haukmarn, snoring on his side. Kion could not bear to look at him, but the repulsive odor and shuddering made him feel as if a great mound of putrid flesh was about to fall on top of him. All the while, the heavy steps of a haukmar guard sounded closer. Then they stopped. All the world was snoring and breathing for many long, quivering, torturous moments.

At long last, the steps returned the way they came.

Kion allowed himself to breathe. Zinder rose, half-crawling now. Kion stumbled after him, pawing at the pavement. Just then, the clouds fluttered overhead, and moonlight pulsed all around them. In one last, heart-squeezing rush, they burst through the open gate and into the vacant haven of the small courtyard.

They collapsed in the shadows. While they recovered from the terror of their long midnight race, which had ended in the most terrifying moment of all, the moon cast off its dark mantle and shone forth once more. Yet no sounds of pursuit came.

A comparatively modest, two-story mansion rose before them, with a squat little stable off to the right. The stable didn't look like it could hold more than two horses and perhaps a very basic carriage. Dead leaves formed an unwelcome carpet across the grounds. A broken window on the second floor glared down at them.

"Now, into the stables," Kithian said. *"And I will tell you how we shall win the day."*

Chapter 29

TRUESILVER'S GIFT

They found the stables as empty as the courtyard. Not even an empty cart or carriage occupied the small space. The hay in the stalls was gray with age.

"Looks abandoned," Zinder said.

"All the better for what we must do," Kithian said.

Kion set the blade against the wall. He needed to sit down for this.

"Truesilver is going to tell us his plan," Kion said. The light within the gems of the hilt sparked with great intensity as it spoke, while Kion relayed the words to Zinder.

"There are two things you should know about glaives. We have each been given two gifts: a common one and a special. The common gift is more like a quality that can be used with or without the swordspeaker's consent. Mine is the ability to see the truth in the spoken word. It is easiest for me to discern among the simple and those who are generally honest to begin with. But if the speaker is more learned, or his mind is wrapped in schemes and subtlety and he is accustomed to deceiving the judicious, it is not so easy. With such folk, I require my glaivebond to be touching the person while I am drawn. In this way, even the darkest of lies may be broken."

"So, that's why you trusted those bumbling gnatters," Zinder said.

"Yes, that makes sense now," Kion said.

"But I have another, greater gift still. Before I tell you of it, know that it comes with a warning. There is a right way to use all gifts of this sort, and a wrong way. The wrong way is always easier, always a temp-

tation, for it is fueled by the glaive drawing upon the life of his glaive-bond. This is forbidden, for though at first it will have little effect, over time, it will slowly drain the glaivebond's spirit until it kills him. True glaives never use their gifts in this way, even at greatest need."

With these words, an edge came into Kithian's voice, both threatening and dire, but it softened as he continued.

"But there is a proper way to use the greater gifts, and that is through a reagent, a catalyst of some sort, which is different for each glaive. My reagent is oil. My pommel is removable, and the handle inside is hollow. When oil is placed within, I am able to use my greater gift for as long as the reagent lasts. And now I will tell you of my gift: it is fire. Fire to push back an enemy, fire to cut through the armor of a foe. You have but to command me and my blade shall burst into flames, hotter than the fiercest blaze, and yet, while you hold me, you cannot be harmed by this fire or any other. Whatever catches fire from these flames will burn in like fashion. What is more, I am able to control and shape the flames to a certain degree, to call them back or send them forth as you command. And that is my gift, Kion Swordspeaker. Use it only at great need. And this hour, I deem the need to be great."

The strange metal of Truesilver's blade glimmered with an otherworldly sheen as he finished.

"Fire. Your gift is fire," Kion said. He sat for long moments in wonder and awe. He would never have imagined such a thing possible, and yet he was not surprised now that he knew of it. Something at the back of Kithian's voice had been burning all along. And yet, how could a sword, a creation of metal, make fire?

Zinder walked over to the blade and pointed to the pommel. "May I?" At a nod from Kion, he unscrewed it. Sure enough, the grip was hollow inside. He voiced Kion's inner thoughts. "The flying part, I was open to. Magnets fly in a way, and swords are metal. Even the truth-telling, I was willing to give it the benefit of the doubt, for those fellows turned out all right in the end, I suppose. But fire? I'm a blacksmith, lad. I know fire. I know what burns and what doesn't. And cold steel—or whatever metal this blade is made from—doesn't catch fire. The only kind of fiery steel is the kind fresh from the kiln. And no one would want to be swinging that around."

"How, Kithian? How does it work? How can you make fire that bends to your will?" Kion gazed the length of the blade, mesmerized by the strange silver metal. The craftsmanship was unquestionable, but there were no markings or indications that might explain how it could produce flame, or where the fire would come from.

"It is through the Spark, but there is no time to speak of that now. We must hurry; the night is all but fled, and we must strike while the darkness lasts."

"My apologies to our talking sword there," Zinder said. "But I for one am unconvinced. If it wants us to trust it with whatever plan it's got, it could at least give us some kind of demonstration."

"We dare not risk the light, nor catching fire to the barn before it is time," Kithian said.

"Before it's time?" Kion said. "You mean, you plan to set the barn on fire?"

"Yes, we will need to generate a significant blaze to be able to overcome so many enemies."

"You really think we can defeat that many haukmarn? Even with an inferno, I don't see how. Won't they just retreat into the mansion? And we can't burn that. Mother and Tiryn might be inside."

"The fire may or may not be enough to defeat them. Which is why we will use it primarily as a distraction."

"A distraction for what?" Zinder leaned in towards the blade, as if he were trying to hear its voice without Kion's help.

"A distraction for Zinder to enter the house and rescue your family —if they are there."

Zinder looked Kion hard in the eye. "It wants to send *me* into the lion's den?"

"Kithian, I thought I would be the one to rescue them. Zinder is no warrior."

"You said it yourself. We dare not burn the mansion down. And a direct assault would surely fail. Even if you got inside, you would easily be overwhelmed fighting in such close quarters. But Zinder is stealthy. I watched him move through the streets. With a large enough distraction, he may be able to enter the house and get your family out unnoticed."

Kion and Zinder exchanged troubled looks. While neither of them much liked the plan, it was probably the only chance they had.

"Ask if I'm supposed to sneak in through the front door, the back door, or just flap my arms and fly in through the window," Zinder said.

"The last one. Though not by flight. Our friend Nar-vel-lis spoke of a tree reaching very near the window on the top floor. That would be the best chance of entering unnoticed. Once inside the house, it should not be difficult to search for signs of your mother and sister. The distraction outside will be considerable."

"Zinder's an excellent climber, but...well, I suppose it would be unexpected. What do you think, Zinder?"

"Well, aside from the fact that I still have no faith in a sword turning into a torch, I do think I would have a chance getting into the mansion if I went alone."

"You know you don't have to—"

"Now, lad, we went through this in the tunnel, remember? It's my family just as much as yours. And if you trust this sword to spit fire and vanquish a battalion all by itself, I suppose you'll have to at least trust me to do my part."

And so it was settled. They filled Truesilver's handle with oil and screwed the pommel back on. Curiously, the liquid inside had no effect on the weight or balance of the blade.

"How will I know when you've gone through the oil?" Kion asked.

"The flames will extinguish," Kithian said. *"But I will warn you when it begins to run low."*

Kion shed his cloak, and Zinder made a few last adjustments to his armor to ensure a better fit. Then the two friends stood facing each other before the door.

"This is even worse than the tunnels," Zinder muttered. "I was prepared to face death by your side, lad. I never thought we'd separate on purpose. But that armor will serve you well."

"It's nynnian made," Kion said. "I'm practically invincible. And I have Truesilver. It's you I'm worried about."

"Me? I'm just visiting the riff-raff at the mansion. They probably put all the weak ones in there for protection."

"I'm serious. What if you don't make it back?"

"I think you'll have plenty of danger on your own without having to worry about me." Zinder gripped Kion's arm tightly. "If things turn grim, remember your family. They're why we're here. I'll be thinking of them—and you—right to the end."

And that was all that needed to be said. Zinder was right. His family needed them—both of them. Kion could not do this alone. Ever since his father's death, he had been trying to restore his family's honor. All the training and suffering, all the long nights and studying the forms, it had all been for nothing. His father's honor was never in doubt. The song of his father had inspired the greatest warrior in the land to fight on when all others fled. But his father had given Kion a charge, long before he had ever dreamed of taking up the sword to defend his honor. "Protect your mother and sister with all that is in you." It was right there in the letter all along. He knew the words by heart, and yet somehow he had missed them. The best way to honor his father's memory was to protect the ones he loved. Maybe all the training wasn't a waste. Maybe it was for this instead, for this hour, when his mother and sister needed him most.

Zinder turned and passed silently out the door. He crossed the courtyard, a mere shadow of motion. In moments, he was lost in the dark wall separating this estate from the next. The wall was taller than Kion by a fair stretch, but the limbs of a nearby tree rustled and, quick as a moonbeam, a dark, nyn-sized shape appeared at the top. The shape lingered a moment before a muted thud told Kion that his friend had passed to the other side.

Good old Zinder.

Kion held Truesilver out in front of him. He remembered how the people of Furrow had chanted against him. He had wondered then if that was what it felt like to charge into the enemy ranks. What he now felt was wholly different. He was not thinking about the enemy at all. All his thoughts were of his mother and sister.

"I hope I don't fail them," he said.

"Whether in victory or defeat, no warrior can fail so long as he stays true to his honor. Go boldly, swordspeaker. For now we fall upon our enemies with glaivefire."

Chapter 30

GLAIVEFIRE

The time for stealth had passed. Kion lowered the visor of his father's helm.

"Truesilver, bring forth your fire," he said. His voice trembled in fearful anticipation.

Crimson flames enveloped the length of the blade. They fluttered and pulsed in silken waves. Truesilver's flames were darker than natural ones, and more opaque. Ordinary fire runs a mix of red, yellow, orange, and even blue, but this had no variation. It was red straight through.

"Strike the air," Kithian said.

As Kion did so, a bright jet leapt from the blade to a nearby bale of hay. In a heartbeat, the flames spread through the straw. From there they flowed up the wall in rivulets of ruby-colored light. A curious warmth enveloped Kion, yet it came neither from the fire of the blade itself nor the rapidly growing blaze around him, but from within.

Another bale caught fire. Flames danced among the rafters. His mind screamed danger. Had he not trusted that the flames were under Kithian's power, he would have fled into the night.

"The time has come. Let us teach these foul creatures to know fear."

Kion flung open the barn door so that it banged against the outer wall. If the haukmarn were not aware of him before, they were now.

Two guards rushed up to the gate. Firelight glowed through the gaps between the walls and roof of the stable, but the fire remained within. One of the hulking figures pointed and let out a satisfied grunt, pleased to find someone who could offer a bit of sport. The other took his spear in both hands and charged forward with a great cry.

"Stay close to the fire," Kithian said.

The light seeping out from the barn lit up the face of the onrushing haukmar in fiendish shadows. The speed of his advance took Kion aback. He was halfway across the courtyard in three steps. If it had been a charging bull, Kion could not have felt more helpless.

"This isn't enough fire! When is more coming?" The only flames in sight were those rippling along his blade.

"It will take a few more moments before it is strong enough. You must hold your own until it is ready," Kithian said. He sounded unsettlingly calm. Did he think Kion could last ten seconds in a fight with this rockslide of a creature barreling straight for him?

Kion was not given the luxury of sharing his doubts. The haukmar leveled his weapon at Kion's chest. Kion lurched to the side, moving too quickly for the guard to adjust. Surprising even himself, he managed to pull off a counterstrike. It had no real force to it, but it clipped the spear's haft as the haukmar passed. It must have been a lucky hit, for it sliced the wood in two.

The guard stared at his worthless weapon in anger, then hurled it to the ground, howling curses into the night. He could still throttle Kion if he got his hands on him, but the flaming sword made him hesitate.

Seeing the haukmar's fear, Kion held forth the blade, trying to keep his enemy at bay. Out in the streets came noise that the slumbering harriers were stirring. Kion had to press his advantage while he had it.

"Crush the skin bag!" The haukmar beckoned the other guard to come help. The one by the gate set his spear and tore across the little courtyard, aiming to run Kion through the heart.

Kion shifted so that the unarmed haukmar was between him and the one charging in. The first haukmar howled his displeasure but was unwilling to risk the blistering fire to maneuver around him. Kion was just about to lunge in for a strike and risk a counterattack when the flames curled out from under the roof and onto the wood shingles.

"Swing me in a wide arc," Kithian said.

Kion had no idea what he was doing but was too terrified not to obey. He shouted, "Glaivefire!" and swung his blade. The flames jumped from the roof in a blazing waterfall. The fire lit into the haukmar's neck and shoulders. His helmet and metal armor, which encased his legs and gut, protected him from the fire, but his arms and chest were covered only in leather. His jerkin and the ends of his greasy hair burst into flames.

"Gahhhhhhhrgh!" the brute screamed.

"That is the way, swordspeaker," Kithian said, his voice intensifying. *"Swing or thrust me in the direction you wish and the glaivefire will smite your foes."*

No sooner had Kithian spoken the words than a spear thrust landed on his side. The impact felt like an anvil dropped on his ribs, but the haukmar had not built up enough momentum to puncture Zinder's fine craftsmanship.

Kion swung Truesilver blindly in the direction of the attack. The blade bounced off something, a grazing blow at best. The ensuing screams of pain came not from his sword strike, but from the channel of fire pouring off the roof and across the second guard's side. Both haukmarn lurched aimlessly, wailing for relief.

Flames claimed three sides of the barn now. They rose into the night, a crimson beacon of destruction. Kion held his side, still smarting from the blow, but a new sight made him forget his pain.

More haukmarn poured in through the gate, wielding great axes that looked heavy enough to crush even nynnian armor.

But seeing what Truesilver had done, and with the blazing pillar of flame beside him, Kion let out a bellowed cry of "Glaivefire!" and rushed to meet them. Swinging Truesilver in perpetual arcs, the relish of swordplay flowed through him. It was as if he were back on the farm, practicing his forms. Only this time, his strokes sent fiery jets shooting from the barn. They rained down upon the heads of his foes, drowning them in a shower of flame and agony.

The haukmar axes never got to strike. The towering figures wilted before him, their faces stricken in horror. Kion took no joy in their screams but pressed on, rushing into the street.

The harriers outside were all roused now. Armored guards shouted orders, barking at others to arm themselves and get into position. Those nearest the gate could have easily closed in, but, eyeing the crimson fire, they held back.

"Archers, form a line!" shouted a gangly haukmar a hundred feet away. He was taller than most, but unusually thin. Around him, haukmar bowmen rushed in and nocked arrows. A few of the haukmarn close by, realizing they were in the line of fire, scattered to the sides or ran back down the street. A handful remained, too terrified of the warrior with the flaming blade to take stock of other dangers around them.

"On my mark!" the leader of the archers shouted, unconcerned by the possibility of friendly fire.

"What are we going to do?" Kion said. This was a danger he had not considered. The haukmarn arrows were longer and thicker than normal arrows. Could they pierce his armor? He wasn't anxious to put Zinder's work to the test. He looked back to the flames. A tree beside the barn had now caught fire, but that was a good forty feet from where he stood. "I don't even have a shield. Should we go back?"

"No, we have enough flames now. Run to the tree and swing. Trust the fire to protect you," Kithian said.

"Ready!"

Kion wanted to ask how flames could protect against arrows, but he dared not delay. He ran toward the tree and shouted, "Glaivefire!" He slashed the air, and a wave of fire cascaded like snow falling from the branches. Carried by some invisible wind, it landed a few feet in front of him.

"Aim!"

A small pocket of fire remained on the tree; the rest of it fanned out in a line stretching the breadth of the street. Though there was no fuel to sustain it, the flames leapt into the air, forming a ten-foot high wall of flames between Kion and the archers. He marveled at this strange curtain of crimson light. It should have died on the pavement, but it clung to the ground as if a crack had opened up from the depths, releasing some conflagration into the world above. The haukmarn nearest to it ran screaming into the night, several of them aflame.

"Fire!"

"Run, swordspeaker, run!"

Kion ran to the far side of the street while zipping barbs filled the air. Judging by the screams, several found their mark in those haukmarn foolish enough to stay in the line of fire. The rest hummed past, set aflame by the flickering wall and quickly consumed once they landed.

"Quick! Another!" shouted the archery commander.

"That was a good bit of luck," Kion said. "But we can't count on it every time."

"Luck had nothing to do with it. The haukmarn fire the arrows, but they do not say where they land."

The opaque wall did not stop them from loosing another volley. This time an arrow whizzed so close to Kion's shoulder, it whistled when it went past, but the arrows failed to connect on the second volley. The haukmarn were spared this time, for most had by now scattered into the city.

"Move to higher ground!" the commander ordered his bowmen. "Get up in those houses!"

"We must keep moving."

The flames in the street spread to a second tree. The fire climbed hungrily through the branches, consuming the living wood like dry kindling.

"But how am I going to get around the wall of fire? It's blocking the whole street," Kion said.

"Do you forget? My flames cannot harm you as long as you hold me in your grasp," Kithian said.

Kion stared at the undulating wall. It was one thing to be told the flames would do him no harm, and quite another to pass through them. Still, he had been holding Truesilver the whole time and had yet to suffer any burns.

"I guess I'll just have to trust you." Not wishing to wait until he had second thoughts, Kion plunged headlong into the wall of fire.

He passed through as though it were a puff of wind. The flames did not so much as singe his hair or stir up a whiff of smoke.

The haukmarn on the other side stood aghast at the armored warrior who could pass through fire unscathed.

"He's not human!" they cried.

"It's a spirit of vengeance!"

"Fall back!"

They turned and fled before him.

"For the Four Wards!" Kion let forth his battle shout and took off running, emboldened at the sight of the fleeing haukmarn.

"Hold, swordspeaker," Kithian said. *"Do not outrun the flames, lest our enemies rally and turn from their flight."*

Kion checked his stride and pulled up just past the second burning tree.

"Right," he said. "More fire." He swung the blade over his head, and a great spurt of flame shot from the tree onto the ground before him, forming another wall of fire, some fifty feet in length, along the right side of the street. A wall of stone ran beside the blaze, creating a corridor for him to pass through. Several overhanging branches beside the stone wall caught fire. The whole right side of the street was now ablaze, every structure between Kion and the barn smothered in red death.

"How are we going to stop this? The whole city will go up in flames."

"I can quench them in an instant should you desire. But we need them yet. We have yet to reach the mansion."

Kion marched steadily down the street, keeping pace with the advancing flames and laying down walls of fire to hasten their spread. The blaze surged forward ever more violently the larger it grew. If Kithian was not able to stop it when the time came, the city would surely be lost.

The only haukmarn remaining in the street were a line of armored guards standing in front of Marlibrim Mansion. But a *zipppt* and a jarring knock on Kion's helm told him that at least one archer had reached higher ground.

"The oil is running low, swordspeaker. We must save the last of it to draw out those guarding the mansion. Hurry! Run!" Kithian said.

Kion sprinted the last stretch amidst a hail of arrows. Only two struck him, but they deflected off his arm and shoulder. The nynnian steel held true, even against the massive barbs of the haukmarn.

When he reached the line of haukmarn guarding the entrance to Marlibrim, the arrows ceased. Kion stopped, momentarily puzzled. The archers had not shown any regard for their own before. But then the line parted, and an armored haukmar, wielding a hefty axe with a notched blade, stepped forth, and Kion knew why the arrows had stopped.

Vayd Mokán stood before him, grim and deadly.

Chapter 31

THE BURNING TREE

C old fear seized Kion at the gates.

Vayd ran his black tongue across his lips. The haukmar leader's dark eyes reflected the crimson fire wafting skyward as it consumed the houses and grounds beyond Marlibrim, but another fire smoldered within, a hateful light, an unquenchable thirst to dominate all who opposed him. The look in those eyes shattered the fragile courage and confidence Kion had built from his victories in the street. He forgot all about the fire and his sword and why he was there. All he could think of was Vayd's gloating face as he stood over the fallen body of Strom Glyre.

"Who dares to threaten the Zaron of Charring? Name yourself before you die," Vayd said. He shifted his mighty battleaxe off his shoulder and gripped the haft with both hands. His shoulder armor, like those of the harriers beside him, was embedded with glowing white stones that gave off a noxious odor, faint at this distance, yet still irksome.

Pools of weakness welled up inside Kion, sapping his will. Vayd was a battle-hardened giant. Kion was just a boy. Every moment he stood staring at Vayd, the larger Vayd seemed to become. This was the monster that had killed the greatest hero of the Four Wards. How could Kion hope to stand against him?

"Speak, fool. What do you call yourself?" Vayd said.

Kion looked down at Truesilver. He was not ready for this.

"What do I do?" he whispered.

"It is not strength that wins the battle, but he who strikes true,"

Kithian said. *"Do what you came here to do. Save your family. Think of your purpose rather than what keeps you from it."*

Kithian's answer told him nothing, and yet it told him everything. Kion tore his eyes from Vayd and looked to the mansion behind him. It rose as elegant and deathly as a mausoleum. A paved courtyard filled the space between the gate and the main entrance. In the middle of the courtyard stood an odd-shaped poplar tree, its branches and leaves in the shape of an upside-down pear. Three stories of windows looked down upon the courtyard and the street. No lights shone within. The house looked empty, but somewhere inside, his sister and mother needed him, and Zinder as well. Their escape depended on Kion creating a distraction. He did not have to defeat Vayd and his guards, only occupy them for as long as he could.

Struggling to keep his hand steady, Kion pulled up his visor. That simple act might have been the bravest thing he had yet done.

"My name does not matter. I have come to give justice to you and your marauding horde. You have no place here. Leave our lands at once or die where you stand." He did not know which came first, the courage or the words, but they fed off each other such that by the time he finished, he half believed he could hold his own against these foul creatures, perhaps even Vayd Mokán. For how long, he did not know, but he would not go down easily. What was it Kithian had told him? *Deeds spent in a just cause are never in vain.*

Vayd's eyes narrowed while the hatred within flashed brighter. "I know you, whelp. I do not easily forget the face of a fool. You are that mouse that came to squeak over the dead body of your fallen lion at the Clefts. You have grown even more foolish since then. Is it you who set Charring ablaze? If so, it's an odd way to save a city."

Yes. The fire. How had he forgotten it? He glanced to his right, where the mansion next door was engulfed in a crimson inferno. He closed his helm and whispered to Kithian, "Do we have enough oil to defeat Vayd and his men?"

"Yes, but we have outrun the fire. And it is too far between this house and its neighbor for the flames to travel. Our best hope is to reach that tree and set it ablaze. The haukmarn will never let us pass, but I believe I see a way. You must challenge their leader to a duel and set the tree on fire during the fight."

"We could try to lure them back into the street," Kion whispered hastily, desperate to avoid the plan Kithian suggested.

"I believe this Vayd is too shrewd to fall for such tactics. If he was looking for battle, we would already be fighting."

"Why the muttering, whelp? Is it madness or just plain fear?"

Kion took in a quivering breath. Defeating Vayd in single combat would be nigh impossible, even with Truesilver. But what else could he do? "Remember what you came for," he told himself.

He raised his flaming sword high. "Yes, I set Charring ablaze. And I will raze the entire city before I see it fall into the hands of haukmar filth. I, a mere boy, am the one who sent your army fleeing into the night. And now I come for you, Vayd Mokán. For you killed a man a hundred times your better. A good man. A great man." And here his voice broke, and he was forced to pause. "You refused my challenge to avenge his death because I had no blade. Well, I have found one now. Do you see it? This is Truesilver, greatest sword of the North. If you wish to stop me, I challenge you once more to a duel. Will you refuse again like a coward? Or will you fight me and end this once and for all?"

It was as if a veil fell over Vayd's face at these words. His rage cooled, and the calculating part of his mind took over. He answered in a way that made him far more dangerous than if he had responded in the unthinking, wrathful manner favored by the rest of the haukmarn.

"What are the terms?"

"We fight for the city of Charring. If I win, you and your army leave. If I lose, the flames die with me."

Vayd snorted derisively. "How will you put out the fires when you're dead?"

"Look at that fire." Kion pointed back down the street. "Have you ever seen flames so thick and hot before, which spread so quickly and stay burning even upon cold stone with nothing to sustain them? It is no natural fire. You know this to be true. It is glaivefire. It is my fire, and it obeys my will. I promise that if you deal me a mortal blow, the flames will extinguish along with my life."

Vayd looked up and down his line of guards. A few pressed forward, itching to be rid of this insolent gnat buzzing at the gates. In any other circumstances, Vayd would no doubt have ordered them to charge in and rip Kion to shreds, or he would have done so himself. But there was something about this boy that gave him pause. He had already routed two hundred of his harriers in the streets. And now the city was all but lost unless Vayd could put an end to the blaze. For all his skill in battle, he was powerless to stop this fire unless what Kion said was true. Vayd wanted Charring badly. A loss here would set them back many days in the war. If there was any chance of saving it, he was inclined to take the risk.

And setting aside the flaming sword, what risk could there be from an untested whelp like the one before him? Once the fire was out, he would have Charring and this strange blade as well. If he could learn the secrets of the red fire raging through the city, it would prove a mighty weapon in the coming war.

"Very well, I accept," Vayd said. "We shall fight for the city of Charring, according to the terms you have spoken."

Kion nodded. Inside, his fears bubbled and threatened to boil, melting the thin wick of his resolve, which alone kept his hopes for his family alive.

"Shall we fight here?" Kion asked, trying not to give away his intentions to get nearer to the tree.

"No, there is not enough room. We will fight in the court-yard." He motioned for Kion to step through.

The haukmar line parted. Kion tried to look unafraid as he passed through the towering corridor of giants. Vayd fell in behind him. It felt like turning his back on a predator. Kion feared for his life every step of the way but did his best to keep a steady pace and not rush ahead, lest his fear be written for all to see.

"Vayd gestured to one of his guards as you passed," Kithian said. *"I do not know what he meant by it, but it seemed to be some predetermined sign. Be wary."*

It was all Kion could do to keep from looking back, but he strode forward as if he had no reason to suspect anything.

The haukmar guards marched into the courtyard and formed a ring around it. They remained silent, but their eyes bored into him with undisguised malice. He would have felt safer surrounded by a pack of rabid wolves.

He stopped in front of the tree. "How long until the oil runs out?" he asked in a whisper.

"A minute or two, no more. You must begin the battle at once, and you must win, swordspeaker, and win quickly."

Kion took up position, ten paces from Vayd. "Shall we begin?"

Vayd rolled his thick neck casually. "I suppose we should start before the entire city crumbles to ashes. But what about your blade? Am I to fight against your fire as well as your steel? That seems an unfair advantage."

"Do you not have the advantage in size, strength, and experience?"

"We cannot make excuses for what fate has given us. I am one of the smallest of my race, and yet no haukmar has ever defeated me."

"Hurry, swordspeaker. Enough talk. My fire is waning," Kithian said.

"My blade has fire. If you wish to fight with fire, bring a blade that has it. Otherwise, let us begin, lest your harriers think your delays and complaints come from cowardice."

"You will learn to hold your tongue, whelp." Vayd glowered at him. He twirled his axe from side to side. It was a pattern for show, meant to intimidate; no one would ever use such a maneuver in actual combat. Even so, Kion could not help but think how one good blow from an axe that size would end his life.

Vayd took his axe in both hands and strode forward, then stopped, eyeing Kion's sword and circling to the left, looking for an opening.

Kion assumed the plow stance, hilt held close to the belly, point raised. It seemed the only possibility given Vayd's height. He waited for Vayd to close, but the haukmar refused to engage.

"Why doesn't he attack?" Kion whispered under his breath. "We don't have time for this."

"He is wary of the fire. You must take the offensive."

It seemed madness to charge within range of that axe. Kion had planned to use his quickness to counterstrike, but he didn't have time to wait for an opportunity.

He advanced with three quick steps and then thrust, extending as far as he could. A wave of acrid fumes from Vayd's stones assaulted his senses, but Kion pushed through it. Vayd gave way, easily avoiding the blow. He swung his axe in return at Kion's head, attempting to end the fight before it began. Kion could do nothing but duck and give ground. He dared not risk getting close enough for any sort of counter thrust.

Despite the ineffectiveness of the attack and the harrowing song of the deadly axe parting the air inches above his head, the brief encounter told Kion something. Truesilver was an exquisite blade, so perfectly balanced, it almost swung itself. If he wasn't imagining things, even his footwork seemed half a step quicker. His every move was more sure while wielding this magnificent weapon. Perhaps he had a chance.

"Hurry—the tree," Kithian said. *"Get me closer."*

Rather than press the attack, Vayd grabbed his axe with both hands again and assumed a blocking posture. He stepped back, all the while circling.

Kion rushed in. He took two steps and made a feint, then switched to the fool's guard to invite an attack; but in all this, his true aim was to get closer to the tree. Vayd, unaware of his plan, circled to the left. Kion swept in, spinning so that his back was against the tree, the ring of flagstones around the roots almost touching the back of his foot.

"Invite his attack and use your counter to set the tree on fire," Kithian said.

But there was no need to bait Vayd this time. Seeing his opponent in tight quarters, Vayd rushed forward, taking half swings on each side to disguise his true attack until he got close enough to land a blow.

He came in faster than Kion expected. Kion's heel caught an uneven flagstone as he shuffled to the left. He fell, but in the end that was what saved him. Vayd sliced at what would have been Kion's shoulder, but it cleaved empty air instead. Kion hit the pavement, rolled twice and shot to his feet with a wide flourish. It was a maneuver he had only attempted a few times in practice but never pulled off.

"Glaivefire!" he shouted. Red fire leapt from the blade towards Vayd. The haukmar leader was caught off guard, but with animal quickness he twisted and managed to avoid most of it. The flames only singed his upper arm, leaving the leather sleeve charred and smoldering. Several of the white glowstones crumbled to dust. Vayd bellowed loud enough to be heard beyond the walls of Charring.

The rest of the flames lit into the lower branches of the towering tree. The fire danced its way up the spidery limbs.

"Treachery!" Vayd shouted, grimacing and moving away from the tree. He smothered the burn on his arm with his right gauntlet.

The haukmar guards, who had been silent until now, growled restlessly.

Kion saw his chance. Even a giant like Vayd couldn't defend himself with only one arm and an axe. He rushed at his staggering enemy, barely aware now of the noxious fumes issuing from Vayd's armor.

Kion didn't bother disguising his attacks or offering feints. He imagined he was fighting Dougan Shaw all over again for the silver medallion. That seemed such a small, unimportant thing now. This—this was the battle that truly mattered. Upon it rested the fate of Charring and his family, perhaps even the whole fate of the North and the Four Wards itself.

He swung the blade effortlessly in tight, deadly arcs. His form, his strikes, everything came to him as if he were the embodiment of the Fiorin Batal. It was as if all his training had been a seed that blossomed at that very moment. It all happened so fast he hardly had time to notice what he was doing. Every swing was flawless, every thrust perfect.

And yet Vayd parried them all. One-armed, wincing in pain, he fought like a caged bear, snarling, slashing, baring his teeth. He seemed to know Kion's every move.

And then Vayd did something unexpected. He let out a deafening shout, grasped his axe in two hands, and began to fight back.

For all Kion's newfound elegance and poise, he dared not parry Vayd's blows. Instead, he gave ground and looked for an opening to counterattack. But Vayd gave him nothing. Hopelessness crept in, like water seeping into his boots from the ground. No wonder Strom had lost. Vayd was everything Strom had been, but bigger and stronger as well.

"Sunder his axe. It is your only chance. Go for the haft!" Kithian said.

Kion was being pushed back to the tree again. Vayd screamed with every movement, grunted with every swing. Sweat poured from him. The long hair that swept down from beneath his visor-less helm was like a soaked rag, clinging to his skin. Kion spun away from his swing and made as if to counter attack but feinted instead. Vayd bit, but Kion did not bother to strike, for he knew Vayd would parry. He parried everything. Instead, Kion feinted again. Again Vayd bit, moving to block the non-existent attack. So Kion feinted again. This time Vayd froze, not willing to be fooled three times. And then, flicking his wrist, Kion spun the blade in a brash flourish that would never have worked if he had tried it again a thousand times, but, paralyzed by the triple feint, Vayd watched as the full force of the blade came down, not on his neck, but on the haft of his axe.

The stroke split the wooden haft like fresh baked bread.

But his strike did more than that. It sliced through the gut plate, and the flames snapped Vayd's girdle and several straps holding it to the tassets protecting his waist. The armor came loose in a disheveled mess, and Vayd stumbled backward in disbelief, tangled in the web of his own armor.

Nearby, the flames had nearly reached the top of the tree.

Kion rushed forward, landing a searing blow that gouged Vayd's chest, cutting deep. The sickening smell of burnt flesh filled the courtyard as Vayd went down.

One more telling strike was all it would take. Kion thrust Truesilver at his foe's exposed neck. But summoning once again from some inner well of hatred and pride, Vayd held up the severed axehead and fended off Kion's blade.

Vayd called out in a loud, pain-choked voice.

"Terroc! Avenge me!"

Kion put his foot on the fallen leader's upper leg and lifted his sword with both hands to deal the killing blow.

"For Strom," he whispered.

"No, Kion, it's a trap!" Kithian's wild warning came burning through his mind. But it came too late.

A *fwwwiiipt* tore through the air, and a burning pain knifed into Kion's armpit, where the armor plates did not cover. An arrow sank deep, and Kion crumpled like his limbs were made of straw.

Truesilver fell from his hands, and a wave of unbearable heat washed over him. As terrible as the arrow wound was, the heat was far deadlier. Instinctively, he shoved himself away to avoid the terrible flames.

Vayd, in perhaps more agony than Kion, struggled to his feet. He cast the useless axehead aside so that it clattered on the pavement.

The haukmar harriers croaked out cheers of triumph.

"Now, I take your sword and finish you with your own blade!" Vayd screamed, covering the deep gash on his chest with his left gauntlet.

"No, Kion, you can stop this," Kithian said.

But, as at Roving, Kithian's voice grew hard to hear behind the roar of Kion's own, terror-filled thoughts. "You..." Kion looked up at the mangled mountain of flesh walking toward his sword. His shoulder and neck convulsed, making it difficult to speak. "You...cheated. No...honor..."

Vayd made a gargling noise, something that must have been intended as laughter. His footsteps pounded the pavement, taking him closer to Truesilver with each thunderous step. "You are a mere whelp, and human besides. You don't deserve honor."

"Kion..." Kithian said something more, but the words were far away. Was the blade speaking, or was it the echo of some forgotten memory?

Vayd's throat let out a continuous scream. He pushed through the torturous heat, his fingers straining for the handle, but each moment was pure agony. Blisters formed on his upper arm, where some of his leather jerkin had fallen away. The air shimmered from the furnace of fire streaming from the blade.

"...In the name of the Mastersmith..." Kion caught the words from Kithian. Something in them brought him back from the brink of oblivion. He gritted his teeth and forced back the pain, if only for a moment, straining to hear Kithian's voice.

"You are my glaivebond. And that bond can never be broken. I plead with you. In the name of the Mastersmith, you were not meant

for defeat here. Call me to you. Take up your sword and win this battle!"

Strength surged into Kion's body, and he shouted, "Truesilver, fly to me!"

Truesilver flicked upward and flew above the flagstones into Kion's outstretched hand.

Vayd howled in pain and frustration, but his cry died in his throat, and the indomitable haukmar collapsed at last, a puddle of dark blood streaming from his chest.

The guards howled and shrieked and wailed, filling the air with full-throated wrath.

"Kion, there is no time. You must call down the flames now!" Kithian's words rang with urgency.

Kion, still lying prone, held the blade up toward the tree and, ignoring the waves of pain, swung it in an arc of bright red light.

"Glaivefire!"

The haukmarn slowed, waiting for the flames to come. But in that moment, the flames went dark. From the houses. From the trees. From Truesilver's blade. The oil had run out. The fire was gone.

With shouts of doom and death, the haukmarn descended upon him.

Chapter 32

IN THE SILENT DARK

The door locked with the faintest of clicks. Darkness swelled around Tiryn. The hushed breathing next to her was the only sound.

"This is the end," she thought. A rough hand found hers and pulled her into the dark.

"Where—?" she said.

Another hand covered her mouth. It scratched her skin like bark, but she did not cry out. She dared not, lest they hear.

A thought fell upon her with shuddering force. The vision. It was coming to pass. She had been in this tunnel before.

She stopped moving. Her premonitions sent waves of dread prickling up and down her skin.

The hand yanked her back into motion.

After three steps, it stopped her again. A shrill creak startled her as the person leading her stepped onto what could only be stairs. She felt for the step with her foot. The stairs screeched again like some secret signal in the dark to her pursuers. Her foot shuffled onto the next step. It creaked, but softer this time, for she put barely any weight on it.

Everything was so much like her vision, right up to her constant worry of missing a step and falling the rest of the way down.

She crept downward, led by the rough hand. She stepped lightly enough to keep the creaking almost unnoticeable, but she cringed each time the noises came, no matter how small. At last they hit the bottom. The cold, packed floor was all too familiar. A damp, faintly rancid smell floated on the air, but it was not as bad as she remembered in her vision. The hand pulled her along at a brisk walk. All she could do was trust that the next step wouldn't lead to a pit or a wall or some sinister thing lurking in the shadows. Darkness wreaks havoc upon those with an over-abundance of imagination, and it played cruelly with Tiryn's.

She felt the passageway close in around her, her footsteps echoing nearer. Her free hand brushed something cold and smooth. Her mind fashioned a monstrous lizard in the dark, but it could have been anything. She bit back a scream.

The hand pulled her in a different direction. She was in a long passage now. The hand turned her again twice more before the pulling stopped and the hand let go. Dust caught in her throat, but she stifled her cough. All went silent. She couldn't even hear the breathing of the person next to her. Was he still there? And where were the shouts and voices from her vision? Had she escaped the danger? Or had there never been any shouts to begin with? She couldn't remember.

A soft grinding noise banished the silence, the sound of stone scraping stone. A waft of stale air blew in her face, and this time she wasn't quick enough to choke down her cough.

Cold hands, colder than the walls, clamped down on hers and yanked her into some new room or passage. The cold hands had yet to let go. She knew their knobby thickness even in the dark. They belonged to Aunt Lizet. She held Tiryn close. The fabric of her dress was soft, just the opposite of the hands.

The odor here was unpleasant in a different way. It was drier and stale. Was this really what she had seen in her visions? What about the fire? Where was that?

The shallow wheezing of two other people came from nearby. One of them belonged to the person who had led her here. It must have been one of the servants, only she hadn't seen which one. The other was too soft to identify.

The stone scraped again behind her, sealing off the influx of damp air from the passageway. Tiryn didn't know why these tunnels had been built below Marlibrim. She hadn't known they existed until today. She read a book once that told how some merchants and higher-born families had their wealth confiscated by the fanes. They used tunnels like this to hide their riches. Whatever the reason for their existence, she was grateful for them now.

They had waited as long as possible before sending her down. Aunt Lizet claimed Charring would easily outlast the haukmar siege until the fane could send his armies, but her faith in the leader of the city, Daysman Ilk, proved to be misplaced. Lizet had very unladylike things to say about him when the gates were opened and the city given over to the haukmar army without a fight.

After a long time, a distant pounding came into the room from somewhere above. Then it came again. And again. And again and again, each time louder than before, until it ended in a great crash. Footsteps, muffled through the dirt above them, scattered throughout the house, multiplying by the moment. Intermingled with the footsteps came shouts of low, bestial voices. She had never seen the haukmarn but knew instinctively the voices belonged to them. The sounds evoked pictures of men carved in stone, with jaws like bricks pounding together and pools of dripping mud for eyes.

Why was Mother not here to hold and protect her? Why did she have to face this with only the cold, uncaring hands of Aunt Lizet for comfort?

Her vision was coming true. The order was all mixed up, and some things had yet to pass, but it was all coming true one way or the other. But how would it end? She had never seen that part.

The image of the burning tree burst into her memory. Would the haukmarn burn Charring to the ground, and Marlibrim with it? Had Tiryn fled down here only to be trapped and die in the flames?

And where was Kion? She could sense his presence, like the sudden cool that comes just before the skies open with rain. He was coming for her. She was sure of it. But she did not know if he would be in time.

Tiryn awoke in the silent dark. The constant pounding of footsteps and the low thunder of voices from above was gone. It felt like night, though in the utter darkness it always felt like night. The hours melted together; she had no way of knowing if she had been here for hours or days.

She had never heard the house this quiet since the haukmarn came. Had they left? For the thousandth time, she wished the vision had told her how it would end.

She listened to the steady breathing of the three others as they slept. She knew the sound of Aunt Lizet. It was quick and crisp and tense, and louder than the others, but only just. This surprised her. Somehow, she'd thought her aunt would have been the kind of person to snore, loudly and frighteningly. Thankfully, Tiryn had been wrong about that. If not, they might have been found out long ago.

The other two sleepers, whom she had learned were Amalia, the head maid, and Lester, the butler, breathed so softly, at times Tiryn wondered if they had not died during their sleep. But then she'd catch a gentle sigh or a faint rasping and know that they were still there.

That was why the sound of a footfall arrested her so, forcing an involuntary and frighteningly loud intake of breath. The sound was not from above, as all the others had been. It was from somewhere in the tunnels.

The first footstep was followed by another. Whoever it was, they were moving very slowly. But as the next step came and then the next, slow as they were, they were getting closer.

She wanted to wake Aunt Lizet but feared the noise would give them away. Better to keep still and hope the infiltrator passed by unaware.

The footsteps stopped. Tiryn held her breath.

Stone scraped against stone. The damp air of the passageway wafted into the room. They were coming inside!

It was all she could do to hold back her scream.

"Annira? Tiryn?" said a familiar voice in hushed tones. Her mind was so wholly given over to fear, it took her a moment to recognize it.

She sat bolt upright. "Zinder?" she whispered. Her skin crawled with excitement and wild, unthinkable hope.

Zinder's voice came back soft and fragile with emotion. "Yes, it's me. Oh, dear one, I've found you at last."

His hand brushed the top of her head in the dark, and she lunged forward and threw her arms around him. She had never hugged Zinder before. He didn't much care for shows of affection. He was rather odd in that way, claiming it wrinkled his clothes or some such nonsense. But this time he didn't say a word of protest. An embrace was the only thing that made sense in that moment. The two of them had found each other in the dark, in the middle of a war, far from home, when all hope of doing so had been utterly lost.

"But how? How did you find me?" Tiryn asked.

"That's a story for another time. We've got to get you out of here," Zinder said. "Where's your mother? I can hear others in the room."

"She—she's not here. She left to find Kion," Tiryn said.

"Oh, my. But there's nothing we can do about that now."

Someone stirred in the darkness.

"Tiryn?" Aunt Lizet whispered hoarsely. "Tiryn, who's that you're talking to?"

"It's only—"

"The name's Zinder, m'lady. Formerly the greatest blacksmith in all the North, but of late, given to burglary and sneakery. I've come to rescue you."

"Burglary? Rescue? What nonsense is this?" Aunt Lizet's

dress rustled, and from the sound Tiryn could tell she had risen to her feet.

"You might keep your voice down, m'lady. There are still two guards upstairs, though there's not much chance they'll hear us. They're too caught up in the raging inferno your nephew's making outside."

"Kion?" Tiryn said, her voice half squeaking from joy. "Kion's here?"

"Yes. And I don't know how much longer he can keep the haukmarn at bay. We must hurry."

Amalia and Lester rose with faint brushing sounds in the darkness.

"Have the haukmarn gone, m'lady?" Lester's withered voice was even more hoarse than usual from disuse.

"Shh! Quiet, I'm trying to think," Aunt Lizet said. "Are you sure it's safe? And how do we know we can trust you?"

"I can handle a single haukmar guard if I get the jump on him. There's one at the front and one at the back. Leaving through the back is our best option." Zinder took Tiryn by the hand and pulled her toward the door. "And I don't care if you trust me or not, I'm leaving with Tiryn. You're welcome to come along, but we've wasted far too much time as it is."

He pulled Tiryn through the doorway and down the hall without waiting for a response. Given Aunt Lizet's temperament and penchant for wanting to control every situation, it was the best thing he could have done in that moment.

"Come on, m'lady," said a new, softer voice. Amalia had yet to speak in all the long lonely hours they had passed in the darkness, but she chose just the right moment, and Aunt Lizet, for once in her life, listened to her maid's suggestion. The footsteps and rustling of Lizet's dress followed Tiryn and Zinder down the passageway.

Little sound was made as they rushed through the darkness along the dirt floor. How Zinder knew his way in the unfamiliar tunnels, Tiryn could only guess, but they soon found themselves ascending the old, creaky stairs. They went slowly, Zinder forcing no sound at all from the boards and the others only the occasional, unfortunate squeak.

Zinder's hand checked Tiryn's advance, and she guessed they had reached the top. A click and a faint, reddish light confirmed that the exit was just in front of them. Zinder pushed back the wall and the cabinet attached to the other side. They shuffled out, quiet as door mice, into the kitchen of Marlibrim Mansion. The house was dark, but through the windows the flickering glow of red fire loomed in the distance. Zinder had said something about an inferno, but Tiryn dared not ask about it now. The haukmarn might hear. But holding her tongue caused a great strain on her heart. What if Kion was caught in that fire?

Zinder motioned for the others to stay near the secret passage while he crept silently into the dining room. Out in the mansion proper, all was quiet, just as below, but troubling sounds invaded from outside. The clank and scrape of steel on steel told that someone was fighting in the courtyard.

Three clicks and a loud *thrump* came from the back of the house. Something large had fallen. Aunt Lizet caught Tiryn's eye with a look of alarm. Lester and Amalia huddled together, their eyes trained on the dining room door.

Zinder reappeared a few moments letter. He whispered, "It's safe," and motioned for them to follow.

When they got into the dining room, the sounds of battle grew even fiercer. A frenzy of scraping metal and clanging blows rang through the house. And Tiryn knew.

"It's Kion," she whispered, crouching beside Zinder's ear. "He's fighting in the courtyard, isn't he?"

Zinder glanced toward the large double doors leading into the foyer. "Yes, but don't you worry. He can take care of himself."

"No." Tiryn stopped. Aunt Lizet rushed past her and stopped

as well. She, too, had heard the fighting. "Kion's in trouble. We have to help him."

"I will, once I get you out of here," Zinder said.

"No, you have to go now, Zinder, there's not much time," Tiryn said. The tone of her voice made even Aunt Lizet turn and regard her.

"My dear, sweet Tiryn, my task is to see you to safety. Then I'll go after Kion. I promise," Zinder said, though doubt riddled his voice.

"Go. Now. Or he will die," Tiryn said. The timid young shepherdess had never spoken with such authority in all her life.

Zinder offered one last, weak-hearted protest. "But there's a haukmar guarding the front door."

"Listen to the girl," Aunt Lizet said.

Zinder, half-dazed, tore from the room through the double doors.

Chapter 33

THE SAFEST PLACE

"**K**ion, stay true until the end." Kithian's voice roused Kion's slumbering strength.

He raised his sword to fend off the first of the haukmar blows. He doubted he could block even one, but he would try. A thought flickered briefly into his mind that Kithian had said there was another way to use Truesilver's fire without the oil, but with the ring of guards bearing down on him, he had no time to pursue it.

The snarling face of the first would-be assassin lit up with bloodlust. The haukmar's ground-shaking charge carried him forward with all the momentum of a battering ram. And then he faltered. He stumbled to his right, into the path of the next-closest haukmar. The other one had too much speed and was too focused on his prey to notice or react in time. Both fell crashing to the pavement stones.

The two large bodies formed a barrier, forcing those nearby to change course and blunting their momentum. But the guards on the other sides of the charging circle surged forward. As they closed, the acrid smell of the haukmar wanstones made Kion's eyes water and his throat itch. The stench fogged his thoughts, but fear cut through. He twisted his body to face the ones coming on his right. Bursts of pain lanced through his body.

He raised Truesilver just in time to deflect a clumsy blow from the first haukmar to reach him. The parry sent a shiver down his arm, and his blade dropped dangerously low. He braced for the haukmar's return stroke, knowing he could not defend against it. But this attacker stumbled as well, careening past Kion with a look of shock and agony.

The thud of his body hitting the ground was followed by a howl of pain as another charging haukmar pulled up short, grabbing at his neck, where dark blood spilled forth. Chaos and confusion now stalled the charge as haukmar eyes shot about the courtyard. Deep, wrathful cries erupted from the throats of several guards, who pointed toward the mansion.

Kion followed their gaze and almost fainted.

Zinder stood in the doorway of Marlibrim, his crossbow flicking left and right as he fired three bolts in quick succession. Every one found its mark. Only one haukmar went down, but the other two bellowed in pain. In a flash, their anger at this diminutive figure who had now felled three of their number made them forget their rage at the one who had slain their leader. Kion was no longer a threat anyway.

"Kill it!" shouted one of them. The others answered with brutal shouts of their own and turned on the small marksman.

Zinder set his teeth and pulled out a bolt case to load in three more shots.

He didn't need to fire them.

At the mansion's gate there arose another cry, not inhuman and guttural like those of the haukmarn, but just as powerful.

A hundred men armed with swords, bows, and spears stormed the courtyard.

The haukmar guards had no choice but to turn and face the new threat. The men rushing in had no armor to protect them, but there were far too many for so few haukmarn to overcome. Still, this was Vayd's personal guard. They grimly hefted their axes and met their doom with vile curses and defiant rage.

Kion, at last overcome by pain, collapsed and sank into unknowing.

The healer closed the door on his way out.

Zinder, who had been there when Kion awoke and throughout the healer's visit, regarded his friend with a deep sigh of relief.

"Well, lad, it looks like you'll pull through after all. You'll not be rid of Zinder Hamryn so easily," he said.

"As if I ever could. If I had died, I've no doubt you would have followed me all the way to the Halls of Majesty themselves," Kion said. It hurt to speak. The healer had made him drink a large cup of water, but he was still parched. "Zinder, could you pour me another glass, please? My throat is as dry as driftwood."

"And what do you expect, after baking half the Merchant's Quarter and sleeping for a whole day?" Zinder filled Kion's cup from a pitcher on the nightstand and handed it to him.

Kion lay propped up in bed, surrounded by a sea of pillows and covered by the warmest, thickest, softest blanket he had ever known. Though he doubted he and his aunt would ever be on friendly terms, this was a good start. He took a few gulps of the delicious water.

"You've got a new hat," he said.

Zinder smoothed the long gray feather nestled in the white band of his smartly sloping, dark-blue hat.

"It was a gift from your beloved aunt." He stood and took a deep and elegant bow, as only a nyn could. "She said she would have given me something more valuable if I had come sooner. Can you believe that?"

"Aunt Lizard. Sounds just like her. Her purse strings are tighter than a nynnian knot, but I am glad she survived—and that she kept Tiryn safe. But I'm terrified about Mother. I should have known she'd come for me. I should never have sent that letter."

Memories of Mother came surging back: her tender touch, the light in her smile, the unique smell of ginger, lilacs, and wood smoke that clung to her, and the thousand ways she had gently corrected and lovingly praised him. How could she be gone? And how could he go on without her?

"You didn't know about the haukmarn, lad. How could you? You did the right thing," Zinder said.

"Did I? Then why do I have this dreadful feeling I'll never see her again?"

"I know, it's a hammer to the heart. But don't dwell on it. No good can come of fixing your mind on what you can't change. You need to get well now. And if she hasn't come back or sent word by then, we'll take that road when the time comes. You're here now, and safe. Be glad of that."

"Listen to your friend, Kion," Kithian said. *"You can only fight the battles before you."* The sword lay propped against the wall in the corner of the room. Zinder had taken the liberty of having a scabbard made for Truesilver while Kion slept. It was of fine quality, with embossed chestnut leather, a burgundy belt loop, and a copper chape on the end.

"I know." Kion looked Zinder in the eye and tried his best to smile. "I am glad we're here. But you still haven't told me how I *got* here, or how we're even still in Charring at all. How is it that the haukmarn no longer control the city?"

Zinder rubbed his hands together. "Ah, now that's a tale that's sure to be put into song, lad. But I don't understand how you can't see that it was all by your hand the city was delivered." He scooted his chair closer to the side of the bed.

"What do you mean?"

Zinder glanced at the door. "I'll tell you the short version, because your sister's been dying to speak to you, and I'm sure she'll be upstairs the moment she hears from the healer you're awake." Zinder dusted off his sleeves, a gesture purely for show. They were immaculate as usual. "Here's how it happened. When you started all those fires, it sent the haukmar army into a panic. I don't know exactly what happened on their side, of course, but the order must have gone out that the city was burning to the ground, because they fled their posts in bucketfuls and ran for the hills! The only ones that stayed were Vayd's personal guard, the ones who tried to finish you off after you beat him. Oh, and by the by, you have to tell me how you pulled that one off!"

Kion's eyes went to Kithian in the corner. The words of the sword had come to him even while he slept, calling him back from the brink of death, as a candle in the window calls a weary soldier home from battle. In time that candle became a torch, and then a bonfire, until it blazed as bright as day, and Kion awoke to find himself in his aunt's mansion.

"It was all Truesilver's doing," Kion said.

"You know I can sense falsehoods when they are spoken in my presence," Kithian said. *"Do not mislead your friend out of false modesty. I may have gifts beyond those given to mortal men, but I am nothing except in the hands of my glaivebond. I was but the instrument. You played the song."*

"The sword put you in your place, did he?" Zinder said. "Oh, yes, I can tell when he's got hold of your thoughts. You get this spark in your eyes, and they turn to glass."

"Kithian told me it wasn't all him," Kion said.

"I should think not. A more fantastic blade you'll never find, but even the most magnificent of blades wants an arm to swing it. And I can assure you, your skill and bravery have already flown through the city faster than that green-breasted loony that got us into this mess in the first place. Sword of the North, they're calling you, and Champion of Charring. Some plucky folk are even calling for you to be named the new bladewarden!"

"After one battle? No. No one could ever replace Strom."

"Well, it's just talk. No commoner will ever claim that title. But still, you're the hero of the day in the heart of Charring, there's little doubt about that. Even so, the both of us would have been haukmar gruel if it hadn't been for those two buffoons from the guardhouse."

"Hormgar and Orvis?"

"The very same. After we left, they got up their courage and woke the rest of the guards. They knew they couldn't make it out all the way through the tunnels, but they figured that if a mere boy and a nyn were brave enough to take on the whole haukmar army, they could at least try to go down fighting. So they snuck out through the tunnels and into an armory in another part of the city. They were just preparing to start a revolt and sell their lives dearly when the flames erupted along the east wall and sent the haukmarn scattering. So they headed straight for Marlibrim. They were the only ones who had the idea that maybe the fires were not an accident. And when they got to the courtyard, they fought like daggers down to the last of them. Twenty men lost their lives saving yours and mine. Charring may owe its freedom to you, but we both owe our lives to those men."

"It was well that you trusted them. Strange bounty often springs from simple acts of kindness."

Kion eased back into the pillows. His shoulder and arm throbbed with pain. They were wrapped in bandages so tight he could barely move, but he was thankful just to be alive.

"Did Hormgar and Orvis survive?"

"Oh, yes. And I had to listen to their chattering for a good half hour after the battle." Zinder pushed up his hat and let out a soundless whistle. "Though, of course, since they'd saved my life and all, I didn't mind it so much."

Kion returned his friend's smile. "So Charring is safe. And Vayd is dead. Does that mean the war is over?"

Shades of doubt dimmed Zinder's countenance. "It's too soon to know."

"Why? Is there something you haven't told me?"

Zinder scratched the back of his neck and looked out the window. Gray skies and spitting rain marred the view. It was hard to tell what damage the fires had caused to the neighboring houses, but it was good to see them still standing.

"Vayd may have survived," Zinder said.

Kion's mind went back to the image of the fallen haukmar leader. If that was not the picture of death, he didn't know what was. "But I saw him. I cut him down. Kithian, tell me he was defeated."

"Like Zinder, I cannot say. I only know that others have survived graver wounds."

"I said the Charring soldiers defeated the haukmar guards, but that's not entirely true. Two of them picked up Vayd's body in the middle of the skirmish and ran to the back of the grounds. The fighting was so fierce, people only remembered seeing it afterward. Vayd's body was never found, and neither were the haukmarn who took him."

Why had Kion ever thought he could defeat a fighter such as Vayd? "I should have known he wasn't dead. I'm sorry. I failed."

"You did not come here to kill anyone. You came here to save your family. In that you succeeded."

"Now, lad, don't say that. You did more than any other warrior in the Four Wards ever could have. You ran into the teeth of two hundred haukmarn and came up smiling. Not to mention—"

A knock on the door interrupted him.

"Is it all right to come in?" Tiryn's soft voice sounded in the hall.

"Aw, lass, as if you have to ask!" Zinder said. He hopped over and flung the door open.

Tiryn came quietly into the room. The tall, prim figure of Aunt Lizet loomed behind her. Tiryn's cheeks flushed rosy and glistened with fresh tears. Her eyes leapt toward Kion's, but her wobbly legs barely managed the distance between the door and the bed before she collapsed onto his good shoulder.

"Oh, Kion," she said, her tears dampening his shirt. "I never should have left. It's all my fault. You almost died because of me. If you hadn't made it, I—" Sobs eclipsed her words.

Kion fought against tears of his own. Even when she had taken sick, even throughout all the long journey to save her, she had never been more precious to him than at that moment. In all the years he had been her brother, he had not known until now how dark and cold the world would be without her and just how much he loved her.

"Tiryn, don't be silly," he said in his old teasing way—for he could not bear the thought of crying in front of Aunt Lizet. "You talk like you personally caused the haukmar invasion. There was nothing you could have done to stop any of this. Hard times come. But the storm has passed, like all storms do, and we've come through it. Now give me a smile, so I can imagine you're at least a little glad to see me."

Tiryn's tears did not stop, but a bright smile now burst through them.

"You always could make me smile—when you wanted to," she said. "Which wasn't very often."

"There will be more smiles from now on, I promise. Speaking of promises, you told me you would come back to Furrow. Don't you remember? But you made me come get you, like always."

"Yes, well, what about your promise? Did you win the tournament?"

Kion chuckled softly. "No. I didn't. I guess we're even, then."

Tiryn sat up, but instead of teasing back, her face turned serious. "I'm not so sure. I think the real tournament was waiting for you in Charring. You faced a lot more than farm boys here. And this time—when it mattered most—you didn't fail. Father would be so proud of you, Kion. You were so brave to face those monsters. You risked everything to save us. I'll never forget that."

Kion glanced at Truesilver in the corner. There was so much he had to tell her.

Aunt Lizet coughed rather too loudly. Apparently, her patience had worn out. Either that or she had a strong aversion to displays of emotion.

"Yes, Kion. Your mother would certainly be proud. You did more than I ever expected. And I...well, I...I thank you. I stand in your debt. And I mean to repay you. I may be many things, but I always pay my debts. You may stay here as long as you like. You may loathe every moment in my house, but your victory has come at a cost, and you must stay until you are well. And then, only when you are well again, will you be free to go. The healer says you are young and have a remarkable constitution, so there is hope for a quick recovery. But for now, I offer you my home and provisions, such as they are." The words were stiff, as if they'd been rehearsed, but they were earnest enough. Kion actually felt bad for her, having to swallow her pride like that. These were indeed strange days when Aunt Lizard the High and Mighty would welcome Dorn Bray's son into her home with open arms.

"Thank you, Aunt Liz—" He almost said "lizard"—some habits were hard to break. "Aunt Lizet. And thank you for supplying my friend with a new hat." He winked at Zinder, whose eyebrows danced like a slithering snake. "He does aspire to be the most fashionable nyn in all the Four Wards."

Kion chuckled, but Aunt Lizet, who caught the wink, rolled her eyes and took in a heavy, unhappy breath. Perhaps she was regretting her offer of hospitality already. Kion would have to watch himself so as not to spend the good graces he had won by saving her life all at once.

"Yes, well, it was the least I could do." Aunt Lizet's lips creased in a terse grin.

"Indeed, the *very* least," Zinder mumbled, a little too loudly not to be heard.

"You two!" Tiryn said, scolding them with a look.

"She is your elder, and your mother's sister, swordspeaker. Treat her accordingly," Kithian said from the corner, the large bright citrine in the sword's hilt glaring at him like a great eye.

"Come, Tiryn." Aunt Lizet drew herself to her full height, straining every inch of her freshly pressed dress. "We shall leave these two wits to mock in peace. If his spirits are any indication, your brother may recover even more quickly than the healer expected."

She turned to go, but Tiryn remained at Kion's side.

"Only just a moment longer, Aunt Lizet. I'll come soon, I promise. It's just I—I need to speak to Kion alone for a moment, if that would be all right," Tiryn said.

Aunt Lizet's jaw flapped open for a sharp response, but she caught herself. "Very well," she said, then turned and left abruptly.

"I'll leave you two to yourselves," Zinder said, making another sweeping, graceful bow.

"No, please stay," Tiryn said. "This is a family matter. And you're as much a part of our family now as me or Kion."

Zinder's eyes softened, and he acknowledged her kindness with a slow and gentle nod. "I am honored beyond words."

"Tiryn, I know what you're about to ask. And I'm telling you right now, the answer is no," Kion said.

"Kion, we have to go find Mother—together. I can't bear to be apart from you ever again." Tiryn's words came out in a rush. Tears welled up in her eyes. Kion knew his refusal to bring her along would break her heart, but what choice did he have?

"I can't put you in danger," he said. "Mother—Father wouldn't want it. I don't want it either. You're too dear to me, Tiryn. And the road will be too dangerous. The haukmar armies are still abroad."

"I know that. But if you leave me here, I will die from grief. Either that or I'll go mad from worry. Please, Kion. You must take me with you. I beg you. Don't leave me again!" She clutched at his neck, inadvertently bumping his bad shoulder, and he winced. "Oh, Kion, I'm so sorry. I didn't mean to do that."

"It's all right, Tiryn." He eased her away with his good arm. "You're not making this very easy."

Zinder stepped forward and cleared his throat. "A few words, if I may, now that I'm officially part of the family." He pulled on the end of his mustache thoughtfully. "I know you want to protect your sister, lad. That's been your sole obsession ever since those fiends showed up at the Clefts. But look over there." He pointed to Truesilver. The warm metal of the blade and the sun-like gems in the hilt burned with a deadly beauty. "I saw only a part of what you did with that sword. And if I live to walk the world twice over, I'll never see such deeds again. You've been given a gift, Kion. I don't fully understand it, and half of it's mad beyond sense, but one thing I know. The safest place in the Four Wards right now is at the side of whoever is holding that blade. So you can stuff your sister away in this mansion and hope the haukmarn don't come charging back again after they lick their wounds, or you can listen to her and let her help you find your mother. The way I see it, it's not even a choice. You can protect her with the sword, or abandon her to the ill winds of war and circumstance."

"The nyn's eyes see ever keenly, swordspeaker. You would do well to heed his words," Kithian said.

Tiryn's eyes shone with gratitude toward the nyn, whose countenance had never looked so sagely.

If Kion had not known it from Zinder's words, Kithian's landed the telling blow. He could not stray from the counsel of his blade. To do so, he knew, would be neither wise nor safe.

"All right, Tiryn." Kion heaved a defeated sigh. "I hope I don't regret this."

Tiryn bounced with joy at his side, nearly bumping his shoulder again.

"Oh, thank you, Kion. And thank you, Zinder. I know we'll find her. I just know it."

"But, Tiryn." Kion fixed his eyes on his sister gravely. "Before we go, I have to tell you about my sword."

Coming Soon

THE SWORDSPEAKER SAGA

RIMEWINTER

BOOK 2

Also by DJ Edwardson

A hero is measured by the size of his heart.

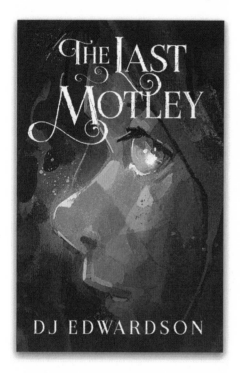

Every century a motley is born. Though only children, their patchwork skin marks them as dangerous, especially to those who know about the first motley. That one nearly destroyed the world.

But a chance meeting with a simple tailor may hold the key to breaking the curse and saving their world.

Read book 1 in *The Null Stone Trilogy*

The key to the future is unlocking the past.

A man with no memories. A device with the power of time. Is it his salvation or the end of humanity? Read the unique, Grace Award-nominated science fiction series as unpredictable as the future itself.

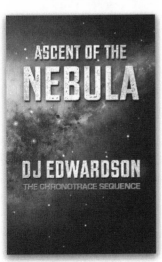

Read all three volumes in
The Chronotrace Sequence

About the Author

DJ Edwardson traveled a lot when he was younger. Now he's busy crafting exotic destinations of his own. Although he has written both Science Fiction and Fantasy novels, he likes to say he writes in the "genre of imagination".

He has a degree in English from Cornell College where his emphasis was on the works of Shakespeare. He's tried his hand at both acting and directing in the theater, but these days is happiest with a pen in hand. He lives in Tennessee with his wife and three children.

For more information about DJ Edwardson's writing please visit: *www.djedwardson.com*